DATE DUE FEB 0 7

AUG 5			
GAYLORD			PRINTED IN U.S.A.

EVERYTHING MUST GO

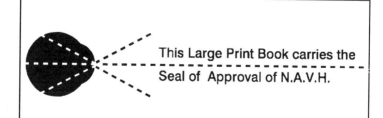

This Large Print Book carries the
Seal of Approval of N.A.V.H.

EVERYTHING MUST GO

ELIZABETH FLOCK

THORNDIKE PRESS

An imprint of Thomson Gale, a part of The Thomson Corporation

THOMSON

™

GALE

Detroit • New York • San Francisco • New Haven, Conn. • Waterville, Maine • London

LIBRARY OF CONGRESS CATALOGING-IN-PUBLICATION DATA

Flock, Elizabeth.
  Everything must go / by Elizabeth Flock.
    p. cm.
  ISBN-13: 978-0-7862-9243-1 (alk. paper)
  ISBN-10: 0-7862-9243-1 (alk. paper)
  1. Losers — Fiction. 2. Adult children living with parents — Fiction. 3. Cities and towns — Fiction. I. Title.
  PS3606.L58E94 2007
  813'.6—dc22   2006037514

Published in 2007 by arrangement with Harlequin Books S.A.

Printed in the United States of America on permanent paper
10 9 8 7 6 5 4 3 2 1

For my brother, Regi Brack

CHAPTER ONE

2001

Five-fifteen p.m. Henry pushes open the door, drops his keys on the front hall table. "Mom?"

He turns into the living room, shut up and dark, the curtain drawn against the brightness of the fall day. His shrunken mother is on the couch balancing a highball in one hand, a cigarette burning out in the other, in clothes that once fit properly but now swallow her up. Her thinning brown hair is flecked with gray and hanging loose from a swirl of a bun.

"David?" she asks, not yet pulling her stare from the television set.

"No, Mom. It's me," he says, "Henry."

She looks over and sees that yes, it is Henry. He can see the disappointment in her eyes, glazed over from the glow of the TV.

He takes the cigarette from her, stubs it

out in the overflowing ashtray on the coffee table and makes a mental note to clean up all the drink rings and ashes.

He opens the curtains with the string pulley and when he turns back to her she is shading her eyes against the light, but then her hand drops back down to the couch.

"How are you?" he asks.

She does not answer him, but he is used to that and so has not waited for a reply.

In the kitchen he opens the refrigerator to see what he'll need to pick up at the grocery store.

Over the din of squealing contestants spinning large dials, Henry asks, "How're you feeling?"

"Are you just home from football?" she asks. "How was practice?"

"I'm home from *work,* Mom," he says, taking a deep breath and leaning down to scoop her up. "Remember?"

She clasps her hands behind his neck, holding on, bumping along in his arms with each step up the stairs.

Henry is gentle placing her into her bed. Moving through the room, he picks up a *Ladies' Home Journal* that has fallen to the floor from her nightstand, and replaces it within reach, right side up. On top of the

Readers' Digest.

"How was work?" she asks, pulling the covers up.

He pauses on his way out of the master bedroom to answer her.

"You know what? It was a hard day," he says. He sighs the kind of sigh that carries a weight. "Bye, Mom. I'm going out for a while but I'll be back later, okay? I'll check on you later."

She is already sleeping when he leaves.

It was not always this way.

1967

"Henry, pass the baked beans, please," his mother says. She rests her cigarette in the notch of the ashtray and reaches across the picnic table toward him.

The clay container feels heavy to seven-year-old Henry and he concentrates very hard to make sure it does not tip on its way over the deviled eggs with the paprika sprinkled on top. Black flies scatter.

"*Thank* you," she says. She is making a point by emphasizing the *please* and *thank you* and waits with an expectation of *you're welcome* from Henry. He stops chewing and with split-second reasoning decides the greater offense would be to talk with his mouth full so he nods his *you're welcome*

9

and hopes his mother will accept this as the best he can do under the circumstances. Did you see I did the right thing right you looked at me like it was good so maybe I did, he thinks, in one jumbled seven-year-old thought process.

"Can I be excused?" Henry's older brother, Brad, asks.

"You haven't finished your hot dog yet," she says. Henry races to finish his own, to escape into the sunny day, away from the fragments of adult conversation floating over his head: Detroit riots. Sergeant Pepper and The Downfall of The Beatles. The Smothers Brothers, which he had indeed watched with his parents one night when they let Henry and Brad stay up past their bedtime, but Henry had not really liked the show and fell asleep before it finished so all he really wanted right now was to be released from the table.

Brad crams the rest of the hot dog into his mouth and says, "Now can I?" Wonder bread bun flicks out of his mouth.

Their mother sighs at Brad and looks away so their father, Edgar Powell, says, "Yes."

Henry's father has a spot of ketchup on the front of his madras shirt, and Henry can tell this is bothering him because he keeps wiping it with his paper napkin and sighing in disgust when it refuses to disappear.

"Can I, too?" Henry asks. The dinner is cutting into the July twilight that won't hold its breath for long. So they squirm to be released because even hot dogs don't make up for lost time in summer light, a conch-shell call to the young boys.

"I swear it's impossible to keep these children in one place for more than five minutes," Henry's mother says to the two other mothers on her side of the bench, who nod sympathetically, yes, yes it is hard to keep them in line so why even try just let them go boys will be boys after all.

"Yes, you may both be excused," she says, leaning across the table so her husband can light her next cigarette with his Zippo lighter.

Henry notices she has not completely stubbed out her last cigarette. He looks up to see if this bothers her as much as it does him, and determining it does not appear to bother her in the least, he finger-stops the Coke in his straw and releases it over the smoking remains of cigarette. Gulping the last of his drink he sighs "aah" like in the commercial but is disappointed nobody notices his attempt at humor so he races off

11

after Brad. On the way he picks up a stick because they'd agreed to play cowboys and Indians and he remembers he is supposed to be an Indian and Indians used sticks not guns to fight the cowboys so he'd better get a good one because Brad is tough competition.

"Wait up," Henry calls out.

Back at the table all are laughing at a joke one of the men makes and the women are shaking their heads at its silliness. All except Edgar Powell.

Edgar Powell is the sort of man who only says "God bless you" after the first sneeze. If multiple sneezes follow he pointedly ignores them. For Edgar Powell this is a pragmatic choice, a studied economy of words, not a malicious wish that the sneezer be condemned to damnation. He is equally frugal with his laughter.

"Boys, watch out for your brother," their mother calls and Henry groans, watching his just barely two-year-old brother David toddle toward them, arms Frankenstein-extended. David David David, it's always *take care of your brother* and *watch out for your brother.* Brad's the oldest so he gets to do older-kid stuff, David's the baby so he gets all the attention, and then there's me, invisible me, he says to himself, kicking at a rock, waiting for Brad to shoot him like he always does. Henry's truth is that he is the one who does everything right. But this seems very little compared to David David David and Brad Brad Brad, and he wishes his parents saw the gut punches, the head locks or the Chinese water torture where Brad pins him down and lets the string of spit hang down almost to his face before sucking it back up. Then there was the time Brad made Henry eat dirt, which still humiliates him even though it happened last year. Thankfully Matt Rollins, who gave Brad the idea in the first place, moved to Baltimore not long after. At least I'm not a tattletale, he thinks. His best friend, Petey, had cautioned against tattling and had told of even worse big-brother tortures. Never ever tell on him, Petey had said in the fort they'd built in back of Henry's house.

Sometimes, though, it was easy not to tattle because Brad would unexpectedly stick up for him at school if the occasion presented itself. Or Brad would talk baseball with him — in a know-it-all way, but still. Life was good when this happened. It made it all worthwhile when, say, the Yankees won and they shouted with joy and leaped into each other's arms and punched their fists into the air with happiness.

"David's a cowboy with you," he calls out to Brad.

"No, he's not," Brad yells, hiding somewhere out of Henry's sight.

"Yes, he is. There are more cowboys than Indians so he's on your team," he says. He turns to David, who has now reached him. "Davey, go over there, Brad's calling you. Go over there to Brad."

"Bad?" David has not yet mastered his *r*'s and Henry has encouraged this coincidental nickname.

"Yeah, *Bad*," Henry says, gently pushing his brother toward the fringe of the park. "Go over there."

"Ha-ha," he calls out. "He's coming over."

"Yeah, well, you just got shot so you're dead," Brad says, standing up from not as far away as Henry had imagined.

Cowboys and Indians gives way to a makeshift series of sticks balanced across rocks at different heights so the boys can leap over them, taking turns being Evel Knievel. But Brad hurts his knee and starts a wrestling match that is incomplete as David repeatedly tries to take part and *boys, watch out for your brother* dots it and it is therefore far less satisfying than any of them had hoped. Henry's cousin, Tommy, at ten is bigger than both of them, and at one point has Brad pinned down requiring Henry to jump onto Tommy's back to peel him off.

"Get off," he says. "Get *off*," because brothers innately stick together against outside foes even cousin foes.

It's two against one. The Powell boys against cousin Tommy carries on until that, too, is exhausted. They scatter then and Henry wanders off into the wood to see what's what. *Let Brad watch David for once how come he always gets out of it anyway,* Henry thinks. *It's such a gyp.*

It is two or three yards into the thick, cool shade of trees when Henry happens on two birds. It's clear they are fighting and he stops to watch. They are well matched — the same breed, the same size. It does not occur to Henry that he has the power to put a stop to this. To intervene. To interrupt the natural course of events. He is frozen and spellbound. He finds it strange how silent they are, the pecking brutal, the feathers — the long ones on top — start peeling off. The bird on the bottom, the one being nailed over and over again by the beak, struggles slightly but Henry sees it is resigned. Horrified, Henry watches the weak one give in. The downy smaller feathers underneath floating in the air like dandelion fluff. The beak pecking pecking pecking red with blood. Henry is surprised at the brightness of the color, so much like his mother's lipstick or like the fake Dracula blood he had smeared on either side of his mouth last Halloween.

The dying bird finally manages a mournful squawk.

"Stop," he says out loud, finding his voice. "Stop it," he shouts, running forward, waving his arms. *"Stop."*

The bloody beak rises and the bird flaps off. Henry's spindly legs walk to the mess on the pine needles. He squats down next to the bird on its side, a beady eye finds his, locks and then shuts.

"It's okay," he whispers. "It's okay now." He is trying to soothe the bird but is sick at his stomach seeing he is too late.

Not so far away the stronger bird waits to finish what he had started.

"Go," Henry yells. Tears in his eyes he rushes at the bird. "Go away. Go."

He returns to the bird on the ground and kneels. This is the closest he has ever been to a bird. He reaches out, and with his index finger, he strokes the top of the bird's head. The only part that is not bloody. It is membrane-soft, smooth and still warm and Henry finds it the saddest thing he has ever ever seen in the whole wide universe.

There is no time to bury it; Brad will be looking for him, Henry thinks. Or Tommy. Or maybe his mother. If he is gone too long. And it feels like he's been gone too long.

"Sorry," he whispers. "Sorry, bird." On his haunches he allows the tears to fall.

It astounds him that he is only steps from his family, from all the picnic activity. He does not tell anyone about it. He keeps it for himself, feeling he alone was entrusted with the weight, the *responsibility* of being the only witness to this spectacularly rare event. It is fine with him that no one notices he is no longer playing. He takes a stick and hits random bushes at the edge of the clearing . . . mad at himself he had allowed it to happen. Come to think of it, he thinks, thank God Mom and Dad didn't find me, not that they really would have, but still — they would have asked why I let the bird die.

The boys are called back to help throw out soggy paper plates and clinking beer bottles. The mothers are stacking the Tupperware and drinking out of plastic cups, giggling at something one or the other has said before the boys reach the table in near darkness.

In the car ride home the boys are quiet, drunk with exhaustion. David has fallen asleep between them, his head bobbing with each bump in the road. In front of them their mother moves closer to their father, who is driving. The station wagon has one long continuous front seat and their father reaches out and drapes his arm across the top of the seat back, across their mother's shoulders, and their murmuring this and that about who said what mixes in with the sound of the engine and Henry next feels his father's arms scooping him up to carry him into the house. Brad trails them, his steps weaving in sleepiness.

Ahead of them on the front walk his mother is carrying David.

Henry dreamily reaches his first finger to his little brother's head he confuses with the bird's, so soft and smooth. But David's head is just out of reach.

CHAPTER TWO

1977

Henry's fingers are too numb to tie a good knot in his cleats so he jams the leftover strings under the tongue and hopes they'll stay.

"Powell!" His coach speaks in exclamation points. "Look alive! You're going back in!"

He tilts forward so he can see down the bench to the running back, who has just hobbled off the field cradling a hurt elbow, steam rising off his body like a cup of coffee, curling up into the cold fall air. Henry wonders how it is he can suddenly feel his own heart beating in his throat. *I'm the last of the Powell men to do something really do something so I can't screw up I really can't please God don't let me screw this up,* he thinks.

"Wake up, Powell!" The coach's head flicks to the right only by an inch or so but communicates exasperation perfectly and Henry jumps up.

He stomps warmth into his legs, and at the sound of the whistle he shoots out onto the field, passing the wide receiver, who had gone in to give Henry a break and who now looks relieved to be coming out. Henry knows why: the smallest guy on the other team is still bigger than their running back, the Fridge, nicknamed more for his eating habits than for his resemblance to a professional football player. At first a source of profound embarrassment, Fridge now calls himself by his own nickname. "Hi, it's Fridge," he'll say into the phone to a teammate's mother. When she calls up the stairs to her son "Fridge is on the phone," she momentarily forgets she is rapidly disappearing from her teenager's life like a Polaroid in reverse.

The whistle blows again. Henry is aware that he very nearly bounces when he is tackled to the ground.

A hand dangles above his helmet but instead of reaching out for it he heaves himself up off the frozen playing field. You take hold of that hand and you might as well hang a *LOSER* sign on your back, he thinks. Henry moves back into position. Inhaling, he focuses. He looks over and across to the quarterback. Steve Wilson. Telepathically they speak . . . the words carried silently through the air, molecules of code that will separate this moment from all others. A ballet choreographed in an instant, *this* instant, one that will set Henry Powell on an entirely different, life-changing trajectory. They nod at each other and turn back to the game. Tick tick tick: time resumes.

Whistles . . . numbers called out . . . grunts all around . . . thumps of bodies hitting the ground.

But then this: Henry is free, the opposing players moving over to the Fridge, forgetting Henry altogether, as both he and Steve Wilson knew they would. The conductor has tapped his baton on the music stand and the ballet begins.

"Twenty-four!" The shout comes from a distance. To clue the others into the Wilson-Powell Plan. Wilson's young voice cracks in hormonal urgency.

"Do it!" His coach is mouthing from the sideline. Henry's legs propel him farther away from Wilson, getting him into place for the grand finale.

For if this catch is not made the game is lost. Like the last five minutes of a television drama at the end of the May season, the suspense hovers in the air and threatens to remain unresolved. The crowd swells collectively to the edge of bleacher seats — perhaps because the spectators sense the beauty of the choreography that is now apparent to all but the opposing team or, more likely, it is so cold the metal makes sitting nearly unbearable.

"Twenty-four!"

The play calls for him to catch the ball, zigzag over, run as many yards as possible and pass underhanded to the running back, Ted Marshall. It will be Marshall's job to run the ball into the end zone. The coach's voice seems distorted to Henry, like slow motion during the turning point in that drama when the main character accidentally falls off a ledge, her lover reaching for her in vain, calling her name that one . . . last . . . time.

His arms extend into the air. He tilts his head up into the dark sky and wonders for a moment how he'll be able to see the ball against the storm clouds, which now seem pigskin-brown.

Thump.

The backslap, good natured though it was, startles him back to 1984 and causes an unfortunate cringe that is noticed all around. "That was something, Powell," the man is saying, eyeing his own profile in the three-sided mirror. "No offense, but I never thought you'd make that catch. It was *impossible.* How many yards was it? Then the *touch*down. Jesus. In*cred*ible," he sucks in his protruding belly and turns this way and that, eyes never leaving the mirror. "You should've seen it," he says to his girlfriend, who is checking her watch. "After that the season turned around. We went to the state championship. *Thanks* to that. Scouts were there and everything. Hey, whatever happened to Teddy that day?"

Henry Powell shrugs his answer and throats are cleared. Neal Peterson, a former teammate, exhales, releases his stomach muscles, and turns away from his reflection. The stilted reminiscence comes to an end as they both knew it would. Henry, who is now kneeling with a wrist corsage of pins, to fold cuffs up so the pants will break just so.

"How about a little longer up front on the left — yeah, that's right," Peterson says. "Great. When do you think these will be ready? I've got to fly to Houston next week."

"I can get them to you by Friday," Henry

says, rubbing another waxy white line along the fold in back. The pins are already in all the way around the pant leg — why bother with the white chalk on top of it, he thinks. He's not as adept as his boss, Mr. Beardsley, and ends up rubbing the white line onto his thumb and index finger.

"You heard from anybody lately?" Peterson reaches back for his wallet with the scratchy Velcro flap that still holds despite years of crumbs and loose threads wedged into the black nubs. His jacket sleeves fall back down and Peterson is slightly annoyed to again have to winch them back up, above his elbows.

"Naw," Henry says. He scribbles tailor notes onto the generic order pad Mr. Beardsley says must be on hand at all times, "in case of emergencies." Henry wonders what kind of crisis would call for a white-green-pink triplicate of a guest check.

"Heard from Benny the other day. From Cancún, that fat bastard." Peterson laughs, certain that Henry, too, appreciates Benny's spirit of adventure. But to Henry, Benny is as anonymous now as he was back in high school. Henry cannot even conjure up his face. But to someone like Neal Peterson the cast of the Class of 1978 will remain photographically burned on the yearbook that is his brain.

"That guy's crazy," he is saying, "drunk off his ass in some Mexican place, calling me. Jesus." Another admiring chuckle from Neal Peterson as his credit card slides back into place alongside another that reads License to Chill along the top, a Carlos & Charlie insignia underneath rattan-style letters spelling out Panama City. "You gotta come out with us, man. We're hitting Blackie's later. Mills'll be there. And Smith-ereens. And Figger. Remember him? He was two years ahead of us? Newton's his last name — *you* know him. Yeah, you do. He's the one with the sleepy eye who got the shit kicked out of him outside Carvel's after that Homecoming game, whatever year that was. Remember? How could you not know Newton? Anyway, come out tonight. Blackie's at ten. Catch you later, Powell!" His finger pointing, thumb cocking an invisible trigger, while the other hand lowers his Ray Bans back down off the top of his head to the bridge of his nose before pushing at the door clearly marked Pull.

The store windows at Baxter's have sheets of amber plastic coating on the inside, to protect clothes from the sun's destructive rays, but Henry sees, when Peterson hurries out the door after his girlfriend (humbled, he thinks, by the pushing-not-pulling thing), it's cloudy out, stormy even, rendering Peterson's sunglasses useless. But if Sonny Crockett wears sunglasses on dark days, Henry smirks to himself, so does Neal Peterson.

Henry detaches the pink copy of the guest check and folds it into the pinned-up slacks. Anticipating a long empty day, he sets the bundle aside so he'll have something to do later.

The truth is Henry does know Newton. *Figger.* A man-child who had facial hair in eighth grade and told everyone Henry had VD when Henry refused to give him his A+ paper on *Tess of the D'Urbervilles* in ninth grade.

Of *course* he knows Newton.

The VD rumor caught fire and Henry found himself at home watching *The Rockford Files* while his fellow ninth graders were pouring Hawaiian Punch into small plastic cups at the Homecoming dance (their first dance *ever*). A week later he was at the water fountain and heard Melanie Parks say, "Ew, I'm using the fountain downstairs instead," and was certain from her tone it was fear of contagion that scared her Fair Isle–sweatered self away. At first he reasoned that they may think he has VD, but at least — he told himself — at least that meant he wasn't a *virgin.* The very word reeked of ignominy and disgrace. As if anticipating this train of thought, though, Figger Newton told everyone Henry contracted VD through sex *with his cousin.*

"Why aren't you out, dork?" Henry's older brother, Brad, asked the Saturday night following the Homecoming dance. He had come up from behind Henry and flicked him on the head before plopping down on the other end of the couch.

"Why aren't *you* out?"

"Good comeback, spaz," Brad said. "Seriously, what the hell's the problem with you?"

Both were staring ahead, carefully avoiding anything that might imply the conversation mattered.

"I don't have a problem," Henry said. "What's *your* problem?"

Chico and the Man is a repeat.

"Is it that Figger fuck?"

Henry winces at his brother's use of the word *fuck.* Brad has a harsh way of saying it. His teeth really cut into his lower lip before pushing out the *f* or something but it always sounds worse coming from him and anyway *it's none of his business* and he's setting me up, I can just feel it, he thought at the time.

"Why do *you* care?" Henry said.

"I don't want a freakazoid for a younger brother, that's why," Brad said.

Henry notices that there was a pause before Brad said this. And he could have sworn Brad had glanced over at him. In earnest. Like he really might have cared. A slight pause, but then with Brad sometimes it was what he didn't say.

And before Brad left, the conversation abandoned just like that, dangling in between them, Henry felt an impulse to cry and to hug his brother, so grateful for the sibling talk, so filled with love that he, momentarily at least, forgot his social misery. The feeling was quick, like a skipped heartbeat. Once it passed Henry got up to change the channel.

The sensor running underneath the floor mat just inside Baxter's front door has triggered the chime that to Henry sounds like the doorbell at his Aunt Millicent's New

28

York apartment. That apartment, a shabby walk-up in Greenwich Village, always sick with the smell of cumin and curry and God-knows-what-other Indian spices Aunt Millicent experimented with, fancying herself the sophisticate of Henry's family. "Just because she went to India once twenty years ago," his mother muttered every time her sister appeared wearing skirts fashioned out of sari material. Aunt Millicent also says *"ciao"* instead of "goodbye," tells them she'll "ring" them later and signs her letters and cards "cheers."

"Can I help you?" he asks, knowing that if Mr. Beardsley were here he'd get a lecture about enunciation and eye contact.

"Just looking," the woman says, fingering the circle of shoulders fanning out from the easy-sportswear display in the center of the store, Mr. Beardsley's attempt to remind this generation that sport coats are, in fact, leisure wear. "Casual Fridays ruined us all," he lamented to Henry when they set the sign in the middle of the rack. "Used to be no man worth his salt would enter a workplace in anything less than a suit and tie," he said, sifting one by one through each jacket, making sure the tiny bright upside-down-cupcake markers indicating size matched the actual garment — "Nothing worse than landing on the perfect jacket and finding out it's not your size after all," he'd say.

Along with sport coats, easy sportswear consists of cotton chinos (straight-legged with one-and-a-quarter-inch cuff), wide-wale corduroys (some embroidered with golf clubs, ducks or whales for the clubby inclusion they suggest), a large variety of oxford cloth shirts ("The largest in three counties," Mr. Beardsley would proudly point out), and a wide selection of classically styled sweaters that are instantly recognizable and therefore comforting to a certain set of customers wary of anything new, anything that varies wildly from what their forebears wore. And so a man could purchase a V-neck tennis pullover, cream-colored with navy and maroon stripes around both the neck and hem. Which is to say he could easily duplicate the Gatsby style his own father had cultivated, complete with red crepe–soled white ducks and the proper white flannel trousers to match. Also for sale, an exact replica of the ubiquitous L. L. Bean Norwegian sweater, navy with white flecks evenly distributed throughout, promising to repel water should the wearer find himself caught in a downpour without a corduroy-collared field jacket, found not so far away in the outerwear section.

Henry tries to busy himself with the week's receipts so his customer doesn't think he is smothering. Mr. Beardsley stalks customers toward the end of every month, so eager is he to bring the numbers up, somehow failing to see a connection between the too-polite, breezy "no thanks, just stopping in for a sec" and the backing toward the door. Henry sees it and winces, knowing he'd do the exact same thing in their shoes. At least they're polite to him, he always thinks. At least they're not simply walking out. Mr. Beardsley does not notice.

"Will this be all?" Henry says, reaching for the three-pack (spelled p-a-k) of Hanes undershirts, size small, and the thin box of twelve one-hundred-percent-cotton handkerchiefs. Though he has been trained to use the new bar code detector meant to simplify transactions, the bar code won't catch the attention of the laser line in the wand. He has to punch in the numbers by hand.

"Yes, thank you," she says. He showily counts out the eleven dollars and twenty-seven cents change so she knows it is exact.

She, he notes, pulls the door open.

Henry returns to the register area and reaches under the counter for the newspaper. He lifts out the classified section, folds it in half, to be transferred to his locker later. The rest of the paper does not interest him.

A little later — minutes? hours? — Henry becomes aware he has been staring at the wall for some time.

The store is empty. Vacant. The air stagnant. Sometimes, on the slowest of slow days, Henry is certain he can feel the atmospheric pressure bearing down and he fears he might choke.

And this is one of those days.

The sun, amber through the plastic window covering, spotlights dust particles suspended in the stale air. Baxter's has bad circulation and on particularly humid days there is an unpleasant and inexplicable smell of camphor mixed in with the old fabric. Intellectually, Henry knows inanimate objects cannot breathe but occasionally finds himself thinking the clothing has sucked up all the oxygen, leaving him with only mustiness.

It does not help matters that the store is packed with merchandise, sparing only narrow aisles that snake to the fitting rooms located in the back. The maze is so cramped that large-size customers are forced, in some cases, to turn sideways while making their way through the store. Every inch of floor space is crammed with some display or another. Upon entering, a customer will encounter the first of seven round racks, this one announcing new arrivals. It is understood that *new* is a loose term at Baxter's for many of the sport coats on this particular rack have been nestled there for several seasons. The new arrivals are flanked by two more circular displays, one set aside for sport coats in the smaller sizes, the other a bit taller, for heavier overcoats. So one must turn either right or left and pass in between these round obstacles just to make it halfway through the store to the square command center that is the register setting atop a glass case featuring cuff links, tuxedo studs, some ties, handkerchiefs — various and sundry items to complete a man's wardrobe. If all the floor displays were magically lifted up and carried away, the old, worn industrial gray carpet would show exactly where they should be re-deposited, thanks to these trails beaten down by years of customers' feet.

All four walls of the store are lined with racks that stretch length-wise, the upper level so tall Henry is called upon to reach the larger sizes of suits or coats. If left alone

Mr. Beardsley is forced to use a pole with a hook on the end of it. Pants are hanging lower and therefore require less attention.

In the beginning, when store owners were called *purveyors,* roads were only recently paved with tar and President Roosevelt's New Deal restored good fortune to many, Albert and Christian Baxter opened Baxter's to great fanfare. Red, white and blue bunting outlined the roof, the glass storefront squeaky clean and sparkling in the sun and nearly everyone in town turned out in fine clothing. Albert and Charles opened the doors wearing paper armbands on top of their high-collared dress shirts. Visors cast green tints on their spectacles and mustaches. Back then, in 1939, Henry's hometown had a population of 6,053 and was considered quite bustling. Fancy. On the rise. And Baxter's exemplified its wealth and promise. Breeding was what most of the townspeople took the greatest pride in. One third of the population could trace their roots back to at least one family member of great national significance. The remaining two-thirds, while not scruffy exactly, were left to cater to the needs of the wealthy. As the town grew, so did Baxter's importance, and shops bloomed on either side of it.

It is hard to pinpoint the moment when Baxter's went from fancy to frayed, but most likely it came after the war, after the nation had perfected frugality. The town (by then population 21,367) felt a collective sense of shame at its preening. Or guilt perhaps. Either way, it was as if a notice had been posted that from that point forward anything that hinted at opulence, anything that drew attention to one's fortune, was tasteless.

Albert and Christian Baxter quickly and sensibly sold the property to a self-made millionaire who kept the name but lowered the standards. The nearby metropolis offered plenty of jobs — careers — but became too expensive and crowded and so Henry's became a town of commuters. The population swelled to forty thousand. The town originals sniffed at the newcomers, thinking them *ordinary:* the workhorses of society who did not know the old Baxter's. They inevitably overlooked the plain and traditional Northeastern wear and flocked instead to whatever was the style of the day. Thankfully, though, some of the quality merchandise remained, so stalwarts continued to shop there.

Strange that the swell of occupants did not translate into town growth. Henry's was mostly a town of ones. One stationery store. One hardware store. One supermarket. One dry cleaner. And for many years a car dealership that by the 1980s had gone the way of the Woolworth's — both moving like moths to the light that was and is Westtown, a growing community three miles away. Baxter's was soon left hanging on to its spot on Main Street by its leather-tabbed, buttonholed suspenders.

Still, the town has a shabby elegance that Westtown cannot duplicate. Try though it might, Westtown has an altogether nouveau sheen to it that is distasteful to all in Henry's community. If there were a town motto it would be *quality not quantity.* The families here take pride in the fact that the previous generation also had house accounts at the hardware store or the stationery store and, yes, for a time, even at Baxter's.

Henry's is a town where honking endures as a form of greeting, not an expression of anger. Where everyone in a certain circle knows their friends' old cars and knows, therefore, all their friends' movements.

It is a place in which thank-you notes are written immediately following dinner parties. Bloody Marys with celery stalks served every Sunday even without company. Cotillions co-exist with salad dressing from packets that promise — with the addition of oil — to produce *genuine Italian dressing.*

This, a town where children make eye contact and call their parents' friends mister and missus and are taught to shake hands at very young ages.

"Do you know," Henry's mother once said to his father across the dinner table, after a bridge game at a friend's Westtown home, "do you know I had to introduce *myself* to her children? She didn't even blink. Not a word. They were little savages, those children. I'm so glad you all have manners. *My* children have manners."

Henry, a boy then, sat up straighter at the compliment. He noticed Brad did, too. Even little David seemed to Henry to be *politely* sleeping upstairs.

From then on Henry thought of Westtown as inferior.

Henry imagines Blackie's at ten. Blackie's is one of the few bars in town (an exception to the rule of ones). But unlike the surly man at Mike's tavern, the bartender at Blackie's ignores the fact that some of his clientele are grossly underage. Most week-end nights his patrons are boys whose voices had only recently dropped a register and girls whose baby fat had yet to redistribute itself. Blackie's is one step above sticky floors, two steps below the brass-and-fern decor slowly springing up in most bars in towns with eyes pointed optimistically to the future.

For a moment Henry is sure the door opened. Positively certain. He whips around to find it just as closed as it was three seconds ago. Maybe it jammed closed when that woman left, he thinks. He gets up and opens it and tries it from the outside. It is, in fact, just fine. No jamming after all.

Satisfied, he takes his seat again and sifts through the receipts in front of him, putting them in numerical order. He arranges himself over the papers so he looks studi-ous. In case someone did come in, he would look engrossed. As if having a customer would be somewhat annoying, actually. You could come back later and I wouldn't mind at all, he imagines his attitude to be.

He checks his watch again and pushes the receipts together, tapping them into align-ment, and tries not to think of the sheer waste his existence is turning out to be. His movements feel clunky and self-conscious.

As if he is being watched closely, the subject of a science experiment. An experiment some cosmic deity had cooked up, he thinks, to see just how deep a human being can sink into waking oblivion.

Or maybe it is a movie, he thinks. *The Life Story of Henry Powell,* starring (drumroll, please) Henry Powell, ladies and gentlemen. His heart sinks deeper into his chest, an imaginary screenwriter scribbles. He sifts through the shoe box under the counter marked Miscellaneous. Stage notes indicate the box is gray. The screenwriter uses words like *pathetic* and *desolate* in his description of the scene. Henry's shoulders are *slumped.* The screenwriter in his sunny California office, so remote from Henry's Northeastern existence. A gray existence. Like the shoe box. The screenwriter tilts back in the ergonomic desk chair all Californians seem to sit in and steeples his fingers together in supreme satisfaction at the metaphor.

Henry can envision Peterson in a pink T-shirt under his blazer (sleeves up) leaning against the bar at Blackie's, swigging his beer — for if anyone *swigs* a beer it's Peterson, he thinks. With, say, Bob Seger playing on the radio he'll fling non sequiturs like pizza dough. Hoping to catch the interest of his audience: "Figger" Newton, Gaynor Mills and Chris "Smithereen" Smith, so called because in tenth grade he took a hammer and smashed the box he'd received a D on in Shop. Though his classmates were admiring of the gesture, deep down Chris Smith knew he'd exploded not because of the grade but because the night before his parents had told him of their plans to separate. They never did end up getting back together, as they'd promised him that night. And Smithereen never quite got over it. Henry knows that at some point "Against the Wind" will give way to something by the Eagles. Serpentine conversation will slither from junk bonds and Drexel Burnham and, inevitably, back in time to Bunsen burners and football games won and lost. Bored heads will be fixed on the game scores scrolling along the bottom of the TV hanging in the corner of the bar. Braves lose. Mets up by two. Henry decides then and there he will not be going to Blackie's tonight.

The magnetic pull of his new answering machine is too much to resist. Not many people have these tape-recording devices attached to home phones. But Henry had his friend, the manager of Radio Shack, order one for him after reading about them in *Esquire.*

He picks up the phone and dials his own number. "This is Henry Powell," his own voice greets him, "please leave a message when you hear the beep." Though he knows what awaits him, he enters his code: 22849. He mouths the words as the robotic voice delivers the news: "*You have* — slight pause — *no* — slight pause — *messages.*"

He knew she wouldn't call him. He'd met her in the birthday card section at the stationery store that morning. Janine. She had moved closer to him at the precise moment he had unknowingly reached for a card with a pornographic cartoon image. Horrified, Henry had held on to the one he had chosen, hoping she had not seen it, and then, to hide the front, he pulled the matching envelope. But she had seen the slot the envelope came from and there was no denying the fact that Henry appeared to be a complete and total pervert.

Henry, beet-red but thinking "the best defense is a good offense," said, "Hi. I'm Henry Powell."

Janine stretched her upper lip out first in disgust but then, minding her manners, forced it into a smile, said, "I'm Janine."

Henry hoped a conversation would distract her long enough so he could back up against the opposing card rack and tuck the dirty card into a section, any section, from behind his back. "Do you work up the street?"

"No. I'm in town visiting my college roommate."

Henry, successful in relieving himself of the card, smiled. "Huh. Who's your roommate? Maybe I went to school with her."

It appears to Henry that Janine might be warming up and even perhaps — please God — forgetting about the card she thinks he chose on purpose. "Sloan Phillips? Do you know her?"

Henry once carried a very bombed Sloan Phillips up her front walk after a party they'd gone to together junior year but felt this was not the time to bring it up to Janine.

"Yeah, I know Sloan. Wow. You're her college roommate?"

The conversation went on from there and culminated in Henry saying, "If you guys are going out later, give me a call," after she'd mentioned wanting to go to Blackie's since she'd heard so much about it. But he had known she wouldn't call.

■ ■ ■ ■

The door chime sounds as Henry replaces the phone onto its receiver. A work fantasy blitzkriegs his brain: the buxom and pony-tailed St. Paulie girl blowing in through the front doors with outstretched arms finally free of the frothy mugs she's gripped ever since he discovered her in ninth grade and lovingly attached her image to the ceiling over his twin bed with circles of Scotch tape. But no. It is Mr. Beardsley, grinning hard underneath the single section of hair carefully directed from the left ear across the top of his head to just above the right ear.

"Henry, my boy, life is good," he says, breezing past him, all Old Spice and mentholated cough drops. "Life. Is. *Good.*"

"How's it going?" Henry asks, defying his boss's admonitions to steer clear of colloquialism.

"I'll tell you *how it's going,* my boy," his exaggerated enunciation a friendly but firm correction. "We're going big time." His arms stretch out, his face clownlike with wide-eyed enthusiasm. *"Big time."*

Henry winces at the "we."

It was not supposed to be *we.* This was to

43

be an interim job, one that supplied just enough income to keep afloat until something better came along. The classified section had conspired, though, to keep Henry here. *Work From Home,* one ad would announce. That hadn't sounded too bad until he called the number at the bottom of the square and found it had been disconnected. *On Your Way to the Top,* another read, but when Henry called he'd learned getting to the top required a significant amount of seed money. "To *make* money you have to *spend* money," the man on the phone had explained. When Henry told him he had little to nothing to give, the man abruptly terminated their conversation, which, until then, had been super friendly. Each week produced more discouragement until finally Henry decided to postpone his job search. Just for a while, he told himself.

"Big time?" His indifference was a way to keep Mr. Beardsley from confusing interest with shared enthusiasm.

Beardsley swings around to face Henry. "I just came from lunch with Arnie Schmidt and Bill Logan." He pauses to bask in admiration he's certain will follow. It appears, though, that this announcement will not have the impact he had counted on.

"Arnie *Schmidt* and Bill *Logan?*" Beardsley repeats himself, annoyed that he must now suffer the indignity of explaining the significance of the meal, diminishing its triumph. "Arnie Schmidt and Bill Logan are legends in boutique men's clothing. Legends. I know it's hard to believe but you know Clarke's over in Westtown? Well, it wasn't always the big draw it is now. Used to be you wouldn't be caught dead in Clarke's — all Sansabelt pants and white vinyl. You wouldn't take your *grand*father in there, much less find anything for yourself, God forbid. Schmidt and Logan went in, cleaned house, turned it into a multimillion-dollar cash cow."

Beardsley's remaining shred of excitement finally dissipates, deflated by Henry's blank stare. "You young people," he says, "you think everything magically works. Everything's *all* taken care of. You don't have to do a thing, businesses just *run* themselves. Bills just *magically* get paid. . . ."

Henry watches his boss's lips move. Their ugly stretchy movements remind him of the eel listlessly snaking back and forth in its tank in the Chinese restaurant near Route 3.

". . . but you and me, we're the *workers.*

We're the ones behind the scenes, making sure when people come down Main Street they've got *choices,* a nice string of shops to go in and out of, family places. . . ."

Carefully, so carefully, Henry reaches his right hand over to his left wrist and pretends to scratch a spot just beside his watch. Twisting it so the face angles up and he can check the time without the giveaway wrist roll, he nods in agreement to Mr. Beardsley's mouth, opening and shutting around the words pouring out his sales philosophy. When Beardsley glances at the front door midsentence, Henry sees his chance and successfully negotiates a quick glance-down.

It is three-fifteen.

It's warm enough to take off the top of the Jeep. It's been smelling like mildew lately but then again it could rain so maybe I should just keep it on.

"Hel-lo? Anybody in there?" The rapping at his skull rattles him out of his head and back to Mr. Beardsley, who is holding up the bundle that is Peterson's pants. "I suppose I'm expected to psychically *divine* what I am to do with these pants balled up here behind the desk?"

"Oh, yeah," Henry says. "I was going to do that after —"

"After what? After your daydream?" Mr. Beardsley jabbers on as he folds Neal Peterson's pants around the tailor ticket. "Honestly, Powell, I can't keep following you around reminding you about how the system works. You never used to need that, as I recall. What happened to those days? What happened to that energetic young man I hired not so long ago? Yes, Mr. Beardsley. No, Mr. Beardsley. Anything I can do, Mr. Beardsley? Now all I get is 'how's it going' if I'm lucky."

He shriveled up and died of boredom, Henry thinks. Rest in Peace. RIP.

CHAPTER THREE

1977

Henry parks his bicycle in front of the shoe repair shop, one store over from Baxter's, so he can readjust his tie and run a hand through his hair. He checks over his shoulder to make sure no one is around before he studies his reflection in the window. But the shoe repairman has not washed the window so Henry does not notice the piece of tissue paper still glued by a dot of blood to his freshly shaved face. The Help Wanted sign is still propped in the corner of Baxter's window so he knows he still has a shot. *Supplemental Help,* Mr. Beardsley said on the phone when he called to inquire the day before. Henry assumed "supplemental help" would be explained and so did not ask what that meant for fear of sounding ignorant.

"Ah, the young Mr. Powell." Mr. Beardsley takes off his glasses and walks to Henry, arm extended for what ends up being a surprisingly hearty handshake for such a delicate-looking man. "How are you, son?"

"Fine, sir," Henry says. "Thank you."

"Right on time —" Mr. Beardsley taps the face of his watch "— I like that. How's the season going so far? Let's go sit over here. Take your pick." He motions for Henry to take one of the two armchairs situated outside the dressing rooms.

"Good, we're just practicing right now actually," Henry says. He pulls his trousers up in front and settles into the chair, mirroring Mr. Beardsley's erect posture. His legs are already sore from the squats and suicide drills they ran that morning.

"Good old FRCP," Mr. Beardsley says. "You're a lucky young man. You've got the world at your feet."

Fox Run College Preparatory is uniforms, leafy walkways between old stone buildings, dowdy teachers, a mutli-million-dollar endowment, a competitive student body in love with Weejuns and bent on trying to appear indifferent. It is a private school as rich in tradition as it is in collective student body wealth, counting a U.S. president, fourteen senators and countless CEOs as alumni. Friendships forged in the dining hall were lifelong and tangled in well connectedness. Its hallways reeked of the carelessness that comes from knowing money will never be far out of reach. Few in Henry's class knew that the bloat of money filling up the pockets of, say, the Sandersons or the Childers offset the relative obscurity of funds in the Powell family. But Henry knew. He felt it when Kevin Douglas drove his sixteenth birthday present to school. Or when tags appeared on zippers after winter break. Tags reading Aspen, Stratton, Snowbird. Or when January sunburns started to peel. His academic scholarship was, he felt, a form of parole. Should some felony be committed, Henry sensed he would be the first one called up for a police lineup. When the headmaster called an assembly to lecture the upperclassmen about pranks and threatened to keep all the seniors from graduating if those responsible for the burning effigies meant to represent himself and his deputy did not step forward, Henry was sure the remarks were directed at him. The scholarship felt creaky, impermanent.

"You understand this is a temporary job," Mr. Beardsley says. His porkchop sideburns impress Henry.

Henry wore his hair long, below his ears — an unspoken uniform at Fox Run. But he made a mental note to aspire to Mr. Beardsley's choice of sideburn design.

Henry was conscious of his looks but not sorry for them. In other towns, in faraway regions, the Powell nose, for instance, would be attached to adjectives like *huge.* But in their Northeastern town Henry's facial centerpiece might be referred to as *patrician.* Befitting his angular, oversize features. Gangly. His limbs long, all muscle and sinew. He had seen pictures of his father in his teens and knew this was just a phase: someday he, too, would grow into his face and body. The cheekbones that jutted out, the chin that pointed from his neck and, yes, the nose, they would all make sense someday. He told himself the girls would be sorry and until then he tried to look at people head-on, postponing the profile view as long as possible.

"We'll see how well you do but I can't promise anything past the winter sale. This fall you'll get a lay of the land and then it's trial by fire. But after the sale I can't promise anything," Mr. Beardsley is saying.

"No, no, that's totally fine," Henry says.

"You make good eye contact," he says, scribbling something on his clipboard. "I like that."

"Thanks," Henry says. The mumbling, though, appears to dent Mr. Beardsley's smile. Another mark goes onto the clipboard.

"You'd be available for overtime work during sale week, right?" Mr. Beardsley peers up at him. Suspicious. The look of a man who has been the brunt of one too many crank phone calls, Henry thinks. A bolt of imaginary lightning illuminates Mr. Beardsley: "I *think* my refrigerator is running . . ."

"Yes, sir," Henry says. "Absolutely."

The Baxter's sale, heavily advertised in the *County Register,* begins every year on New Year's Day and lasts one week. The towns that circle this one like a skirt invade the store during the weeklong event — an event as much about acquiring new clothes as it is a hibernation hiatus. A chance to compare Christmas gifts and vacations. Henry and his brothers had gone with their mother every year when they were little. They would run through aisles with friends while their mothers chatted and picked through bins marked by sizes.

Between working the stockroom in the fall, on the floor during the holiday season and then during the sale, Henry hopes to save enough money for the used Jeep he has his eye on. A CJ-7.

"Those suck," Brad said to Henry just

before he left home for good. Henry, ripping out a picture from *Car and Driver,* said, "No, they don't," and regretted it because it had made him sound like a baby.

Sure enough: "No, they don't," Brad whined back at him.

"The thing is, it pays well," Henry says to his father a few hours later. "And Mr. Beardsley says I could make a schedule work around football practice and all. So I could work Thursdays when he stays open later anyway — after practice till close — and Saturdays. And days we don't have practice. Yeah, I'm pretty sure about that."

Henry has not quite thought it all through, this job at Baxter's. He pauses to check his father's reaction and to figure a way to spackle up the holes in his speech. His father's tie in muted diagonal stripes of pale yellow and brown is barely back in fashion after two decades off. In the dim light Henry can hardly see the frayed flecks of pulled silk.

"The away-game days, though, I know Mr. Beardsley won't mind," he says as much to himself as to his father. "He said so, actually. Oh yeah, I remember he said he wouldn't mind if it was different week to week. So then it's fine with the away games.

And it pays well."

Henry stops there as he notices his father's spoon has stopped circulating in his coffee mug. He has made a bad choice in ending with the pay factor. He knows that now and knows his father knows. But it is too late to rectify so Henry remains quiet, watching his father's wrist resume the trips around the perimeter of the chipped mug they had picked up on a family road trip to Vermont in the summer.

It is the great unspoken understanding in the Powell house that any discussion that points to their lack of fortune would be in bad form. In theory the Powells came from money. In theory. Their name a good, solid-sounding name sure to be connected somehow to English nobility somewhere deep in the rings of the trunk of the family tree. But in actuality Henry Powell's parents were Brontë penniless. A small trickle of money from a family trust fund kept them above the below, but the fact of the matter was they were below the above. Still, his mother's grandfather had had a lot of money that was to be stingily disbursed "in perpetuity" and that enabled them to continue the illusion — with manners and bearing — that they came from old money. They surrounded themselves with wealthy friends.

They wore shabbily preppy clothing. But most of all, they wore their lack of great fortune proudly. And so they were accepted into society.

It was just not done in the Powell circle, the speaking of money. A previous mention had ended badly, with Edgar Powell crying a single, solitary Native-American-looking-out-at-a-now-littered-land tear. Henry had only heard about the heartbreaking spectacle from his cousin, Tommy. Henry Powell had never seen his father cry. But he suspected seeing someone perpetually on the brink of crying is worse. The way nausea makes its victims pray for vomit. To be rid of the sickness. "How come your father cried?" Tommy had asked, unaware that he would now be eternally disliked for his Holy Grail sighting. From that point forward Henry refused to allow Tom into his fort. Henry sometimes imagined it was *he* who had seen his father show such emotion. He even concocted a scenario that entailed him offering his father a tissue, a kind pat on the head thanks for the thoughtfulness of the gesture. All fantasies ending with Henry and his father in a loving embrace, Henry inhaling the wet-dog tweed of his father's clothes, his father — eyes closed in reverie — inhaling his son's smell, the smell of childhood.

"So? Can I tell him yes?" Henry asks.

The spoon resumes clinking against the rough-hewn pottery, its surface purposely uneven in that craft-fair style.

"You can tell him yes," his father answers after a moment. Henry has no way of knowing that these would be five of only a dozen or so words ever spoken by his father about his job at Baxter's.

"Thanks, Dad," Henry says, already backing out of the room. He is eager to get out of his father's dark, tiny study, to get back out into the sunshine of the day. He would not know that his father will continue stirring and stirring his coffee until it grows cold and undrinkable. Obsolete.

In the two weeks that follow, Henry and his father do not see much of each other as his summer vacation gives way to football practices twice a day. In fact, there are many days in which the only signs that other people live in the house at all are the plastic-wrapped plates of food in the refrigerator. Henry leaves the house at first light to go to morning football practice and by the time he returns his father is gone for work. The afternoon practices stretch into the twilight, the heat mercifully lifting off the grass, which finally cools in the summer air. Once home Henry, bad posture and tired limbs, hunches over a plate shoveling his cold dinner into his mouth in silence, his parents having eaten long before he returns from the playing field.

One afternoon, Henry finds his mother in the kitchen.

"Your father wants to talk to you," she says. Henry's mother does not watch her hands when she is cutting. Cooking-school cutting. She is gazing out the window at the house across the street.

"Why?"

"I don't know, talk to your father about it," she says. Henry pictures a huge invisible watch dangling in front of his mother's eyes, hypnotizing her. Tick-tick-tick. Henry looks to see what has her so entranced and is not surprised to find it is the geranium-filled wooden-duck planter at the edge of the driveway.

"Mom," he says.

Tick-tick-tick. His mother's stare never wavers. She has finished cutting, but still she holds the knife in place on the cutting board.

"Mom."

The head turns, eyes tearing away from the driveway duck at the very last minute. It is a smooth turn that suggests the hypnosis is still in effect.

"Yes?"

"Why . . . does Dad . . . want . . . to talk . . . to . . . me?"

But slowed speech is not enough to hold her. Tick-tick-tick. The knife resumes its tempo on the cutting board. Over and over again, an even rhythm so familiar it has become the white noise of every dialogue.

Henry makes a show of leaving the kitchen but knows his mother probably will not notice he is no longer there. Though her knife is moving, nothing is under it to slice.

As he leaves the kitchen he glances up the stairs and, in Henry's mind, the soap opera Vaseline-on-the-lens effect kicks in.

The carpet runner, like a Slinky attached to each stair, is no longer beaten down and Henry's mother is bounding down the stairs, toward her boys, her tennis skirt flouncing with each step. Tretorns. Socks with little pink pom-poms at each heel. Her white Lacoste shirt tucked in. A pink headband to match the socks.

"I'll be back in an hour," she says, whisking past them to the front hall closet and her tennis racket with its needlepoint cover. "Betsy's here. If I hear you boys got into any trouble I'll be telling your father. Betsy? I'll be at the club if you need me. You can call the main number and remember to page Helen Wellington."

Helen Wellington invited Henry's mother to play doubles once a week as her guest at the country club twenty minutes away. But Henry's mother never thinks of herself as a guest. She has made a point of knowing the server's names at the grill where the foursome has iced tea and crust-less chicken salad sandwiches following their game. She pulls in to the same parking spot in front of lower court number eight each week. But the inescapable fact is that if there were ever an emergency that required her presence she would have to be brought to the club phone by Helen Wellington, her own name unrecognizable to the club operator.

"Be good," she calls out while climbing into the family station wagon.

Though he did not know what name to put on it at the time, a feeling of euphoria would overtake Henry every Wednesday when his mother left for her tennis game. It was not the fact that Betsy the babysitter was cute and let them do whatever they liked as long as they left her alone to read *Tiger Beat*. She even let them eat two Devil Dogs if they wanted (Henry always took two of whatever was offered but stowed the spare in his tiny desk drawer, to be savored later in little bites).

No. It was the sight of his mother so carefree that meant the rest of the day and night would be okay. She might even talk his father into taking them all to the drive-through for hot dogs for dinner. Anything seemed possible on Wednesdays.

But then a Wednesday came and went without the tennis game. Henry checked the calendar to make sure he had not gotten the day of the week wrong but he knew it was Wednesday because Wednesday was sloppy joe day at school and on that same day he had a stain on his school shirt to prove it. When he got home from school his mother was out in the backyard, on her knees pulling up weeds. No tennis whites. No pom-poms.

The following week was the same except this time his mother was in the kitchen sitting at the table, angrily flipping the pages of a magazine. Henry could not have known the subtle gaff that banished his mother from the country club (Helen Wellington had grown tired of Henry's mother, who had developed a nasty habit of arriving early at the court and greeting the others as a hostess would), but he felt its sting as acutely as she did. Wednesdays became like any other day of the week for Henry's mother. Except on bridge nights, but by then there was an unmistakable hollowness to her that dulled even the joy of playing cards with friends.

Two weeks after her last tennis game, Henry's mother burned the roast but only Brad brought it up with a mean "this tastes like my shoe" that felled whatever tree of hope was left standing in the center of the family that night. Moments later she got up from the table, carried the platter of meat into the kitchen and threw the whole thing out. The flick and hiss of her cigarette lighter could be heard through the swinging dining room door that slowly swung itself back to center.

Henry watched Brad look down at his plate, his mouth open in shock at the effect his words had had on their mother. His brother's face moved from shame to sadness and then, on looking back up, to surliness. "What are *you* looking at?" They both knew that Brad had been about to cry.

"Boys, go to your rooms," their father said.

Henry stopped in the kitchen before going upstairs. "I thought it tasted fine, Mom," he said. In a whisper so Brad would not hear in case he was still nearby.

On his way to his father's study he stops at his mother's purse and fishes past lipsticks, a compact and her wallet to find the pill bottle. He pours the little blue pills into the palm of his hand one-two-three . . . it is clear she has taken three today instead of the one that is prescribed by the family doctor he has never liked because he still offers Henry a lollipop after every annual visit. Usually she only doubles the dose.

"Dad?" he stands at the doorway to Edgar Powell's study. "Mom said you wanted to see me." With the toe of his shoe he traces the strip of metal that is meant to smooth the transition between carpeted and hardwood floors.

Henry's father looks up from his work and takes off his glasses, a signal that this will be a difficult talk.

"Have a seat," he says to his son. "How was school today?"

"All right, I guess." Henry shrugs and shifts in the chair that faces the desk.

"Good, good," Edgar Powell says. He clears his throat and Henry shifts again, aware that his armpits are tingling in sweat preparation. "That's what I wanted to talk to you about, actually. School."

Henry sits up straighter. "What about it?"

"I've noticed the light in your room stays on later and later into the night," he says. "I am concerned your schoolwork might be suffering under the pressure of all your . . . ahem . . . *commitments*."

"My grades will be fine," Henry says. He concentrates on keeping his voice from climbing into the fear register. "Classes are going to be easy this semester, I can already tell. It's senior year."

"Nevertheless," his father continues, "I want to raise the possibility of streamlining your schedule. Your allegiance must be to the academic curriculum, after all."

"I'm not going to cut football," Henry says. "I know that's what you're getting at and I'm just saying I'm not quitting the team."

Henry's father tilts his head and even though his glasses sit on his desk blotter he gives the impression of looking over bifocals at his son.

"You're not playing, Henry," he says. "I wonder if the coach has any more intention of putting you in this year than he had last year. And if this year is a replication of last then I suggest we take a long hard look at your mission. At your objectives."

Henry hears a rushing sound in his ears,

like the ocean in a seashell. He feels his face burning.

"My mission? What do you mean my *mission?* He doesn't want me to push my ankle, is all. He said the next game I'm starting and staying in."

"Watch your tone, young man," Edgar Powell says. "And I do not appreciate that look on your face."

"Yes, sir," Henry says. "But he said I'd start." His jaw is clenched through this last bit.

He starts to repeat himself but stops when his voice cracks and his tear ducts tingle. "He said . . ."

Every family has its own sign language. Every family has its own complicated set of signals, unintelligible to outsiders but loud as a shout in a tunnel to its members. In the Powell family it is Edgar Powell's habit to clean his eyeglasses with the end of his tie when he wants to be finished with a conversation.

"I simply don't want to see a scholarship evaporate because of some fool's errand on the football field. Or because of an after-school job."

"It's senior year — they're not going to take my scholarship away senior year,"

Henry says, now composed.

"Attitude, young man."

Henry notes the glass cleaning and decides not to challenge his father any further because the end of their talk is in sight. Which is, of course, his father's original intention in rubbing the tie on either side of the tiny square of prescription glasses. *No more words from you,* the subtitles say.

"Yes, sir."

"Good," he says. "I'm glad we had this talk."

Edgar Powell turns back to his work. He holds the glasses up to what little light is coming in through the small window and inspects his cleaning. That is the signal that Henry is dismissed.

The old headphones are huge, the springs have remained factory tight so that if he wears them too long they give him a head-ache. But at least they seal the sound of music into his head so none of it leaks out. Henry sees himself in the mirror that hangs over his dresser and thinks he looks like a fighter pilot.

But this image is in contrast with the one he has cultivated in his mind so he is care-ful not to look in the mirror once he clamps them on.

He tilts open the Plexiglas top of the record player with one hand, places the record on the turntable with the other. Henry has always liked this part. This is the part — the pops and nicks of the dust hitting the needle — when his room transforms itself into a recording studio. He closes the plastic top and readies himself for today's session. The window that overlooks the backyard becomes the soundproof window that separates the studio from the room full of producers, a record company executive and, in many cases, a *Rolling Stone* reporter leaning eagerly forward in his seat, ready to be dazzled by the notorious Henry Powell Band.

It started with "Rock On." That echoey, bass-driven song sounded so cool to him back in '74. He bought the David Essex album and played the song over and over and over after he was sure Brad was out of the house. Brad hated the song and called him a fag whenever he played it — Brad liked Three Dog Night and the Allman Brothers. Once Henry had saved enough allowance he bought the earphones.

Standing on the far side of the room (as long as the headphone cord would allow) he mouthed the words to the song piped into his ears. Soon it wasn't enough to be the lead singer so he began playing the bass guitar.

"Not many bass-playing lead singers," the *Rolling Stone* reporter would lean over and say to the producer at the sound board. "He's incredible, this guy." His producer would nod and say things like "Man, that was a great take" and "Right *on*," and then "Let's lay down some more just in case" which ultimately justified his playing the song over. And over. The record company executive was fetched by the assistant producer, who thought this Henry Powell so talented, "So *revolutionary,* man."

Rolling Stone came on board after Henry recorded "Goodbye Yellow Brick Road." A reporter was dispatched to absorb all things Powell. He tagged along with Henry and scribbled notes in between takes and tracks, recording Henry's wonderful wit and self-deprecation ("Seriously, I know it can be better. Let's do it one more time," Henry would say, apologizing to his band and crew for keeping everyone late.) Words like *workaholic* and *perfectionist* would litter the *Rolling Stone* guy's notes.

Over the years the Henry Powell Band

branched out and recorded all kinds of songs, defying all sorts of genres. "Dream-weaver" was followed by "Lay Down Sally," "All By Myself," and then, of course, the seminal "We Are the Champions." *Rolling Stone* had already put him on the cover but after "Champions" they did another cover that involved Henry standing, hands on hips, with a menacing look on his face. "Just the Way You Are" gave his public a glimpse of the private Henry. The one who never discussed his personal life. "They're eating it up, man," the reporter would tell him. "Men want to be you, women just want you," he said. "I just love the chance to play music," Henry would reply.

This particular session was interrupted by his brother early on in "Band on the Run." Henry hadn't really given it his all.

"What the fuck are you doing?" Brad says. He stands in the doorway. Henry frantically pulls his headphones off and throws them onto the bed, running a hand through his hair to try to be cool.

"What?"

"What the *fuck* were you just doing?" Brad asks.

"Nothing," Henry says. "What do you want?"

"I'm going out," Brad says, shaking his head. "Dad said to come get you and tell you to keep an eye on Mom. He's at a meeting."

"Yeah, okay."

"You freak."

Henry rushes across the room to close the door on his brother, who is already several steps away so the door slamming does not have the effect Henry had hoped. He calls out "knock next time."

"Freak," his brother calls back from the bottom of the staircase.

Henry cancels the rest of the session, his heart is beating so fast from this interruption.

Later that night he takes a ball of string from the messy miscellaneous kitchen drawer and ties one end to the inside doorknob in his room. He unwinds the ball across his bed to the far side where the mike stand (with its spit guard) stands. Before cutting the string he makes sure it is fairly taut in his hand. He cuts it and ties it to his finger. This way if it goes slack he will know the door has opened, his privacy compromised. It is too late in the game to change vantage points so he can be facing the door. He has to be facing the window in order that the team of admirers and producers working the boards better see him in action.

Rolling Stone (RS): I know you're really busy — like, insane busy I know — but there's this kid I know. Actually he's the son of a guy I work with. Anyway, this kid is a huge fan. Is there any way I could . . .

Henry Powell (HP): Bring him in! Sure, sure. Bring him with you tomorrow.

RS: Are you kidding? I was just going to ask you to sign a picture or an album cover or something.

HP: Yeah, fine. But if you want to bring him into the studio it's no problem. We'll put his name on the list at the security desk.

The *Rolling Stone* reporter shakes Henry's hand and runs off to make a call. Incredible, he'd say into the phone. Just like I told you, man.

By the time "Handy Man" comes on, the kid-who's-the-huge-fan has cancer and Henry's generosity grows accordingly (backstage passes, trips on the private plane, song dedications, the usual stuff). He's so down-to-earth, *Rolling Stone* will write. He's a megastar on tour but he still finds time to make a dying kid's dreams come true. Incredible.

"Hey, Steve?" Henry calls over to the quarterback on his way off the field, his father's words from the night before still ringing in his ears. "Any chance you could throw a couple before heading in?"

Steve Wilson drains the last of his Gatorade and nods, turning back to the dusk-lit fifty-yard line after tossing the empty plastic bottle aside.

"God, thanks," Henry says. He tosses the ball to the quarterback and sprints downfield.

The ball comes fast over to the left . . . then to the right . . . sometimes down the center . . . always spiraling. Henry and Steve speak in numbers hollered in near darkness. The evening fills with the music of whooshing and panting and feet pounding across the field. The others have long since showered and gone home.

"Last call," Steve says. Henry catches the final throw . . . a perfect thirty-yard pass . . . and tucks it under his arm to run it to the opposite end of the field, past the quarterback. The crowd roars as he scores a touchdown in his mind.

"See ya," Steve calls out.

"Hey, thanks, man."

And so it is that Henry Powell and Steve Wilson forge a relationship silently sealed with grass stains and sweat and a shared love of the game. After most practices, they hang back, tossing the ball back and forth to each other until their teammates are far away in the locker room or in cars heading home to pot roasts and mashed potatoes. Then the drills begin. Tosses turn to throws. Henry's long legs take him up and down the field. Until Henry begins to anticipate what Steve will do next. Until it is so pitch-black that the ball is invisible. Henry straggles into the showers so tired he does not see the coach's car still in the dirt parking lot.

CHAPTER FOUR

1984

Mr. Beardsley passes, his voice directed at Ramon the stock boy but intended to alert Henry that he's on deck, question wise.

"We'll see you on Sunday, right, Ramon?" Ramon is sweating under a huge box of outerwear and therefore cannot answer properly.

"Yeah," he says.

"Good." Mr. Beardsley looks back down at the checklist that's never far from reach. "Good." A check next to an item that by Henry's reckoning is most likely "make sure Ramon is coming on Sunday."

"Roughly what time will you be getting there, Henry, do you know? Just roughly." He tries to sound casual but Henry knows that whatever time he quotes him will be etched in a Moses tablet in Mr. Beardsley's head so he answers carefully.

"About three or so."

"Good." Another check on the list. "Good. I'll be in the back room if anyone needs me."

Sunday is the annual company picnic, an excruciating event dreaded by both Henry and Ramon, the sole invitees not counting the UPS man, whose name is mumbled by all because no one is sure if it's Robby or Bobby. But the UPS man never shows. This year Mr. Beardsley ventured a cheerful "You're working too hard . . . obby," varying the volume on the name. (R/Bobby managed an equally cheery combination head nod and shake accompanied by "Don't I know it, don't I know it" on his way out the door, hands never leaving his dolly).

Once Mr. Beardsley has wandered off, Henry dials his own phone number to recheck his answering machine. But the new toll-saver feature alerts him to the fact that he has no messages. Three rings. No calls.

He had really thought his brother would return his phone call this time. Brad knew very well he was at work and Henry had assumed he'd have taken the occasion of his not being home to leave a message, avoiding a conversation altogether. It had been three days since he had left the message on Brad's answering machine in Portland, Oregon.

"Brad? Hey, it's Henry. Um, I just thought

you should know, ah, Mom's not doing very well right now. She's been asking about you a lot lately and I was wondering if you were thinking maybe of coming back for a visit. Just wondering. No big deal if you can't. But Dad asked me to call you so I figured what the hell. Okay. Well. You have my number. Or you could just call the house. Hey, Brad? Come home, okay?"

"Hi, Henry." Kevin Douglas appears smaller, thinner, than he did at Fox Run. He had been the yearbook editor two years in a row but was ousted senior year for picking the most unflattering faculty pictures he could find. He lived in the city but had inherited his family home in town. The last time Henry saw him they had been at the pharmacy and had both been preoccupied with getting their prescriptions filled, and Henry was concerned about keeping Kevin from seeing the ointment meant to curb the alarmingly dry flaky skin he'd developed on various parts of his body.

"Hey, Kevin." Henry smiles as he replaces the receiver behind the desk. He comes out from behind the counter and shakes the delicate hand that is offered. "How are you?"

Henry claps Kevin on the back but the

friendly gesture is mistaken for a malicious one as little Kevin Douglas is pushed forward and has to right himself on a rack of jackets.

"Oh, jeez, sorry," Henry says. He guides him into the middle of the store where all the new arrivals have just been unpacked. Away from Mr. Beardsley and his picnic planning.

"So how's it going?" Henry asks.

"Fine, fine," Kevin says. Henry knows Kevin is waiting a moment for the business at hand to take precedence over small talk, which he has never mastered. "I'm looking for a suit," he says. "Maybe something double-breasted? I don't know. What do you think?"

"Double-breasted's one way to go," Henry says. "I like single, but that's me. Double-breasted can be a little boxy if you don't get the right one. Let's look over here."

Henry is hoping to dissuade Kevin, who will be further dwarfed by the extra fabric of a double-breasted suit. But he does not want to alienate him, especially after the unintended shove and because Kevin Douglas has always appeared nervous around him. Henry takes care to be gentler, quieter around him.

"Let's see." Henry bypasses the Pierre

Cardin, trendy in the late sixties, holding on in the seventies, and now in the mid eighties, Henry thinks, sadly on its way out. "Are you looking for pinstripes? Solid? Okay. Good. Yeah, I like navy, too. Perfect. Here it is. How about this?" Kevin, after careful examination, carries Henry's choice off to the dressing room.

"We do free alterations," Henry calls after him. "Just so you know." The back-clapping has poisoned the entire exchange: Henry would remind any customer of their alteration policy but now worries Kevin will think this a subtle reference to his size.

"I'll take it," Kevin says. He has not come out of the dressing room. Henry's eyes shift from one side of the store to the other, thinking of what to do to rectify this misunderstanding.

"What's that?" he asks, pretending not to have heard. Buying time.

"I said I'll take it," the tiny voice answers. "I'll be right out."

When Kevin Douglas emerges, Henry decides he will act as if the suit is a perfect fit.

"Good?" He looks at Kevin hopefully.

Kevin avoids his eye and hands the clothing over to be carried up to the cash register.

■ ■ ■ ■

"Henry, my boy," Ned Beardsley greets him, "what's your poison?" His arm sweeps over the foam cooler, the generous host. Henry curses himself — he didn't note when Ramon would be arriving and now he's paying the price by being the first there.

"Beer's fine," he says.

"Beer it is," Mr. Beardsley says. He pulls the pop top off before handing it over. "Aah," he says, swallowing a sip of his own beer, "this is great. Isn't this great?" He's looking out from his apartment's rooftop across others just like it, out into the distance. The tar of the rooftop has been painted an industrial silver-gray. The metal door that leads back into the building stairwell is propped open by a brick that has also been painted gray. There is a hibachi and an old radio that's tuned to the easy-listening station Mr. Beardsley favors. But the wind carries the sound out, away from them. Henry notes the flank steak marinating in a long Pyrex baking dish, grateful it's not the bratwurst his boss had served last year. An abnormally huge black fly circles the bowl of coleslaw, landing on the edge then rappelling down to test it with a stick leg.

"Yeah, it's great," Henry says. "Great view."

"I'll tell you," Mr. Beardsley says, "I was so lucky to get this place. I'm not sure I told you about that. Did I?"

He had, but Henry feigned ignorance and interest, figuring the story, however boring he knew it to be, would require little in the way of response and would fill the time until Ramon arrived.

"Oooh, it's *incredible*," Mr. Beardsley says. "I didn't tell you? I could've sworn I did. A lady comes up to me in the store one day, this really funny look on her face. I'm telling you, I couldn't read it. You know me — I can usually tell in five seconds what they're after but with this customer, nothing. So I waited. I let her come to me in her own way. That's something that's always good to try to do, by the way. Let them come to you. Anyway, she comes right up to me, doesn't even try to look for something on her own, looks me square in the eye and says she has a strange request and hopes I won't be too offended by it. Of course I won't, I told her. I'd be happy to help with anything she might need, I said. She clears her throat and says she has to buy a sport coat for a dead man. Just like that. She looks at me and squints a little, like she's not sure how I'll take this news."

Though Henry has heard this story multiple times and could even recite parts of it by heart, he politely raises his eyebrows and nods to his host.

"I tell her I am not in the least offended, that we have seen to the clothing at funerals in the past and that we'd be happy to help her. Then she asks me if I could come up to the apartment and measure him for it. Asks me to come measure him because he's never had a sport coat or something like that. Or maybe he had one and he lost a lot of weight or something, I can't remember that part but the bottom line is I agree to go over to his apartment, which I think is strange but who am I to question another's culture, I think to myself. She seemed a bit *exotic,* if you know what I mean. So I assumed at the time that this was an ethnic thing where they don't like funeral homes. This is what I'm thinking at the time." He taps the side of his head, a visual aid now built in to the fabric of the story, it's been told so many times.

"Anyway, I agree to meet her at the front of her apartment building and I go there right after I close up for the day. Remember I'm thinking it's their religion or something. Maybe he's laid out at their apartment instead of a funeral home for religious reasons. To each his own, I tell myself. We shouldn't judge."

Henry nods, shrugs and takes a gulp of his beer.

"So, I get there — you want another beer? Let me get you another one," he says, eager for his audience to be totally focused on his story, not waiting patiently for it to be over in order to get another beer. He's pleased at his own attentiveness.

"There you go. *Anyway,* I get there and she's right out front, like she said she'd be. Everything's going just as she said it would. Except that I notice her key chain is huge. One of those rings like jailors have in the movies, you know? I think it's strange but I follow her in through the main door to the lobby. We go over to the elevator and while we're waiting for it she thanks me again for doing this. She's very grateful and so on. We get in the elevator and then we're on the top floor of the building, walking down the hall to the apartment. That's when I realize it's not *her* apartment at all, *she's the superintendent of the building.* She's fishing through the keys on her ring, she doesn't know for sure which key it is. That's how I know."

He explains his detective work to Henry as an aside. Many of his listeners must have wondered about this part so he has worked the explanation into the story.

"Anyway, she gets the door open and that's when it hits me. The smell. I'm telling you, Henry, it almost knocked me over, the smell was so bad. I look over at her and she's acting like she doesn't notice a thing. So I take a gulp of air before I go in and try to hold it as long as I can. But how long can you hold your breath, you know? You've got to exhale sooner or later. So I try to breath in and out of my mouth. It works for a few steps but then I'm tasting the smell. *Tasting* it. Can you imagine? It was so strong *it actually tasted.* And there she is, motioning me to come over to this chair, where I can see the back of a man's head. This isn't right, I'm thinking. He's not laid out all official-like. I get around to the front of the chair and I see what's going on. She's his landlord and he's *passed* and she hasn't called anyone about it! He's sitting upright, his eyes are still open! For a second I think this might be a sick prank — like he might reach out and grab me or something. Like a *Candid Camera* thing. If it weren't for the smell I would've thought that for sure."

Henry senses this is where he should interject something verbal.

"So what'd you do?"

"I'll tell you what I did." Mr. Beardsley beams at the question, listlessly executed though it was. "I excused myself and practically ran out to the hallway. She followed me out. You've got to call someone about this, I told her. I'm ashamed to say I may have raised my voice. The police. The coroner. *Someone.* And she just looked at me like I was speaking a language she didn't understand. Does he have any family? I asked her. She said no. Are you his landlord? I asked her. She said yes. That's all. Just 'yes.' Like it's twenty questions and I'm supposed to piece it all together. What about friends? Are there any friends of his you could call? None, she said. As it turns out he was a loner, stuck to himself mostly. He was old. Ninety, I believe."

Mr. Beardsley takes a sip of his beer and luxuriates in his wonderful tale, so sure is he of Henry's complete fascination.

"Wow," Henry says.

"Wow is right," Mr. Beardsley says. "I

talked her into calling the police and we went back inside, where I figured I'd just stand by her for moral support — maybe she's in shock or something, I think to myself at the time — but the way she looked at me . . . I couldn't believe it, she still wanted me to measure him. She was standing by the phone, not saying a word, but standing there looking at me like it's a bribe — she'll call the police if I take his measurements. I'm sorry but if you've got an unreported dead man in one of your units — I think you've got bigger things to worry about than whether he'll be dressed right in his casket. I don't say that, I just think it. Of course I don't say it out loud."

"*There* he is!" Henry says with an emphasis that reveals he's been wondering about Ramon's arrival for some time now. He practically hugs Ramon when he sees him emerging from the stairwell onto the rooftop. The metal door clanks back in place next to the gray brick doorstopper. "He-ey, man!"

Ramon squints at Henry, who has never seemed so happy to see him.

"Mr. Rodriguez." Mr. Beardsley's demeanor shifts back into that of a host, jovial formality. But Henry knows he is slightly annoyed by the interruption so close to the story's climax. "Good to see you, good to see you. What can I get you? I was just telling Henry here how I came to live here."

Ramon's eyes crinkle in a stifled smile of recognition — he now understands Henry's false enthusiasm. Henry nods back with a miserable gulp of his beer.

"I *know* I've told Ramon this story," Mr. Beardsley says with a clap on his guest's back.

"Yeah," Ramon clears his throat. "Yes." He accepts the beer.

"So, to make a long story short —" he directs this back at Henry along with a pointed finger uncurled from the bottle neck "— turns out she's crazy. Certifiable. She called the police to report him dead — I had to make a show with the measuring tape and let me tell you I almost lost my lunch doing it. The police showed up, asked a few questions and the next thing I know they're taking her out to the cruiser, wanting to talk to her downtown, et cetera, et cetera. She's nuts."

Big gulp and Henry knows he's rounding the corner into home plate.

"They hauled her off to some nut hut and her son took over. Anyway, I think about it —" again the visual aid indicates where his

85

thoughts are taking place "— and I think the man's place isn't half bad. If you want to know the God's honest truth, I was thinking that to myself even when I was measuring him — this place is great, I thought. So I let a few days go by, but I'll tell you in this market you can't wait too long, things get snapped up. I called the son and voilà!" Henry's French teacher would have disapproved of the *v* pronounced as a *w*. Mr. Beardsley continues, "I'm signing a contract before he's got all the old guy's stuff cleared out. I looked around and told him I had half a mind to keep some of it, if it weren't already spoken for and you know what the son said? Two birds, one stone. That's what he said to me. Two birds, one stone. Great guy."

Mr. Beardsley beams. "Soooo," he says with a monologue-ending stretch, "you never know what a customer's going to come out with, I'll tell you what," he says. "Little did I know that day the woman came in the store I'd end up with a whole new life by the end of it."

"Two birds, one stone," Henry says, flush with happiness that the never-ending story has, in fact, ended. "That's something."

"*Qué peso,* Ramon?" Mr. Beardsley calls

86

over to his other guest, unaware that Ramon Rodriguez doesn't speak a lick of Spanish even if the greeting were correct.

The rooftop door clanks against the brick and Mr. Beardsley's smile fades. "4-C," he mutters.

"A-hem," he loudly clears his throat, a signal Henry recognizes as being a precursor to Mr. Beardsley's version of anger. "Can we help you?"

"No, thanks," the woman says, unfurling an oversize beach towel that says "Love is . . . never having to say you're sorry" underneath a cherubic cartoon couple holding hands. But before 4-C can grease up an arm with the baby oil she's pulled out, Mr. Beardsley descends.

"Aah, hold up there. I signed up for roof use a month ago," he says. "Check the sign-up sheet. I reserved the roof — what was it? — a month ago. Henry, Ramon? When did I first talk to you about the picnic? About a month ago, right? Anyway, you'll see my name there, clear as day. Ned Beardsley. 14-D."

"Okay, okay," 4-C is folding up her towel. "Take it easy. No biggie. I'll go to the park down the street." It strikes Henry that 4-C looks like Patty Hearst from the side. Patty-pre-SLA not Tanya, he thinks, noting that

4-C's breasts are not half as big as Patty Hearst's.

Mr. Beardsley clears his throat, this time more gently. "Thanks," he says. "If I hadn't signed up it wouldn't be a problem but I signed up and everything . . ." He trails off, unsure what to say, so unaccustomed to getting his way so easily. He brushes an invisible fly off his short-sleeve madras button-down Henry knows was remaindered and finally set aside to donate to Goodwill before being rescued by his boss who praised its "classic cut" that would no doubt come back into style once all the hippies grew up and shaved, he said.

"Can I use your bathroom?" Henry asks, eager to walk down with 4-C.

"Sure, sure." Mr. Beardsley turns from 4-C, grateful for the diversion from the awkwardness. He reaches into his breast pocket and hands Henry a single key. "You know the way, right? Want me to come with you to let you in?"

"No, no." Henry waves him off and holds the roof door open for 4-C. Richard Marx comes on the radio and once his back's turned to Mr. Beardsley Henry rolls his eyes theatrically for the sunbather's benefit.

"Sorry about that," he says to her once the metal door falls back against the brick.

"No biggie," she says again, her flip-flops slapping down the stairs. "Is that your family?"

"No!" Henry's voice seems louder as it echoes in the concrete-and-metal stairwell. "No." He lowers the volume back to a level that is meant to indicate he's cool. "He's my *boss*. He has this cookout thing every year. It's like — Jesus. It's painful. Every year."

"Here's your stop." She smiles, and thumb-points at the hallway entry door with "14" stenciled on it army-style so the lines on the number four don't exactly meet. "See ya later."

"Yeah," Henry says. "See ya." 4-C's flip-flops clack down the stairs so quickly she does not notice the deflation of Henry's shoulders.

Mr. Beardsley's hallway is dark and smells of disinfectant. The key works so well Henry suspects Mr. Beardsley polishes it and then uses some vacuum attachment to suck any intruders out of the lock. No detail is too small for Mr. Beardsley.

Mr. Beardsley's apartment, Henry thinks, could be an advertisement for the witness-relocation program, so generic, so devoid of any personal effect. Even the record albums are covered in brown wrapping, like schoolbooks meant to be passed down from one class to another. Ned Beardsley has carefully erased any clues to his personality; any crumb of identifying style has been banished from this clean, airless living area. The furnishings, if not rented, are equally noncommittal. The couch merely serviceable, a place to sit. The overhead light simply existing to eliminate darkness — no mod globes here. Nor are there any trendy macramé hanging plant holders.

In the bathroom, a towel rack across from the sink offers three neatly folded medium-size towels Henry knows Mr. Beardsley positioned with deliberate care should one of his guests have to use his bathroom. Curious, he pulls back the blue-and-white seersucker shower curtain and sees the one thing that he knows gave Mr. Beardsley pause for thought this morning. It is the towel used for the morning's shower. Since it would have been too wet to put into the hamper lest it mildew or emit a strange smell, Henry could picture his boss struggling with what to do before deciding on spreading it out from end to end on the towel rack. A pragmatic and neat solution. But one that leaves Henry sick. That very morning, after dragging himself numbly out of bed and showering, he too stretched his towel perfectly between ends of the towel rod, even untucking the final inch or so of the right side so every centimeter of towel would air dry evenly.

And so Henry Powell uses the toilet, flushes and leaves the seat up. Just like that. An act of defiance that restores the acids in his stomach and puts a smile on his face that becomes even broader when he emerges into the sunny rooftop where, according to the song on the radio, Brandy is a fine girl (though, sadly, not fine enough for a seaman to marry) and Mr. Beardsley is flipping the flank steak.

"Hey." Ramon juts his chin out at him.

"Hey," Henry says. "How's it going?" He reaches into the cooler for another beer.

"Oh, you know," Ramon says. Though Henry doesn't know. He's never really clicked with Ramon and has attributed this to the fact that they went to rival high schools.

Henry is uncomfortably aware that to Ramon, Henry is another rich white guy who feels working in a retail store beneath him. It's like a pebble in his shoe; this thought chafes every time he sees Ramon.

"How'd it go with 4-C?" Ramon asks. But not too eagerly. He looks out at the view while Henry tries to decipher Ramon's sphinx smile.

"I'm too much of a man for her," Henry says. Fake chuckle.

Ramon nods and chuckles back. But Henry can't tell if it, too, is disingenuous laughter — one trapped picnic guest to another.

"How's Melissa?" he asks. Ramon's wife has managed to be "busy" at every single company picnic.

"Oh, you know," Ramon says.

CHAPTER FIVE

1985

Six fifty-nine. Every day it's the same. The alarm is set to go off at seven but Henry's eyes blink open at exactly 6:59. Henry Powell has never overslept in his life. Not once. Much to his disappointment. He has tried to sleep in — on weekends and holidays certainly — but attempts have ended up with frustrated flips under the covers, trying to shimmy his body into a position that will prolong sleep that never lasts beyond seven in the morning.

The room is so quiet he can hear the clock's three metal plates fall over, turning 6-5-9 into 7-0-0. A gentle click of a sound. The radio lazily comes on (ten seconds after the changing of the numerical guard, he notes) and the room fills with shootings, traffic backups, baseball disappointments and heat indices.

"O-kay," he exhales, and pushes himself

to the edge of the mattress, legs dangling, feet brushing the dusty hardwood floor.

Soon the two-room apartment fills with the sounds of morning: shower spray hitting the tub, clock radio blaring, the blip blip blip of the coffeemaker forcing water through the tiny hole into the small glass pot beneath it. Once the shower's been on a full three minutes Henry gets in, sure it's hot enough. The mirror above the sink is already fogged up.

Four minutes into soaking with eyes closed, he feels along the tiled wall to the soap shelf. Lather is created. Private parts are soaped and rinsed. Two more minutes under the shower head that's so old errant streams of water break rank and hit at odd angles. Water is turned off. Towel is found by groping hands. Body is dried and ready to step out onto the cold floor.

Like the childhood game of red light/green light, Henry freezes in exactly the position he's in: toweling out his right ear. Was that the phone? He waits three seconds and yes, sure enough, the phone is ringing.

"Hello?" He holds his towel around his waist even though he is alone.

"Henry? Henry, it's Mr. Beardsley." He doesn't wait for Henry to murmur hello, which he does, inaudibly. "You've got to come right in. Can you? Can you come in right now? I need you right now."

"Yeah, sure," he says with a glance over to the clock. It's seven nineteen. "What's going on?"

"Just come in as soon as you can get here." Click. Mr. Beardsley — of all people — didn't say goodbye. Just hung up.

He pulls a pair of briefs out of his underwear drawer. Boxers are too free form for a day that very well may require some kind of physical exertion. Better to go with briefs. Then khakis, his staple blue oxford and blue blazer. The neat sound of the tightly woven silk tie being pulled off the rack and he's out the door. No time for his customary commuter cup of coffee, he's pleased that at least he remembered to turn off the coffeemaker before locking up.

England Dan and John Ford Coley are singing far too loudly, the sound a shock to the morning quiet — it takes a moment for him to turn the knob down. Lite rock never is, in the morning.

His jaw is clenched in what's become his natural expression. "You mad about something?" his friend Tom Geigan asked him not too long ago even though they were enjoying a Mets game on TV. Indeed, when he opened his mouth to answer no it was a relief to his jaw muscles. Since then he has to consciously relax his mouth throughout the day.

The hard rain that lulled him to sleep the night before has changed the landscape of his morning drive. He passes three plugged-up gutters on his way in to work, pools of stagnant water circling out into the middle of Main Street. The single traffic light that forces hesitation between his apartment complex and his job blinks red and no one else is on the road so he makes it downtown in minutes. He skims through the last pool and sails into a parking space right in front of the building.

But instead of rushing in, his hand remains on the gearshift long after he is parked. For here she is. The girl he noticed two days ago getting into her car, parked alongside his. Even though she's got a whole street full of empty parking spaces, she is once again pulling in to the one alongside his.

"Hey," he says, careful to appear casual with a half-head nod in her direction. He tries to look as if he, too, is juggling too much to fully concentrate on the morning greeting. But he doesn't have a coffee cup or an armful of papers and books like she does. He is holding his tie in one hand, keys in the other.

"Hi." She says it as more of an apology than a greeting. "Some rain, huh?" She juts out her chin and blows her bangs out of her eyes since her hands are full. Then she moves up to the curb, where he's standing.

"Yeah," he says. "You need some help?" he reaches out to indicate he means the books she's loaded down with.

"Uh, no," she says. "I've got it. Thanks, though." He turns to go.

Then, providence intervenes. The sound forces her to reconsider. They both turn and face the source, knowing that it will require her to submit to his offer.

Splayed out on the wet pavement is her key chain, mocking the distance between them.

"Here, let me . . ." Henry doesn't finish the sentence, aware now that she is strangely embarrassed at having to accept help. He leans down and scoops up the keys and tries to hand them back to her but quickly realizes she's got no free hand with which to accept them.

"What d'you . . ." "Could you . . ." They speak at the same time. Then she starts over. "Could you just . . . would you mind just grabbing that door — no, down there. I work at Cup-a-Joe," she explains while walking. "You probably think I'm nutso, drinking coffee on my way to a coffee shop."

"I didn't even notice —"

"It's just that it takes a while to brew. At the store. It takes a while to get everything up and running so I drink coffee on my way in. The key with that purple dot? Yeah, that one. I put permanent marker on my keys to tell them apart better. It's the bottom lock first. No, turn it to the right. I know it's stupid. My roommate makes fun of me. Counterclockwise. No, other way. Yeah. But this way I don't waste time trying every single key on my key chain before hitting the right one. Okay, then the top one is the key with the black dot. . . ."

"Henry!" Mr. Beardsley bellows down the sidewalk. "What're you doing?"

They turn to Henry's boss, the dripping mop an explanation for his early-morning call.

"I'll be right there," Henry calls over. He knows this exchange has cost him response time.

"I can take it from here," she's saying, "thanks so much. I can get it. Oh, great."

Henry's unlocked the top lock and is pushing the glass door open for her.

"Thanks a lot." She collapses her load of papers and books onto the bar-height counter along the front window that enables coffee drinkers to face out and watch nothing happen. "Phew." She pushes her hair out of her face with a finality that blown air cannot achieve. "I hope I didn't get you in trouble for being late."

"Oh, no." He waves his hand dismissively. "Don't worry about it."

"I'm Cathy," she says, extending her hand for a shake. "Cathy Nicholas."

The morning is spent pressing water out of the sopped carpet in the front of the store. The plastic sealants surrounding the double glass doors failed to keep the rain out, most likely because the wind blew it sideways throughout the night. Henry's job is to twist the soaked mop out, which he does over and over again out at the curb. Like the Sorcerer's Apprentice he marches to and from the curb and each time he glances down toward Cup-a-Joe. It takes three hours before most of the heavy damage is controlled. Mr. Beardsley has set up little yellow sandwich boards that read Caution: Wet Floor and depict stick men falling.

For the first time in Mr. Beardsley's years at Baxter's the store is closed during regular business hours. Customers would track this all through the store, he tells Henry, and then the whole carpet would be ruined. The smell of mildew is already threatening the inventory.

Henry and Mr. Beardsley set up two industrial-size fans on either side of the worst part of the damage and face them out to the street, opening up the double doors. The hope is that the moisture will be pulled from the ground and carried off, like a drunk is peeled off the sticky barroom floor and deposited elsewhere to sleep it off.

By midday Henry's back aches. He stands up and stretches, tired from pressing the floor with beach towels Mr. Beardsley has run out and bought down the street at the dollar store.

"This is terrible," Mr. Beardsley says. He is standing alongside Henry but has to yell to be heard over the fans. "Just terrible."

"It'll dry up," Henry says. "It won't be too bad."

"No one wants to buy smelly clothes," Mr. Beardsley says. "I'm going to go out and get some air freshener. I'll be right back."

Henry sits behind the counter and thinks about Cathy Nicholas.

He curses himself for not noticing her body. He'd taken in her face at the time and now, trying too hard, he cannot even conjure that up. She has brown hair. The kind of brown that he is willing to bet was, in childhood, white-blond. It's straight, he thinks, though he's not quite sure.

He has to get back into the dating game, he knows this much. His last date had a lazy eye. He had not known which eye to look at and frankly it felt creepy. He'd nicknamed her *Cross-Eyed Mary* for the Jethro Tull song of the same name and he'd joked about her with his friend Tom and felt bad about it.

Since Cross-Eyed Mary there had been no one. He worried that dating was a muscle that needed to be exercised, so one night, for practice, he pulled two plates out of the cabinet above his tiny kitchen counter — only big enough to accommodate his coffeemaker and a toaster oven on one side of the sink, a drying rack on the other. Two forks. Two knives. Even two place mats — the ones he had taken from his parents' house when he had found this apartment. They had long since stopped using place mats at the Powell house so he figured they would not miss them. At the time he had figured it would be a good thing to have two place mats for dating purposes.

He set up the pair of places on the rickety thrift-store dinette table and stood back to admire it. Not bad, he thought. But after a few minutes he decided the place mats cheapened the look of the whole thing, being plastic foam and somewhat picked at the edges. He carefully put it all back — cabinet door opening and closing, drawers doing the same — it felt sad to him. Like the plates had gotten their hopes up. And the forks. Knives can fend for themselves.

The drying rack has the single plate he uses for dinner, the bowl he uses for cereal, a single spoon, fork and knife and at times a pot that is drying, depending on what he has cooked. Every so often he replaces each one to give them all equal rotation.

He tells himself he will ask this Cathy out for dinner. He feels certain she does not have a lazy eye.

The problem will be her falling in love with him. They all do, he shakes his head. It gets tricky extricating himself from these relationships. Cross-Eyed Mary had called and called. He didn't know for certain it was her — she never left a message — but he could just tell. He didn't answer — Jesus, no way, she'd hear my voice, tears would follow so better to just let the phone ring.

The ghost writer leans forward to make sure his tape recorder is getting all this and appears relieved to see he still has time on the miniscule tape cassette. *All the women love Henry Powell,* he scribbles in his note-pad. Yes, Henry nods silently and then says, it's always been the way. I guess it's like fat people hearing thin ones complain about having to put on weight so I maybe shouldn't say this out loud, Henry says, but really it is difficult to be me in these sorts of situations. Oh, yes, I'm sure, the man gives a sympathetic nod. I cannot imagine how difficult, he adds.

"Henry? I could use your help with this," Mr. Beardsley says, pushing his way past the wind tunnel the fans have created, handing Henry one can of Lysol. He takes the other and starts spraying.

"Won't this be worse for the clothes?" Henry calls out over the fans.

"What?"

"I said, won't this be worse for the clothes? This spray sticking to them? This smells worse than the water did," he shouts.

Mr. Beardsley stops spraying and sniffs the air.

"Shit, you're right," he says. It is the first time Henry has heard his boss swear. "Jesus, what're we going to do?" He drops the can of Lysol to the floor and it rolls under a rack of pants.

"Let's just let the fans go for a little while," Henry says. "I think the fans are all we need." He lowers to one knee to reach the Lysol.

"What?"

"Let the fans do it," Henry shouts. "It'll be fine."

He rolls his sleeves back down and buttons them. Mr. Beardsley is staring at the carpet as if willing it to dry.

"How much longer do you want me to stay?" Henry asks.

Mr. Beardsley motions to the area just past the counter and points to his ear, indicating he cannot hear, though Henry is sure he has.

"What'd you say?" he asks Henry once they are farther away from the fans.

"Um, how much longer did you need me, do you think? I can come back . . . I've just . . . I've got to run a quick appointment, you know."

Mr. Beardsley nods. "Yes, yes, five-fifteen. I know. Go ahead. You don't need to come back."

"If you need me I can come back. I mean, if you need me."

There is a pause.

"It's okay," Mr. Beardsley finally says. He is so tentative Henry decides against offering again, as he was going to do a moment before the pause. To be polite.

"Okay, thanks," he says. "Um, I'll come in early tomorrow to clean up what doesn't get done tonight. Don't worry. I think the fans will really do it."

Mr. Beardsley looks back out toward the doors. "You think?"

"Yeah, totally."

"I don't know. I hope you're right. Okay, well, go on then. Have a good night."

"Thanks. See you tomorrow," Henry calls out over the sound.

Cup-a-Joe is already closed he notes, getting into his Jeep. Most of the stores along the street are closed. Henry starts up the Jeep and puts it right into Reverse instead of waiting the thirty seconds he normally does to let the engine warm up. He hurries along Main Street and soon pulls up in front of his parents' house.

"Hel-lo? Mom?" he calls out, shutting the door behind. "Mom?"

He hears the refrigerator door closing so he goes into the kitchen.

She is mixing the orange juice into the vodka, ice cubes jingling.

"Hey, Mom," he says.

"Hey is for horses," she says. She is alert, her smile full of recognition, but Henry has been fooled before. He steels himself and sure enough the impulse to rush to her, hug

105

her, bury his head in her chest, dissipates as she teeters past him to the living room. Imperious. Regal. And very, very drunk.

"You doing all right? You seem better today. Did you take your pills?"

"*Did you take your pills,* listen to this. My son doddering over me like I'm an old lady."

"You okay on groceries?" Henry ignores her comment and goes back to see how they are holding up, food-wise.

"Liquid lunch," she says, toasting the air in front of her and spilling a little in the process.

"Mom, you really shouldn't be . . ."

"Don't even finish that sentence, Henry Powell. Where's my Brad? He came by yesterday but only stayed a few minutes."

"That was me, Mom," Henry says. "Brad's in Portland, remember?"

"That was most certainly *not you,*" she says.

"It was me. You want to watch something? What's on now?"

"I want to watch something with *my Brad,*" she says. "He was always so sweet. Did I ever tell you about the time he tiptoed into the kitchen after I'd burned a roast that tasted like an old shoe?" She leaned over conspiratorially as if this were not her own son she was speaking with. "He tiptoed in and whispered to me that he'd liked it just fine. He said it just like that, 'It was fine, Mom. *Just fine.*' So sweet, my Brad."

A little later Henry pulls his Jeep into space number twelve in front of his apartment building. There are two visitor spots for every unit in his building but his have never been used.

He unlocks the top lock, then the bottom, lets himself in and closes the door. He throws his keys like dice to the counter and reaches for the phone book.

"L, m, n . . . n . . . ni . . . Nichitas . . . Nicholas," Henry says. "C. Nicholas. Bingo. C. Nicholas, 452 Railroad Avenue."

He looks up and squints while tracing the back roads of town in his head. Railroad Avenue should be familiar as he knows where the tracks are and how they cut through town, but he is quite certain the road that runs alongside it is Lockridge. The train tracks are not so obvious in their division of the town for they cut through like a knife into a sandwich, separating east from west to no effect. Rather, the real distinction lies between the town's north and south.

After the cluster of Victorians and small Cape Cods huddling near downtown, the roads wend their way north past larger properties, set farther back from the road. In many cases, tucked nicely in the center of manicured and landscaped lawns, more likely called *grounds.* Homes protected by gates, some wrought iron, others fashioned to look like barn locks, crisscrossed-and-painted wood. Mallard mailboxes, stone walls, forsythia, boxwood and rhododendron, in different combinations, complete the complexion. Over there the Petersons', where Henry drank too much beer after their senior prom and passed out in the pool house next to fat Sally Evans, who had vomited up her drinks. Over here the Childers', where Henry walked in on Steve Wilson, a junior at the time, in the master bedroom with a classmate's college-age sister. Just up that hill, behind the Alcatraz gates, sophomore Henry brokered a peace agreement between John von Sutter and Kitty Connors, who were on the angry side of the breakup-reconcile pendulum.

In one motion the phone book is closed and keys are grabbed. The light is fading and Henry wants to set out while he can still read street signs.

The Top 40 station is playing "Owner of a Lonely Heart," and it crosses Henry's mind that 1985 is not a good year for music. He hasn't bought a record in two months. Turning from his low-rise apartment complex he drives down Elm to Lockridge and follows the tracks, slowing at each intersecting street to read the signs. Mason, Brookridge, Shore and one that has no sign at all but could not be Railroad as it dead-ends into the town dump.

Two verses into Billy Ocean's "Caribbean Queen" he sees it. Railroad Avenue. He takes a chance and turns right but it is wrong, as all initial directional choices turn out to be. The numbers are going lower from 132, not higher. So he pulls into a driveway in front of a decrepit boxy house and flips the Jeep into Reverse, lowering the radio before backing out.

He slows in front of number 452, a brick apartment building that yields no clues, as he had hoped it would. He parks the Jeep across the street and waits. Other than a discarded plastic bag jellyfish dancing along the sidewalk, filling up then deflating with wind, there is no movement anywhere on the block. An empty Tab can rolls under a car across from his. He turns up the radio even though it's "Ghostbusters," a song he hates. He rests his head back and closes his eyes, remembering her trying to blow her hair out of her face. Then shaking his hand. Then saying her name. Cathy Nicholas.

By the time he opens his eyes, "Purple Rain" is ending and it is dark. No plastic bag in sight. Several lights are on in the apartments facing the street and he regrets not getting out earlier to see which is hers. He cannot do it now, he reasons, because someone may have seen him — *she* may have seen him — and he feels he must go home.

In the dating world there is a finite amount of time in which date requests can be made following random meetings. To Henry's way of thinking, this period is not greater than forty-eight hours. The sooner the better, he tells himself. And so the next day, the day after meeting her, Henry goes in to Cup-a-Joe before going in to work.

"Hey," he says once it is his turn to place an order.

"Hi, there," she says. "What can I get for you?"

"We met yesterday," he says, coloring. "The flooding? You dropped your keys?"

"Oh, yeah," she says. But she does not appear to remember. "How are you?"

"I'm Henry," he says. "It's Cathy, right? I helped you unlock the store in the morning."

"Oooh, yeah," she says, this time with genuine recognition. "Thanks again." She glances around him to the line that has developed. "What can I get you?"

"Ah, actually I was wondering if you wanted to grab a bite later," he says. "Lunch, maybe?"

"What? Oh, ah, I don't know," she says. "Um, do you mind . . . I'm not supposed to . . . um, can I just help this . . . ah, lemme see." The stammers are meant to encourage Henry to move over to the side of the register so others can order.

Before he can do this the woman in back of him in line tilts Von Trapp-family-style to the side to catch Cathy's eye and orders a decaf. Henry now sees the line and moves over.

"I'm sorry," Cathy says, turning to fill the order, "it's a really bad time right now."

"Oh, yeah, sure," Henry says. "Sorry. I'll come back. I'll try you again later."

"Yeah, thanks. Sorry," she says.

"No problem."

But it does indeed present a problem to Henry, who is now unsure of when he can revisit the topic with her. Did she mean it was a bad time now as in time of day, he wonders, or as in time in her life? He decides she must have been alluding to the early-morning rush for caffeine.

Baxter's is dark and locked, as Henry knew it would be this early. It is eight o'clock, two hours before the store is set to open. Even though he told Mr. Beardsley he would open the store, he had half expected his boss to be there himself to assess the damage.

Henry separates the store key from the others on his key ring and unlocks the door. The smell is like a punch. Mildew. Unmistakable. It reminds Henry of the boathouse at Fox Run where they jockeyed for the newer, less-smelly, life jackets before sailing class.

Henry knows Mr. Beardsley will unravel when he arrives so he hurries over to the phone.

"This better be an emergency," Tom Geigan says in lieu of "hello."

Geigan has worked at the local hardware store for as long as Henry could remember. His specialty is cutting keys. There is a sign reading *Key Korner* above his tiny nook toward the back of the store. Henry at first thought him much older but in fact only two years separate them — Geigan dropped out of high school and Henry assumed this adds to the division.

They met soon after Henry began working at Baxter's in his senior year of high school, but both seemed to sense his impermanence so, while they were cordial to each other (no smiles, just respectful head nods and the occasional "How you doing?"), they more or less kept to themselves. It wasn't until Henry was full-time at Baxter's and found himself sitting on the bar stool next to Geigan that they both spoke to each other in complete sentences and the friendship took flight. Still — Henry being *completely* honest here — he had the itch of a thought that the friendship was temporary. The feeling that it would not be the sort of friendship to withstand a geographical move or a major life change. There was something that kept them off kilter. Fox Run? Henry was not sure.

"You don't even know who this is," Henry says.

"I don't care who it is. If you're calling at this hour, it better be an emergency," Tom says. "There's a construction site banging away in my head."

"Yeah, well, get up, it's an emergency,"

Henry says. "You've got to come down here."

"What is it?" Henry can tell Tom's eyes are now open with yawning curiosity.

"How fast can you get here? Seriously."

"Seriously, you better tell me what the fuck is so damn important and then I'll tell you how fast I'll be," he says. Another yawn.

"Just get down here," Henry says and hangs up.

The phone rings before Henry has moved away from the counter.

"I'm serious," Henry says, sure that it is Tom calling back.

"What? Henry?" It is Mr. Beardsley.

"Oh, sorry," Henry says. "I thought you were someone else. Actually I was just going to call you. . . ."

"Jesus. How bad is it? Did the smell go away? Is it dry?"

"Everything's fine," Henry lies. "I was just going to check in, you know, see how it went last night."

"I was there until one in the morning," Mr. Beardsley says. "But really, is it okay?"

"Yeah, sure, everything's okay. Actually, why don't you come in late. Since you were here until one and all."

"So now you're setting my hours? What's going on, Henry?"

"*No.* I mean I'm not trying to set your hours. I'm just saying, I've got everything covered here and if you wanted to take your time getting in that'd be fine. Sorry."

"I *am* a bit tired."

"There. See? Just take your time. I've got it covered."

There is a pause and Henry cannot be sure but he thinks he hears Mr. Beardsley stifling a yawn. That, he thinks, would be perfect: if Mr. Beardsley could go back to sleep that would be perfect.

"All right," Mr. Beardsley says. "I'll see you in a little while."

"Take your time."

Henry hangs up and goes back to the front doors, opening them one at a time so he can unfold the gateleg rubber stoppers that prevent them from closing. Fresh air wafts into the store. He imagines it a fight between superheroes: the strong, evil Mr. Mildew standing, feet apart, hands on hips defying the lightweight but equally powerful Captain Fresh Air, master of all that is good and right and decent, to try to thwart Mildew's diabolical plan.

Because Baxter's is a storefront in the middle of the block there are no windows to open. But it occurs to Henry that the backroom door, the emergency door, could be opened. This would create a crosswind. He looks out the front doors, up and down the sidewalk, to make sure gangs of looters aren't lying in wait for the opportunity to make off with armloads of men's clothing. Then he moves through the store, dodging displays as if they are players on an opposing team, Henry with the golden football under his arm.

The back door is metal and has a menacing brace across it that cautions it is not to be used or "alarms will sound." But he happens to know the alarm will not sound because the company that installed the fire door went out of business two years ago. The door is issuing empty threats. The crossbar makes an official-sounding clang as it unlocks the door to Fresh Air's troops, hurrying in as Henry lowers the bridge across the moat.

"Yo! Powell!" It is Tom. Henry can hear him say *Jesus frigging Christ* and knows the smell has hit him.

"I'm back here," Henry yells out. "Hang on. Be right there."

He is looking for something to prop open the door and finds a cinder block mercifully close to the door in the alley.

"Hey," he says in greeting Tom.

"What the hell happened? It smells like shit in here," Tom says.

"Shit." Henry had hoped Tom would arrive wondering why he'd been called in.

"Beardsley's gonna freak *out,* man," Tom says. He is shaking his head.

"What should I do? You've got to help me think of something," Henry says.

"Did you do this?"

"Did I do what?"

"I don't know, *this,"* Tom gestures to the problem area, including a wave of his arms meant to include the smell.

"No! Why would I do this? The store flooded yesterday. With all the rain," Henry says.

"Why are you so worried, then, man? You guys got insurance to cover flooding, right? Plus it's not like it's *your* store. Let Beardsley worry about it. Why've you got your panties in a wad?"

Henry steps out onto the sidewalk to see if it is not windy out or if there is another reason air is not moving through the store as he had hoped. No wind.

"Seriously, man." Tom has followed him out. "I can't believe you hauled me down here when you could be dialing frigging State Farm. You should've come out last night. Blackie's was packed. I got two numbers."

Geigan was perpetually gathering pretty girls' phone numbers. Even not-so-pretty girls. He held on to them like lottery tickets.

Henry stalks back into the store. It's one of life's great mysteries, Henry thinks. How that shitty — yes, shitty, so there — mullet can get women and I can't. Screw him. Screw State Farm.

Still, and for different reasons, a tiny part of Henry cannot believe he *is* so concerned with the store carpet. Not because it very well may be an insurance issue but because this is not what he had in mind. That tiny little voice in his head thinks *this is not how I thought my life would go.* But this only annoys him more so he shakes it out of his head, like a random piece of lint, picked off clothing, that won't float off from a hand.

It occurs to him that the fans will create what Mother Nature cannot: a perfect crosswind. "Just give me a hand, will you?"

"Did you hear a word I've said?" Tom asks, following him to the backroom.

"I heard you," Henry says, handing Tom a fan. Just drop it, he thinks. For God's sake, drop it. "I've got an idea. Here. Take this one and set it up facing the street up toward

118

the middle of the store. I'm going to plug this one in here so it can get it started from back here." He has to yell over the whirring fan as he plugs it in.

Henry comes up to just past sportswear and pushes pants and jackets wider apart to accommodate the fan. "Here."

"It's not gonna reach," Tom says. "Where's your outlet? You got an extension cord?"

"Yeah, let me go get it."

"This is stupid, man," Tom calls out across the store to him. "I'm telling you."

"Here." Henry hands him one end and snakes the coil along the floor to the closest outlet.

The second fan starts, taking the ball passed off from a huffing Captain Fresh Air and carrying it to the gray cement end zone.

Henry checks his watch. It is eight-thirty so he has an hour and a half until he should start looking for Mr. Beardsley. He knows Mr. Beardsley will, in the end, not be late.

"I'm going on a coffee run," he says to Tom, who is lighting a cigarette outside in front of the store. "What do you want?"

"*Now* you're talking," Tom says, inhaling. "Black. Large. Just how I like my women." Which Henry knows is not true — he has never known Tom Geigan to date a black

119

woman. What he does know is Tom Geigan adds this phrase — *just how I like my women* — to anything ending in an adjective. If a traffic jam is slow and snarling Tom would follow up with *just how I like my women.*

"I'll be right back. Can you stay right in front here just in case?"

Tom nods but says, "In case of what?"

Henry walks over to Cup-a-Joe. This time it is empty. He hurries in when he sees a car pulling up out front.

"Hey," he says to Cathy.

"Hey," she says back. She pushes her hair behind her ears and smoothes her apron.

Is she blushing? I think she's blushing, he thinks. She definitely smiled at me. Be cool. Be cool.

"Could I get two coffees to go?" Henry asks. "Large. Both black."

While she is filling the first cup, pulling down the black knob on the tall round metal container behind the register, he has the opportunity to appreciate her backside, which, he realizes, is perfect in size. Her Levi's are tight and faded. With her back to him he works up courage and is surprised at his ability to say out loud what only moments before he had wished he could say.

This is an infrequent but welcome occurrence.

"So I'm wondering," he says, "I'm wondering if you want to go out sometime? Like to lunch maybe? Or dinner."

"Oh," she says, setting the two cups down in front of him. "Um, well . . ."

"Or we could get a drink after work maybe."

She looks up at him and pushes the keys on the register. "That's $3.25." This time he is certain she is blushing.

He takes his wallet out of his back pocket and hands her four dollar bills. The register rings open and she fishes out three quarters.

"I guess," she says finally. "Yeah, I guess."

"Great. Tonight? After work tonight?" he asks, looking over his shoulder to where her gaze is leveled. His time is up. The man behind him already has his wallet out and two dollar bills in his hand, ready to order and pay in one motion.

"Yeah, okay."

"Great. See you then."

"Lids are over there" is all she says.

"Can I help you?" she is asking the impatient man with the two dollars.

Henry turns and backs out the door because his hands are full and because it affords him one more look at her. She is looking at him, too, and pinpricks of energy stab his skin. When she smiles at him — however quick it may have been — he feels himself becoming aroused.

His light-headedness might be because he is hungry and the first sip of coffee on an empty stomach does from time to time make him a little nauseated. Or it might be because he has a date with Cathy Nicholas. He cannot be sure which.

"Nice face," Tom says, reaching for his drink.

"What?"

"Nothing. You look weird is all. So what's the game plan here?"

Henry deflates as he looks inside at what is promising to be a lost cause.

"I don't know. There's got to be something else we can do."

Tom shakes his head and ventures another sip of black coffee. "Not your problem-o."

Henry imagines Cathy watching him. Admiring him from a distance — across the street maybe? No, he thinks, she's closer. She can hear us. And once again he says the sort of thing he usually shies away from. Which is to say he speaks his mind.

"You know what? It *is* my problem," he says to Geigan. "I *work* here, man. This is my *job*."

Funny, he thinks, funny how Geigan does not seem to notice the change. He does not seem to mind being challenged. Huh.

"Yeah, well, I got a job, too, man, but if the whole place burned down tomorrow I'd walk away, find myself another job easy."

"Yeah, well, it's not that easy."

" 'Course it is. See, that's the difference between you and me, Powell. My job's just that . . . a job. Your job's . . ."

"What? What's my job?" Henry faces Tom.

"It's your *life*, man," Tom says. He shrugs and turns to walk away. "You've got to get a *life*, Powell."

Henry watches him go. "*You* get a life," he mutters.

He goes back into the store to think of some new way to get rid of what is now an old smell.

After an hour of letting the fans do their work, Henry goes to the back of the store and turns one off, unplugs it and coils the cord. He carries it back to the storeroom and then closes the heavy emergency door, testing it, pushing against it to make sure it is locked back into place. Then he turns the middle fan off and stows it, eventually moving up to the double front doors and closing them. After the noise of the fans the silence is more powerful.

At ten-oh-two Mr. Beardsley walks in, sniffing the air.

Henry watches him and finds himself anxious about Mr. Beardsley's reaction.

"Good morning," he says. He knows this is what Mr. Beardsley likes to hear and on a morning like this one figures he may as well give his boss a break.

"Good morning," Mr. Beardsley says. "It's not so bad. I thought it would be worse but it's not so bad."

"Yeah, it's not bad at all," Henry says after exhaling.

"This we can deal with. I've got a professional cleaning crew coming in at eleven so that should do the trick."

"Good."

"Any calls?" Mr. Beardsley asks.

"Nope."

"I'll be in the back for now," he says.

Henry looks around and tries to think of something to do that will take his mind off the clock, which appears to have stopped altogether it is moving so slowly. He pulls yesterday's paper out from the shelf underneath the counter and scans it for anything he has not already read. It cheers him up to think the job classifieds are already separated out, taken home for study. Henry feels disloyal circling things while at work. Lunch hour is fair game but at the counter he could be spotted. He thumbs through the remaining paper. This takes about seven minutes from the day which, because of the date with Cathy, is now like an abacus: beads pushing time from one side to the other. He stands and takes a fistful of change from his pocket, separating out a quarter for the news box on the sidewalk a few steps from the store.

Today's newspaper is not much different from yesterday's. Except that an extra second has been added to the calendar year. And leaded gas is now officially banned in the United States. More fighting over Karen Ann Quinlan and whether or not she should be allowed to die. Sixteen minutes slide across the abacus. Henry wonders how on earth Billy Joel could land Christie Brinkley. Music is power, he tells himself, noting that she appears to tower over her new husband in the wedding photo the paper has printed. He thinks of Geigan, his mullet and slightly pockmarked face, and figures that even though he is not Billy Joel, he *acts* like he is and so will probably land someone beautiful.

The cleaning crew arrives and as he is

helping move racks out of the way he is aware that this will take up time.

"We can take it from here," says the man with "george" in script on an oval over his heart, the *G* lower case.

"I'll be over here if you need me," Henry says.

"They're here?" Mr. Beardsley says, checking his watch on his way to the front. "Why didn't you come get me? How long have they been here? Hi, how are you? I'm Ned Beardsley." He extends his hand to lower-case george.

Henry goes back to his paper and purposely does not check his watch so he can be pleasantly surprised later to see that there is not much time until Cathy.

That Live Aid would be the ticket to score, he thinks, reading the list of bands scheduled to appear. Philadelphia is not that far away and he contemplates calling Ticketmaster to see about cost. But then turns the page. *Back to the Future* is number one at the box office. He imagines Cathy sitting beside him at Main Street Cinema. Reaching into the tub of popcorn they are sharing. Smiling over at him during previews. Or better yet nodding after a preview saying "That looks good. We should see that one for sure." She'd like *Back to the Future,* he thinks.

Soon, gloriously soon, it is lunchtime. Twelve noon. Henry Powell never eats lunch before twelve noon. Even if he is starving. Noon is the magic hour. After the final chime of the church bell down the street he stands, stretches and steps over the cords and big yellow-fabric-covered Slinky that snakes ominously out to the matching yellow van parked out front.

In the storeroom he pulls a Tupperware container out of the minifridge. A strip of masking tape with H. Powell written in black capital letters is peeling off the top and Henry reminds himself he must replace it. He always liked having his name on his uniform, his gym locker. In fact he was happy to note that the dry cleaners had stamped H. Powell into his laundered shirts, "H" and not simply "Powell" to distinguish him from "R" Powell, a scowling man who works at the bank and has a bad case of eczema.

The leftover Chinese food is cold and tasteless and Henry wishes for the millionth time that Mr. Beardsley would invest in one of those new microwaves everyone's talking about. It occurs to Henry that he should get one for his apartment and then rave about it to Mr. Beardsley, who would hopefully be convinced of its usefulness.

He finishes and puts the empty container on the top shelf of his locker, indicating it is to go home with him that day for cleaning. But then he remembers he is going out after work and it would not do to bring a smelly, dirty plastic lunch container out on a date. Bottom of the locker. To be moved to the top shelf tomorrow.

" 'Sup?"

Henry, startled, turns to see Ramon shedding his baseball jacket in front of his locker next to Henry's.

"What's up?" Henry says.

Ramon tilts his head toward the front of the store. "What's going on with Ned?"

"Oh, we got water in the store yesterday, er, two days ago. No, yesterday I think. Whatever. Whenever that storm was," Henry says. "You should've seen it. It was pretty bad."

"Glad I dodged that bullet."

Henry closes his locker. "See you out there."

George and the professional cleaners have gone and Mr. Beardsley is beaming at Henry.

"Look at that," he says, but his facial

expression is one of smelling, not looking, so Henry too inhales the artificially freshened — *professionally* freshened — air.

"Money well spent," Mr. Beardsley continues.

The rest of the afternoon drips by. Henry busies himself with whatever tiny or not so small chores occur to Mr. Beardsley, who is aware of and pleased with Henry's newfound industry.

At four-thirty Henry asks if it would be all right if he could run a quick errand and hurries home to check in early. He does not help his mother to bed at this hour (even though forty-five minutes later he would have) because he will be returning after his date. He leaves a note for his father in the off chance Edgar Powell comes home early. *I'll be back later tonight,* Henry scribbles. He jumps in his car and drives back to Baxter's so he can saunter over to Cup-a-Joe's from there. He does not want to appear rushed.

At five-oh-one Henry closes his locker door after again noting the Tupperware and thinking he must remember to transfer it to the top shelf tomorrow.

"Well, I'm out of here," he says to Mr. Beardsley. Careful to conceal his triumph in making it through a day that at first looked to stretch into infinity.

"Good night, Henry," Mr. Beardsley says. "Thanks for your help with the water situation."

"No problem. See you tomorrow."

He has never been one to consider skipping but Henry now understands its allure. For he nearly skips up the street.

At Cup-a-Joe the sign in the door reads Closed but he shades his eyes and looks through the glass at Cathy, who is untying the half apron from around her waist. She looks up and sees him and waves. He watches her reach under the counter for her purse and, though he can't hear her voice, he knows she is calling "good night" to the back of the café where an unseen boss is probably saying the same back. He is pleased to see that she has changed from her faded jeans to black stirrup pants. A sign that she is looking to impress him, he thinks.

"Hi," she says once outside.

Be cool, he is telling himself. Be cool. "How's it going?"

"Pretty good," she says.

"I was thinking we could go to Sweetwater," he says. Sweetwater, a bar hoping to be thought of as a music club, is in the next town over.

She shrugs and says, "Sounds good." But the shrug makes him unsure of his choice.

"You want to go someplace else?"

"Sweetwater's fine," she says. "I'm parked over there." She points to a silver Celica with a banged-in bumper.

"You want to just leave your car and I can drop you back by after?"

"It's okay," she says. "I'll just follow you."

"You sure? Parking's sometimes tough around there. Two spaces might be harder to find."

"It's all right, I'll just follow you there." She crosses the street.

"See you there," he calls out.

As it turns out, since she is in her car before he is in his, he ends up following her there. Henry is not so disappointed that she is not riding with him but really he is relieved not to have to make conversation in the car. Then again he pictures them laughing by the time they got to Sweetwater — climbing out of the car mid-laugh, the way he sees so many couples on dates. The shared jokes. The intimacy of even the shortest of rides. Screw it, he thinks. Screw it, we'd just have run out of things to talk about. This way is much better, he is satisfied at the thought.

"Hey," he greets her inside the bar. Tuesday nights are women-drink-half-price nights and he worries that she will assume they are there, at that particular place, for that particular reason.

"How about over here?" He motions to a small, round table for two.

She drapes her coat on the back of her chair before sitting down. "This is nice," she says, looking around. "I've never been here before."

He tries to remember whether this place has table service or if customers are expected to order up at the bar.

"What do you want to drink? I'll go up and order," he says.

"What? Oh. Um, a glass of wine I guess."

"White or red?"

"Ah, white, please. Thanks."

Up at the bar he orders a chardonnay and a merlot, because it is what he remembers his father always ordering. Truth is he is more of a beer drinker.

"I'll bring them over," the cocktail waitress says after he has paid the bartender.

"They're bringing it over," he tells her when he pulls his chair back out. It makes an ugly scraping sound that startles her.

"So how long have you been working at the coffee place?" he asks.

"I don't know . . . a year maybe?"

"A year, huh?"

"Longest year of my life." This is loud enough for him to hear but she is really muttering to herself.

"You don't like it there?" he asks, leaning forward to hear her.

"I *hate* it there," she says, in a tone that suggests surprise that there is an alternative.

"Are you looking for something else? Another job, I mean?"

"Yeah. Hell, yeah," she says.

"Where are you looking?" he asks. "Actually — oh! — I hear Transitions is about to lay someone off. Just don't say I told you about it. My friend works there."

Transitions is an ironically named women's clothing store in the same block as Baxter's. Ironic because the only transition it seems to be making is one from prosperity to bankruptcy. Henry's friend there, Amy, is really an acquaintance he occasionally sees out in the back alley that runs behind their stores, when they are both breaking down cardboard boxes so they do not take up too much room in their Dumpsters. For months they called out hello to each other and then met more formally in line at the post office. Amy is a woman about his mother's age and he has always felt sorry for her without really knowing why.

"Ugh." Cathy's lip is curled up when she says this but Henry does not see it as a sign of disgust but rather an opportunity to see her perfect teeth. "Actually, I'm trying to get a temp job at this ad agency in the city. A foot in the door, you know? Plus even if that didn't work out permanently at least once I'm there it'll be easier to hear about other stuff."

Henry finds himself wishing she would stop looking around the bar — it makes it seem as if she is talking to herself. It makes him feel like the date has not yet begun. He wonders if maybe he should bring over a bowl of pretzels from the bar so she can focus on that, and then, perhaps, him.

Finally, she looks straight at him. "How is it working at Baxter's?"

"Fine," he says. To keep her attention he adds, "But . . . you know . . . I'm not *always* going to be working there, either. But whatever. I'm always looking."

"What're you looking for?"

"I'm not sure," he says. He does not want to talk about the classifieds because it will look as if he is copying her job search. He looks around, hoping he'll see a friend who can see him out on this date.

But it is a slow night at Sweetwater and he recognizes no one.

"Where were you before the coffee place?" he asks.

"What? Oh, um, around. I worked in Norton for a couple of years. After school."

"Where'd you go to school?"

"Buckton," she says. "Where'd you go?"

He had meant high school, not college.

"Um, I'm on leave from Westerfield. Just for a little while."

"Really?" He notices her brighten at the significance of the name. Westerfield always elicits this response and he is aware she now thinks of him as pedigreed. Most graduates, Henry has noticed, mention it in the first minutes of conversation for this very reason. But he feels as if he is misrepresenting himself and hurries to change the subject.

"Where'd you grow up?" he asks.

Before she can answer, the waitress places square napkins down in front of each of them followed by their wine.

"Cheers," he says, offering his glass to clink. She takes a sip of her drink.

After a few silent sips he says, "This is great," and she nods and smiles as she looks into her wineglass.

"Where'd you say you're from?" he asks, two sips later.

"Oh. I'm from Rhode Island. Where're you from?"

"Here," he says. "I grew up here, actually. My brother moved away a few years ago but I'm still here." He does not know why he has offered this.

"Where'd your brother go?"

"Oregon," he says. "Portland area. He's supposedly got this really great house right on the river. I haven't been out to see him."

She nods and takes another sip of her drink. She touches her hair when she notices him staring at it. "What?" she asks, pushing it behind her ears.

"Nothing," he takes a sip of his drink and looks down. "You've got nice hair."

"I do?" She sits up straighter in her chair but looks down, as if memorizing his compliment.

"Yeah," Henry says. "So. This is great. Isn't this great?" He looks around so she does, too. "I mean this, us going out."

"It's good," she says, looking back up at him, checking to see if he is being sarcastic.

After several conversational dead ends they leave the awkward first-date phase and enter the we-have-so-many-shared-interests-how-is-it-possible-we-have-not-yet-met phase.

"Sometimes?" Cathy lowers her voice and

leans in over her third glass of wine. "Sometimes I pretend I'm this really rich heiress — like a billionaire's daughter or something — but I'm disgusted with the materialistic, capitalistic life and I'm trying to make my parents mad by working at a coffee shop. And all these guys — the rude ones who yell if I'm taking too long — all those guys find out about me. About how I come from all this money. And then they're sorry they treated me that way but it's too late. I've already seen how they really are. What they really act like."

Henry is nodding. "Yeah, yeah," he says, "I know exactly what you mean."

They trade customer stories and shake their heads and smile. "Wow," he says. "So funny." He eases back into his chair.

"Yeah," she says. "Yeah." And she smiles.

"I should probably get going," she says, checking her watch. "Wow. Guess what time it is? Don't look at your watch. Just guess."

"Seven?"

"It's eight," she says, thrilled to be able to surprise him with the amount of time that has elapsed.

"Time flies," he says. "You sure you don't want another glass?"

"Yeah. Actually, no," she says, and he feels a surge of happiness to see that she says this with a degree of reluctance matching his exactly.

He reaches around and lifts her jacket off the back of her chair, holding it open for her.

"Thanks." She smiles over her shoulder at him and he cannot believe a smile like this one is directed at him and for some reason it reminds him of the time his mother brought home a Boston cream pie. *It's your favorite,* she had said, looking him straight in the eye. The miraculous thing about it was, it was not his birthday. She had just done it out of the blue. On an ordinary day.

He walks her out to her car.

"Have you seen *Back to the Future* yet?"

"What?" she says, turning to face him, car key already facing her door lock.

"I was wondering if you wanted to go to see *Back to the Future* this weekend," he says. "It's supposed to be really good. But I don't know. We could see something else if you want."

"I'd love to," she says, fitting the key into the lock.

"Great," he says. He shoves his hands into his pockets, hoping slouching body language will help balance out his enthusiasm. The moment is approaching where he will be called on to give her a good-night kiss. This body language is also meant to show he is not in the least bit nervous, no sirree.

"Okay, so," she says, pausing before lowering herself into the driver's seat.

Henry is horrified to find his legs have gone leaden. He is unable to move. Making matters worse is his apparent inability to pull his hands out of his pockets — something he would like to do in order to make his intentions clear.

"Okay, well," she says, now settling in behind the wheel. "Bye. Thanks for the drink."

"I had fun tonight," he says, moving closer to her car as she shuts the door.

But her window is up and she does not hear, offering a feeble wave once she has reversed out of her spot and is pointing forward.

On his way back to his parents' house for a quick check in, Henry erases the last few clunky minutes of the date from his mind and instead imagines his car tires suspended over the road, floating. Like the Jetsons, he thinks . . . like how their bubble vehicles glide through the air to and from work.

He carries his mother, who has tilted sideways and fallen asleep on the couch, up to bed, and it very nearly ruins his mood to find his father sleeping soundly there. Henry makes no effort to be quiet. If he wakes up, Henry thinks, he wakes up.

Why the hell can't *he* do this? Henry works hard to be gentle with his mother, lightly pulling the covers up over her. He tries not to take it out on her. His father has not stirred.

Seriously. He's got arms. And if he can't lift her he could at least shake her awake long enough to make her walk up. He's teaching me a lesson he's trying to make me feel bad once just *once* I miss my five-fifteen and here he is teaching me a lesson well it's not working . . . I *always* do this, this is nothing new so that's how much *you* know.

Like laser beams he shoots these thoughts off to his sleeping father, hoping they sink in by osmosis the way as a middle-schooler he used to put his notebook under his pillow, hoping its contents would seep into his head on nights before tests.

Minutes later he lets himself into his apartment, spare but for a hand-me-down couch and a few other pieces of furniture his brother left behind when he moved out to start his new life.

In the kitchen the drying rack alongside

the sink the one plate and one glass appear to mock his bachelorhood and so he quickly puts them away — ha, I just might have company over, so there. He takes a beer out of the refrigerator and snaps the top off with his bottle opener. Back in the living room he settles into the nubby chair that faces the television, remote control already on the arm. He sits in silence, replaying the date, wishing his visit to his parents' had not poisoned the evening as it did. As it always does, Henry thinks. He finishes the beer quickly and fishes another out of the refrigerator.

Stop thinking. *Stop it.* What's on TV tonight? he asks himself. She blushed a lot. A *lot.* Maybe more than most, he imagines the biographer scribbling, looking up to gauge Henry's reaction to this fact. Is he cocky? the writer is wondering. Is he humble? Self-deprecating? He certainly is a good-looking man — probably has no idea his effect on women, the writer scratches onto his legal pad full of the tiniest of Henry Powell observations. No idea whatsoever.

Henry smiles and flicks on the television.

The following morning he is up and out of bed long before six fifty-nine. Showered, he stands in his underwear in front of his closet, sifting through the clothes, mindful of what he has worn lately. He selects a black Pierre Cardin blazer that he has not worn in a while, a white tab collar, plaid pants, the tie a solid color so as not to compete with the pants.

He purposely does not prepare a lunch to bring in to work. Keys jingle on his way out the door. The weather is unseasonably warm.

There are three cars outside the coffee shop, one is idling with a passenger inside leaning forward fiddling with the radio dial. Henry hops up on the curb and ceremoniously opens the door for the woman on her way out holding two cups of coffee.

He sees Cathy and feels like an ice cube that's been dropped into boiling water.

"Hi," he says.

"Hi, Henry," she says. He soars hearing her speak his name.

"Can I get a large one? For here," he says. "Black?"

His smile stretches that much wider that she has remembered how he likes his coffee. "Yeah."

"You look nice today," he says when she hands it over to him.

Her hand flutters up to her hair. She

smiles and presses keys on the register, ringing him up.

"One-fifty," she says.

He hands her the money. There are two small tables in the place, one already taken up by a large man reading the paper through spectacles that are too small for his face. Henry sits at the unoccupied table, not the bar-height ledge along the window that would have meant his back to her.

He blows on his drink, cupping both hands around the mug, waiting for it to cool.

When the last customer in the cluster of commuters that has descended leaves he gets up and goes over to her.

"So, what about the movie this weekend?"

"Yeah," she says. "Sounds great."

"Cool," he says. "Which —" But before he can ask her which night, Friday or Saturday, a customer interrupts.

"Which what?" she asks once the order is filled.

"Um," he says, "Friday or Saturday? Either one's fine with me." He wishes he had not added that last part as he knows this makes him sound like he never ever goes out ever and hopes this won't have registered with her.

She shakes her head and shrugs. "You pick."

"How about Friday?" This will mean one less day for them to be apart.

"Great. Cool."

"Great," he says. "I'll see you before then and we can work out which showing and stuff. Okay, well, I'll see you later."

She itches her head and turns red. She tries not to notice the customers in between them, smiling at her shyness and at Henry's boyish courting.

He lets himself in to Baxter's. One-two-three-four all the light switches are flipped up and to Henry the light bathes the racks in golden hues. The carpet, thanks to *george,* lends a fresh smell to the entire store. He goes to his locker and is pleased he remembers to transfer the Tupperware to the top shelf. Instead of slamming the flimsy metal door closed he lifts the handle and lets it settle quietly, neatly, into its docking.

Back out in the store he moves self-consciously through the aisles, touching this pair of gabardine slacks, marveling at the whisper of lining in that linen jacket, straightening the trouser socks hanging from individual black plastic half hangers, making sure the ties are fanned out just so. He imagines his biographer jotting down potential chapter headings: Henry Powell

Meets the Woman of His Dreams or, better yet, Mutual Infatuation. The book would be a fascinating read, his love life especially salacious — an inspiration to the lonely-hearted everywhere. The Extraordinary Life of Henry Powell. A *New York Times* best-seller. His mother's voice rings in his ears. *Happy happy happy,* she used to say — sing, really — when he was little and they would pour themselves into the car on the way home from the Hot Dogger, stomachs bloated. The three words one by one climbing the musical register. And it would perfectly capture the moment. He had thought it so wonderful that his mother felt the exact same way he did at the exact same time. Later on when Henry was older she would say it under her breath before taking a sip of the highball that was always within reach. *Happy happy happy,* lips in motion up until the rim of the glass, the sip turning into more of a gulp as his father stalked out of the kitchen, the end of a mysterious conversation always trailing off before Henry entered.

The voice ping-ponging through his head now, though, was that earlier, younger voice — the one that smelled of ketchup and mustard, of summer nights, paper-thin pajamas worn while it's still light out, Evel Knievel stunts and cowboy vests with brown plastic fringe hoping to be taken for leather. *That* is the *happy happy happy* Henry is feeling.

It occurs to him that he might enjoy a new shirt. You can never really have too many shirts, he tells himself as he sets out across the store. The new rugby shirts look appealing to him at first but he reconsiders when he imagines Cathy dressed in a skirt. Better to go with a buttondown, he thinks. The new polo shirts are the obvious choice but he scans the rest of the rack just in case something has slipped his mind. No. He returns to the sherbet-date colors and chooses a blue, thinking the rest too effeminate.

Eventually the shirt, tried on and paid for using his thirty-percent employee discount, is stowed in his locker and the sign is turned from Closed to Open a few minutes before Mr. Beardsley arrives. The biographer's pencil furiously taking it all down. Words like *diligent, trustworthy* and *dependable* are scattered throughout.

The first customer of the day is the unfortunately named Mrs. Waddleton, who has met Henry numerous times over the years — Henry tutored her son at Fox Run — but has managed to remain ignorant of his name.

"He's about that size," the woman says to Mr. Beardsley, pointing at Henry. "What size would *he* wear?"

"Henry? Could you come over here for a moment, please?" Mr. Beardsley's voice had a lilting quality to it in the way that all voices-for-show do.

Henry puts down a box of undershirts in between the pant racks and the formal-wear display.

"Hi, Mrs. Waddleton," Henry says.

But she looks genuinely confused that this stranger should know her name.

"What size shirt do you wear?" the lady asks him. But she doesn't wait for an answer. Her words are directed at Mr. Beardsley. "See that gap between his neck and the shirt? That's what I'm trying to avoid. Should I just go with a size smaller than what I would normally buy him and he can come back and exchange it if it still isn't right, or should I just get the same size as this one wears?"

"Thank you, Henry, we can take it from here," Mr. Beardsley says.

"Do we know what size he wears,

though?" the lady asks, reluctant to dismiss him.

"Now that I know your Patrick is roughly the same measurements as our Henry I can find him something," Mr. Beardsley says.

"Good," she says.

Henry retrieves the box he'd been carrying to the back room. He imagines Cathy Nicholas sleeping in an XL, so large on her it nearly reaches her knees. The image lingers and becomes slightly pornographic as the undershirt size gets smaller.

A few minutes pass, or maybe more, when he is interrupted by Mr. Beardsley, "Henry, your friend is asking for you."

Henry hurries out to the floor to greet his friend Joey Young, the manager of the movie theater, wanting to find something warmer to wear at work as it is air-conditioning season. Joey lives two units down from Henry and spends much of his free time washing his black Camaro in the apartment complex parking lot, weather permitting.

"Hey, by the way," Henry says. "I'll be seeing you this weekend I think."

"Oh, yeah?" Joey's tan is the rough and leathery kind acquired after years of summers spent in a lawn chair ogling young girls at the town beach.

"Think so," Henry says, trying to appear

casual. "You think it'll be busy? Should we get there early?"

Henry knew he would try out the "we" but was unprepared for the rush of internal excitement it would generate.

"You might want to allow a little time," Joey says. "It just opened and all. Did gangbusters last weekend. Is this a hundred-percent cotton? You think it's going to shrink?" he asks hopefully. In addition to his reverence for the sun, the theater manager has a penchant for wearing his shirts tight, the better to show off his pecs.

Henry remembers this and hands him the medium. "I think it's preshrunk, so try this one just to see."

"Preshrunk? They're washing things before you even buy them now?"

"Wave of the future, man," Henry says. "Ned says they're doing it with jeans now."

Henry would never call Mr. Beardsley "Ned" to his face but does so behind his back with customers close to Henry's own age so as not to look like a brown noser.

"Huh," Joey says. He emerges from the changing room dressed in the clothes he came in, handing the medium to Henry. "I'll take it. You want me to hold a couple of tickets aside for you this weekend? What night are you guys coming?"

"Friday."

"I can hold a couple for you. We're not supposed to do it but since I know you . . ."

"Yeah, thanks. Thanks. You paying cash or do you want to put it on your store credit?"

The biographer takes note of Henry's attention to detail. A chapter certainly.

CHAPTER SIX

"Mr. Murray? How are you, sir?" Henry is startled by the fragility of the old man's bony hand. "It's Henry. Henry Powell."

Like a windshield defrosting — fog dissipating from the glass — the eyes become clear with recognition.

"Oh, my goodness," he says, squeezing Henry's hand. "Oh, my. Henry Powell, of course."

Is it a wince that crosses ever so slightly across Mr. Murray's eyes? Henry cannot be sure. Gently he withdraws his hand and allows himself to be studied.

John Murray looks away at first, visibly bracing himself for the grief to flood in intravenously as it does without fail every time he sees an old friend of Jimmy's. A friend who does not scurry across the street, head bowed not in deference to the stricken father, but more in the hopes that old Murray won't recognize them. They tell themselves he wouldn't want to be reminded — maybe he'd managed to push aside the memory of his son, forever fourteen. Besides, how does one begin mindless conversation with someone who has been shattered to bits? Easier to duck and run, they think. But here, *here* is Henry Powell. Tall, good posture. Polite. This is what Jimmy would look like today, Henry can tell Mr. Murray is doing the math. Figuring out how old his Jimmy would be. Now of course he would go by Jim, anxious to be taken seriously. Murray's old eyes study Henry. Would Jimmy have the same hint of crow's feet, the same gravitational shifting of weight and mass to the middle of his body?

Henry thinks: this is mature of me. This is right of me. He regrets that he has, in the past, been one to duck and run.

At first it was easy for Henry to position himself in the middle of the pack of bedraggled tenth-graders, steaming, stumbling off the field to the showers. Mr. and Mrs. Murray were good to keep going to the games. They stood off to the side, away from the huddle of regular parents who weren't sure what to say, weren't sure what they would call out or if they even should call out to the couple. Every parent's worst nightmare, someone mumbled. Such a horrible tragedy, someone else said, by way of agreement. Still, no one called them over.

Tragedy had attached itself to the Murrays like barnacles to a forgotten boat. First it was Laura, the eldest child, who spent an inordinate amount of time in the intensive care unit of Good Shepherd Hospital. They said she almost died. They said she *did* die, she saw a white light and everything. Henry heard his mother whisper into the phone that she had always said not *all* feminine products were to be used by young people. Her tone accusatory, Henry thought, and mean. The illness a *syndrome. Toxic shock,* they whispered, for it was the sort of disease one never spoke about out loud. Not in good company. The casseroles were still rotating in and out of the Murray house when they got the word from the doctors: brain damage. Too long with too little oxygen. Laura Murray would never be the same.

Two years later her younger brother, Jimmy, was reaching for the eight-track cassette of the Bay City Rollers he'd just unwrapped — it had clanked out of his hands to the floor of his friend's car —

when the Ford Fairlane barreled into them. Killed instantly, they said. Didn't feel a thing.

When Ethel Murray was rushed to the hospital the following year the news was met with remarks like *are you serious?* Massive stroke, they said. She'd always suffered headaches. He had to pull the plug, they said. So sad, they agreed. Tragic, really.

And so they began to cross streets when John Murray came to town.

"Well, Henry Powell, looks like you're going to have to help me find myself a pair of trousers," Mr. Murray says to Henry. "These just won't do." His tone has always been courtly — Henry finds himself wondering if Mr. Murray had even spent time in London . . . he had that kind of flair to his voice.

"No problem, Mr. Murray," he says, steering the old man to the part of the store devoted to the lower half of men's bodies. It feels strange to Henry to call this man "mister" still but there is a general understanding with those who enjoy a wide-enough gap in age that the younger will always refer to the elder formally.

Henry notes how much he enjoys the

intensity of Mr. Murray's focus, even though he knows the old man is not seeing *him* but the ghost of what might have been. When Mr. Murray averts his eyes, Henry is sorry to feel the attention come to an end.

"What kind of shoes will you be wearing?" he asks.

They both look down at Mr. Murray's shoes: loafers misshapen by overuse and inappropriate weather conditions. Mr. Murray is still staring at his feet when Henry gently touches him on the back, silently suggesting forward movement.

"I think I know exactly what you need," he says. "Here we go." He selects a pair of chinos. "These pants are good for just about any occasion." The heavyweight khaki material is crisp enough to hold up under a blazer's demands but comfortable enough to be worn on trips such as this one. Weekend errands.

Mr. Murray fingers the material and nods a Chinatown-turtle sort of nod, softly tapering off, giving way to a skeptical tilt. "They're not too dark?"

"Naw," says Henry. "I don't think so. Try them on. I bet you'll really like the color."

"I don't go in for these trendy things," Mr. Murray grumbles on his way into the dressing room. "I hate these trendy things. . . ." he is saying.

"I promise," Henry says, "these aren't trendy. They're classic. I don't like the trendy stuff, either. I really think you'll like them. But if you don't we'll just find you something else."

The chimes are tripped off and Henry glances to the front door. It's Clarence, the mailman, depositing a neat, rubber-banded packet of mail onto the counter. The daily wave over his shoulder his only acknowledgment of Henry.

"I don't know." Mr. Murray nearly stumbles back out through the saloon doors, the extra-long pant legs tangling with his socked feet. "Except for the length, they fit, that's for sure. I just don't know about the color."

"Let me just fold the leg up so we can get an idea how they look," Henry says, kneeling to roll up one leg. "There. I like them. I like them a lot. You still don't like the color?"

"They're comfortable," Mr. Murray says. "I suppose I should get them. I sure don't want a trendy pair of pants, though."

"They're not trendy, I promise," Henry says. He stands back from the three-way mirror and lets Mr. Murray turn this way and that, deciding whether he needs more

156

convincing. Henry can tell Mr. Murray had planned on spending all afternoon searching through the racks of pants, trying to find something to replace his worn trousers. He appears surprised it is going so well. This Henry is a godsend, he sees his biographer taking it all down.

"Can you hem them up for me? My sewing's pretty limited," Mr. Murray says. "I can put a button back on but Ethel never did let me near that machine so I don't think . . ."

"Oh, please —" Henry holds up a hand to stop Mr. Murray from even completing the thought "— we take care of all of that. Let me just go grab my pins, I'll mark them up and the tailor will have them done by the end of the week."

"Oh."

"Why don't you put your shoes on so I can get an idea of the length and I'll be right back."

Henry is in formal wear when he hears it. The hangers clanging together in alarm, then a thump.

"Mr. Murray?" Henry stops in his tracks, in case he'd misunderstood the sounds.

The silence carries a special frequency heard perhaps only by dogs and by those who have an acute sense of danger. Henry shoots back through the racks so fast there are cartoon lines streaming from his back, indicating speed and direction.

"Mr. Murray? Mr. Murray, can you hear me? I'm going to turn you over." But he hesitates trying to recall what it was he saw on television about this very subject. About moving someone elderly who has fallen. He remembers now: it was on that show *Emergency.* Johnny Gage. That was his name, Henry thinks. Johnny Gage is the one who said never move a fallen old person.

The voice is muffled by the carpet, "I think I broke something. Oooh."

"I'm going to call an ambulance." Henry rushes back to the counter and dials 911. "Hello? We need an ambulance. Please, we need an ambulance. What? Oh, Baxter's. On Main Street. Please come quick."

"They're on their way," Henry calls out on his way back through the obstacle course of racks to Mr. Murray. Looking down at him Henry realizes that the pants are indeed too dark.

"Damn pants," Mr. Murray says. His head is turned unnaturally to the side, an angry right angle that looks painful. "I went down so fast . . ." he trails off.

"I don't think I should move you," Henry

says, by way of comforting him. He is squatting down alongside him. "You might have broken something. I don't think I should move you. Or should I?" Johnny Gage be damned, he thinks.

"It's okay, son," Mr. Murray says. "I'll be okay."

Mr. Murray's using the word *son* has an unexpected poignancy even though Henry knows that most older gentlemen will use this term with younger men. It's different, of course, when Mr. Murray uses it.

"Maybe I *should* flip you over." Henry moves off to the side and hunches down so Mr. Murray can see his face. "What do you want me to do?"

"Ambulance'll be here in a minute," Mr. Murray says. "Let them deal with it."

"I'm so sorry," Henry says. "I should've folded up both legs. I thought I'd just do the one. I'm so sorry. God, why didn't I just do both?"

Mr. Murray's eyes are closed.

"Mr. Murray? Oh, God. Oh, Jesus."

Henry stands up and races out to the sidewalk in front of the store to look for the ambulance. He looks east first, but then remembers the hospital is west of this block of Main Street. Nothing in either direction.

Back in the store the chimes sound underfoot as he moves quickly, gracefully, between racks back to Mr. Murray.

"It's on its way," he lies. "Mr. Murray? Mr. Murray, it's almost here. Just hang on."

"I'm okay, boy," he says, though his eyes remain closed.

This time the silence telepathically urges Henry to come up with something comforting to say. Something that will fill the time until the paramedics arrive. He clears his throat.

"I bet it's just a bruise or something," he says, thankful that Mr. Murray can't see his own eyes roll in disgust at his feeble attempt at comfort. He knows it's bad. He knows Mr. Murray's eyes are closed against the pain.

"Where *are* they?" Henry asks, standing, shooting back to the front door, through it and onto the sidewalk. Just as it pulls up. He can see that above the hood with its backward spelling of Ambulance one of the paramedics is carefully wedging a to-go cup of coffee into where the dashboard connects with the windshield.

"He's in here," Henry calls out to them, motioning them out of the van. "In here."

The paramedics bear no resemblance to

their televised selves, nearly always exploding out of ambulances, expressions grave, movements efficient: equipment grabbed with minimal effort, speaking in a complicated code of vital stats. Johnny Gage'd be disgusted with these two, he thinks.

Henry, fidgety, moves closer as they slide the gurney out of the back.

"I think he must've fallen getting off the tailor block," he says, "I didn't move him. Oh, let me get the latch from the inside so I can open both doors. They open out so . . . here, let me — oh, okay. It fits through one? Oh, great. You want me to . . . ? Yeah, just straight back. By the three-way mirror."

"What's his name?" is the only thing the paramedic asks.

"Murray," Henry says from only just behind. "His last name is Murray."

"Mr. Murray," the other paramedic says a bit too loudly. "Looks like you got yourself in quite a fix, eh?"

Henry scowls at the condescension.

"Paulie, hand the board over," one says to the other. Henry looks from one to the other and thinks they look exactly like Tweedledee and Tweedledum. "Okay, on the count of three we're going to flip you over, Mr. Murray. One. Two. *Three*. Good. You doin' okay?"

But instead of answering the emergency technician, John Murray looks into Henry's eyes and says, "I'm okay, son. Don't worry. I'm okay."

"Mr. Murray?" Tweedledee is strapping him onto the board. "We're taking you up now, into the ambulance. Okay?"

"Don't worry," he says to Henry again.

"On three, Paulie. One. Two. *Three.* Here we go."

The gurney is secured into the back of the van — a completeness comes with the sturdy sound of doors shutting — and Henry falls alongside Tweedledum, on his way into the passenger seat.

"That pant leg," he says. "It was the pant leg he tripped on. I should've at least tucked it up or something."

Tweedledum now heaved into the front seat says, "Doesn't look like he tripped on the pant leg, kid. Looks like it was his shoes: the right sole's practically falling off. Probably got folded under on his way off the block there."

Mr. Beardsley is at a doctor appointment, Ramon is not scheduled to come in today. Henry finds himself miserably pacing back and forth in front of the counter, wondering what he should do. His instinct is to follow the ambulance to the hospital. Who else is going to check on Mr. Murray? he wonders. He has no one else. No one to drink bad coffee and hold vigil by his bed until he wakes up from the surgery Henry assumes he'll undergo. Laura Murray, he had heard, is in a home for the mentally disabled. And as far as Henry knows she is Mr. Murray's only living relative. What to do, what to do. Henry chastises himself he did not fold up both pant legs. It would have taken three extra seconds, he laments. Three frigging seconds.

The sidewalk in front of the store is empty. No cars appear to be heading in his direction. So Henry makes the executive decision to close the store. He reassures himself it is only for a few minutes. It is an emergency after all.

He tells himself Cathy will know just what to do. He needs to talk it through with someone clear-headed. Yes, this is the right thing to do, he says to himself, pushing the Cup-a-Joe door open. Once he sees her he is sure. Once he sees the place empty he knows it is a sign that he has made the right decision.

"Henry?" She comes over to the cash register from the coffee filter area. "You look weird. What's wrong?"

"Oh, Jesus," he says. "I don't know. I

messed up."

"What happened? What is it?" She comes out from behind the counter and steers him to a seat. "Lois? Can you cover?" she calls out to the back of the place. Henry looks up from the tabletop to see the mousey-looking Lois emerge from her steamy job washing mugs.

"Tell me," Cathy says. Under any other circumstance Henry would have been thrilled to feel her hand touching his, but here, now, it makes him feel worse about Mr. Murray.

So he tells her about the accident. All in one sentence practically. His words travel hurvy scurvy through the air into her ears, into her head, awaiting interpretation. A jumble of words needing straightening out. She nods in all the right places. Coos, really. Comforting verbal hugs. When he gets to the part about the second pant leg she says, "Of course you wouldn't have folded it up — you thought he'd stay in one place." Already she is making sense of it for him. It is as if the words weighed a pound each and in speaking them, in getting them off of his mind, he is shedding the weight.

"I just feel so bad," Henry says. At the end. Her hand is still resting on his. He is now aware of the stroking motion. And presto, he now feels the thrill of her touch.

"I know," she says. "But it's not your fault. You just feel bad for him . . . like, as a person. You know? But it wasn't your fault."

Henry is suddenly horrified to realize that he may have used Mr. Murray as an excuse to see Cathy after all. Because when he looks up into her eyes he no longer feels anything for the old man. Just relief that Cathy is here, touching him, talking to him. What else could explain his newfound elation? he wonders.

"I guess I better get back to the store," he says.

She nods and gives his hand a squeeze before withdrawing.

John Murray died twelve hours later and was buried later in the week. In that same pair of loafers.

CHAPTER SEVEN

1977

Finally. . . . *finally* . . . Henry knows what he has to do. A can of paint can't cost that much, he reasons. He stops by the Murray house on his way to the hardware store.

"Hi, Mrs. Murray. Is Jimmy home?"

"Hi, Henry," she says, and holds the door open for him to come in. "Jimmy? Henry's here." She calls upstairs.

Jimmy bounds down the stairs and the boys are off. The walk to Main Street is long and seems longer if alone so it is an arrangement they have — Henry and Jimmy — that if one has to walk into town the other will keep him company. They never discussed it but just happened on it and it stuck. They silently kick a rock ahead and back and forth, careful not to lose it.

"Hey there, boys." Mr. Hillman at the hardware store is the father of a friend of Henry's from school. "What can I do for you today?"

"I need some white paint," Henry says.

"Aisle three. Satin finish?"

Jimmy is fiddling with the power tool display.

"Oh." Henry had not considered the finish. "Um, I just need to touch a few things up. I don't know. What kind would I use for inside? For a door. For the frame around a door."

Mr. Hillman smiles. "A door. Well, there're lots of different options. Do you have the can of paint that was used originally? An old can? Maybe your father kept it. That would tell you for sure."

Henry blushes at his own stupidity. He had not even checked his father's rarely used workbench. And that would be just the sort of thing his father would do: save an old can to make an exact match. Dammit, Henry curses to himself.

"What if I don't need a match?" he says, a light bulb of an idea winking in his brain. "What if I just do the whole area over?"

"Well —" Mr. Hillman ponders this "— better go with semi-gloss."

Aisle three is bursting with white choices that depress Henry, who had started out the day sure that this was a good idea.

Mr. Hillman suggests this and that, pointing to different brands and consistencies. Henry shrugs at each one, wanting a decision to be made for him. At last he settles for the semi-gloss in linen, the shade of white, Mr. Hillman says, that is most popular. So Henry fishes the money out of his pocket and pays almost exact change.

"Nice to see you two," Mr. Hillman calls out over the friendly bell that tinkles on their exit.

"What're you painting?" Jimmy asks.

"Just a stupid project my dad needs it for," Henry lies. "What're you doing later?"

"I don't know."

"I'll come by when I'm done," Henry says. This is the easy exchange that has always existed between them.

"See ya," Jimmy calls out as Henry turns back up his front walk.

Back at home Henry goes straight to the basement and sure enough there are the old paint cans he should have thought about before his errand. Dried paint is petrified on the sides of most. Pompeian drips. In some cases, on a few cans, the old paint has covered up the label so Henry cannot be sure which is which. His father had not labeled any of them. Which is a sort of relief: if asked he can say he tried to match colors but — here's the beauty of it — he can effectively turn it around and make it his father's fault for not writing something indicating what color went where in the house.

Buoyed by this he takes a paintbrush from the Peg-Board and, on his way back upstairs, grabs an old newspaper to use as a splatter guard he knows he will not need but, just in case, he wants his bases covered.

He has barely made a stroke when rattling ice cubes announce his mother's arrival.

"What do you think you're doing?" she asks. *"Stop."*

"What?" he stands up to face her. "I'm just touching up . . ."

"Stop," she says. It is three in the afternoon and she is still in her nightgown. "Edgar?" She yells this part.

"Mom . . ." He reaches for her. "It's no big deal. I'm just . . ."

"What is it? What's wrong?" His father towers over both of them. He takes in the can of paint, the brush in Henry's hand, his wife's highball.

"Do you see what your son is doing?" she says, stumbling off to the living room. Or maybe upstairs. Henry is not sure. He is looking at his father.

"I won't have it," she shouts on her way

to settle somewhere else. "I just won't have it."

"You heard your mother," Henry's father says. "You'd better put that away."

"Dad," Henry says. "Let me just paint it over."

"Put it away, Henry," his father says before stalking off.

For a moment Henry considers defying them both. One stroke up and it would all be erased. That would be all it would take. One longer stroke and all the height marks with their corresponding names and dates would be gone. A fresh door frame.

The brush is dripping semi-gloss Linen onto the newspaper. It hangs in his hand.

Henry kneels to close the can, using the handle of the screwdriver he had opened it with to hammer it back closed. He rinses the brush in the sink, watching the milky paint circle the drain. He is surprised the brush has retained that much paint since he'd only dipped it into the can once, imagining he could take his time and inch slowly up from the bottom. Why hadn't he moved quicker? How had he thought he'd have so much time? Stupid, stupid, he thinks.

He shuts himself into his room and his parallel headphone universe. With "Bridge

Over Troubled Water" piped into his ears, Henry the recording artist is called upon to lend his celebrity to worthy causes. Jackson Browne calls to see if he could play the No Nukes rally. Graciously Henry accepts and the guys in the booth shake their heads at his generosity. Nuclear power's a scary thing, man, he says in between laying down tracks. We've got to do something, he tells them. His agent mutters that he worries Henry is spreading himself too thin. *I don't want him tired out,* he says. Henry laughs and says, "Don't worry, man. I'm fine." *What? I can't worry about you?* his agent says.

On this particular day he comes into the session all set to record "Horse With No Name," greeting everyone by name as he always does (*that Henry Powell is so down-to-earth. You'd think fame would go to his head but he knows everyone's name,* they say in his wake), but he notices something is not quite right. By the time "Goodbye Yellow Brick Road" is playing, Dan the engineer is looking away and Hal is mumbling "sorry, man."

"What's going on?" he asks them, noticing the sympathy, concern, alarm, echoed from face to face. "What's up?"

His agent would be the one to break it to him.

"You better sit down," he says.

The booth is just big enough to accommodate an old couch and three swivel office chairs always askew because the producers slide from board to board. Henry sits on the arm of the couch.

"Someone better tell me what's up," Henry says.

"You haven't seen any news yet?" Hal asks. "You don't know?"

"It's your family," his agent says, shushing Hal.

"They're on their way to Egypt," Henry says. This part changes depending on Henry's mood. Sometimes his family is traveling to Egypt, sometimes it's to Colombia or Chile. All trips in all scenarios are funded by Henry, insisting his parents and brother need a break — "see the world" he'd tell them — and he'd surprise them with first-class tickets.

"They called from a pay phone at the airport before they boarded," Henry says. "I talked to them before I went to bed last night."

"They stormed the plane," his agent says. "Guys with masks or something, they're not even sure yet what group they're with. They stormed the plane and took hostages."

"What?" Henry says. "What the heck are you talking about? If this is some kind of joke . . ."

But he knows from the looks around the room it is no joke.

"How many hostages?" he asks, looking from face to face. *"How many hostages?"* he yells, not getting an answer.

"Just your family, man," his agent says. "I'm so sorry. It looks like they were gunning for your family. They figure maybe you'd have the most money to offer for their release, I guess."

This part calls for harder rock. The Stones. "Gimme Shelter" with its building guitar tension. Kansas. "Point of No Return." Zeppelin. "What Is and What Should Never Be" (the real drama saved for the angry chorus).

In all cases Henry — still in the recording studio — works with the FBI to secure his family's freedom. "Any amount of money," he tells the special agent in charge. "I'll charter a plane. Any amount they say."

"The government's position," they tell him, "is that we do not negotiate with terrorists."

"I don't care about *the government's position*," Henry yells. He is pacing, running his hand through his hair. "I'll fly over there myself and hand them the money. I just want my family back. *Get me my family back.*"

The FBI scurries in and out while The Who is playing. Sign this, sign that, they say, shoving documents under his pen. "You understand we can't be liable," they say.

"Are you sure you should be doing this, Powell?" his agent says, taking him aside. "It's dangerous."

"I'll be fine," he says. And all applaud him on his way out the door on his way to secure his family's release.

Which, to the tune of "Don't Fear the Reaper," he does.

"Henry!" His father's shouts reach beneath the round, cushioned rim of the earphones. "I've been calling you for five minutes!"

"What?" Henry says, throwing the headphones down. "Sorry. What do you need?"

"Let's get dinner started, shall we?" his father says.

CHAPTER EIGHT

1985

Henry can vacuum his entire apartment from one electrical outlet. In the living room he makes sure to move the armchair facing the television so the vacuum can inhale crumbs that have tumbled to that no-man's land between the chair legs and the coffee table. The chair is then pushed back into the divots in the carpet that show exactly where it has sat in the years since it was deposited there, a hand-me-down from his parents. The machine combs the carpet, the little zaps of debris making its way up the metal tube into the bag, affording Henry a sense of accomplishment. He makes sure to go east-west in his pushing and pulling, like ballpark groundskeepers mowing the outfield, cutting patterns into the grass.

The hallway is short and just wide enough to fit two vacuum columns. He will erase his advancing footprints on his way back to the utility cabinet once the job is done. He finishes the bedroom easily, remembering to get under the bed as best he can. He had heard of a guy who shoved his porn magazines under the bed when a date came over only to be discovered when she reached for the shoe that had somersaulted beside a copy of *Oui* during the haste and sexual fervor the night before. Unfortunately, the girl had only just been convinced that her small to the point of being nonexistent breasts were in fact preferable to the overblown variety featured prominently on the cover of the well-thumbed contraband, a headline screaming *Going for the JUGular*. So Henry cleaned underneath his bed in the off chance Cathy Nicholas was repulsed by dirt.

He backs out of the room and removes all foot imprints (vowing to tiptoe along the wall on his way to bed that night to safeguard his work) on his way to the kitchen.

The vacuum packs up nicely, cord wound neatly and looped over the neck of the upright. The kitchen floor is small enough to be wiped not mopped so that is what Henry does. Finally he is confident the apartment is clean enough to make a good first impression.

The bathroom will be tackled the following day at the last minute. He calls his friend Tom after surveying his efforts.

"Hey," he says into the phone.

"What's up," Tom Geigan answers.

"Not much. Want to grab a beer?"

"Yeah, I guess. You want to meet there or, actually, can you swing by and give me a lift?"

"Yeah," Henry says. "Your car's in the shop?"

"Kind of," his friend says. "I'm good to go whenever so . . ."

"I'll be over. Seriously, you better be ready this time."

"I will, I will, *Jesus,*" Tom says.

"I'm not parking this time."

"O*kay.* See ya."

Twenty minutes later Henry is muttering "goddammit" while parallel parking along the curb in front of Tom Geigan's apartment building.

He bangs on the door, the sound unexpectedly and angrily loud against the flimsy pressed-wood door.

"What did I tell you?" Henry says once the door is answered by his friend. "What, are we going on a date or what? You're showering for me?"

"I'll be right there, *Jesus,*" Tom says. He

is already back in his bedroom. "What'd you do, fly here?"

"You should really think about throwing some of this out, man," Henry says. "It's disgusting in here. It's like a science experiment."

"Feel free," Tom says. "Go to town, man."

Henry is careful not to touch anything. He stands, motionless, in the middle of the room eyeing the calling cards of sloppy bachelorhood: old pizza boxes and empty soda and beer cans.

"Seriously, let's go," he says.

"I'm waiting for you, man," Tom says, walking into the room holding up his hands in a shrug. "Let's adios this joint."

"What's wrong with your car, by the way?" Henry asks as he climbs into the Jeep.

"Huh?"

"Your car's in the shop, I thought, right? That's why I'm picking you up?"

"Oh. That. Yeah. Um, it's not in the shop, really. It's just . . ."

"You cheap son of a bitch," Henry says. He turns onto the main street that will lead them to Blackie's. "You're too cheap to pay for gas."

"I'm doing my part for the environment, man," Tom says. "Trying to conserve energy."

The conversation at the bar skitters from baseball to the new prevalence of salad bars ("I just don't see who would want to make themselves a salad. Don't you go out to a restaurant so they can make the food for you?") to music ("I'm telling you her name's pronounced *Shar*-day, not Say-dee"). Henry is happy to be thinking of anything other than his date the following evening.

But the fact that he is even thinking that he is thinking of things other than his date proves he is, in fact, not thinking of anything else but Cathy Nicholas.

Finally, with enough beer, his anxiety is numbed and they settle up and leave.

"See ya," Tom calls out on his way up the walkway that leads to his building.

Henry turns up the radio on his way home, the theme from *Miami Vice* reminding him of Neal Peterson's pushed-up blazer sleeves.

The following day — Date Day — Henry walks up the street to Larry's Diner for lunch.

"The usual?" Michelle, the waitress, asks, already writing *Philly cheese steak* on her order pad.

"Actually, hold the onions," he says. He

tries to look preoccupied with the newspaper to give the impression it is a whim this no-onions thing, an afterthought.

"You got it," she says. She pins his order to the round metal tree perched on the kitchen ledge.

On reflection it occurs to Henry that the cheese steak itself might leave his breath smelling foul even minus the offending onions.

"Michelle? Could I change my order? Sorry," he says.

"Hold up on the cheese steak," she calls out to the short-order cook. "No problem, Henry. What do you want?"

"Sorry. Thanks. Um, could I get just a turkey on rye?"

But the rye seeds might become embedded in his teeth and he might run into her before he can pry them loose in the Baxter's restroom.

"Do you have seedless rye, actually?" he asks.

Michelle, pen poised above the pad, eyes him before answering. "Do we have seedless rye? What's going on, Henry? You're never this picky. In fact, I think this is the first time in the three years I've worked here that you've ordered something other than the Philly cheese steak. And now you're changing orders, you're wanting special bread . . ."

"Seedless rye is special?" Henry tries to steer her off course. "Well, ex-cuuuuse me," he says, trying but failing to mimic the Steve Martin routine he'd seen on *Saturday Night Live.*

"All right, all right, don't tell me then," she says. "We don't have seedless rye, though, I can tell you that right now. How about white?"

"Turkey on white is great, thanks," Henry says.

He is exhausted from the effort to maintain freshness. Giving up onions is one thing, he thinks. But he made a mistake in cleaning his apartment too early in the week. He knows that now. After two days of hugging the wall on his way to and from his bedroom in order that the carpet stay neatly vacuumed he finally gave up and performed an early-morning sweep before heading out the door to work. The kitchen floor, too, had to be rewiped after a sloppy transfer of coffee from his mug to his commuter cup only moments after stowing the vacuum. His face hurt from the aftershave he slapped on following an especially fastidious bout with his razor in the hopes of avoiding the emergence of a five o'clock shadow, about the time he is meant to pick her up. Freshness takes work, he thinks.

After reading the same sentence five times and still not taking in its meaning, Henry folds his newspaper in half and stares out the window. He eats the turkey sandwich with the very energy its blandness requires, chewing in monotony. The sandwich has no condiments — too threatening to his cleanliness — but he safeguards his lap nevertheless with two large napkins unfolded lengthwise.

He returns from lunch to find Baxter's uncharacteristically busy for a Friday. Mr. Beardsley waves him over to take the phone, a customer wondering if a certain golf shirt could be secured before the weekend.

"I'll check," Henry says. "Just a minute."

"I know what you're going to ask and the answer is I don't know. I called the shipping department and they can't give me an ETA," Mr. Beardsley says to him. He turns back to his customer. "I'm sorry, Mr. Warren. The jacket I have in mind is over here."

The golf-shirt phone call ends just as a woman approaches him.

"Excuse me, are you Henry Powell?" she asks, glancing back at a boy who is most certainly her son but appears to wish it weren't so, his pimple-ridden angst exacerbating into redness the moment she poses the question.

"Yes," he says. "Can I help you?"

"I'm Cheryl Eddy," she says, "and this is my son, Craig."

Henry shakes both their hands, which given the ever-widening gap between Craig and his mother, took a moment to complete. "Hi."

"Constance Garvey — from Fox Run? — told me I should come and talk to you," she says, "about the football program. I don't want to bother you while you're at work but I didn't have your phone number. Everyone knows you work here so I hope you don't mind us coming in like this. . . ."

"No, no, it's no problem," he says. He glances around and sees Mr. Beardsley is helping a customer but otherwise there is a lull.

"Oh, great, thanks," she says. "My son's getting ready to start there this fall and, well, I know you were the big hero there. . . ."

Henry colors and shifts his weight. "Oh, God, no . . . the team . . ."

"No, you were," she interrupts, "everyone knows *that*. But what I'm wondering is if you ever do any private tutoring. . . ."

"Mom, *God*," Craig says from as many feet away as he can remain. His embarrassment now borders on the kind of humiliation only teenage sons feel around their mothers.

"Tutoring?" Henry asks.

"Private coaching," she says. "Once or twice a week? Just to get Craig ready for the season? We'd pay you, obviously."

It is at this point that Craig gives up and skulks down the aisles out of earshot.

Cheryl Eddy lowers her voice. "He really wants to get better and his father works with him when he can but he's out of town a lot for work so it's not really a regular thing. And you . . . well, to be coached by you would definitely give him the edge."

"Mrs. Eddy, I just —" Henry starts to speak.

"Are you kidding? Call me Cheryl," she says, smiling and pushing her hair behind her ears. "Mrs. Eddy is my mother-in-law."

"What? Oh," Henry says, clearing his throat and offering a wan smile. "Um, Cheryl —" more throat clearing "— I don't know. I've never really done that kind of thing. I'm sure your son'll be fine. The coach is really good."

"He needs help, Henry," she says. She looks across the store at her son. "I know it doesn't seem like it right now but he really wants help. He's just . . . shy."

"Oh, totally," Henry says. "But . . . won't he feel kind of weird since I'm, like, about his age?"

Cheryl cocks her head and smiles. "You graduated in 1978, right?" she asks. Then she pats his arm knowingly. "Welcome to my world."

"Ah, well, can I think about it?" he asks, not quite understanding her comment.

"Of course, of course, sure," she says. "Let me give you our phone number and you can just give us a jingle whenever. But maybe it'll be soon? I don't mean to rush you or anything, it's just I was hoping things could get started on the soon side. Here, oh, you have a pen? Great." She scribbles out the seven digits and hands them to Henry.

"No problem. I'll call you early next week if that's okay," he says.

"That'd be great," she says. "In the meantime we need to find a sport shirt for travel days. Craig?" She motions him to come over, a signal that the uncomfortable part of the exchange is over.

"What sport jacket will he be wearing?" Henry asks, recalling the day he left the house for his first away game. He had felt so grown-up, like a man leaving for work. He had copied the bored but hurried expression he had seen so many of the fathers wear every morning on their way out the door. The air left the balloon when he climbed out of his mother's station wagon and saw they were to board a bright yellow school bus.

"Oh, I *wish*," Cheryl says. "Craig? Did you hear that? Why don't you wear a sport jacket like Mr. Powell here says?"

"Yeah, right," Craig says.

"The coach'll bench you if you *don't* wear one," Henry says.

This remark — in that it is directed at Craig — requires a response equally personal. Cheryl can no longer serve as interpreter between them. A classic mistake old people make, Henry thinks.

"Um, that's not what they sent home in the packet," Craig says, uncertain. He has mustered all his courage to address Henry but quickly looks at his mother for confirmation.

"Apparently nowadays," Cheryl says, "they're not required to wear a sport jacket for game travel days."

"Just a sport shirt," she is saying. "So maybe you can steer us in the right direction? And since you're picking it out it will be Craig's lucky shirt!"

Craig's horror is now complete, Henry

thinks. He takes them over to the tall stack of clear Lucite cubbyholes filled with neatly stacked folded sport shirts separated by size. One cubbyhole for smalls, two for medium, three for large (the most popular size), one for extra large. XXL and XXXL are too few to warrant their own space so instead are shamefully hidden in the back room, brought out only by request or implication. The entire display is Henry's least favorite as it reeks of straight pins, cardboard squares and origami-like folds impossible to replicate once a shirt is undone and then passed over. He wishes he could erect a sign above it saying Please — *for the love of God* — Only Undo These Shirts If You Are Prepared to Buy Them. Cheryl holds up various colors and patterns to Craig's chest, which is collapsing in agony with every passing minute. After a feeble point from Craig to a dark blue polo buttondown they move to the cash register.

"You ready, hon?" she asks, knowing the answer. She fumbles in her purse for her car keys and then turns back to Henry and flutters four fingers. "Hope to hear from you soon."

"Bye," Henry says. He watches them go, Craig stalking past him, barreling through the door in front of his mother. Outside he sees Cheryl is shaking her head and preparing the lecture on rudeness he is sure will occupy most of their drive home.

At stoplights he has seen this going on in cars alongside his: a mother chiding a child either backward via the rearview mirror or sideways to the passenger seat. Her lips moving angrily, hands gripping the steering wheel, waiting for the light to turn, even though that won't interrupt the tirade, the steady flow of words. Once or twice he has caught the eye of the victim, who silently telegraphs "help me" just as the light changes and the car speeds up to match the words racing out.

And when this happens something inside Henry aches with envy.

He replaces the mercifully still-folded shirts and tidies up the stacks. Then he checks his watch.

Each step is deliberate, one foot carefully, self-consciously, placed in front of the other like an amputee learning to walk with a new prosthetic. He is pretending to amble, as if he'd only just thought "Oh, *that's* what it is. I have a date tonight. I knew there was *some*thing I was forgetting." He is hoping that pretending to be nonchalant will give way to genuine indifference. And so one foot steps slowly in front of the other continuing the optimistic charade as he walks down the sidewalk to collect his date.

From the very slip of the outer edge of the most remote part of the front window Henry peeks. He sees Cathy laughing with a girl he recognizes as Cup-a-Joe's equivalent of a stock boy. They are folding up their aprons, Cathy throwing her head back in laughter at something the other one has said. Now it is Cathy's turn to amuse her colleague, which she does with apparent gusto — hands are involved, gestures, an exaggerated facial expression theatrically thrown in. He imagines her equally animated with him this evening, regaling him perhaps with similar stories, anecdotes from the front lines of the service industry. He finds himself smiling at her happiness. And it is with this smile still lingering on his face, in his eyes, that he pushes open the door — not yet locked for the evening (maybe she has forgotten in her eagerness to go on her date, he thinks) — and joins their mirth.

But the revelry stops the moment the girls turn to face him.

"Hi," he says. "How's it going?"

"Hi," Cathy says. She blushes when she

looks at him.

"You all set?" he asks. The girl, the colleague, scurries away, calling out "Bye, Cath" in a singsong way girls have, on her way out the door.

Cath. He stores the nickname away, thinking it will be so nice when he, too, can refer to her casually in this way. Then again maybe he will continue to call her Cathy — Catherine even — to distinguish himself from her friends. In the way husbands call their "Liz" wives "Elizabeth."

"Yeah," she says. The fact that she blushes when she looks at him ignites an animal surge of protectiveness in him.

"I'm psyched to see this," she says. And then she forces and stifles a cough. He is aware she is trying to be cool. First-date cool that requires a measure of nonchalance he, too, is gunning for. But strangely his nervousness decreases as hers increases. He imagines there to be a finite amount of it between them so when one is using it, the other has to wait.

She holds the door open so he can exit first and she can lock up, taking the key with the little purple dot out of the bottom lock and then inserting the key with the black dot into the top lock.

The walk down Main Street to the theater

is short and involves passing Baxter's, the hardware store, a long-boarded-up storefront that used to house a children's toy store and before that a beauty parlor. Next to that, the real estate agency (Train and Assoc. in chipping gold stenciled lettering) that has so many pictures of houses for sale an interested buyer could barely see in through the window to the bustling office. Next to the real estate office is a liquor store that has begun to carry various incongruous items like milk, tampons, razors, dog food and Kaopectate. At the end of Main Street, after Transitions, the women's clothing store, but before crossing to the small theater where their tickets are already on hold, is a two-pump, full service gas station with a dirty office where, if you don't pay the attendant with cash, he will take your credit card inside and clip it to a small plastic board. In the winter that plastic board barely ekes through the slit in the window his patron will allow, unwilling to let even a moment's worth of heat escape the cozy interior. A receipt is traded back for the board and the window is sealed back up. Shutting out the freezing and jump-suited attendant who will then inhale exhaust fumes while blowing on his bare hands on his way back into the tiny office to await his next customer.

They wait at the corner for the light to change. Henry is aware of a suffocating need to speak. To say something — anything — to fill the silence that is bearing down on both of them. He has already asked her about her day at work, a question that elicited a shrug and a simple "fine." Panicking, Henry fears silence is rapidly becoming the third wheel on this date. Finally and thankfully Cathy coughs.

"Are you cold?" Henry asks. "Do you want my jacket?"

"No, thanks," she says. But she coughs again so he slides out of his coat.

"Seriously, I'm hot," he says. "I was going to take it off, anyway."

She smiles at him as he drapes it over her shoulders and his chest swells with a caveman sense of control. He sees her tiny hands — less-benevolent eyes might view them as scrawny — clutching the lapels of his jacket, pulling them closer together, and it stirs an animal pride. He has created warmth where once there was cold.

When they walk in, Henry's friend Joey Young waves them over.

"Hey," Henry juts his chin out as a greeting, reasoning that anything more enthusiastic would be uncool.

"Whatdya think?" Joey points to himself and Henry recognizes the shirt he'd sold to him a few days earlier.

"Looks good, looks good," Henry says, smiling. And to Cathy says: "I sold him that shirt earlier in the week."

"I got your tickets right here," Joey says. He moves into the booth, edging out a confused teenage ticket-taker, and rings them up.

The problem is this: because they are at the first showing — the five-thirty — there is no line. Having tickets on hold makes him look too eager. Completely uncool. Henry clears his throat and decides to look surprised that this man would set aside two tickets for him. Cathy does not appear to understand the nature of the transaction, anyway, he thinks, so this won't be too hard.

"Wow, thanks." Henry bends his knees and says this through the mousehole opening in the booth window. "Huh. How about that?" He turns to Cathy in faked surprise.

"I thought . . ." Joey starts to give away their plan but Henry interrupts him quickly.

"Thanks again, man." He takes his change while steering Cathy to the concession counter. "What'll you have to eat?"

"So what, you're some big star, getting tickets on discount? Jeez," she says, smiling into the Milk Duds and Jujyfruits.

Her interpretation is, of course, misguided, but he does not correct her. He is pleased by it. Joey Young is safely back in his movie office doing God knows what movie theater managers do in their offices and Henry revels in her characterization.

"H-hardly," he stammers on purpose, to convey just the right "aw shucks" mix of modesty and pride.

The date is now going well. Henry imagines his biographer following not so far behind, like a private detective. There goes Henry, he writes, pulling two napkins from the dispenser. Henry with his hand tentatively and ever so slightly on the small of Cathy's back, somewhere underneath his jacket. Henry letting his date lead the way to whatever seat she prefers. Henry helping her remove his own jacket, depositing it on the empty seat beside him. Henry offering the tub for her to hold — "or I can hold it here in the middle if you want."

"We're here early," Cathy says. "It's only five-fifteen."

"What?"

Several rows behind them, the biographer's head snaps up. *Uh-oh,* he says under his breath.

"It's five-fifteen," she whispers even

though the lights had not yet dimmed and there are only six other people in the theater.

Five-fifteen.

Shit. Five-fifteen!

"Oh, my God." He turns to her and nearly upends the popcorn. "I completely forgot something."

"What? What're you — where are you going?" In one hand she is holding the soda he has handed her, in the other she clutches the bucket of popcorn. "I'll come with you."

"No!" he practically yells at her. Really it is a regular volume but for a movie theater it comes across aggressively. Calibrate, he tells himself silently. Calibrate. "Don't get up. I'll be right back. No, seriously . . . sit back down. I just forgot something. I'll run up the street and be back before the previews even."

Reluctantly she sits back down, clearly bewildered at his frenzy to leave.

"Is it the store?" she asks.

"Yeah," he says, crab-walking out of the aisle. "It's something I forgot to do at the store. I'll be right back."

Main Street is a straight shot perpendicular to the theater but never has Henry been more aware of its slope. The muscles in his legs are twitching by the time he reaches his car.

He nearly runs the only red light at the top of the street, turning right just in front of an oncoming car that justifiably honks.

Bridge Avenue — the road he is now careening along — takes him past mostly single-family homes. Starter houses. Houses young families are thrilled to pay mortgages on.

Five minutes have passed. Henry pictures Cathy looking over her shoulder for him as the theater starts to fill up. Sorry, she will say, this seat's taken. And other couples will file past her winched-up legs — women never stand to let people usher past.

Six minutes. He pulls up to his childhood home and lets himself in the side door.

Don't look — no time today. There is no time. This is Henry talking to himself under his breath as he rushes past and through the door that leads into the kitchen, stale with the smell of spattered grease from meals long ago. He figures he has gone back and forth past it probably more than a million times in his life. The thing is — in telling himself not to look he is thinking about it. So he might as well have looked. The time expended thinking *don't look* is undoubtedly greater than the time spent taking that one glance at the inked-in names and height marks on the door frame. There has not been a time he had passed through the doorway and not noted the markings. It is superstition. Like when the Yankees won the pennant in 1976 and he happened to be wearing a checked flannel shirt and so from then on he pulled out that same shirt every year during the playoffs.

"Hello?" Henry calls out without bothering to close the front door. "Mom? Dad?"

No lights are on in the house.

The living room is silent. Empty. The only sign she has been here is the glass on the coffee table with melting ice cubes. So she's not too far away, he thinks.

Heart thumping with hurry, he takes the stairs two at a time, practically vaulting up to the master bedroom with its upholstered headboard and matching comforter that used to be fluffy but now is flattened with years of bodies punching down any remnants of the synthetic down.

"Mom?"

She is facedown on top of the comforter. He puts his face right up close to hers and is reassured to feel her thick breathing. Out cold.

He turns her over and sees the imprint of the comforter on the right side of her face.

But then he remembers about the vomit and how someone can die this way . . . choking on their own bile . . . and half turns her so she is on her side.

He takes her shoes off and pulls her up so that her head rests on the pillow.

Back downstairs he scrawls a note to his father on a blank legal pad in the center of his father's desk in the darkened study. *Hi, Dad. I was here. Mom's upstairs asleep. See you tomorrow. H.* He turns on the desk lamp to serve as a spotlight on the evidence that he had indeed checked in but he purposely leaves the time off the note. Normally he would have written 5:15 p.m. at the top. His father won't question it. He is sure of this.

Unless . . . unless his father was here at five-fifteen, checking his watch, waiting. Five-twenty even. He might have just left, only moments before Henry's car came screeching up the block.

He has no time left to figure out what to do. He pictures Cathy standing up to look back over the sea of heads in the now-darkened theater. He imagines her leaving. Worse, he imagines Joey Young walking up the aisle with his flashlight landing on her, puzzling out why he had left her there alone, telling her how Henry had even requested tickets put aside for this date.

The car screams back up Bridge. Its blinker, signaling a left turn down Main Street, sounds Edgar Allen Poe loud. "Why is this light so *long?*" he says out loud. *Jesus.*

To save time he should drive directly to the theater, but he can't because he'd told her it was something at the store. He would have had no need to get into his car, which had been parked in a now-occupied space directly in front of Baxter's. Maybe she hadn't noticed where he'd parked. Several spaces down — twelve to be exact — there is an empty one which he jerks into, barely remembering to lock the doors in his haste.

He sprints back down Main, now grateful for the gentle hill. Ticket stub, ticket stub, he is saying to himself, trying to wrestle it from his pocket as he is running.

The rush of cold outside air floods into the seat with Henry.

"Hey," he says, stifling his panting, "sorry about that." The glow of previews lights her face.

"Is everything okay?" she whispers sideways, without tearing her eyes from the screen. In between previews for *The Jewel of the Nile* and *Fletch* she looks at him and hands him back his drink.

"Yeah, no, everything's fine," he says. He takes a deep breath and exhales as quietly as he can.

CHAPTER NINE

1977

"Boys, I've got to tell you, I like what I'm seeing out there," the coach is saying. "So I've decided, Powell, you're starting this week. We're going to feature you if you can keep up some of the stuff I been seeing after hours. . . ." He pauses to let it sink in that they've been watched. "You think you're up to it?"

Henry's attention does not waver from the coach but Henry feels Steve Wilson nodding, too.

This is one of those moments, he thinks. One of those moments I'll tell my kids about. "I remember the day it all turned around for me, kids," Henry hears his elderly self talking to the children gathered at his feet. "If you apply yourself like I did back there on that football field, every day, after practice, bone tired," Elder Henry says, "then you can make it happen for yourself. Like I did." It occurs to Henry this will warrant at least one chapter in his biography. Words like *underdog* will join *triumph* and, again, the reader will be reminded of the Extraordinary Life of Henry Powell.

Somewhere off in the distance a radio is playing Leo Sayer. Henry is thinking he wishes he had dried off properly before talking with the coach because his wet skin is now covered in goose bumps. Also, since Steve Wilson was already dressed, he feels naked even though he has his towel around his hips. But the towel is ratty, threadbare after so many washes.

"You with me, Powell?"

"Yeah," Henry says. "I mean, yes, sir. Coach."

"Good," the coach says. "Tomorrow we'll get started building plays into the rotation. Go home. Get some sleep."

"Yes, sir," they say in unison.

Outside the gym locker room Wilson says "way to go" to Henry.

"Huh? Oh, yeah. Thanks," he says. "See ya."

Henry wonders if this means they will no longer be able to work drills after practice.

It is still light out when he emerges from

the gym. He shields his eyes salute-fashion, letting them adjust before setting off for home. He does not mind walking home when the weather is still relatively nice. His knapsack does not start to feel heavy until he turns onto his street so he has no reason to complain. The only drawback, he thinks, is that the two-mile walk sucks up time. There is barely enough time as it is between school, practices, work and homework.

But then, a miracle.

"Henry!" The arm is waving out the driver's side window, accompanying the voice calling his name. He turns toward his mother's voice, so startled to hear it but so happy not to have to keep walking. The sun is hitting the windshield so he does not know until the family station wagon advances toward him that his mother is in her nightgown.

"Mom? Jesus, Mom," he says, closing the passenger door just as she presses down on the accelerator. "What're you doing?"

"Can't a mother pick her son up from school?" she says, turning to smile at him. The trouble is she doesn't look back at the road.

"Mom! Look out!" Henry says, grabbing for the steering wheel. "Here, pull over. *Mom.* Pull over and let me drive."

"I most certainly will not, you silly," she says in a sodden voice. "Since when do first-graders know how to drive?" She laughs and tousles his hair.

She does not let up on the gas and an oncoming car honks and swerves to avoid her.

"Mom!" Henry slides across the front seat and bullies her right leg aside with his left to reach over to the brakes. He has the steering wheel and, though it is not smooth, he manages to pull the car over to the side of the road and put it into Park. His mother, in her summer nightgown, is crumpled up against the driver's side door. The tears start before he takes the keys out of the ignition, a safety move in case she decides to jump out while he walks around to her side of the car.

"It's okay, Mom," he says. He pats her arm. "I'm going to come around and get you out, okay?"

All her weight is against the door so that when he opens it from the outside she tumbles out to the ground. Fortunately they have pulled over far enough so she does not fall onto pavement, but unfortunately it is dirt they are on and it mixes in with the tears she is crying so she is a mess before he can help her up.

"It's okay, Mom," he says, crouching down beside her. "I'm going to lift you up now. One. Two. Grab hold of my neck. There, that's good. Three." He scoops her up and immediately wishes he had thought ahead and had the back door open in advance. Now it's too late. The handle will be impossible to grab hold of; it is all he can do to keep her nightgown pulled down far enough over his mother's legs.

The back gate of the wagon, with its easy push-button release, is his only option. We'll be home in no time, he thinks. She won't even notice.

"Here we go," he says, "I'm just going to slide you in here." He folds forward so he can deposit her far away from the back hatch. "There. Good. Okay? You okay, Mom?"

"Everything okay, Powell?" The coach is pulled up alongside the station wagon.

Henry has just closed up the back of the wagon. He cannot be sure how long Coach has been there. Did he see Mom? He panics. *Click click click* his mind shuttles through excuses like those slide viewers that look like binoculars until you look through and you see different parts — all clear and crisp — of the Grand Canyon.

The backseat's torn up. Click. My mother's leg is hurt and she needs to stretch out. Click. She's sick. Click. She's just fine. Click.

He sees his starting position evaporate as the coach will no doubt think he is a liability — too much craziness going on with that Powell guy, the coach will think.

"You okay, son?" the coach asks him again. He puts his own car in Park and Henry is horrified to think he might be climbing out and then would certainly see inside the station wagon.

"Yes," he says. He scales his reaction back from a guilty-sounding voice. "I mean, yeah, sure, everything's fine, Coach. I just . . . ah . . . my baseball cap flew out the window." He looks down at his empty hands.

They look at each other and Henry sees the words as they float across the air from his mind into Coach Cahill's. *Please let it be please just forget what I know you saw please just drive away Coach please.*

One moment more for the message to be fully received and the coach says, "Okay, son. You drive safe, you hear me? I'll see you tomorrow, Powell."

"Thanks, Coach." He watches as the car pulls away.

Henry exhales and climbs behind the wheel. He adjusts the rearview mirror so he can see his mother.

"Mom? We're going home now, Mom. We'll be home in no time."

She cannot wipe her nose — her hands are wrapped around her knees, a sloppy fetal position — so the sniffling continues the whole ride home.

"Almost there," he says a moment or two later. "Almost there."

On the field Henry hears nothing beyond the coach's calls, the numbers shooting back and forth between players, the occasional cheers from parents gathered in the bleachers and along the sidelines. Even these he barely hears. On a good day. Which is to say that to Henry, football is beauty. It makes sense. Leaving the field is like stepping off a moving airport sidewalk: regular steps feel heavy, clumsy, mincing compared to the smooth ride of the long treadmill that reaches lengthwise down the center of a terminal.

It is Henry's first starting game and the crispness of a fresh start is echoed in the cloudless sky. Its shade of blue particular to fall in a Northeastern town: Canada geese gliding southbound overhead, leaf piles burning, butternut squash, pumpkin patches.

Because Henry is tall and comparatively skinny he can out-jump other players. And that is precisely what he does on this breezy day. On the first pass spiraling through the air.

Steve Wilson gives a sidelong nod and makes the calls they've agreed on in the huddle.

The running back inches forward but it is Henry, all limbs, who makes the catch and runs the ball into the end zone. Shouts. Backslapping. Henry Powell. Who'd have thought it? a teammate's father will mutter on the side.

Henry does not feel elated so much as he feels he has come home.

Second quarter. Another play called, signaling Henry is to save the day again. Which he does . . . to more clapping, raised expectations, shoulder pads shuddering under teammates' pats.

And soon, after three more games, his coach calls a meeting.

"We need to work out a system, Welly," Coach says after another victory. This is a nickname that spontaneously appeared the day of his first start. Henry can't decide whether he likes it or not but is happy for the feeling of inclusion it evokes. The two of them are straddling the bench facing each other in the steamy, smelly locker room after everyone else has showered and gone home.

"A system?" Henry doesn't understand. He was sure this meeting was to be complimentary and now the coach is going to lecture him. He searches his mind for what went wrong. As fast as this starting position came, it could disappear with equal rapidity. It seems to Henry that if he can land on what he did wrong, if he can identify it before Coach does, he can retain his position and regain Coach's respect. Show that he is aware. Looking out for his own errors just as closely as his coach. But what had he done wrong? For a moment he cannot bear to have his tranquil game, this game he loves more than anything else in the entire world, torn apart by the coach. It will ruin it. He feels he would do anything to keep this from happening. If the coach starts to rip on me, he thinks, I'll just run out. I'll run out of here so fast his head'll spin.

"We've got to figure out what to do about this job of yours," Coach says.

"Baxter's?" Henry resists the urge to cry with happiness. This — *this?* — is the system they need to work out? Henry is seized with the desire to reach across to hug this man facing him. This straight-backed, Brylcreemed, wrinkle-faced coach.

"Yeah," the coach says. "Look. You've got to be here. I've got to have you here not just for practice and games but for films, too."

Saturday mornings the team reviews the films of Friday night games. The coach, pointer in hand, stops and starts the whirring movie projector to make sure his players see what went wrong and what went right. They also review films of other teams. To prepare for the upcoming game.

"But I work all day Saturday," Henry says. *What?* Why'd I just say that? It sounds like I won't do whatever he says, Henry thinks. I will. He'll see. I'll do whatever he says. Just let me stay in the game, he thinks.

"Not anymore you don't," Coach says. "We need you here for that. Before it was okay for you to miss Saturdays and the occasional practice here and there, but now you're my blue-chip. Everything's different now. You're a player now."

"You want me to call your boss for you?" the coach is asking. "I can talk to him. Explain the situation."

Coach talking to Mr. Beardsley is a mental image Henry simply cannot abide. As distasteful as imagining one's parents having sex. Mr. Beardsley is the type of person who actually pronounces the *t-h* in the word *clothes,* which, to Henry, has always implied a lisp. He looked it up in the dictionary one bored night at home and saw that the *t* and *h* are meant to be pronounced. But Coach, along with the rest of the general population, pronounces it *close.* No, they would not see eye to eye. Henry is sure of it.

"No," he says, "I'll talk to him. I can cut back on my hours. I don't think he'll mind."

"Good. That's what I want to hear. 'Cause you need to be here, Welly. You're looking good out there."

"Thanks, Coach."

"Now, get out of here," Coach says. "Go home. You need a ride?"

Henry would in fact like a ride home but instead hears himself say "no thanks" because he doesn't want to make the coach go out of his way. He knows the coach lives where a lot of the other teachers do, not far from campus. Faculty housing. On a street that has less space between houses. Small squares of yards in front, bricked patios in back just big enough for barbecues and small picnic tables. Henry's home is out of the way.

"See you tomorrow."

"Thanks, Coach."

He waits long enough to be sure the coach is gone and slings his backpack across one shoulder (blue-chip players certainly wouldn't put both straps on, he smiles to himself) and pushes out of the locker room. Swaggers out. The Extraordinary Life of Henry Powell. Now this . . . *this* will be a good read.

For secretly Henry has always thought something wonderful — something *special* — would happen to him. He has always suspected he is destined for greatness. He kicks up the leaves in front of each step. The two miles home are barely enough for him to sort out the trajectory he is now on.

His eye is on setting a school record, one with a big-enough gap to hold for years and years to come. Stenciled up under the other names on the plaques on the gymnasium wall. Immortality. This is my immortality. This is all I want. If I can have this, God, if you can just let me do this, I will never ask for anything else ever again. Most yards gained in a season. Just let my name be on it.

"Go long, go long!" he calls out. The field empty but for the two who are after-hours fixtures there. Henry practicing his own passing. Receiving is one thing but Henry has decided to work on his throws. Well-rounded players have more of a chance of setting records. But this pass spirals and drops short.

"Okay," he calls over to his new receiver, who picks it up and jogs it into the end zone, anyway. "It's okay," he says. He knows it will take time. They've traded roles and it will take time to get used to the switch.

"Wilson!" he calls out. "Go wide this time."

The pass is completed and he knows they are both feeling better. Getting into a groove. Before daylight is gone. A couple more of these and we can end on a good note.

"Wilson! Long. Go long!"

Long, wide, far, they share three more completions and finally jog toward each other to call it a day.

"That was good, huh?" Henry says.

"Yeah. But why do you keep calling me Wilson?"

Henry looks at the boy and turns toward where the old locker room used to stand. He looks back down at the brown patches on the field. Where no grass ever has a chance to grow for the feet stomping it down.

He pats Craig on the back. "Good work today, pal."

"Thanks, Mr. Powell," the boy says. "See you Thursday?"

"Yeah, I'll see you Thursday."

CHAPTER TEN

1986

If he could just know *why* she didn't want
him things would be all right. He could
move on, he tells himself. He could stop
driving by her apartment building, slowing
to see if her lights are on and dreaming
about what she might be doing inside.
Sometimes the blue glow of television
would illuminate her windows and he would
watch the images flicker and wonder what
she was watching. Perhaps it was a cop
show. No, she wouldn't watch a cop show.

If he just knew *why* things would "never
work out between them" as she had said,
then he could maybe even throw out the
perfume. The sales clerk had thought he was
a queer when he asked about it, he could
tell.

"Um, do you have a perfume called, um,"
Henry had said. He was trying to look like

the name had slipped his mind. Like he hadn't already committed it to memory. "Let's see. It's Baby Soft . . . something. . . . Oh, yeah, Love's Baby Soft."

He had colored at the name, which hadn't sounded so feminine when he'd turned it over in his head. Cathy had blushed when he asked her what perfume she wore. She always smelled so good.

"Yeah, we have it," the clerk said. "We might even have a tester of it." She slid the glass door open to fish a bottle out.

His plan had been to pretend to be thinking about the purchase just to get a quick whiff of it. To tide me over, he thought at the time. I just need something to tide me over.

He hadn't planned on buying a bottle. But when he sniffed it, Cathy was inhaled up into his nose, down his throat, directly into his lungs. It was too intoxicating to pass up, the idea that this feeling could be constantly replicated in private. At home. He pulled his wallet out quickly, hoping his erection would subside.

"I'll take it," he said. The fact that the clerk used only her thumb and forefinger to take the twenty dollar bill from him registered but did not matter. He was consumed by Cathy's scent.

Her favorite things became his favorite things. On their fourth date she mentioned she liked fried chicken and now ten Swanson's fried chicken dinners were stacked in his freezer. He'd overheard her telling a friend to "have a happy," and now this is what he says to every departing customer. That or "take it easy," which she had said to him directly at the end of that same fourth date. Which hadn't really been a date, come to think of it. She had needed a ride to pick up her car in the shop. He offered and stretched it out to include an ice cream run. There she ordered mint chocolate chip and presto Henry had a new favorite flavor. In the car she turned the radio up when Steely Dan came on so Henry went to the record store the next day and bought *Pretzel Logic.* And then pored over the liner notes, memorizing first the band members' names then the song lyrics.

How could she not want to be with me the way I want to be with her? he wondered. How can she live without me? Henry found this mind-boggling. Because he had a hard time *breathing* without her. He sometimes thought he was suffocating he missed her so much.

If he had to pinpoint the moment it took

a turn for the worse he would pick the day following the first time he took her to his parents' house. That was when things started to head south, he told himself. That was when she started looking at me differently.

His apartment was off limits due to an unfortunate plumbing problem in the unit above his. The super was waiting for a replacement part to arrive from the toilet manufacturer in Ohio and in the meantime the smell was too foul to ignore. So Henry was staying with his parents for the week.

"Nice house," she said. They were standing in the front hall. Henry hung her jeans jacket on the coatrack.

"Thanks. Let's go upstairs."

He hadn't wanted to take her to his old bedroom as much as he wanted to keep her from seeing any family members. Wait, he tells the invisible screenwriter, that's not entirely true. I *did* want to take her to my bedroom. Did not: Screenwriter. Did so: Henry. Dramatic license, the screenwriter says.

They were halfway up the stairs when the voice reached them, hooking them, reeling them into the boat. Don't bite, don't bite, he thought at the time.

"You don't want to introduce me to your family?" Cathy had smiled at him from two stairs below.

Catch-22, Catch-22, he thought. Don't bite.

"Henry? Is that you?" his mother's feeble question fooled him into thinking it might be averted, this potential powder keg. The Powell Powder Keg. That's perfect, he thinks. The Powell Powder Keg. The screenwriter takes note of it.

"Henry?"

"Come on, we'll make it quick," he says.

"What's your *problem?*" Cathy says. She takes his hand and lets herself be led into the den.

At least she's dressed, he remembers thinking when he sees his mother. But the drink in her hand should have been a red flag.

"Mom, this is Cathy. Cathy, Mom."

"Nice to meet you, Mrs. Powell."

Henry's mother extends her hand. "Nice to meet you."

"Okay, so, we're going to go upstairs," Henry says.

"What's your hurry?" his mother asks.

And Cathy chimes in with, "Seriously," in agreement with Mrs. Powell, an alliance she assumes will garner faux annoyance in

Henry. That would be the normal course of events. But she doesn't know this is not a normal family, he thinks. He looks at her innocently trying to win over his mother.

This looks pretty normal right now, Henry thinks.

And so he leaves for a moment — "I'll be right back" — to go to the bathroom so he can be sure there's nothing stuck in his teeth. He also wants to swig mouthwash because the pizza left a bad taste in his mouth and he doesn't want Cathy to be grossed out.

"Sure, take your time," his mother says. "How was your dinner?" Henry hears her asking Cathy. Perhaps this is why he doesn't hurry. He goes to his parents' bathroom to use his father's Listerine.

He hears his mother's laughter from the third stair on his way back down. It sounds more like funny-ha-ha than funny-insane.

When he enters the room he sees Cathy is no longer trying to humor Henry's mother, who is laughing quite hard. Cathy looks defeated, as though she has already seen their relationship play out start to finish and it's the finished part she's on right now.

"What's so funny?" Henry asks his mother. But the question is to both of them, hoping to increase his odds of an answer by putting it to two people instead of one.

Cathy stands. "Um, I've got to go."

He looks from her to his mother and back at her. "Let's go upstairs." He holds his hand out for her, to lead her away. But they only make it as far as the hall.

"Actually I'm just going to take off," she says, pulling her jacket off the coatrack.

"Okay, okay," Henry says. "Let me grab my car keys." He knows they're in his pocket but uses this as an excuse to go back into the den.

He squats in front of his mother, now collapsed back into the couch, back into her haze as if the five minutes she spent socializing with Cathy had wrung her out.

"What did you say to her?" he hisses at his mother, inches from her face.

"Henry, I'm going to walk," Cathy calls from the front hall. "You don't need to drive me. I'm going to take off now."

"Wait," he says.

She is halfway down the front walk when he reaches her.

"Cathy, wait up," he says, getting in front of her, blocking her path. "Can you just — can you just hold on a second?"

She shifts her weight from one leg to another. "Yeah?"

"Look, I don't know what my mother said

to you back there," Henry says. He is hoping she will just come out with it so he knows what to refute, where to begin, but she is silent. So he continues, "But, you know, um, my mom's like psycho kind of. I mean, not psycho like she's going to kill someone in a shower or something. Just, you know, not, like, *normal.* So if she said . . ."

He trails off with the instant realization that what he most feared has actually come to pass. The thought quickens his heartbeat and his panic reaches fox-limb-gnawing proportions.

Cathy says, "I just have to go home, that's all."

"Cathy, wait," Henry says, his breathing shallow. He is walking backward step for step with her forward movement. "Seriously, can we just talk? Can you just tell me what's wrong?"

"Henry, move," Cathy says, trying to step around him. "I've got to get going."

"But . . ."

"Seriously," she says. "I just have to go. Take it easy."

She darts around him and speed-walks away, hugging her purse to her side like a nervous American tourist on a cobblestoned Italian street.

He watches her until she has turned the corner and then he stalks up his front walk into the den.

His mother is still on the couch, still clutching her glass, but now her head is tilted back, mouth ajar.

Henry pries the glass from her hand and sets it on the side table. He is so furious he purposely does not put it on a coaster.

She does not stir when he forklifts her up into his arms. Her head — mouth still wide open — falls back. Dead weight.

"You told her," Henry says. The impulse to cry folds into anger like a coal mine caving in. "You *told* her." He is speaking to her but really just to himself since she is unconscious. "I swear to God, Mom. Jesus."

She's lost weight, he thinks to himself, noting that carrying her isn't as difficult tonight as it's been in the past. She must have lost weight.

He lays her on the bed alongside his father but shakes the bed when he stumbles into it while extricating himself.

"David?" His father's voice is hoarse with sleep.

And just like that Henry belly flops. It takes a moment for the air to reenter his lungs.

"No, Dad," he manages, "it's me, Henry."

His father, though, has slipped back into sleep. He won't remember, Henry thinks. He won't remember his mistake. It wouldn't matter if he did, though. It's not like he'd say anything about it, anyway, Henry thinks. He is reassured by the fact that it does not happen that much anymore, anyhow, being confused for his dead brother.

But oh how it hurt at first. Hearing the name was bad enough, but seeing the wave of disappointment and grief when he entered a room — living proof that he was not in fact David Powell but Henry Powell — to know that the mere sight of him brought this tidal wave of nausea . . . *that* was excruciating.

Brad wasn't there when it happened. He was at his baseball game. Or somewhere, Henry couldn't remember that part. His father was working late. His mother was in the kitchen making meat loaf. Show late 1960s, early 1970s house, the screenwriter jots down in the margin. Mother with the apron on, a cigarette perched on the edge of an ashtray on the kitchen table. Raw meat on the counter, he scribbles, adding a note to look up other ingredients so he can set the scene.

But I only remember what was happening

upstairs, in the bathroom, Henry tells the screenwriter. *That's why we're such a good team*, the screenwriter says. *You say what you saw and I'll take care of the rest. Just trust me*, he tells Henry. *Don't worry about it. Go on.*

Where was I? Henry thinks. Oh, yeah. The bathtub.

He stops. The image shrivels up.

Oh, no. Not this again. The screenwriter is shaking his head and leans in toward Henry. *Hey, kid*, he is saying. *Hey, listen to me: it happens all the time. Kids taking baths . . . you look away for just a second —*

Stop. Henry says this out loud. *Stop.* Just stop, okay? I don't want to think about it.

Okay, okay. I'll take over, the screenwriter says. *Just relax and let me tell it.*

Seven-year-old Henry had wanted to make up for the fact that he had helped Brad put firecrackers in Mr. and Mrs. Rockton's mailbox. The box was knocked clear off the wooden stake to which it had been nailed. Mr. and Mrs. Rockton demanded an apology — and got one — but it was their mother's anger that concerned Henry. She shook her head and grimaced all the way back into their house.

He thought cleaning his younger brother

up would make their mother happy. Get him back into her good graces.

Little David is always getting into something. That is what Henry heard his mother telling neighbors time and again. Just trying to keep up with his brothers, she'd say. They'd all chuckle and marvel at the adventures of the Powell boys. David the fearless and dirty one.

Especially that day. May 13. It was a warm day and the boys were outside for most of it. Henry had not wanted to blow up the Rocktons' mailbox but Brad had ratcheted his arm up high behind his back and told him if he didn't do it he'd die. Plus Henry had nothing better to do, really. So the firecrackers were fetched from the shoe box under Brad's bed and matches were swiped from their mother's purse.

The explosion was not as gratifying as they had hoped. Mostly smoke snaked out of the opening. All in all a bust if you asked Henry. But Brad liked it. "Cool," he said before running off to God knows where. Leaving Henry to face their mother and angry Rocktons.

David's being dirty only added to her misery. So Henry saw his way of making amends in the way all middle children try to apologize for their too-troublesome older siblings and their too-trouble-free younger ones.

He had taken care to get the temperature right, cool enough for his little brother, not hot like he himself liked it. David allowed him to soap his little body up, splashing and laughing at the attention. But Henry had not counted on the fact that David would not want to stay put in the water for very long. To keep him there long enough to get the suds off his head, Henry went to fetch a toy from his brother's room, one that might create enough of a distraction.

On television Henry had seen amazing feats: an average-size man lifting a whole car up with his own two hands; a kung-fu chop breaking a cement block in two. He had always imagined that in a real emergency he, too, would have superhuman strength. But David's sodden, upside-down body was so heavy, it took some doing to pull him up and over the edge of the tub. When Henry flipped David right-side up on the bath mat, he knew his brother was dead because even though David's eyes were open, he wasn't blinking.

The last thing Henry remembers from that day is choking back vomit long enough to call out for his mother. Neighbors later spoke of hearing her scream but Henry never could conjure up the sound. Nor did he recall the ambulance, the people rushing in and out, his mother's wailing. He had heard about it later but could not picture any of it.

The days and weeks that followed were snapshots in his mind. Cluttered night tables, filled with pill bottles on his mother's side. Doors opening and closing. Food appearing and disappearing.

And Henry being called David.

CHAPTER ELEVEN

1978

"I must say I was surprised to get your phone call," Mr. Beardsley says. "Not that I wasn't thrilled, mind you. Once people hear you're back we'll have a steady stream of customers. Why don't you take this long locker? It's over here so there'll be a bit more privacy. And I've had a new lock installed on the bathroom door, just so you know. I got your call and you know the first thing I did? I made a copy of my key. See, otherwise you'd have to go out and get the communal key I keep under the register. But this way you have your own key to the restroom. The executive washroom, ha. I'll leave you to get settled in. Take your time coming out onto the floor.

"Oh, and Henry? Welcome home."

Henry pulls out the folding metal chair from the tiny round table Mr. Beardsley has set up — another change since he left nearly five months ago. This table used to be folded up in the corner, he thinks. And then he remembers that it was used for his going-away party, for the sheet cake that read *Good Luck, Henry!* He sits down and leans forward, resting his elbows on the table. After a moment his forearms fold down and he lowers his head onto the pillow they create.

The scene enters his mind and disappears, the way a shard of eggshell eludes a fingertip, pushing farther into the glop of raw egg as the intensity to retrieve it builds.

Finally Henry lets it play from the beginning.

"So this is effective starting the day winter break officially begins, which is the day after tomorrow," the dean said. "I know I'm repeating myself but the devil's in the details. We'll need a good four weeks' notice to reactivate the scholarship, remember. Let me just get you to sign there, on that line there, and then initial on the next page just confirming I told you about reactivation. There. Great."

"Thanks," Henry said, sliding the paperwork back across the desk where the dean neatly stapled it all together.

"No problem. This should be nice and

smooth. I'm assuming you've taken care of things in the sports complex. I'm sure they'll want you to turn in your lock and locker number and so forth? That's frankly out of my area but I'm sure . . ."

"I'm doing that after this," Henry said.

"Good, good. Now, you have a safe trip home, Henry. And you take care of yourself. Don't be a stranger. And don't forget about the notice we'll need. We'll be seeing you back here in no time."

The dean's smile was matched by Henry's but the difference in the two was marked on that cold December day. Henry's mouth was turned up but his eyes were dead.

The door to the dean's office closed behind him and he exhaled and soldiered on to the sports complex. The wind nearly knocked him off balance, its gusts were so strong. And its direction annoyingly unpredictable, like a child playing a prank by tapping first one shoulder then the other. It pushed him from behind, a signal, he had thought — even then at that precise moment he thought — this is a good thing. The wind seemed to be encouraging him along the footpath: this is the right thing, Henry Powell. But then, after a momentary lull, it came full force from the front, assaulting him. You only *think* you're going to get there, it said. Not on my watch. Sideways directions were harder for him to interpret. What did it mean? he wondered. He trudged along the shoveled footpath that snaked back and forth across the snow-covered quad. Henry always felt like a dolt walking on this path, so he usually walked on the grass, weather permitting. Why not just pour the concrete in a straight line from point A to point B? To Henry it is a "lions and tigers and bears, oh my" path. Dorothy finding her way across the poppy fields to the Emerald City. Which is exactly what the sports complex had represented to Henry only months earlier when he arrived as a freshman. Now it loomed. On that day, in the middle of finals, it sneered, the building did. "Quitter," it said to him. As if the sports complex (the plex they'd called it, he and his fellow teammates), almost as if it had overheard his phone conversation the previous week.

"I found a ride," Henry had called his father to say. "The bulletin board at the campus post office has lots of notices on it for ride shares and I hooked up with this guy who lives in my dorm. He's going farther south but he's taking 95 so it's perfect. He doesn't mind dropping me."

"That's good," Edgar Powell said. "What kind of car does he drive?"

"How should I know?" Henry says. There is silence on the other end of the phone. Breathing fills the air. Finally an intake of oxygen and this:

"I wonder if he has enough room," his father says. Henry waits for the thought to complete itself. The explanation to become clear.

"I'm thinking you'd best pack up most of your things, son. Just to be on the safe side."

"What?"

"Please don't take a tone with me, young man," his father says. After a moment he scales back on his sharpness. "This is not easy for me, Henry."

"What's not easy? What's going on?"

"My asking you to come home."

"I'm *coming* home," Henry says. His jaw relaxes on hearing that his father is simply worried he might decide to spend the holidays with friends, as he had threatened to do on a particularly stilted pre-Thanksgiving phone call. "I just told you, I arranged a ride and everything."

"That's not what I mean, Henry," his father says.

"What do you mean, then?"

"I mean I have to ask you to leave school and come home. For a while."

They are tiny specks, the holes in the phone receiver. It is hard to believe, Henry thinks, that they can suck all the oxygen out of a dormitory room. But that is exactly what they must have done because Henry gasps for air. One gasp but still.

"Henry?" the voice is coming from his hand. Henry's hand is still holding the phone but not up to his ear as it was doing only moments ago.

"Henry, are you there?"

He imagines his arm is mechanical. Bionic. A crank winding it up into place, adjusting for angle and comfort. Finally the phone is in place on the side of his face, matching nicely with the protruding of his ear. He pictures the Six Million Dollar Man running in slow motion because the naked eye would not be able to see him otherwise. And Jaime Sommers, who can squeeze and collapse a tennis ball with her bare hand. The two of them with those bionic hands. Just like Henry's, now clutching a phone to his head.

"Yeah, I'm here," he says into the phone.

"This isn't easy, Henry," his father is saying. "But your mother isn't well and . . ."

"She's never been well," Henry says, aware that his father is probably bristling at the increased volume. "She's *never* been well, Dad. Since when is that anything new? Ever since . . ."

"Stop," his father says. "Don't you dare talk about your mother that way. Stop that."

"Dad . . ."

"I'm not saying it's forever. But just to be on the safe side you'd best bring most of your things home this trip."

"Dad . . ."

"That's it, Henry. That's all I will say on the topic."

"But . . ."

After he'd replaced the phone into the receiver he realized neither of them had mentioned Brad. The very idea of Brad returning home — to this unnamed and unappealing drama — was ludicrous. Brad's name conjured up slamming doors, strewn trash and stereos at catastrophically high volumes. Anger. Pure, deep anger.

The worst was years ago when Brad yelled out, "Why don't you just say it? Huh? Just say it — you wish it was *me* that drowned, not him. *Say it!* See? I knew it. You can't even *look* at me." Henry looked at his parents and saw that Brad was right. They had both turned their heads. They hadn't denied his accusations. They hadn't told him to *check your attitude, young man* like they always said to Henry. They hadn't even told him to be quiet. They just looked away. Until Brad, raging and squeezing his eyes against tears, stalked out of the living room. One by one they peeled away: his mother lurched out of the room. He heard the kitchen faucet come on and then off a few seconds later, just long enough to fill a glass with water to wash the pills down. His father heard it, too, but pretended he didn't as he left through the other doorway that led from the living room into the front hall. Henry heard the door to the study seal itself shut. Henry climbed the stairs to his room and sat on the edge of the bed. He remembers staring at the poster of C-3P0 and R2-D2, admiring the shine on 3P0's gold suit of armor, his robot arm draped — if that is possible for a robot arm to do — lovingly on top of R2-D2's dome head. Brotherly, he thought. That arm looks brotherly.

After that Henry and his parents tiptoed around Brad. None of the Powells could risk another explosion like that. No sirree.

■ ■ ■ ■

He raises his head from the edge of the table and sits up in the chair, stretching his back before standing. "Let's do this," he says out loud to himself before opening the door that leads back out to the store. The same thing he said to himself before games, on the trek out the tunnel to the field. As the door opens into the belly of Baxter's he imagines the same roar of the crowd that always greeted the team as they hit the university field. That stadium, those cheers, the dial-tone roar that remained steady throughout games . . . all of it equaled adrenaline. Baxter's is transformed: jackets chanting the fight cheer, pants echoing and clapping. Sportswear would most certainly start the wave. That's sportswear for you, he thinks. Up ahead, the end zone. The doors to the outside world. His day will be spent trying to score a touchdown, the doors flying open, releasing him to a triumphant dance, spiking the ball on the pavement, arms raised in victory. The rush of the applause deafening.

"I'm going to run up the street for a minute," Mr. Beardsley says. "Can you hold down the fort? Gee, it's just great having you back." He doesn't wait for an answer from Henry.

He walks up to the counter, the register, the stool. The Windex on the shelf below, a half-used roll of paper towels next to it. The lidless grey shoe box filled with odds and ends, paper clips at the bottom. All the same.

The front door chimes sound but he barely looks up until the man is nearly directly across the counter from him.

"May I help you?"

This question does not come easy to Henry Powell. He would like to be able to substitute the word can for may. It doesn't seem like that would make that much of a difference. In the beginning — back before he left for college ("b.c." is how he thinks of it), it was "Need help?" but to Mr. Beardsley that was an unpardonable offense so Henry adapted to suit his employer. The words, though, have not adapted to suit the speaker, often resulting in making the customer equally if inexplicably uncomfortable.

"Naw, just looking," the man says, fingering the ties.

The small-town reaction to any face not immediately recognizable is very much like a dog that, before lying down, circles and circles to beat down the tall grass that plagued his ancestors. Henry wonders if he should know this man. Refusing to follow up with Mr. Beardsley's suggested "My name's Henry if you need anything" he checks his watch and moves toward the front window. Almost lunchtime.

Looks like snow, he thinks.

"Tell you what I'm looking for," the voice cuts through the silence. Henry swings around to face it. "I'm looking for a tie clip. You got any tie clips here?"

"Absolutely we have tie clips," Henry answers, already in motion. He has learned people love hearing the word *absolutely.* His communications professor (Interpersonal Communications 101) told them it was a mark of charisma to use that word. That and *exactly* as in: "I know *exactly* what you mean." She'd lectured that these and other similar words instilled confidence. She'd read aloud bits from presidential press conferences to prove her point. Seems Harry Truman used the code words a lot. You'd think FDR, she said, but not so much. He didn't really need to, she said.

"Tie clips we got. Right over here. Are you looking for gold or silver?"

"Whatever's cheaper," the man replies.

"Silver, I guess."

"We've got a sterling silver one right here." Henry struggles with the lock and then finally shimmies the glass along the metal runner enough to fit his arm in.

"Sterling," the man says, "I don't need sterling. You got anything cheaper?"

"Let me just see what the price is on this one." Henry turns the dangling price tag over. "Sixteen-fifty for this one. Sterling's usually not too expensive. Plus this one's pretty simple, not too big."

"I'm gonna have to think about it," the man says. "What else've you got, maybe cheaper?"

"Let's see. There's this mother-of-pearl one. I think that's less. Yeah, $12.99. Then there's this turquoise one. Let's see . . . no, that's more. It's Indian. Made by Indians, I mean. Somewhere out in Nebraska or South Dakota or something. Let's see . . . what else. The rest are all gold and going to be a bit higher. This mother-of-pearl one's nice. Doesn't look like it's only $12.99, either. Looks much more expensive."

"I'll be back." The man's backing away from the counter. "Lemme just think about it. Thanks a lot. I'll be back."

"You're welcome," Henry says to the man he knows he'll never see again.

An hour later Mr. Beardsley returns with "What'd I miss?" but though Henry shrugs he has not really waited for an answer. Not long after his return it is noon. Lunchtime.

The bologna sandwich isn't filling — bologna sandwiches rarely are. Henry curses himself he forgot the bag of Fritos. They were right there on the kitchen counter, he thinks. Right there. His hand — karate chop formation — irons out the wrinkles of the paper bag. After it is folded and tucked back into his bookstore tote bag, Henry pulls his wallet out from his back pocket and counts his money. Nine dollars.

Mr. Beardsley comes into the break room. "Just double-checking: you'll be here to work the sale, right? I'm assuming yes but you know what happens when you *assume.* Ha."

"Yeah," Henry says. "I'll be here for the sale."

"You make an ASS out of U and ME," Mr. Beardsley says.

"What?"

"That's what happens when you assume. Get it? You make an . . ."

"I get it," Henry says. He closes up his locker. "Good one."

"Mr. Football Hero? You think you could

come over here for a minute?" Mr. Beardsley says. Henry can't see who he is shushing
but he knows it must be a child because his
boss is looking down at a head that is not
clearing the shirt display.

"I wish you wouldn't call me that," Henry
says.

When the little boy sees him he holds out
a pad of paper. "Could I have your autograph?" he says.

Mr. Beardsley is beaming over the little
blond head. "I told you you'd be good for
business."

Henry reaches out for the paper, not
wanting to embarrass the boy, who he
estimates is about six. In college Henry did
in fact sign his share of autographs, even
though he was a freshman bench warmer.
Mostly they were children like this one, lining the walkway that led from the locker
room to the parking lot, which Henry would
cross on his way back to his dorm. The older
players climbing into sports cars even
though they lived within walking distance.
The kids were children of die-hard alumnae
who, in their younger days, would have
painted faces — or worse, painted bellies —
in team colors at similar games. He knew
his autograph was insurance in case he
became famous some day. No matter. Who

wouldn't enjoy signing an autograph here and there? he wondered with a smile. That was only two months ago, he thinks.

"What's your name?" Henry asks the little boy.

"Frankie," he says. "But you could just sign it to Frank if you want."

Henry nods with the solemnity the remark deserves: a little boy wanting to be a grown-up. "To my friend, Frank," he writes, "from Henry Powell."

He frowns at his signature. He has never liked his handwriting.

The boy says "thank you" and hurries over to his mother. He holds the pad up for her to see and when she looks up from it, smiling, Henry recognizes her. She is somewhere around his brother's age, he thinks. In his class, maybe? Maybe Frank isn't six, he reasons. Maybe he's five.

"Hey," he says, nodding at her and smiling.

"Hi," she replies. "Thanks." She tilts her head toward little Frank and Henry sees that it is likely she who has christened him Frankie. Her freckles and red hair intone Irish roots that explain — justify even — the nickname.

"I'm Henry Powell," he says, extending his hand for a shake. Unself-conciously, thanks to college.

"I'm Paige," she says. "Paige Graves."

"You went to Fairhaven High, right?" he says. And when she nods he adds "My brother went there."

He realizes his mistake too late. Her eyes widen as she puts two and two together and it is only a matter of time before the pleasant recognition gives way to the pall that accompanies every recollection of Brad Powell. Here we go, he says to himself.

"Powell, Powell," she is racking her brain. "Oh, my God, Brad Powell is your brother?"

He has perfected the nod that younger, better-behaved brothers offer when the embarrassing exploits of their older siblings are cataloged. "Yep, that's my brother," he says. He no longer adds the look that reads: *don't hold it against me.* He long since gave that up as futile when he realized the road was littered with the fallout from his brother's misdeeds.

"Wow," she says.

In his younger years Brad Powell was the sort of boy who rode a bicycle four sizes too small, knees angled out to avoid knocking into elbows. The whole picture a circus act were it not for the menacing curl to the boy's lip, a look that left no doubt that

244

somewhere a swollen-eyed weakling was standing on a curb missing his beloved bike.

"It was nice to see you," she is saying, ushering little Frankie out toward Henry's end zone.

"Bye," he says. "See you, Frank." Little Frank waves over his shoulder.

And there's the flaw, he says to himself. After the Confrontation his brother had washed his hands of the Powell family, and they of him. The Confrontation — always capitalized in Henry's mind — probably would have been considered nothing in another more expressive family, but in the Powell house any display of emotion, any outburst whatsoever, nearly shook the earth off its axis. The unspoken agreement was that everyone stay out of Brad's way until they were delivered from his presence with either a college scholarship or a prison sentence. Whichever came first. Henry steered clearest of him.

Henry wonders if Frankie will keep his autograph.

"Will you do the honors, Mr. Football?"

"I *really* wish you wouldn't call me that," Henry says, taking the sign from Mr. Beardsley.

"All right, all right," his boss says. "Let's

keep it in the same corner. The right side, remember."

"I know, I know," he says. He tucks the sign into the corner of the front window.

Within minutes of unlocking the doors, Henry knows the crowds will start and will not let up until five o'clock that evening. He takes a deep breath and turns the key in the lock, then carries it back, with exaggerated fanfare, to Mr. Beardsley, who mistakes his irony for sincerity.

"Exciting, isn't it? Every year it's the same feeling," Mr. Beardsley says. "Butterflies. A buzzing sound in the air." He rubs his hands together as if he is warming them in front of a bonfire. "It never gets old. Never gets old."

Henry checks his watch and Mr. Beardsley says, as much to himself as to Henry, "Those poly suits are great . . . that'll save us a lot of headache today, I'll tell you. We won't need to be straightening that section as much. What's really going to be tough is keeping the shirt area presentable. Just remember, whenever you can, go over there and fold. Not when customers are around, mind you. But if there's a lull. If there's a lull, fold. The polyester area over there —" he points to the New Arrivals section "— is fine. Whoever came up with that blend knew what they were doing. It just does not wrinkle. Remember to tell your customers that, by the way. I told you that, right? No? Well, it doesn't wrinkle, that's point number one. Number two, it's less expensive than the silk weaves, the wool blends, even. And number three, it's selling like hot cakes. Stores can't keep it in stock. You made the yellow pages in polyester it'd be your next bestseller, I'll tell you. Bottom line, it doesn't wrinkle. Just try to remember that one point."

"Got it," Henry says.

"Mr. Warren! Welcome to the sale," Mr. Beardsley says. "Good to see you again. What can I steer you to today?"

Henry watches his boss float across the store. A haberdashing debutante, he thinks.

The second customer of the day punches Henry in the arm.

"You don't remember me," he says, smiling at Henry's wincing bewilderment. "That smack should've reminded you. The last time I saw you, you were going, 'cut it out, cut it out,' like this. . . ." He held his hands up in a defensive gesture, indicating Henry must have had serious concerns for his upper-body region. Primarily his head.

The laugh gave the customer away.

"Oh, my God, Tony Coulson," Henry

says, a wan smile as much as he can muster. "How are you?"

Henry feels the need to toughen up even though he is now quadruple the size he was when he was at Tony Coulson's mercy.

"Good, good," Tony says. "Talked to your brother just last week, actually. Funny seeing you now."

Henry resists the urge to ask details about his brother's life. "Yeah. No kidding."

"I heard you're like this huge hometown-hero football guy," he says.

"Naw," Henry says. If they had been on a beach, his toe would have been drawing circles in the sand. He looks up. "Did my brother say that?"

"Just heard it, you know. I hope you're saving your paychecks, though. You're a freshman, right? Yeah, well, they never tell you what those scholarships cover, and if you want to do anything that's worth anything in college you'll need your own spending money. Trust me."

As if for emphasis he punches Henry's arm again. Henry recalls that Tony went away to the University of Nevada at Las Vegas on a basketball scholarship. He was the only white boy on the team for two years and then got kicked off. Henry couldn't remember what the story was.

"Yeah, okay," he says. No point in telling this guy my whole life story, he thinks. "You live here in town now?" Oh please God, no, he thinks.

"Shit no. I stayed out west. In Vegas, buddy. In town for the holidays. You know, log some face time with the 'rents. Vegas is fucking incredible, man. You've got to come out. Your brother just came for the weekend, what was it, like a month ago or something? Man, took me three days to recover from *that*. Shit. But I don't have to tell you . . ."

"Yeah, no shit." He is so unaccustomed to using profanity, it has the effect of making Henry feel even more insecure, not less.

"You got any of those shirts with the sailboats on them? Those KOOL sailboats, you know? Actually, wait. Show me some of those polyester suits you guys got," Tony Coulson says. "They're on sale, right? Everything's on sale?"

Henry was tempted to say *No Shit, Sherlock* but did not. His brother would have.

"Yep, everything's on sale. The poly suits are over here, I'll show you."

"Look at you," Tony says, "mister clothing-store guy. Little Henry Powell selling me a suit. Shit. This is hilarious." And then that laugh. A laugh that — in Tony Coulson's teenage years — might easily have accompanied cruelty to animals or the sight of a mentally handicapped child.

"Hilarious," Henry says. They walk to the leisure-suit rack.

"All right, kid," Tony Coulson says, ignoring the sarcasm in Henry's comment, "hardsell me. Why do I want to buy a polyester suit from you."

Henry looks at him, and before looking back at the clothes they are standing in front of, he scans the store for any potential distractions. Anything that might, say, require Henry's immediate attention elsewhere. But they have thought of everything, he and his boss and even Ramon, who has been called in for the week to be a floater.

"They don't wrinkle," he hears his own voice saying.

"What? I couldn't hear you, what'd you say?" Tony says. "Speak up, kid. You want my sale or what?"

"They don't wrinkle," Henry says louder. "And they're flying out of stores, the poly suits are. We can barely keep them in stock. We just had to reorder."

He is making this last part up but wants this to be over.

The laugh. "Shit, man, I'm just yanking your chain," Tony Coulson says. "I can't wait to tell Brad. Shit, that was too funny.

They don't wrinkle . . . we can barely keep them in stock. . . ."

The high-pitched voice Coulson is using to mimic him catches Mr. Beardsley's attention.

"Henry, could you trade places with me and pin up Mr. Warren's trousers, please?" he says. When they pass each other Mr. Beardsley says, "I told him we wouldn't charge, just so you know. But still write up the ticket, so when I send them out we can keep track of them."

Though he is halfway to the dressing room area he hears Mr. Beardsley addressing Tony Coulson. "Now. What can I help you find?"

Was there an emphasis on the "you" in that question? In fact there was: Mr. Beardsley had overheard the entire exchange.

"Oh, my God, there's Henry," he hears a female voice say and hurries to finish Mr. Warren's pants.

"Shhh, wait till he finishes," another voice says, muffling a giggle.

He pretends he has not heard them so he can remain professional with Mr. Warren. "There you go, sir," he says. "Just hand me the trousers when you've changed out of them and we'll call you when they're back from the tailor."

"Oh, my God, Henry, *hi.*" The two girls

descend as one. Henry fancies himself one of the Beatles. The Cute One. The girls rushing in . . . ravenous . . . hoping just to touch him. Maybe one even passes out from the excitement.

"Hey! Wow, hi," he says. "Look at you guys. You look great."

"Thanks," they say in unison. "How's school" and "My mom said you were back in here working over the holidays" and "What're you doing tonight?" all tumbles out at once.

"What's going on? How's school going for you guys? Wait, you're at Brown, right?" He points to the girl on the right. Alissa. Alissa with the Farrah hair. "Oh, yeah, Tulane, that's right. Where're you going again?" is directed at Jory. Jory with the too-tight fuzzy sweater that has pilled up in the spots where her arms rub against her torso. Two former classmates he saw at all the games but never really talked to since they both had boyfriends who did not appear to appreciate their girlfriends befriending a football player. But these two had always waved, smiled, lingered just a little longer than the others after games.

College stories pour out, accompanied by shrugs to keep enthusiasm in check. Most tales center around the excess of alcohol. But Henry is more aware of the ambient sound. He nods at the girls and smiles — laughs even — at the right places, but all he is hearing is "excuse me" and "just trying to inch by you here" and "oh, sorry. I'll switch places with you" with increasing frequency.

"I'm really sorry but I better go," he says. He rolls his eyes as if to say "It's a drag, this whole working thing." "My boss'll kill me if I don't get busy here in a second."

"Oh, yeah, totally" and "Sure, no problem" and "Maybe we'll see you later — at Blackie's?" and then they turn to the shirt section. As he helps one man to a fitting room and another find the sport coat, he glances over to see the girls holding up rugby shirts over their down vests.

A little while later tightly sweatered Jory asks him if they sell army jackets, which they do not. "I think there's an Army Navy store in Newbury," he tells her.

"God, mellow out," Farrah-haired Alissa tells her. Then, for Henry's benefit she adds, "Don't have a shit fit" and they are gone. "Bye," they call out in unison.

The next day the names change but the faces remain remarkably similar: Jory and Alissa are followed by Dawn and Heather, neither of whom had said more than three words to Henry before his success on the football field landed him on their radar screen.

"Ohmygodthisis*perfect*," Dawn called out in one long exclamation. "This is *perfect*." She is holding up a butter-yellow V-neck lambswool sweater. "Tell me this isn't perfect," she says to Heather, though it is understood Heather will do no such thing.

"It's perfect," Heather says. "Shit, you're so lucky. Help me find something for Michael."

"God*dammit* this is perfect," Dawn says, still holding it up. "What size? What size do you think?"

"I don't know," Heather says. She is rummaging through the thirty-percent-off bin. "Seriously help me find something, will you? What'm I going to do?? This was my last shot. I already went to Mitchell's and Saks. Dawn, seriously. You've got to help me."

Her voice has reached just the right pitch of frantic — only heard and recognized like a dog whistle by other like-minded girls.

"Okay," Dawn says, with magnanimity reserved for those who have satisfied a quest. "What color, first of all? What is he, a Fall?"

"Shit," Heather says, tossing aside her own version of perfect in a not-so-perfect size. "What? Oh. Um, I don't know. He's blond."

"No, he's not," Dawn says. "In the picture he's got brown hair."

"Blond-ish. Not really blond. Just kind of dark blond. What do you think of this one?"

"It's *pink*," Dawn says.

"So? It's cute."

"If he's dark blond he's a Summer. Plus you can't get your boyfriend a *pink* sweater. Jesus."

Henry has caught snippets of the exchange but has been busy helping with two receipt-less Christmas exchanges.

"What about this one?" Dawn pulls out a blue crewneck.

Heather reaches for it. "Let me see."

"It's blue and blues go with Summers and Springs," Dawn says. Henry knows she is ready to go. He noticed her checking her watch.

"It's okay, I guess," Heather says. "Do you think it's big enough? It looks small for a Large." She checks the label and then holds it up to her body.

"How tall is he?" Dawn asks.

"I don't know. Six feet, I think. I don't know."

"Just get it," Dawn says. "He'll love it. Just

get it and let's go."

"Hey," Henry says. "How's it going?"

The beam of attention turns from price tags to him.

"Hey," they say. "How *are* you?" Dawn asks.

"Good," he says. "You guys okay?"

"Yeah," Heather says. "You're working here?"

"How's school?" Dawn asks.

"It's good. Fine."

"Are you playing football? Not now. I mean, at school. Are you playing at school? Football?"

"God, who taught you how to talk?" Dawn says. "You? Playing? At school? Football?"

Heather has turned red.

"Yeah, well, season's over now."

"Oh, yeah, of course. Yeah."

"Duh," Dawn says to Heather. "Um, Henry, ah, do you guys give friend discounts?"

"Everything's on sale right now," Henry says. "Those are both already thirty-percent off, I think." He is careful not to appear too knowledgeable.

"Yeah, I know," she says. "I'm just wondering if . . ."

"Yeah, we were wondering if you could

like — I don't know — like mark them down a little more, maybe?" Heather says, completing her friend's question. "For us? 'Cause we're friends, you know?"

"That'd be so great," Dawn says. Heather nods her agreement. Their backs arch at precisely the same moment.

Henry hears himself say "yeah, sure," and looks both ways to make certain he is not overheard. Then, "Don't tell anyone."

Up at the register he writes up the true price minus thirty-percent discounts and then, off to the side he stretches a Mc-Donald's napkin tightly under his blue ball-point pen, making note of the added ten percent he awards the girls' breasts. The numbers are scrawled across the embossed M. He folds the napkin up and slides it into his back pocket for later when he can count out the eighteen dollars from his wallet.

"Thanks," they say. Their smiles — no longer necessary — are not so bright. "See ya."

"Yeah, see you," Henry says, watching them go.

The week is like a marching yearbook. Classmates Danny and Will come in to use gift certificates they'd each received for Christmas ("Is there anything here that's not faggy?" Will asks). Jack comes in alone. Allison and Megan and Beth ask the same questions the rest do but in triplicate. Neal comes in, shows off a flask he's just bought himself, and leaves to go "beaver hunting."

"Have a happy!" and "See ya" and "Take it easy" are all called out to Henry, who smiles, shakes hands and refolds.

"Another year, another sale under our belts," Mr. Beardsley says. He settles onto one of the two bar stools behind the counter and scans the store, which now resembles a Soviet market: picked over and low on essentials.

"I'm going to take off," Henry says, "if we're done for the day."

"We're done for the day," Mr. Beardsley says. "We're done for the week. Nice work, Henry. Good work. You worked real hard out there, don't think I didn't notice it. I did. And I want to give you a little something extra — no, don't wave me off — it's just a little something extra for all your hard work. I know how money comes in handy in college, believe you me. I could tell you some stories . . . but you're trying to leave. I know, I know. You're probably meeting the gang for some brewskis. I remember those days. I'm not some old fogey. Anyway, I thought you could put this to good use back at school."

He slides an envelope across the counter to Henry.

"Um, actually, I could probably come in this next week if you need help," Henry says. He is looking down, not at the envelope that is still lying between them on the counter but at his feet. Their eyes meet only for a moment when he looks back up, and after a pause Mr. Beardsley clears his throat.

Mr. Beardsley says, "I'd love to have you. I sure could use the help, let me tell you. Ramon has next week off and the guy I've hired for spring help doesn't start until February."

"Great, thanks," Henry says. "Okay, well, see you then."

He walks away. Mr. Beardsley looks at the envelope on the counter and opens his mouth to call after Henry that he's forgotten it. But then he sees the slump to Henry's shoulders, the way his head is hanging, the resignation in his step, and knows at that moment that Henry is not going back to college.

He reaches for a pen and writes Henry's name on the envelope and stows it safely in his own locker.

At the same moment his boss closes his

locker door, Henry closes the front door to his house.

"Hey, I'm home," he says.

CHAPTER TWELVE

1979

"Hello?"

He closes the front door quietly. The house is dark and still smells like morning coffee since it has remained sealed shut all day.

"Mom? Dad?" Henry calls his way through the front hall to the kitchen.

"Who is it? Who's there?" her voice calls.

"It's me, Henry," he says. The refrigerator is filled with condiments. He takes note of what he'll need at the market. He checks the pill bottles by the sink to see that she hasn't run out. Shaking each one. The third one is light. He opens it, sees only two pills left and curses himself he hasn't done this earlier, while the pharmacy was still open. This now means he'll have to fill it tomorrow on his lunch hour and somehow get it back home to his mother before she hits her midafternoon dose.

"Hello?" his mother says. He can tell she is on the couch. Her voice has a just-woken-up sound to it.

"Hey, Mom," he says. He leaves the kitchen and passes through the living room on his way to the stairs, to his room.

"Oh, *Henry*," she says when she sees him. "Oh."

"I'll be upstairs."

"What're you doing here?"

"What?" he calls down from only two steps up.

"What're you doing here? Where's your father?"

"I don't know where Dad is. I'm home from school, Mom. Remember? I came home a couple weeks ago? Remember?"

She settles back into sleep.

Upstairs he hangs up his jacket and loosens his tie, sliding it out from underneath his collar.

He flips through the albums. *Breakfast in America, Some Girls, The Long Run, 52nd Street* . . . none of them catch him. *Tapestry,* The Carpenters.

Finally: *America.* You can't go wrong with America, he thinks to himself, lowering the needle, closing the top over the turntable.

As "Horse With No Name" begins, its

steady, calming vocal drumbeat, Henry is stepping onto the field. Henry before everything changed. He luxuriates in the fact that he did not know the scouts were there for that particular game. Thank God Coach didn't tell me. Thank God.

To Henry it was just another game. Just another beautiful game. Starting. Catching. Running. Bending over to catch his breath before taking his place for yet another play. The symmetry between Powell and Wilson subliminal. And beautiful.

Henry isn't recording today. Instead the music plays in the background of the game.

He comes off the field to an extended arm. "Henry, I'm Don Lambert from Westerfield. I'd like to have a word with you, son," the man is saying.

He resets the needle on "Horse With No Name" — he never thinks to play it but whenever he does he wonders why he never thinks to play it. It's a great song, he thinks.

He had not known what it was about. Why this trench-coated stranger wanted to talk to him. He remembers being more concerned with what Coach would say about the game. He'd fouled up. A pass intended for him had been intercepted. The first time in a three-game streak that he'd allowed that to happen. He tells himself that nothing the coach could say could make him feel worse than he already did about it. They'd won the game, but still. It was a catch he could've made. If he'd only caught more air on his reach.

They are headed into the locker room. Coach falls into step along Henry, but before Henry can say anything in the way of an apology the coach asks, "Did you meet Mr. Lambert?"

"Yeah," Henry says, sloughing it off. "I know I should've gotten that ball."

"He's from Westerfield, you know. Did he tell you? Top-ten school. He wants to talk to you."

Henry is starting to get the picture. Coach isn't sore after all, he says to himself. And that guy is here to talk to me *about college.* The twists in his stomach start to relax.

Underneath the headphones Henry revels in this moment. The moment before everything happened. He tries to remember that flood of feeling he had as it dawned on him that good things really were going to happen to him. Before that moment he truly had not considered college. His parents had not brought it up — funny now that he thinks about it, since his father was always pushing him to put his studies first. Huh. Strange he wouldn't have mentioned college even once. Or maybe he did and Henry just can't remember. This could be. Naw . . . it wasn't that long ago. Oh well, get back to the moment, the screenwriter says. No, it's not the screenwriter this time taking notes. It's a reporter from *Sports Illustrated.* That's who's saying it as Henry replays "Horse With No Name." What were you thinking right then? When you realized that Mr. Lambert with the Bear Bryant hat and trench coat was there to talk to you about Westerfield? Henry sighs patiently as yet another pen is poised above yet another pad.

Ah, yes. That moment. What was I thinking?

Henry does indeed remember the change in the way the others started looking at him. He knew it the minute he walked into the locker room. It is awe. Mixed with resentment. With some jealously thrown in. Mostly, though, at that minute, it is awe.

Now of course Henry wishes he'd taken it in. Appreciated the moment. Soaked it all up. All his hard work paying off. He should have met their eyes. Then, though, Henry remembers feeling guilty. Tremendously and unequivocally guilty. For being the one Lambert'd come to see. Steve Wilson should have been the one to "have a word" with the man. Lots of the guys were good: why weren't any of them talking to Lambert? He had looked down, hurried through his shower and rushed out of the locker room without speaking to anyone.

I should've taken it all in, Henry thinks.

The door to the locker room closes behind him and, come to think of it, the coach hasn't followed him in to talk to the team. This time it's just the guys. Just the team. Welly talking to the team.

"Hey, guys?" he says. Calling their attention. They've been whispering about him, he can tell. No matter.

"Listen up!"

Now that he has their attention he puts one foot Caesar-like up on the bench.

"Look, I know what you're thinking," he says. He pauses to let the muttering die down. "I know what you're thinking and I don't blame you. I'd probably be thinking the same thing."

Henry thinks he's seen this speech somewhere in a movie. *Brian's Song?* Naw. Different speech. What movie is it? Huh. That's going to bug me. Keep going, tell me tell me, the *SI* guy says. Oh yeah, Henry says. Sorry.

"I didn't ask for this, you know," Henry

says to his gathered team. "I don't even want it, to tell you the truth."

Actually — he corrects himself to the *SI* guy — I didn't say "to tell you the truth" because I hate it when people say that. It's like everything else they've said before saying "to tell you the truth" is a lie. I think I said this:

"I don't even really want it. I just love playing the game, you know? Same as you. That's why we're all here, right? Because we love to play the game? Why else would we do two-a-days and then bust our asses out there every game?"

This time the mutters aren't mutters so much as agreeable smiles. A few nods of recognition.

"Let's face it: this is hard. It sucks to have to do homework with ice packs. I hate how it hurts to even walk down the stairs to dinner. . . ."

Chuckles. I swear there were chuckles, he tells the reporter. I believe you, the *SI* guy says, writing fast to keep up. So he doesn't have to interrupt and slow Henry's memory down.

"So, please," Henry says to the team, now gazing at him in admiration. Their eyes twinkling with pride. "Don't be pissed.

Know that that guy — whatever the heck his name is from whatever corn-cob school . . ."

Henry has to stop here to let the laughter subside.

"That guy wouldn't *be* here if it weren't for *you. All* of you. We're a *team*. Right? Am I right?"

And a cheer went up, swear to God, Henry says. Then they applauded.

Henry cranes his neck over the *SI* guy's head to make sure he's getting it all down.

The coach walked into the locker room and had to say "Okay, quiet down, everybody, quiet down" before he could do the post-game.

Wow, *Sports Illustrated* says, finally able to look up from his pad. Incredible.

When Henry laid his headphones to the side of his stereo he'd nearly forgotten that his coach had entered the locker room when he did. That he'd gotten to his locker and found someone had put a soaking-wet towel on top of his now-also-soaked backpack. And that sopping-wet backpack had to be stowed on the floor of Mr. Lambert's car — the man had insisted on giving him a ride home "so they could talk" — and Henry felt embarrassed the whole way back to his house that this man's nice floor mat would be left wet.

The very idea that the *SI* guy would refer to this present period of his life as the Time in Which Henry Powell Moved Back in With His Parents . . . would perhaps even write a chapter about it . . . so shamed him he vowed to bring it up with his father as soon as the right moment presented itself.

Henry considers his making dinner a step closer to his goal of moving out. Edgar Powell hates to cook and generally avoids it altogether: nibbling at cheese and stale crackers rather than have to prepare a meal. Henry figures this will put his father in a better mood, his cooking.

Not that Henry's mother particularly liked to cook. In her current state she most certainly would not tackle it, but Henry cannot conjure up a single image of his mother at the stove. Before — *before* — he knows she used to take care of these daily household chores. Marketing, cleaning, cooking — this was expected, required even, of nearly every wife and mother of her generation. And while he cannot recall her ever actually cooking, Henry does indeed remember her speeches. That is what Edgar

Powell would call them. Your mother's *speeches,* his voice reeking of amused condescension. Henry always checked his mother's face when his father turned to pour himself a Scotch. He saw her flinch. She didn't know he saw it but he did. Many times. Her smile tight, her own drink inches from her lips, the wince flickered across her brow and five-then-six-then-seven-year-old Henry knew there was something slightly amiss.

Back to the speeches, the biographer is saying. He has settled into one of the four kitchen chairs. Yeah, oooh yeah, Henry says. Sorry about that.

The speeches. On many occasions Henry's mother would announce — whenever a task presented itself — that this was not what she had had in mind. "You know what they're doing right now?" she would ask over the loud vacuum motor. "I'll tell you what they're doing. They're out catching a show right this minute. A musical. Something they read about in the paper." She would pause by the ashtray, vacuum still running, to take a good long drag from her cigarette. A minute later, Henry on the couch would hold his legs up so she can get the crumbs under his feet.

"And here I am," she says, "here I am making sure the carpet is perfect. Just perfect. They're having the time of their lives right now."

The angry and intermittent vacuuming would carry on, and as her cigarette burned down and her drink emptied, her speech would expand to include not just education but the Merits of Childbearing and — her favorite and the topic voted by the Class of Topics the one Most Likely to Crescendo into Total Abandonment of the Task — the Institution of Marriage.

"What was the damned rush?" she would ask the polished coffee table, moving her cloth down each leg for any dust fragments she might have missed during the first pass. "I was in such a damned hurry to get married. What was the rush? Like it was a lottery ticket. I thought I held the winning numbers, meeting your father."

Other times Henry would be rolling his Matchbox cars to the sound of his mother snap-shaking the clean pieces of laundry before folding them. "That Phyllis is a dope," he'd hear her say, "dumb as a stone." Like a raccoon at the edge of a river washing its food, she would stare straight ahead, occasionally shaking her head at Phyllis Hartley's stupidity, marveled at in silence then, while her hands felt for the seams along his jeans, lining up the ridges so they are perfectly folded in half lengthwise before being halved then quartered and stacked neatly on the pile.

"You boys won't have to worry about this," she would say. "You'll have *wives* to take care of all of it. The house will miraculously run itself." The word *miraculously* slurs its way out of her mouth. "The laundry will be done and put back into drawers and you'll hardly even notice. You'll just always have clean undershirts whenever you reach for them. Because you're men. Because women take care of all those things so you *men* won't have to."

Sounds pretty good to me, young Henry would think. But he sensed this was not something he should say out loud.

"And you know what your wives will be concerned about? Lipstick shades. Not the presidential election. Not civil rights in the Deep South. Nooo . . . they'll be talking about *wallpaper.*" She said the word *wallpaper* as if it was the most vile conversation topic ever to be discussed.

"Ah," Edgar Powell would say on entering, "your mother is giving one of her *speeches.*"

A week or so later it was his mother's turn to host the weekly bridge game and, as one card or another is slapped down on the square card table unfolded for just such occasions, Henry hears this:

"I *have* to ask," a disembodied, unidentifiable voice says, "what detergent do you use? You just smell so *clean.*"

"I noticed it, too," an enthusiastic addition weighs in, "when I hugged you at the door. Something *fresh.* Like a meadow."

"Is it a perfume?" yet another voice.

A card slap.

Henry hears his mother's answer. "You won't believe it but it's Oxydol. I don't even wear perfume anymore, the scent's so good. And it's always on special at the store."

The murmurs of disbelief carry through the air to Henry, who is quietly coloring at the kitchen table.

"Isn't it always the way?" another voice says. "It's always better to stick with tried-and-true."

"I've been using Wisk but I'll tell you now I'm switching. You don't mind? I just love that smell."

"Of course I don't mind," his mother says. "It's great, too. The boys' clothes have never been cleaner."

"Speaking of stores, did you hear A & P is closing?" Phyllis Hartley says. Henry can tell it is her voice because no one else sounds like Phyllis Hartley. She is a grown woman with a little girl's high voice.

"Who needs a refill?" his mother asks. Her chair is pushing back from the table.

"Mom, look." Henry holds his picture up for her to see how well he has colored the fire truck and its station.

She sets the glasses on the kitchen counter. "That's nice, honey." She pats him on the head on her way to the freezer for an ice tray. "Will you go check on your brother? I haven't heard a thing from upstairs. That's a good boy."

She pulls the metal lever and pop, pop, go the ice cubes from the tray into the glasses. She is pouring the drinks when he leaves to check on David.

He does not see her pause before carrying the drinks back in on the black-lacquered tray that he thinks looks like something James Bond would have — does not see her brace herself at the sink, her wingspan ending in white-knuckled grips at either end of the sink.

Henry pours water into the pot and silently practices his own speech.

Dad, I'm moving out, he will say. I'll still be here to take care of Mom when you need me but I'm getting a place of my own. I don't care what you say. You can't stop me. I'll be moving out at the end of the month. Just so you know.

No. This is too harsh. He imagines his father saying "watch your tone" and then it's all downhill from there, he thinks.

Dad, here's the deal. Brad can come back and we can tag-team it. The Powell Men, just like old times. We'll all three take care of her. But I've got to have my own place. I've just got to.

The trouble with this option, Henry knows, is that there is no old time that recalls — fondly or otherwise — the Powell Men tag-teaming anything. This will baffle his father and he'll be back at square one. Plus, Henry thinks, Brad would no sooner move back to help out than he would drive a railroad tie into his own foot.

Dad? Can I talk to you for a second? He would start that way: Gentle. Calm. Dad, I really want to move out. I don't want to leave you in the lurch with Mom but I really think I need a place of my own. I'll come by every day and check on her. You'll see. You won't have to worry about a thing.

Five-fifteen. I'll come every day at five-fifteen.

That's good, Henry thinks. I like it. His posture reflects his resolve: straight-backed, chest puffed out. He waits for the water to boil.

His eye wanders around the kitchen and lands on the door frame.

There is Bradford, age two. They had started out calling him Bradford. Henry knows it is a ridiculous thought but still wonders if Bradford became Brad because the surplus letters *plus* the height mark *plus* the date were too tight to fit in before the wood indentation dropped off. No, he thinks. That's a stupid reason to give someone a nickname. But sure enough there it is: BRAD, age three. All capital letters. Announcing to the world this child is now several inches taller. Henry's lines are in blue. David's are red.

He drops the frozen square-shaped bag of chipped beef into one pot of boiling water and shakes out three cups of rice into the other, replacing the lid and lowering the burner to simmer.

"Smells good in here," his father says, rubbing his hands together on his way into the kitchen.

"Nothing's cooking yet," Henry says, looking up at him.

"Did you wake your mother yet?"

"No, I thought I'd get this started first."

"I'll go up. How long?"

Henry checks his watch. The instructions say to let the bag boil for twenty-five minutes. He's not sure about the rice.

"I don't know," he says. "Half an hour?"

"I'll be back."

"Um, Dad?" Henry turns from the stove to face his father. "Before you get Mom . . ."

"Yes?" His father pulls the cuff of his right sleeve out from under his sport coat.

"I wanted to talk to you about getting a place in town," Henry says. "Closer to work."

This isn't at all what you said would happen, the writer says, flipping through his reporter's notebook to find the exact speech Henry had planned. I thought you were going to put it off for now, he says. Look, Henry says, I couldn't help it. It just popped out. Oh-*ka*ay, the writer says, fiddling with his miniature tape recorder placed carefully in the middle of the kitchen table. Go ahead. They both know this will be a momentous chapter in his life story. Very dramatic, the writer scribbles.

"I don't understand," Henry's father says. "An apartment."

"We've lived here for over twenty years."

"Not for *us*," Henry says. He takes a breath. "For me. My own apartment."

His father looks down and adjusts his left sleeve.

"I saw a For Rent sign on Stone Avenue," he continues. "I thought I'd call them tomorrow. Just to check it out. It may be out of my price range, anyway."

"I wasn't aware you had a price range," his father says. "You only just got back from school. I can't imagine they're paying you enough at *your job* to afford an apartment."

"I saved a little bit," Henry says. "And I can ask Mr. Beardsley about an advance."

"What about your mother?" his father asks.

"I've thought about this — I'd still be around to help do stuff. I'll check in every day after the store closes. She sleeps all the time, anyway."

"Your mother is *ill*," his father says in a stern voice that seems to Henry one Dickensian sentence away from *young man, tonight you will have only porridge.*

"She needs looking after," Edgar Powell says. "That was the whole point."

"I'll look after her, I told you. I'll come by every day. I promise. Same time every day. Plus *you're* here. It's not like you're not here, Dad."

"Tone, young man. Watch your tone."

"Sorry." Henry paces himself.

"I'm just so busy with work," his father says.

They both look down, knowing this is not the case.

There was a time Edgar Powell was indeed very busy with work. The bank afforded him a salary that placed them one or two inches over the line that separates a blue-collar existence from a middle-class one. Not comfortable middle-class. That would have meant Edgar Powell could have joined his colleagues on their noon-time restaurant jaunts (instead he waited until they left and drew out his brown bag from his lower desk drawer). Comfortable middle-class would have meant buying a new, not secondhand, car. It would have meant reupholstering furniture that had been in-law hand-me-downs they were happy to take as newly-weds but now, in middle age, looked worn and — even more offending to Edgar Powell — cheap. No, the Powells were just barely middle-class.

Just Barely Middle-Class is perhaps the most difficult place for a proud man like Edgar Powell to reside. For it requires a full-time effort to keep up appearances, which are paramount to Henry's father. It pleased him that young loan-seeking couples peering across his wide standard-issue credenza saw a man they could only hope to become someday. Nameplate polished, suit fitting just right, glasses lending an air of intellect, of confidence, of *wealth.*

Henry looks at his father standing here in the kitchen beside him and remembers the first time he realized there was a difference between Edgar Powell the banker and Edgar Powell the father.

"Hi, Dad," he said, appearing at the side of his father's desk, startling him.

"Henry, my boy," his father said a bit louder than was necessary. And Henry noticed his father smiling hard — an unfamiliar smile — and scanning the bank to see who was watching their interaction.

"Is that little Henry Powell?" a bored and overweight colleague two desks over calls out. "My, my, my, you're a grown boy now."

Henry's father's hand propelled him forward to her desk. "Henry, you remember Miss Merkin."

"Hi." Ten-year-old Henry allowed his hand to be shaken though he dearly resented the fact that they were treating him as if he were a child.

"How would you like a piece of candy?"

This colored Henry's cheeks, so offensive was her tone.

"Here you go." She ceremoniously held out a butterscotch and very nearly pinched his cheek. That would have been just too much.

"Dad? Can I borrow five dollars?" he said, holding the candy in his hand just to prove he is old enough not be governed by candy. A child would have gobbled it up immediately.

"What do you say to Miss Merkin? You know better than that. . . ."

"Thank you for the candy," he said. And then, "Can I?"

"Five dollars? Sure," his father said, and fishes his wallet from his back pocket and with fanfare rivaling Miss Merkin's candy presentation, produces a five dollar bill. Nice and crisp. He barely had to hunt for it among the bills as he organized his money in descending order: twenties along the outer edge (the line that is created when a man's wallet is unfolded), then tens, fives and ones.

He pats Henry's head when his son thanks him and then says, "I'll walk you out, son."

They leave the building and stand, out of sight, at the edge of the parking lot — an asphalt square optimistically filled with white lines enough for twenty-five cars on a busy day. Now only seven cars are parked there and one is employee of the month, the other reserved for the bank president, a dour man not given to appreciate something as trivial as a conveniently located parking space. Edgar Powell's hard smile disappears. "You'll be paying me back of course."

It didn't take long for the bank to recognize that the town was not growing at the rate of, say, Westtown, so it closed and reopened there. Henry's father then had to drive, not walk, to work every day. Which he did from then on.

Every day Edgar Powell trudged out of the house with his briefcase and returned in darkness, never letting on that he had driven to his bench in the park on the outskirts of town. The bench out of view. The bench where, after nightfall, couples might be found necking. During the day, though, this bench saw the deterioration of a man with eyeglasses that lent a whiff of intellect, of confidence, of *success.*

When Henry was in high school and got

lunch privileges that enabled students with no demerits to leave campus in between classes, he piled in to his friend Connor Segman's car with four others to pick up burgers and fries from the McDonald's seven minutes out of town on Route 7.

"If we eat in the car my Dad'll kill me," Segman said that sunny day. "He has a shit fit if we even open a candy bar in here. Let's go to that park down the road."

It seemed like a fine idea. But it had rained the day before and the ground was still soggy so they looked around for an unoccupied bench.

"Hey, Powell, isn't that your father?" someone said.

It only took a second for Henry to size up the situation. Why would his father have brought his briefcase along with him on his lunch hour? He wasn't eating anything — he was spread out neatly, newspaper on one side, a legal pad on the other, a coffee cup he recognized from home balanced on one of the bench slats, his father dropping crumbs to pecking pigeons. The bench was his office.

"There's one," someone else called out. "Let's go. We've only got twenty minutes left and I've got a quiz in English I've got to cram for on the way back."

Mercifully they changed course to an opposite end of the park.

His burger was ruined with the thought that the check that arrived in the mail every month, the check from a law firm carrying out the wishes of a long-dead great-grandfather, was what was keeping them alive. The French fries were ruined, too, though he assumed that it was simply that French fries don't travel well. They only taste good on the spot, wherever they're ordered.

The picture of his father sitting on that park bench seared itself onto Henry's brain while the others chattered between bites about the upcoming game, about Heather Lewis and her big breasts, about Jack Vernon going all the way with her and how he said she wasn't a virgin when he got to her. So who else had she done it with, they wondered.

"Let's go," Segman said. Someone called "shotgun" and Henry found himself squeezed in back.

As his father leaves the kitchen to awaken his mother Henry realizes he has been holding his breath. His exhalation is relief, fear, excitement and hunger. For he knows that the way is paved. His father will not stop him, as he had feared. After Henry mentioned a daily five-fifteen check-in time, his father had simply said, "You are nothing if not a man of your word, Henry. I expect you will continue to keep your promises."

Plus you're over eighteen now, the biographer ahems from the middle of the kitchen. There's really nothing he could do to prevent you from leaving — legally speaking I mean, the man points out.

Henry looks over at the door frame and knows he won't have to live with it any longer.

The door frame with the lines, the dates, the names. Bradford. Then Brad. Then Henry. And then, close to the ground . . . David. He must have had to have been propped up for it, judging from the date and the fact that his little brother would only have been about a year old at the time. David's lines were in red, amplified by the darkness (and dullness) of Brad's black (faded almost to gray by now) and Henry's blue.

A foot or so up from that first entry is the final David entry. Just high enough to really catch your eye. It all stops after that last line. Henry and Brad were never again measured.

CHAPTER THIRTEEN

1986

Henry slides the letter into the mail slot in the bottom of the front door and worries for a moment that it might have flipped upside down. The lobby floor of Cathy's building is white and he curses himself he did not put the letter into a colored envelope, one that would stand out. What if it got stepped on? Or, worse still, what if it got ignored? Days might pass, weeks, and she might not know how he feels. She might never get the letter: her superintendent might just sweep it up and carry it off with the market-savings mailings.

This is a disaster of gargantuan proportions.

On the drive back to his apartment he constructs another letter. One that would include an apology to her for his repetition (in the off chance she does find and read that first letter). One that would go even further than the last. Now that he thinks about it, Henry is sure he was vague. He loves her. He loves her even more now than ever before. She is the only one for him: of this he is sure. So why hold back? he asks himself as he pulls into the parking space in front of his unit. He will not make the same mistake in this letter. He will spell it out for her. He will fight for her!

He takes the stairs two at a time and is sitting at his kitchen counter with a legal pad within minutes.

Dear Cathy,
Strike that.
My love, he writes.
Yes. That's right. She is my love so why not say it? Life's too short to hold back, he tells himself.

My love,
From here, though, every first sentence sounds like a song lyric. *I can't breathe without you . . .* he is sure this is a line in a song, he just cannot remember which one. He crosses it out. *I miss you like crazy.* No, that's cheesy. A line is drawn through that one, too. *You are everything to me. You are my world. We belong together.* He curses himself for his completely unoriginal thoughts. All have been put to music. Goddammit.

Dear Cathy,

He starts again, certain that by using her name he will stay the course. Using her name reminds him of her face . . . a face unlike anyone else's. She is original. She is unlike anyone else he has ever met. That's it! She's unlike anyone he's ever met! That's how he'll start. Perfect.

Dear Cathy,

You are not like anyone I've ever met.

He groans at this line but does not cross it out. He decides to keep going and — at the end — pledges to go back and change whatever sounds corny.

Dear Cathy,

You are the most fantastic person I've ever met.

But wait. His eleventh-grade teacher told him not to use contractions in letters. He is pretty sure of this. So . . .

Dear Cathy,

You are the most fantastic person I have ever met. You are incredible. It is YOU who keeps me up at night (remember how I told you I can't sleep very well?). I know you know exactly how I feel. You and I go together. It is a fact.

Look, I know my mom talked to you

that night and maybe she scared you off about me. But if you'd just let me talk to you and explain. She can make stuff sound different than it really is. Trust me. I know.

I'll *(damn! A contraction again. Oh well, he thinks. The other way sounds stupid)* I'll admit you might not need me as much but I need you. You called me the other night and I felt so tremendous! I never knew a phone call could do this to me. I just can't believe this feeling inside me. It's tremendous! Right before the phone rang I was thinking about you and thinking I'd love to hear your voice and sure enough you read my mind. That's proof right there. No girl has ever made me feel like this. You're all I think about every minute of my day. It may sound corny but don't laugh. It's true. I'll do anything for you. I love you. When we look at each other I can tell you are thinking some of the same stuff.

I wish I could just tell you this in person. I wish you'd just let me talk to you. Write me back.

Love, H.

P.S. Sorry if you already got a letter from me. It wasn't as good, anyway.

He sits back in his chair with relief. Looking it over he decides the contractions aren't so bad. It's a pretty damn good letter, he says out loud. Damn good. But the only envelopes he has are white so he folds the letter up and goes back down to his car to go to the only stationery store in town.

Hal's Hallmark smells like Christmas all year round, a scented candle-chocolaty smell that Henry does not mind one bit. He smiles at the kid behind the counter and sees, in the return nod, that this boy does not like his after-school job. It does not dent Henry's mood one bit, this thought. He happily heads to the blank stationery section. He is not discouraged to find the envelopes are only sold as a package deal with matching sheets or cards. In fact, he buys a box of yellow fold-over notes and envelopes that is the most expensive package on the shelf. The fact that he will have one fold over note leftover (without a matching envelope) does not bother him in the least.

After a predictable monosyllabic exchange with the high school kid, Henry gets back in his car and takes out an envelope, proud of his choice of color. This will stand out on the floor of her entry, he thinks. Definitely.

The light above the door to her building

has not yet come on. Henry checks his watch. It usually comes on by now, he thinks. The super had better get that fixed.

He wishes Cathy hadn't seen him parked out front the other night. This recollection threatens to ruin his mood. Still, he picks at the scab of thought.

She'd been dropped off in front of her building and, before he'd ducked, their eyes met. He cursed himself for the impulsive ducking. He knew it showed him to be "getting out of hand" — something she had accused him of the day following her meeting his mother.

"Let's just take a break is all I'm saying," she'd said. They were standing outside Cup-a-Joe. He'd gone in to talk to her and the minute she saw him she called to the back to ask Lois to cover for her for a minute and then she suggested they talk outside. Even though it was cold. Henry sensed it was rehearsed.

"Things were going so well," Henry said. "Things were so great just, like, a *day* ago."

"I don't want a serious relationship, Henry," she said. "I don't want you to get the wrong idea."

At first he'd tried to be cool. But "I don't want a serious relationship, either." But his reply came out sounding whining and defensive. "I'm falling in love with you." A popped blister of a statement.

"You don't even *know* me," she said. "And I *really* don't know you."

"What did she say to you?" He'd meant to touch her arm gently — a gesture intended to encourage disclosure. But he'd forgotten how tiny her bones were.

"Ow! Let go of me," she said.

"Sorry! I just . . ."

"You're getting out of hand." She backed into the store shaking her head. Fear mixed with disgust.

The door closed behind her so she did not hear him say, "I didn't mean to kill him."

Miserably he stalked back to Baxter's, kicking at a pebble, "I didn't mean to kill him" softly murmured on the way.

For he knows this is what his mother has told her. That he is a murderer. Lately she'd begun using that word: *murderer*. At first it punched his rib cage. But he'd been working on tuning it out. He'd almost succeeded: the last time she slurred it at him it barely registered as he tucked her into bed at five-fifteen.

CHAPTER FOURTEEN

1987

"Hold still," Carol Douglas is rodeo-wrangling her son. One little arm is just barely stuffed back into a jacket sleeve when the other shrugs itself free and the whole process starts over right to left this time. Henry remembers someone telling him that the Golden Gate Bridge is in a constant state of repainting because it takes so long to reach the far end that by the time the painters get there the beginning is once again in need of touch-ups. "I'm so sorry about this," Carol says in Henry's direction. "If you don't *hold still* I swear to God . . ."

"It's okay," Henry says through pins between his lips. "Almost done down here. Just . . . one . . . more turn for me and we'll be all set with your pants then I'll do your arms and we're all done."

"Bunny? Did you hear the nice man?" his mother asks, her voice childlike but so heavy with bitterness and frustration Henry looks up at her. She softens, mostly for his benefit. Her conversation patterns are staccato Tourette's outbursts disconcerting to others but completely unnoticeable to her. "*Bunnyholdstill.* I swear, Henry, when did I become my mother? You know? Oh. Well. You know what I mean. *Jesus.* My brain is fried. Sorry. If I'd've known what a pain in the a-s-s him being in this wedding was going to be I never would've said yes. *BunnyImeanit.* I thought it was a *compliment.* Can you believe they're actually going through with it? She's a fool, I'll tell you what. *Bunnyholdstill.* That Neal Peterson's always been a loser. Total loser. But she's hung in there this long so I guess she just figures — *Bunnyifyoudon'tholdstillIswear* — why not get something out of it, you know?"

"Yeah," Henry says. The child's hand, sticky from lollipop residue, is resting on Henry's head. Henry has unsuccessfully tried moving his head slightly back, hoping it would encourage the boy to remove his hand. He even jerked his head once as if in spasm but that backfired as the boy leaned even more weight onto the hand to prevent tipping over should Henry jerk his head again.

"I can't believe how *cute* he looks," Carol says.

Here the wavy picture lines begin. A fun-house mirror in which Carol's face distorts this way and that until finally coming back into the focus of a lens trained on her in 1976.

"I mean, doesn't he look so *cute?*" she asks Henry. "Oh, what am I asking *you* for. You're a guy. What do you know?"

Last year's yearbook is open, binding long ago broken so that its natural part is on the ninth-grade class picture. Carol is sitting cross-legged on her bedroom floor, her long hair pooling on either side of the picture she is poring over. Henry leans in, too, not to get a view of Carol's latest crush but to inhale the patchouli oil she rubs into either side of her long neck because she read that's what Gloria Steinem wears.

"He's a fag," Henry says, tired of Carol's obsessions. Gloria Steinem doesn't have psycho crushes, he thinks.

"Hey," he says. "Punch me as hard as you can in my stomach. Seriously. As hard as you can." His voice reflects the fact that he's tensing up every muscle in his midsection in anticipation of a fist.

"You're a retard," Carol says, flicking her hair over her shoulder. "I'm not going to punch you."

"Just do it. As hard as you can," he says.

"No," she says.

"Come *on.*"

Whomp comes the punch and then Carol is shaking her hand.

"Yeah, uh-huh," Henry nods at her. "Does Albert Brinkman have a stomach that hard? Huh? Huh?"

Carol rolls her eyes, closes the yearbook and slides it back into the bookshelf alongside the other yearbooks.

"I better get going," he says.

He watches her spread her books out around her in preparation for homework.

"Are you walking me out or what?" he asks.

"Oh," she looks up at him. "Yeah, okay."

He had been planning on trying to kiss her but loses his nerve when she says "So long, see you tomorrow" and closes the door behind him without even waiting for his reply.

"There," Henry says. He prepares to stand up and winces when the little boy pulls his hand off the top of Henry's head — the gumminess of little Bunny's hand has claimed a dozen hairs at least. Henry stands back up and stretches. "Be careful getting him out of those pants — there's pins all over."

"Bunny, wait — *wait,*" she's saying from inside the changing room. "You've got to be *careful,* honey. Jesus. Hang on. Hang *on.*"

Henry can see the two sets of legs under the double doors that just cover the middle of the changing rooms. One set is struggling to extricate itself from the fabric, the other more solid set is squared off, hands working in between, feverishly untangling the octopus child.

"You need this by Friday, right?" Henry calls out to her. He's filling out the tailor notes on the guest check.

"Is that okay? That'd be great," she says.

"How's Kevin doing?" Henry calls out. "That suit work out for him? The navy one?"

He has not seen Kevin since the accidental backslap-turned-shove. It is something he has felt bad about ever since and has been hoping to rectify the next time they met.

The doors push open, saloon-style, and Carol waddles through, Bunny's tiny tuxedo pants and jacket draped over one arm, an overloaded tote bag in the crook of the other bent arm.

"I just sewed a button back on last week," she says. "Funny you should ask."

"If there was a button missing he should've brought it back," Henry says. "We'd take care of that right away."

"Even after three years? Wow. Now *that's* service," she says, smiling and fishing into her bottomless bag. "Time flies, huh?" she says, noting Henry's confused look. "Kevin bought that suit three years ago. The year before Bunny was born. Jesus, *those* were the days." She sighs as she hands over the tuxedo. "Thanks, Henry. How're you doing, by the way? How're your parents? How's your mom doing? Bunny! *Get your foot out of there.* I'm so sorry, lemme just go grab him. *Bunny!*"

The boy, at first gleeful in his discovery of the electric shoe buffer, had in a matter of twenty seconds wedged his little foot deep into the bristles in between the red side and the black side and was howling.

"Your parents are good? *BunnyIswearto-God.*" Carol talks in two different volumes, adjusted accordingly while fishing in her purse for something that has eluded her throughout their exchange. "Sorry," she says.

CHAPTER FIFTEEN

1989

It starts with the movie theater. *Back to the Future* is long gone and still he goes. Buying tickets for *Cocoon,* then *Crocodile Dundee, Moonstruck, Big, Driving Miss Daisy.* Slowly he walks through the years, unnoticed, to the concession stand. Same size popcorn. Same size Coke. He is only out there, getting food and drink, because he knows he has already draped his jacket across the seats. The same two seats. "Will you guys watch my coat?" he asks the couple in the seats directly behind his. "I'll be right back."

"No problem," they'd said in unison.

So he stands there accepting his change back, savoring the fantasy — however fleeting — that she is in the bathroom. That he will wait there in the lobby for her and she will come out and together they will happily settle in to their chosen places in the theater. That she will take turns holding the tub of popcorn until they've eaten enough. That she will whisper, "Do you want any more?" and, when he shakes his head no, she'll put the half-finished bucket on the sticky floor. That they will laugh at the same moments and look at each other in confirmation of the hilarity. That she will clutch his arm in suspense — not even realizing she's doing it. The way driving mothers' arms swing out when they need to stop short whether or not there is anyone in the passenger seat.

Unhurried he allows others to push past him on their way into the theater from the candy stand. He knows his jacket is there. He prolongs the lobby moments as long as possible. When he, too, enters the theater it will jar him. The reality of a coat holding two seats for one will spell it out to him.

And still he goes. Time and again. To the theater. To the same two seats.

That becomes the ritual. So does the ice cream place. And the pizza parlor.

He tries to put out of his mind that last visit to Cup-a-Joe. He had stayed away at her request but then could not resist.

"Can I help you?" the stranger asks.

"Where's Cathy?" he says. Maybe it is her

day off. Maybe she's switched her schedule around.

"She doesn't work here anymore."

He looks around and is shocked to find no one else seems to notice the subtle shift in atmospheric pressure. He tries to keep his voice steady:

"Oh, yeah? Where'd she go?" Maybe up the street to the stationery store, he thinks.

"Don't know. She left town, I think," he says. "Anyways, what can I get you?"

Henry turns and leaves without a word.

It had been a comfort, until then, a security blanket, knowing she was still there. Even though she had made it clear she did not want to see him, it had remained a steady part of his day — this knowledge that she was moving around in the world just a few storefronts up from his.

Back at Baxter's he pleads a stomachache and asks to leave.

"Sure," Mr. Beardsley says. "Feel better."

In his car it takes a few minutes to catch his breath, which had become shallow, as if when she left she took all the oxygen with her.

He drives first to her apartment building. No wonder he hadn't seen her coming and going from his spot down the street.

Out of his car he walks as if in a dream.

Straight to the buzzers. To the spot where once "Nicholas" was affixed. That label now peeled off seems to him the cruelest cut of all. As if she'd been erased from existence.

At his apartment he reaches for the headphones.

It seemed like a good choice at the time: Michael Bolton. "How Am I Supposed to Live Without You." Once the song starts he realizes his mistake and lifts the record from the turntable.

Instead, he slips the Richard Marx record out of its sleeve. "Right Here Waiting."

The Henry Powell Band gears up to lay it down. They have groupies now. Girls — and a couple of die-hard guy fans just digging the music — who have gathered in the studio. But no. The studio becomes a concert stage. The groupies multiply and soon he is holding his microphone out to the crowd, for them to finish the lines they've memorized. Crowds love this. And so does the band. To have their words sung back to them.

Like a disc jockey he quickly switches out records and Bad English is playing the concert encore. "When I See You Smile." The audience is singing along with it, the throngs packed into the arena. But this time he keeps the microphone to himself, sings to them entirely. Gives it his all. And their manager tells them they "killed" once they collapse backstage in the dressing room.

Glossies are signed for radio stations and contest winners and soon they load up and head out to their next gig.

Henry sings Bob Seger's "Turn the Page" a cappella on their way onto the tour bus. Someone laughs. Someone else — probably the drummer — calls out for shots of JD. Henry retreats to the tiny bedroom in the very back of the bus. Wrung out, he flops onto the custom-made mattress and tries to get a little sleep.

Chapter Sixteen

1990

"Hey! What in the hell're you doing here, man?" the huge mitt of a hand swallows up Henry's. "Good to see you! Wow, it's been a long time, huh?" The voice a smiling one, familiar and warm like Toll House chocolate chip cookies or James Taylor's voice to a certain generation.

"What're *you* doing here's the question," Henry expertly shifts the focus of attention to Connor Segman, their hands still pumping up and down. "Looking good, man, looking good." He smiles back at the open skillet face he'd known for the first eighteen years of his life.

"Ah, well, you know," Connor says. "Every goddamn Christmas my folks are at my throat to come back to this goddamn town so I finally caved. Plus I couldn't miss the famous annual sale," he says.

Henry nods. "The famous annual sale," he says, knowing this is the point where Connor will realize he's talking to someone who still lives in "this goddamn town."

Right on cue: "I mean, it doesn't take much!" Connor's voice now transparently jovial. "I miss it here. I really do," he says. And now, Henry thinks, and now the familiar subject change: "How's it going with *you*, man? Jeez, how long's it been? I don't think I've seen you since that summer after graduation, man. You look great. Jeez."

"Yeah, it's been, what, ten, twelve years?" Henry says. "Jesus, we're old now. Hey, you know who was in here a while ago? Peter Campbell. In fact you just missed him. You wouldn't've recognized him, I'm telling you."

"Campbell's back in town? Unbelievable!" Connor says. Henry knows Connor is relieved, grateful to Henry for his willingness to rebound away from Awkward Topic to Comfortable Third-Party Topic. "What's *he* doing these days? Jeez, I haven't heard that name in years."

"Turns out he's a big-time Hollywood agent or something," Henry says with a laugh. "He comes in here all tanned — middle of December — all tanned and slicked back. Like he's Mr. California now or something. You've got to see him. You won't recognize him."

"Oh, man, I've got to call over there," Connor says. "His parents still living in the same place? They got the same phone number you think?"

"Yeah. They're still out there in that old barn," Henry smiles. "Remember that barn? God, I haven't been out there since tenth grade."

"What're you doing after work?" Connor asks. "Let's drive out there. Pick up Campbell, go out drinking. What time're you finished here?"

"I'm out at five but I've got something to do and then I've got to go back to my place first," Henry says. "I can be good to go by six-thirty-ish."

"That's fine," says Connor. "I've got to have dinner with the folks, anyway. Hey, guess where we're going? DaSilva's! Can you believe that place is still around?" But Connor colors when Henry says, "Um, yeah."

"Fuck me. Okay well, come by my folks' house at about eight. They like to eat early now, Jesus. If I let them they would've had us going out at four in the afternoon for dinner. So just come over."

"Same place?" Henry asks, even though he knows the Segmans are still at 423 Hillside, their home since they first moved to town when the boys were two.

"423 Hillside," Connor says.

"Good. By the way, what're you looking for? You need a new jacket or something? We've got an unbelievable sale going," Henry says. "But come to think of it, not much in your size. What're you, like six eight now or what?" He means it admiringly but Connor suddenly appears in a hurry to leave.

"Naw." Connor colors again and moves toward the door. "Came in to see you, man. Came in to see you."

"You didn't even know I work here!" Henry says. "You're such a crappy liar."

"I'm not lying! Anyway, I've got to go. Gotta pick my mother up from her eye appointment."

"You need a suit, right?" But if Henry further pursues his old friend he will surely appear to be hounding him.

He knows it is Connor Segman's reluctance to have his old friend wait on him that has him in retreat mode.

"See you later, right?" Connor Segman's hand is reaching for the door.

"Connor, wait," Henry calls after him,

wanting to let him know it is okay. He won't feel weird about it one bit.

"Turn here, *turn here,*" Connor says. He is hunched over in the front seat of Henry's car. Stuffed in like Alice in Wonderland in the tiny rabbit hole after swallowing a magic pill.

"I think I know where they live, man," Henry says.

"I'm telling you, you just missed it."

"I know where I'm going . . . oh, *shit.* What the hell?"

"I told you," Connor says. "I told you."

"What're you, like, five?" Henry is annoyed.

The night did not get off to a good start. Mrs. Segman, eyes dilated after her afternoon eye appointment, appeared startled to see Henry standing at the door, then quickly abandoned her post for the downstairs powder room where she could be heard retching from vertigo. Her nausea, though brought on optometrically, hurt Henry's feelings nevertheless. Nothing like someone vomiting when they lay eyes on you, he thought. "Let's go," he mumbled to Connor after he clomped into the front hall from outside the bathroom door ("Mom?

You okay? I'm going to take off, okay? Dad's upstairs. You'll be okay? Okay, so, bye").

"I don't know why you're taking it out on me," Connor is saying. "Jeez."

"I'm not," Henry says, looking over his right shoulder into the black night, negotiating a hasty three-point turn in the middle of the road, "taking it out," he huffs the steering wheel back to the left, "on you." Headlights showing trees in relief against the spookily dark woodsy backdrop with each angled turn.

Soon they are back on the right side of the double yellow lines in need of road crew touch-ups that always seem to get done when no one's looking. Suddenly the yellow lines are fortified, the paint mysteriously dry and flawlessly within the lines. It's a machine paint blower, Henry knows, jerry-rigged to the back of a beat-up municipal pickup truck. But still. It's perfectly within the lines. And no errant tire tracks smearing the lipstick from the lips.

"Aw, jeez," Connor is saying. "I puked in those bushes. After Campbell's graduation party. Remember? I think I drank a whole bottle of Southern Comfort that night. Look at 'em. They're still there." He is proud. As though his vomit is the compost that's enabled the bushes to thrive. Then again,

Henry thinks, maybe it *is* compost.

"I hope he's home," Connor says, almost to himself, as he reaches for the door handle.

"You didn't call him?" Henry puts the car in Park and turns to face Connor. "He doesn't know we're coming?"

"What?" Connor says. "I thought it'd be a good surprise! What's wrong with a little surprise?"

"Jesus, Segman," Henry says.

Segman's body unfolds itself from the car, like a tiny dried-up health-food-store sponge that finally meets water and triples in size.

"Don't slam your door — Jeez! He'll hear us!" Segman lopes along after Henry.

"This is so great," Segman whispers, after the doorbell is depressed. "This is *so great.*"

Henry looks over at him and, for a moment, feels eighteen again.

"Who's there?" the voice calls out from not quite behind the door.

They look at each other and surpress laughter.

"It's Henry Powell —"

"Shh" Connor jabs Henry's rib cage. "Let him open the door." Theatrical whisper again.

Petey Campbell's father, Fred, has always been a source of hilarity to them. Petey's mother was his father's fourth — and very much younger — wife. "Old Shrivel Dick" they had called him.

"It's my *father* you guys are laughing about," Campbell said once. And he gave Powell a shove because, unlike the others, Henry had been unable to stop his laughter after a particularly graphic and yes, pornographic, image was described by Connor to Henry.

Petey's mother divorced Fred and had already remarried before they'd graduated. "Old Shrivel Dick" called it a day after four wives and the accompanying four costly settlements, no doubt figuring it would be cheaper and more to the point simply to hire a housekeeper/nurse named Jenny to take care of things.

"He'll have a stroke." Henry matches Segman's volume. "He's gotta be a hundred by now."

"Who is it?" The heavy oak door barely muffling age and bewilderment tinged with annoyance. "Who's there?"

"Candygram," Connor says, and Henry bursts into unexpected laughter.

"Dad, just open the damn door," another, younger, voice says.

Henry and Connor look at each other

once more and the door moves backward. Revealing Peter Campbell alongside a squinting Fred Campbell, a Dorian Gray reminder of what thirty-year-old Petey could look forward to in a few decades.

"What the hell?" then "Hey!" and "Look at *you!* How long's it been?" all tangled up in the three-way greeting.

Smiles. Exclamations. A tangle of manly hands reaching out across the threshold of years, clasping one another in genuine warmth and recognition of the history they share.

"Who is it?" Fred Campbell keeps asking in the background. "Who are these people in my house? Who is it?" As though the door had not yet been opened.

"It's Henry Powell, Dad," Petey is saying, clapping his friends on their backs as he shuts them into the front hall, "and Connor Segman. From Fox Run. Remember?"

"Who?" Fred Campbell pads behind the three men, now heading into the room once called the den, now the study. "Who is it?"

"Dad," Petey says, clearly trying to cover his exasperation, "they're old friends from school, okay? Now, why don't you go to the kitchen. I think Jenny's in there. In fact, I heard her calling you a second ago."

"Jenny's calling me?" the elder Campbell

turns and shuffles off. "Jenny?"

"Hey, man." Connor extends his entire arm out and draws Campbell in to his side. In younger days he might have completed the move with a noogie but now it's more of a vibrating half hug. "You surprised?"

"How're you guys doing? What can I get you? We've got everything. Beer? You want a drink? What'll it be, Powell? Hey guess what, Segman, you're in luck — we've got Southern Comfort."

Henry looks over from the bookshelves of dusty family pictures. "Beer's good. Whatever you've got. I can't believe these pictures. When was this one taken?" He holds up a picture of the three of them playing Frisbee in an unrecognizable park.

Petey squints at it. "That was, what, like eighth grade or something? I don't know. Jesus, we were young. Segman? Beer okay?"

"Yeah, thanks," Segman says from another section of pressed-wood shelving, vertical holes finally given up hope that they'll be called on for pegged shelf adjustment after years of dormancy. "Peter S. Campbell. State Champion. Peter Campbell. First Place. Jeez, I forgot we were in the presence of not one but two sports heroes."

When Henry turns in Segman's direction

the years have magically melted away.

Their high school bodies, freshly showered, scrubbed cheeks still ruddy with athletic flush after the game, wait in the Segman den for Petey to steal the hard liquor so they can celebrate their victory. Henry is hoping to catch sight of Petey's pretty younger sister, Nonnie.

"Okay, guys, let's go," Petey says, out the front door, the half-empty bottle of Jim Beam wedged up under his arm, football jacket puffing out to hide its bulk.

"A bet's a bet," Segman says, blocking the driver's door, holding out his hands for keys.

"Oh, ma-an," Henry says. "Get in the back, Segman. Seriously. You're not driving the Jeep."

"Hey, man." Segman is not budging. "A bet's a bet. You said she'd never say yes and — what's that? Oh, yeah, *you were wrong.* Not only did she say yes but she pretty much jumped my bones after. So hand 'em over. I'm driving the Jeep."

It is prom season and the males of Fox Run were one by one facing the frightening task of asking girls for inevitably uncomfortable dates. The three had bet that Connie DaSilva (whose family owned the only bona

314

fide restaurant in town) would turn him down.

Segman jumps into the driver's seat and reaches for the bar underneath to make room for his legs. "A bet's a bet," he repeats, adjusting the rearview mirror.

"You have to go readjusting everything?" Henry says, miserable at the thought of his settings all mucked up. He had really thought Connie DaSilva had better taste or he never would have made this bet.

"I'm being a responsible driver," Segman smiles, pulling the bar under his seat again, pushing it back just one more slot's worth.

"Aw, man," Henry says.

"There," Segman says. "Just right."

"I'll never get it back to where it was," Henry says. Campbell leans into the radio, scrolling the knob up and down. "You already *moved* the mirror. Jesus, Segman!"

"Just drive already," Campbell says. Then whoops as he pulls the bottle out once they turn the corner away from the house. He takes a gulp of it and passes it to Henry.

"Where're we going?" Henry asks, trying to draw attention away from the liquor and the involuntary scowl it produces with each chug.

"I don't know," Campbell says. "Where should we go? There's no place to go, man.

I'm so sick of it here. That's why we've gotta leave. I'm telling you . . ."

"*Here* we go," Segman says. He looks back at Henry and makes another minor adjustment to his mirror.

"I'm just saying," Campbell says. "We decide on a city to meet up in after college, right? What's so bad about that? Powell, right?"

"Sounds like a plan, Stan," Henry says. Not minding being a passenger in his new Jeep as much as he thought he would.

"I'm thinking L.A.," Campbell says. "The girls are all babes. Every day is like, what, eighty degrees and sunny. What's not to love? Let's make a plan. Seriously. No, *seriously* . . ."

"I'll tell you where we're going," Segman says, shooing away the bottle that is again offered him. He swings the Jeep around in the middle of the road and heads in the opposite direction.

"Jesus, Segman!" Henry and Campbell say at the same time. Campbell is holding the roll bar over his head.

"We're going to the pit," Segman announces. "Wooo-yeah!"

The high-pitched holler all three break out in is a sound that would never be ventured without "My Sharona," playing on a car radio.

"Shit," Campbell says after it sinks in. He swallows hard before he turns to look out into the blackness. "The pit."

The rumors had started back when he was in Boy Scouts — somewhere in the quarry the body of a mobster was buried. The quarry became "the pit" because it sounded more *Godfather* than *Breaking Away.*

"Hell yes, the pit," Segman says. "Powell's up for it, right?" Segman's checking the rearview mirror. "You're in, right?"

But the alcohol is reattaching the synapse in his brain so the words sound like gibberish to Henry's ears. He nods his head along to "Stairway to Heaven," the only words that make sense to him right now.

"Right *on,*" Segman says. He honks for emphasis. The sound of the horn barely audible over the radio. To Henry it sounds far away. A car stuck in traffic heading in to dinner and a show in the city, perhaps, impatient to stay on schedule.

"Who the hell's honking out there?" Petey Campbell says, handing out the beer. He goes over to the window to look out into the darkness. Henry is startled to see it is not varsity-letter-jacket-Campbell turning to face them, shrugging at the mystery of the honking car.

"Goddamn, it's good to see you guys," he says. Segman and Henry nod and settle in to the couch and armchair. "Seriously, what's going on with you guys? I'm so fucking out of touch."

"I'm back for the holidays," Segman says.

"I know *that,* Segman, Jesus," he says, looking at Henry to confirm that their friend Connor Segman is still the court jester. "I mean what're you doing for a living? Where are you living?"

Segman, Henry is pleased to note, remains nearly impossible to offend, realizes his mistake. "Oh, yeah. I'm in Chicago now. Married. Two kids. I'm in the insurance business. Cars and homes, not life . . ."

He keeps talking and Henry takes longer gulps of his beer.

When Segman trails off Henry says to Petey, "Hey, I told Segman about your job, man. So cool."

On cue Campbell explains that his career is "artist representation," and Segman cocks his head to the side and says, "Wait, Henry said you're a big Hollywood agent."

"I'm an agent," he says, smiling at Henry.

"Whose? Whose agent are you?" Segman asks. "That's so cool."

He names an Oscar winner, a major television star and a teenager bent on parlaying her G-rated films into darker independent R-rated pictures.

"Whoa." Now Henry and Segman are exchanging looks.

"Oh, you know who else I represent? You'll get a kick out of this, Powell — Art Washington."

Henry finishes off his beer and feigns impressed surprise, as he knows he is expected to do. Art Washington is the star of many blockbuster action films but mainly he is known for winning the Heisman Trophy. Henry knows people will always gauge his reaction to football references, but the fact that he will also have to bear the scrutiny of two of his oldest friends makes him feel exhausted.

"Is that right?" he says. "Can I get a refill?" He offers Campbell his empty bottle.

"Yeah, yeah, sure."

"This is great," Segman says to Henry while Campbell is back in the kitchen. "Chicago's good. It's great. But . . . I don't know . . . it's good to be where people know you, you know? It's a fucking job, you know? Roof-over-our-head kinda thing.

319

When the fuck did we turn into our fathers, you know?"

Henry nods and turns this thought over while Segman continues. "But Chicago's awesome. You've got to come out and visit us, man. You'd love it. And you could stay with us. All you'd have to do is get the plane ticket, the rest would be free since you'd stay with us. Come in the summer. Well, duh. Who'd visit Chicago now, huh? Duh. But in the summer we grill out, seriously, like every night. You should definitely come out."

"Here you go." Campbell hands Henry a fresh beer, then sets Segman's new one in front of him. "Cheers."

They clink bottlenecks.

"Hey, Henry, how's your brother?"

"Jeez," Segman says. He picks at the label of his beer. "God, remember that night? At the pit? Shit."

"We're going to the pit," Segman called from the driver's seat. "Wooo-yeah!"

"Shit," Campbell said. Gulping Jim Beam and staring out into the blackness of the chilly night.

"Hell yes, the pit," Segman said. "Powell's up for it, right?" Segman checked the rearview mirror. "You're in, right?" Henry remembers it still: their eyes meeting in the mirror in spite of the black night.

He remembers tapping his fingers along to "Jackie Blue," a song he now switches off on the rare occasion an oldies station plays it.

"Right *on,*" Segman said.

Soon they pulled over. "Someone's already here," Segman said. He switched off the ignition.

"Whose car is that?" Campbell said. "I know that car. Hey, is that Figger's car?"

Henry, buzzing, leaned into the space between the two front seats to see if he could recognize the car. "Oh, shit. Let's get out of here."

"What? Who is it?" Segman and Campbell both turn to face him.

"That's my brother's car. Let's go."

Campbell looked at Segman and said, "It's three against one and I want to stay. He can leave."

"Yeah," Campbell says, swigging the Jim Beam. Laughing.

"It's a mistake, I'm telling you," Henry says. He stands near the Jeep.

"Brad Powell," Segman says. Henry sees he is shaking his head. "What the fuck, give me that." He reaches for the bottle. "Shit that sucks."

"What's with your brother, anyway?" Campbell asks. "Seriously, how come he's always got to be such an asshole?"

All Henry can think of to say is: "I don't know. We're not close or anything."

"Apparently . . ." Campbell said. He wiped his mouth with the back of his hand — like a character in a movie — and handed the bottle back to Henry.

"Yeah, yeah, okay fine," Henry said, taking it. "But seriously, let's go, all right?"

"No fucking way," Campbell said. "Come on."

By the time Henry caught up with them they were already on the trail that led from the road through the woods to the edge of the quarry.

"Bad idea," he said out loud. "I'm telling you now this is a bad idea."

Branches snap and break underfoot. Truth be told Henry never liked going to the pit, liked it even less at night, even less than that when his own brother is already there.

"Shhh." He heard one of them up ahead. "What was that? I heard something. . . ."

He was right behind them now. "It's me, you idiots."

"Jesus." "Shit, Powell." "Shhh."

There was no mistaking the sound coming from up ahead. A sound that surprised

Henry so much it was he who hissed "Shhh, *quiet,*" this time.

They stood still listening to Brad Powell . . . sobbing. Followed by the male equivalent of a scream. A hybrid yell-howl-voice-breaking-midstream-scream. Then more sobbing.

It was out before Henry could caution against it:

Cutting through the angst of this dark fall night, Connor Segman hollered, "Hey."

"Shit."

"What're you *doing,* Segman?"

"Heeey!" Followed — and this is the part that made Henry wince — by "Hey, *Powell.*" In bass relief against the Jurassic silence of the ravine.

If he turned to run, as he badly wanted to do, he would no doubt lose two friends. But if he stayed something worse might happen. Henry knew he had to remain there, frozen, instantly sobered by fear, at the edge of the pit.

"Where'd he go?" Segman asked. "You hear anything? It's like he disappeared. Hey, maybe he was beamed back up into the spaceship. . . ."

The hit came hard from behind and plus it was dark, but the next thing Henry knew he was gasping for air. He didn't feel the pain on his left side until after the oxygen returned to his lungs.

By then another of them was down, followed by the third, all rolling around on the dry leaves, sticks breaking and thuds of flailing limbs.

It was never clear where he came from or where he disappeared to, but Brad Powell knocked all three boys to the ground, pummeled them and then evaporated. Henry never saw his brother again.

"That was bizarre," Peter Campbell says, standing, back in his thirty-year-old Los Angeles tanning-bed skin. He stretches and twists his spine Jack La Lanne–style. Then he sits back down.

"What was up that night? What was wrong with him?" Segman asks.

"I don't know," Henry says. Another swig of beer.

But he does know. They had fought the night before. Brad returned from God-knows-where (he had become a magician: disappearing and reappearing in the Powell house every few months). Henry was filling out his scholarship forms — tedious work that required a lot of table space so he had commandeered the long-since-abandoned dining room table.

It started out with the usual sparring. "You still a virgin?" Brad asked on his way through to the kitchen.

"It depends. Are you?" Henry answered, not looking up from his paperwork. Their father was not home, their mother was staring at *Family Feud.* The broken capillaries on her cheeks, the thinning hair, the wasted body, all had shocked Brad on re-entry. Henry saw this and looked at his mother with an outsider's eyes and saw, with alarm, she was killing herself from the inside out. So that may have put Brad in a bad mood, Henry thought as he skipped to "Part B" as the application advised. Then again just about anything put Brad in a bad mood so you never knew. Henry remembers thinking this. He had no way of knowing it was only about five minutes until escalation point so he was at leisure to let his mind wander.

He had jumped in his seat when he heard his brother's voice coming from just above his head.

"God, it's suffocating in here," Brad said.

"Jesus, you scared the hell out of me," Henry said. Involuntarily. Normally he never would have said such a thing to Brad as it made him too easy a mark. "Take off your sweater, then," Henry said. "It's not that hot."

He glanced up at Brad and saw him looking at the forms, a beer in his hand, shifting his weight to the other leg casually, as if he were taking brotherly interest in Henry's project.

"No, I mean it's *suffocating,*" Brad said, looking into the living room. Appearing bored now by Henry's work. "Don't you think?"

"Not really," Henry said. He filled in his home address for the six millionth time, muttering, "Jesus, how many times have I got to fill this in?" to himself.

"Come to think of it," Brad said, trying very hard to sound conversational, as if this thought just popped into his head. "That'd suck, don't you think? Worst way to die. I mean, I'd rather take a bullet in the brain than suffocate. Think about it — gasping for air. Choking. *Shit.*"

Had Henry not been preoccupied with his social security number, taking care to fit the first three then the next two and the final four into the squares provided (he had not memorized his number so had to check and double check his wallet-size blue-and-white card) — had he not been concerned with

326

this he might have been alerted to the direction Brad's discourse was headed. But he had waited until the last minute — the forms needed to be postmarked the following day and he had a creative-writing assignment he had not even started also due the next day.

"Why are you just standing there? You're creeping me out."

But Brad did not budge. He tilted the bottle into his mouth and swallowed hard.

Henry shrugged and turned to the application checklist to go over what had yet to be tackled. Teacher recommendations were in this pile, check, character reference over there — he had chosen the coach for this — check. Okay, what am I forgetting? Henry looked back and forth from checklist to pile.

"And just think," Brad said, moving in for the kill, "that's exactly how our brother died."

Henry's hand stopped but he did not dare react yet.

"He *suffocated*," Brad said. Making it sound like the thought had plagued him, the pity had eaten him up all these years. "Choking on water. Wondering why his older brother had just left him there. That was probably his last thought — where's *Henny?*"

That name — the name David had called Henry. Henny.

The chair scraped back but Henry did not straighten. He remained near half seated — tackle position — and went right for Brad's midsection, knocking him to the ground. The shattered beer bottle sounded far away to him. His eyesight narrowed even more to hear his brother, on his back now, on the floor of the dining room *laughing.*

"Shut up," Henry said. His hands went around Brad's throat with no resistance.

"Or what?" Brad said, finally trying to push Henry off, to get out from being pinned, "or you'll *kill* me?"

The punches got harder and came faster. Wrestling, tangled, they traded one for one. Chairs knocked to the ground. Fists becoming bloody.

"Boys." Henry was aware of their mother's feeble voice but it was too little too late it was time for someone to take care of Brad once and for all and dammit it's got to be me so stay away Mom just stay away and let me take care of this.

"Fuck you," Henry said to Brad. The word — however extraordinary it was for Henry to say — was ordinary to Brad, who littered every sentence with it, diminishing its meaning in the process.

Gasping, turning from a gut punch, Brad said, "At least I'm not a murderer." He kicked his way to half standing.

"Boys," the word barely shy of an exclamation point from the doorway. *"Stop."*

More punches, now slowing from pain and near exhaustion. Still the punching continued.

"You know what?" Henry said, again straddling his weakened brother — finally pinning him back down. "We all wished it was you."

He pulled more air into his lungs past what he was sure was a broken rib. A half-hearted punch thrown again but Brad left his head where the punch put it. "You know how you wanted them to say it out loud back then?" Another breath. "I'll say it now — *we all wanted it to be you that died. You* should've died in that tub."

Henry was suddenly aware of the sobbing from the doorway. He was also conscious of his brother's limpness and in one motion, mustering all his strength and not bothering to hide a wince in the process, he hauled himself off of Brad to stand.

"What's he up to these days?" Campbell asks.

"He's out in Portland I hear," Henry says. He shrugs as if being in Portland explains everything.

CHAPTER SEVENTEEN

1993

The door chimes alert Henry and his boss to a potential customer. They look at the door simultaneously. As Mr. Beardsley deflates for the lack of retail possibility, Henry smiles involuntarily.

"Hey," he says, "how's it going?"

"Same-o, same-o," Tom Geigan says. "How's it hanging here? Hey, Mr. Beardsley."

"Tom. Nice to see you," Mr. Beardsley says on his way to the back room. "Slow day?"

"You could say that," Geigan says. "It's a ghost town over there."

He turns back to Henry. "I'm about to blow my frigging brains out. Collins wants me to reorganize the key racks so all the car keys are on one side and the house keys are on the other. Motherfucker. I'm going to get a Coke," he says to Henry. "Want to come?"

"Yeah. Hang on, I'll go tell Beardsley."

Mr. Beardsley is punching numbers into an old accounting calculator.

"Mr. Beardsley? I'm going to go on a break now, just letting you know." Henry brings his own lunch and eats in the storeroom or outside on the bench across the street from the store (weather permitting) — never taking more than fifteen minutes . . . not even close to the allotted hour. Official breaks are unnecessary as the store is rarely that busy anymore.

Mr. Beardsley looks at his watch. Henry knows it is meant to discourage a long break, something he is wont to take when Tom Geigan is involved. They both know this. Breaks are one thing, Mr. Beardsley said the last time Henry returned from an hour and forty-five-minute excursion with Geigan, but this is more like taking advantage, if you ask me, he said that day.

"I won't be too long," Henry says. "You want anything?"

Mr. Beardsley considers this and Henry resists the urge to roll his eyes. He wants to get going. "Where are you going?"

"Just down to the Mobil Station for a Coke."

"Yes! That's the ticket," he says. "Will you bring me back a Coke?" He leans over to make pocket access possible. "Here's fifty cents. Thanks. If it's more let me know."

"Okay."

"Jesus, let's go," Tom says when Henry reappears. "I don't got all day."

"You 'don't got all day'?" Henry says.

"All right, all right, Fox Run," Tom says.

Outside it is sunny and warm. They turn left and Henry enjoys the feel of the spring breeze coming up Main Street. It is the promise that winter is over. Put away those heavy coats, the air is saying. Don't worry. No more surprise cold snaps. He inhales the scent of bulbs pushing through the soil. Days like this they would have had class outside.

"So." Henry clears his throat and prepares for Geigan's rapid-fire reaction to what he is about to say. "So it turns out she lives a half an hour away."

Casual. He puts his hands in his pockets and tries to appear as if this is just a silly bit of trivia tossed out to make conversation on this shiny, happy, bright day.

"Who?" Geigan asks, preoccupied with the box that sells newspapers on the corner. "Can you believe that Buttafuoco story? Did you see the picture of the wife? The one who got shot? She looks like a night-mare now. That's his punishment, you ask me. He's now gotta wake up to *that* every day. That face. It's like it's collapsed in or something."

Henry clears his throat and is aware of his quickening heartbeat. He is about to say her name out loud and that is what hap-pens when he says her name out loud. He practically has a heart attack.

"Cathy Nicholas."

Geigan stops walking. Freezes is more like it. Slowly, for effect, Henry knows and wishes it were not so but was prepared, anyway, he turns to Henry, who is busying himself with looking anywhere but at his friend.

"What the fuck? I *knew* it. You've still got a hard-on for that girl. I fucking *knew* it."

It has not escaped notice, this increase in profanity over the years, and it bothers Henry quite a bit. Not that he doesn't and won't toss one out every now and then if the situation calls for it. But what happened to everybody? he has wondered many times. Why is everybody swearing all the time now? Just the day before he had been startled to hear a woman using the f-word in the supermarket with her children in earshot. First of all, a woman using the f-word . . . that offends his sensibilities right off the bat. But in front of little kids?

"I do not," Henry says, continuing the walk down the street. "Jeez."

"So what are you saying," Geigan says, catching up. "You just *happened* on this information? I think not." Henry knows Geigan is pleased with himself for saying "I think not" — that's how well he knows his friend. He probably got it from watching *NYPD Blue.* Sipowicz is interrogating some guy in what appears to be the station's only interrogation room. A room with inexplicable pen marks in a cluster on one part of the wall. That's all Henry sees when he watches the show and they get to those scenes. Why all the pen marks? he asks the television set out loud.

"Hey, Ernie." They greet the Mobil attendant as they walk past to the Coke machine on the side of the building.

"Hey, guys."

Henry picks out a dollar fifty from the change fished from his pocket.

"I got it," Henry says, plugging the quarters and dimes into the slot. He has always enjoyed the sound of the can dropping down the chute to the tray. A substantial sound. Like he's really *getting something* for the money.

"You sure? Here," Geigan says, offering his fifty cents.

"Yeah, no, I got it."

"See ya, Ernie."

Ernie nods, scratches his nose and looks back down at his magazine.

"Who's the extra soda for? Your *girlfriend?*"

"Will you stop?" Henry says. The Coke is cold, super cold, as if they keep the machines ten degrees colder than the average refrigerator, he thinks.

The walk back is easier, the wind at their backs. Henry relieved of the burden of saying it out loud: he has found Cathy. After all these years. Just half an hour away.

"So what're you going to do?" Geigan asks. They have passed the same newspaper box and he can't resist a glance. His question seems off hand enough, easy enough. So Henry answers honestly.

"I was thinking of calling her."

"Aw, man," Geigan says. "This has *shitty* written all over it."

"You think I shouldn't call her?"

"No. I don't think you should call her."

Now Henry stops not so much because they are almost in front of Baxter's but because he is surprised at the resolve in Geigan's tone.

"Why not?" He tries not to sound whiney. Or pleading. Like he's asking for permission. He tells himself he knew this would be Geigan's reaction so it should not come as any surprise. Henry is annoyed at the way Geigan is gulping his soda. He sure drinks *loudly*, Henry thinks.

"When that ended," Geigan says, finally done with crunching his can and tossing it into the trash can a fair distance away (impressing them both), "you were a mess. You never left your apartment, man. When it comes to that girl you get all weird and shit."

"No, I don't."

"Listen to you. *No, I don't,*" he mimics Henry in a higher pitch than Henry thinks is necessary. "You're already getting weird. Whatever. Call her if you want to. I know you're going to. In fact *please* call her. How about that? You *have* to call her."

"You're crazy," Henry says. He waves Geigan off and reaches for the door to Baxter's.

"This way I can say I told you so when you get the shit kicked out of you again." Geigan doubles back a couple of storefronts to the hardware store, which they passed in order to continue their break. "I'm going to Blackie's tonight if you change your mind. Which you won't . . ."

Geigan's smugness ruins the Coke for Henry.

"Who died?" Mr. Beardsley asks Henry, who has wordlessly handed him his soda and walked past on his way to the back room to think about the phone call he is indeed going to make.

It wouldn't be so bad, Henry thinks, if people didn't cringe when they catch themselves in their stupid death references. Mr. Beardsley's expression had wrinkled up in dismay at his thoughtless remark, squinching his eyes into pinpricks. He looks like a mole, Henry thinks. Like a fat little blind mole.

"It's five o'clock," Henry says, making his way through the racks toward the end zone, "I'm heading out."

"Okay, sport," Mr. Beardsley says. "See you *tamale.*" His chuckles reach Henry, who has rebounded from the negativity of Tom Geigan and has returned to the thought that this could be *the day.* The day we tell our grandchildren about, he thinks, pushing through the goal-posted front doors back into the spring air. Henry can imagine them marveling at the miracle of timing. Of fate. "If he hadn't called me right then, on that day," Cathy will say to the children who would never tire of hearing the story, "at that precise moment, you would not be sitting here right now. I would have married —" No. Henry doesn't like this to be her alternative. Rather, "I would have died old and alone, pining away as I was for your father."

And they will gaze lovingly into each other's eyes.

They must have gotten the light fixed at Bridge Avenue, he thinks, because the wait for it to turn green is only a few seconds and for God's sake why are people so quick to honk it's only just turned green and so I didn't turn right on red that's my prerogative so lighten up.

He reminds himself to call the gutter guy when he pulls up in front of his parents' house and sees that there is ragweed sprouting up from the chipped metal wells trimming the edge of the roof. Or I guess I could get up there and clean them out. But it's a pretty steep pitch.

"Hi, it's me," he calls out. He closes the

door behind him. "Mom?"

In the kitchen by the sink he checks the pill bottles. The one from Dr. Hellerson is nearly empty. On a scrap of paper by the phone farther down the counter he scribbles a note to himself that it is Dr. Clarke he should call this next time for the refill. The last time he called Dr. Hellerson for a refill the nurse gave him a lecture about Valium addiction and refused to take a message, saying that he needed to speak directly to the doctor. Between the four doctors in three different towns he had managed to help her stay afloat. But he knew this would soon come to an end. They were all becoming reticent to prescribe.

His mother wanders into the kitchen and startles him by patting his back. He had not heard her enter. Bare feet.

"Hi, Mom."

"How was work today?" she asks, pleasing them both with her lucidity.

"Good," he says. "Boring. How're you feeling?"

"Good," she says. She fills a glass of tap water and sips from it. From the looks of it she has bathed. A good sign.

"You know, Mom," he says, broaching a subject he has had little luck with in the past, "it's probably time to start cutting the pills in half. Dr. Hellerson said . . ."

"Dr. Hellerson said," she mimics. "Dr. Hellerson thinks I'm a Valium addict."

This surprises him. He had not thought anyone had broached the subject with her. She reaches for the bottle in his hand and says, "You know what Milton Berle says? Milton Berle says a Valium addict is a patient who takes more Valium than her doctor."

Her laugh is more of a burp.

"Yeah, well, he said we should be halving the dose. I think he's right."

"Have you seen Dr. Hellerson? He's barely able to string a sentence together," she says. "So by Milton Berle's standards I'm doing just fine."

"Yeah, well, next time I need a medical assessment I'll be sure to call up Milton Berle."

"You're funny." She pats his back again and teeters into the living room. The TV is switched on, the game shows are starting and he has lost her attention.

He peeks into the room to make sure she is appropriately glued to the glow of the old set (another mental note to look into the price of a new one). He empties the remaining Hellerson pills and pulls a steak knife out of the slanted wood block. He presses the knife down along the line indentation in each one, careful to keep it straight so that each half is more or less even. Each pill is cut. He pushes them off the counter with one hand into the palm of the other and repeats the exercise with the three other bottles.

Now the trick will be to keep her from taking two halves. This is a trick to be sure but something's got to give, he thinks. Maybe this will do it. He looks at his watch.

"I'm going now, Mom," he says, leaning down to kiss the top of her head. "See you tomorrow, okay?"

"Bye," she says in the offhanded way someone dismisses anything that distracts from television viewing.

Within a few minutes he is pacing in his apartment.

"Cathy? Hey, it's Henry Powell. How *are* you?" Too girlie.

"Cathy. Hey there, it's Henry Powell — how are *you?*" Why the emphasis on *you?* Plus *Hey there* sounds weird.

"Cathy? Hi, it's Henry Powell. How are ya?" *Ya?* I'm a sixteen-year-old *girl.*

Should he not say Powell? He worries this might put too much distance between them, this use of last names. Better to stick with Henry.

"Cathy? Hi, it's Henry. How're you doing?"

Hey sounds more laid-back. I should say *hey.*

He takes a deep breath and reaches for the phone. He has already memorized her new phone number. It's an easy one: numbers in more or less descending order. It rings once . . . twice.

"Hello?"

His first impulse is to hang up. In fact she has to say hello again before he finds his voice.

"Cathy?" Heart attack heart attack heart attack.

"Yeah? Who's this?"

"It's me, Henry." What now? *What now?*

In the intervening pause — slight in reality but minutes long to Henry — he panics and thinks 1) she knows another Henry and is trying to figure out which one it is; 2) she's forgotten she even knew a Henry; 3) I should have taken one of Mom's Valiums.

"Henry? Henry *Powell?*"

He is so grateful for this he nearly cries "yes." But then he reins in his excitement and relief and gratitude. "So, how're you doing?"

"How'd you get this number?" she asks.

"What?" He had not thought this would be her reaction. Does she sound happy he has found her number? He tells himself yes, she does.

"I just looked you up, that's all. So how are you? God, it's been a long time, huh?"

"You know what?" she says. "I was just running out the door. . . ."

"Oh, yeah, sure, sorry, um," he says, cursing his bumbling reply.

"Can I call you back in, like, about an hour? I'm just running out to do one quick thing and I'll be back."

"Sure, sure," he says. "No problem. I'll be here."

"What's your number?"

"It's the same," he says, and then tells it to her, anyway.

"Okay, great," she says. "I'll call you back. Jeez, wow. Henry Powell."

"Yeah, huh? Okay, well I'll talk to you in a bit."

"Okay, bye."

Henry wills himself not to look at the clock. Or at his watch. Just to be on the safe side I'll take it off, he thinks. Put it in the drawer.

But then I might forget it, he thinks. Better to leave it on and just forget it's there.

He knows that watching the clock casts a slow-motion effect on everything. Even this thought process, he thinks. In thinking about not checking the time I'm still slowing it down. This is the longest hour since the dawn of time, he thinks.

He checks the time once more and then vows to forget it all together so he can be pleasantly surprised at its rapid progression when it does occur to him to look.

The room is so quiet, though, he can hear the second hand of the clock that is hanging on the wall. He closes his mouth and breathes through his nose to listen for it. At first it is something he does not realize he is doing but soon he is conscious of the fact that he is counting in ten-second intervals.

Stop! Stop it right now. And he *will* stop . . . right after this last . . . neat . . . minute . . . is counted. Okay, there. He is done. Time will have no meaning to me now, he thinks. Starting now.

Henry reaches for the book that has remained untouched on his night table for so long he is forced to unfold the dog-eared page twelve and start over from page one. *Jonathan Livingston Seagull.* The book everyone talked about so long ago but he never got around to reading. But the first line has to be read twice. The second line three times. By the time he hits the end of the first paragraph Henry decides the book will most likely never be ticked off the list of Books One Must Read in Order to Be a Part of the Collective Conversation and replaces it to the exact same spot it had been occupying. The list was one he had cut out of the paper, imagining it to be just the sort of thing one might need in order to liven up date conversation.

Sleep, he tells himself. Sleep is just what I will do. I will take a nap. I never take naps, he thinks, justifying this idea to himself out loud. Plus he read somewhere that the human biological clock requires naps in the afternoon. It is why Europeans take siestas, he thinks. Or was that biorhythms?

He lies down on his back across his bed. His arms along his sides and his feet hanging off the bed, he wonders what he might look like to an ant crawling on the ceiling. Splat. He imagines the ant thinking: splat went the human.

Tick tick tick goes the wall clock so he turns over so at least half of his problem is solved: one less ear to take in the sound.

And maybe with one less he won't be able to bionically hear time trickling by.

Then again he hasn't checked in a while. All this thinking must have taken up a good lot of time.

Only seven minutes have passed. Damnation. That's *exactly* why I'm not going to check the time again, he thinks.

The phone ring makes him jump.

"Hello?"

"Hey, yo, get off your ass and come out tonight." It's Tom.

"I don't think so," Henry says. He waits for his heartbeat to catch up with his mind in his realization it is not Cathy calling back.

"Why the fuck not? Come on. You can't stay locked up forever, man. Jesus. You're like the smelly old man."

"Who?"

"The smelly old man," he says, "the guy down the hall from me. Never comes out of his place unless he's emptying the trash. Once I was stuck behind him on the stairs and I figured it was the bag of trash that smelled so rank but he dumped it and passed me on the way back up and it wasn't the trash . . . it was him."

"That's a good story."

"Yeah, fuck you. You're the smelly old man now. So scrape the dirt off and get your ass in gear and come out."

Henry pauses to consider this but worries that the phone might ring while he is gone and what if it's her — Cathy never leaves messages. She hangs up when the machine picks up. No way. He can't risk missing her call.

"No thanks, man."

"You're so pussy-whipped it's sick."

"What are you talking about?"

"You called her, didn't you?" Geigan asks him.

"Shut up. No, it's just . . . I . . . I don't feel well. I think I'm coming down with something."

"Come to think of it, smelly old man is sick a lot, too," Geigan says. "Plus you're a liar. You called her."

"How do you know so much?"

"This is not going to go well."

"I've got to go," Henry says.

"Whatever. Smell you later."

Henry waits a second after hanging up before picking the receiver back up. He listens for the dial tone and hangs up again.

Then he thinks of something else.

"Operator, may I help you?"

"Um, hi," he says, "I'm wondering, ah, is there a power outage?"

"What's the prefix, sir?"

"307."

"That's your area code, sir. I need the first three numbers of your local phone number."

"Oh, yeah. Sorry. It's 339. And I'm fine. I mean my area seems fine. I can see lights on in other people's houses and stuff. I was just wondering if . . ."

"No. I'm not showing outages of any kind in your area. Is there anything else I can help you with?"

"No. No thanks. Thanks for checking. I was just thinking . . ."

"You have a good evening."

"Yeah, you too."

Chapter Eighteen

1999

The stick figure begins flashing red, indicating a limited number of seconds in which to cross the street.

"Powell? Henry Powell?" The voice comes from behind.

The recognition does not come so easily on his end, leading to an awkward explanation. "Michael Dean," the stranger says. A hand is extended.

The traffic starts up.

"Mike!" Henry says. "Wow, Mike Dean. How the hell are you?"

Smiles, handshakes, steps taken back from the curb.

"Good, I'm good," Mike says. "How about you? What are you doing back in town?"

"I'm here," he says. "I live here. What're you doing? How's it going? I heard you were out in San Francisco, man."

350

Mike Dean is shaking his head. "I just moved back. I'm moving back, I should say. Next week the movers come so I'm staying in the city until my place is ready. I just took the train out to check on it."

"Oh, yeah?"

"Yeah. Which way are you heading? I'll walk with you."

The stick figure is again blinking red but Henry knows: there are eleven blinks before the man in the electronic box stays permanently red. Mike looks both ways to make sure they've got time to cross. When his head hits center again he realizes Henry has already started across.

"What's going on with you? What're you up to?" Mike says, once he has caught up.

"Can't complain," Henry says. "How about you?"

"Not bad," he says. "Sick of the rat race, I'll tell you that much. Glad to be back in town."

"Yeah?"

"Taking some time off," Mike says. "Planning my next attack." His sigh is more of a snicker to Henry's way of thinking.

"What was the last plan of attack?"

"Dot coms."

The two words explain everything.

"Heads up," Henry says. The car doesn't

look like it's going to wait for them to cross the street, so eager it is to tuck into the empty space in front of the stationery store. Henry hasn't broken his stride but Mike flinches and waits for the car to park. Again he has to hurry to catch up.

"How about I take you for a beer later?" Henry asks.

They're stopped in front of Pier One. "Sounds great, actually. I'm heading in here. Where're you going?"

"Baxter's," Henry says.

"That place is still around? Jesus, I remember getting my confirmation jacket there. I can't believe it's still there."

"I work there, actually," Henry says. He pushes his shoulders back and stands up straighter. "You want to say six? At Blackie's?"

"Oh, sorry," Mike says. "No offense."

"None taken." Straighter still. "Six?"

"Six it is," Mike says. "See ya."

The Pier One potpourri smell wafts out as Henry continues down the street back to Baxter's.

The pavement blurs and shoes clicking by are now carrying bodies twenty years younger.

"Seriously, congratulations," Mike says.

"Thanks, man," Henry says. "I really thought you had it in the bag."

"Don't say that. Don't do that. I know what you're doing. I never had a chance. I know that. Not with the *football hero* in the race," Mike says.

"Naw," Henry says. "Look, it's not a popularity contest."

"What? How could you say that? That's exactly what it is. I can't believe you even said that," Mike says. "You think I don't know what everybody says behind my back? You think I don't hear? You think because I've got glasses I've got a hearing problem, too?"

"Dean, Dean, slow down," Henry says. "I don't say anything about you. I've never said anything about you. You're a good-enough guy. Paranoid maybe but a good guy. Jesus. Lighten up."

"Yeah, yeah, yeah. Anyway, class president goes better with varsity football than with computer club. I know. I'm not blind. But this way in college interviews I can say I ran for the office."

"College interviews?"

"Oh, Jesus Christ, Powell, you don't ever think about college interviews? Of course you don't. I bet they come to you, don't they?"

"Dean, Jesus."

"The colleges come to you, don't they? Just tell me."

"They talk to everybody," Henry says unconvincingly.

"Shit. I knew it. I *knew* it. Why am I not surprised? Look, I gotta go. Congrats, Mr. Class President. Shit."

Mike Dean walks away and back into contact lenses and Italian loafers.

Henry steps into Baxter's, where Mr. Beardsley is looking at his watch.

"Nice of you to join us this afternoon," he says. "Could I trouble you for a stockroom run, do you think? Would that fit into your social schedule? I wouldn't want to inconvenience you."

"What do you need?" Henry asks.

"Oh, *thank* you, Mr. Powell," Mr. Beardsley says. Henry knows his boss is disappointed in the lack of apology. Which is precisely why none is offered.

"I need you to unpack the Izods. I just got a call from Mrs. Langley. She's looking for a canary-yellow, two-button, size large. I've got to call her back a-sap." Instead of A-S-A-P, Mr. Beardsley makes a word out of it.

"Will do," Henry says.

"Chop chop."

Mr. Beardsley couldn't be sure but Henry knows he notices him moving just a tad bit slower than he had been only seconds before.

The box opens easily and Henry unfolds the top panels to reveal the flat, folded technicolor shirts now all the rage after patiently waiting for a decade of grunge to run its course.

Henry reaches into the cardboard box and the shirts are now cans of nonperishable food.

"What's your system?" Mike Dean is standing over him, arms full of Bumble Bee tuna and minestrone soup.

"My system?" Henry says. He doesn't look up but reaches for the cans on the gymnasium floor to his right.

"Your system. Are you separating soups from condiments or what? What's the plan?"

"No plan, just pile them over there. Or here. Just put them down here and I'll start the next box in a sec."

"Jesus. You need a *system*," Mike says. "Move over. Move. I'll do it. I'll show you."

"Dean. Get lost, I got it. Hand me that tape over there, will you?"

"If it's all mixed up together," Mike says, handing him the packing tape, "what happens on the other end? You gotta think of the end game. What're they going to do when they get all this stuff? They're going to have to sort on their end, that's what. And that's not community service, that's chaos. You've heard of the chaos theory. Or did you have a game that day?"

"Incoming!" One of Henry's teammates elbows Mike Dean aside as if he were invisible.

"Ow, Jesus, *excuse me*," Mike says. He rubs his stringy arm and checks it for bruising.

"Step it up, Powell," his teammate Will Sanderson says. "We got two more loads after this one and I want to get out of here sometime this century."

"Put them over there on the table. I'll get to it after this next box," Henry says.

Sanderson dumps the cans, which roll indiscriminately and clang to the floor, the deviled ham making a break for freedom across the polished floor, nearly reaching the gym door.

"Your friends are *geniuses*," Mike says. He fetches the deviled ham and moves closer to Henry once the coast is clear and once he has neatly restacked Sanderson's cans.

"Dean. What do you want?" Henry says. He is stretching the tape across the bottom flaps of the next box. "I'm busy. What do you want?"

"I just don't think it's fair, that's all. I've been in charge of the food drive since eighth grade. That's four years of running the show. Ow! Jesus, stop," he says.

"Then move out of the way, loser," Sanderson says. More cans are unloaded, more cans roll, more cans clang to the floor.

"I don't see why I can't play a role here, is what I'm saying," Mike says once he is sure Sanderson's gone out for another heaping armload. "Number one it's unfair, number two it's idiocy since last year Mrs. Hendricks said my organizational skills were unparalleled. Unparalleled. But *nooo.* This year the *football* team is sponsoring the drive so all my expertise is ignored for pure chaos. I can't wait to see what Mrs. Hendricks says about your system. Ow!"

"Three strikes, you're out," Sanderson says. After emptying his arms of cans he bends over and faces Mike. "Fourteen, twenty-seven, twenty-three, hike!"

He charges Mike Dean, hits him square in

the midsection and hoists him over his right shoulder, carrying him out of the gym.

"Hey! Put me down!" Mike Dean's voice echoes, now an octave higher than usual, throughout the gym.

Henry tapes up the box he's just packed full and slides it to the side. He pushes himself up off his knees and stretches his back.

"Leave him alone," Henry says to Sanderson, who is pinging Mike Dean's head. Flicking it first on the right, then on the left.

"Ow! Cut it *out.* Ow. *Ow.*" Mike's backing up but holding off from running away altogether because experience has taught him that running will only ignite a chase.

"*Sanderson.* We've got to carry the boxes out to the truck. You want to get out of here, don't you?"

Will Sanderson turns from his prey and hurries back into the gym.

Mike is rubbing his head, which appears two sizes too big for his body. Henry is gone by the time he turns to thank him.

"Any day now," Mr. Beardsley says. Henry's hands jump into action and lift out the orange shirts. Below them are the yellow ones. Following the yellows are whites. It occurs to Henry that Mike Dean would be pleased. The packer had a system.

"Here you go," Henry says. "Size large."

"*Thank* you," Mr. Beardsley says.

Henry straightens up and winces with the pain in his lower back. He rubs it away and reaches for the shirts he has unpacked, setting them neatly on the folding table. He takes each one out of the plastic, careful to maintain the perfect factory fold.

Out in the store the sun is streaming in dark amber through the window but is nevertheless bright enough to magnify the floating dust particles that choke the life out of fresh air.

"Henry, give me a hand here, would you?"

He crosses the store to the formal-wear display as if he is cutting his way through the jungle of airborne debris. It depresses Henry to think this is what he has been inhaling every day for twenty years. He makes a mental note to schedule a physical soon.

"I don't know how it happened," Mr. Beardsley says, "but this rack is off about a foot. It needs to go to southwest about a foot."

"I forgot my compass today so which way do you mean?" Henry asks.

"Toward you. On three. One. Two. Three — stop! That's good. Now a little north. Too much. No, *north.* That way," Mr. Beardsley says, angling his head in the direction he is intending. "There you go. Perfect. Let me back up and see. Yes. It's perfect."

"Want me to mark the latitude and longitude in a ledger so we'll know for next time?"

"Very funny, very funny. You know what needs doing?" Mr. Beardsley asks. "Those fisherman knits need to get moved back. Actually, most need to get packed away. Just leave a couple out."

It has always surprised Henry that these sweaters sell at all. Baxter's sells the authentic Pringle-made sweaters still smelling of wet Edinburgh afternoons. Itchy and ill-fitting on most everyone but the man with a walking stick and border collie in the catalog that is packed in the woolly box, the bulky sweaters are a perennial favorite. He has seen the fisherman knits he has sold dart from station wagons to supermarkets and dry cleaners.

"Here's the sign for the shelves, once the sweaters are cleared out," Mr. Beardsley says. The sign is handwritten, proclaiming deals for those who have the foresight to buy cold weather clothes in hot weather. Twenty percent off. As far as Henry knows no one has taken advantage of this deal, but still the laminated square gets Scotch-taped back up to the shelf year after year. Fisherman knits are remembered only when rakes are pulled out and leaf piles are burning.

The stacking eventually gets done and winter turns to spring and summer on the right side of Baxter's. The left side is seasonless. Suits, jackets, ties, formal wear proudly keep their places all year round.

"You okay to close tonight?" Mr. Beardsley is already putting on his trench coat. Henry Powell is always available to close the store up at precisely five o'clock.

"Yeah," Henry says.

"Okay then. Don't forget to put the UPS cardboard out tonight, tomorrow's pickup day. And change out the bulb in the exit sign over the door, will you? It'll go out any day now — I changed it out six months ago today. I don't want a violation in case we get a pop quiz, if you know what I mean."

"Okay."

"Got any plans tonight?" Mr. Beardsley asks. He is tying the sash of his coat and is turning to go without waiting for an answer.

"Yeah, I do actually," Henry says.

"Yes?" Mr. Beardsley is halfway through

the door. He looks back at Henry.

"Old high school friend," Henry says. "His dot com went bust so he's back in town."

"Ah! The dot com bubble," Mr. Beardsley says. "What did I tell you? What did I say? All good things come to an end. I said it before anyone else, remember? I called it. Everyone out there on a gold rush in California and I knew the bottom would drop out. Remember that day? The day that thing — Webvan? — skyrocketed and the Dow went through the roof I told you then it would all go to hell. You can't *hold* dot coms. You can't *wear* dot coms. You can't *eat* dot coms. Nothing good ever comes from things you can't wear or hold or eat."

"I thought money can't buy happiness," Henry says.

"Precisely," Mr. Beardsley says, missing the point entirely. "Poor guy, your friend. I bet he had everything sunk in it. Well, I guess you're buying tonight! Don't forget the exit sign."

" 'Night."

The metal brackets holding the four-letter sign in place are hot. Henry curses himself for forgetting they would be and steps back off the ladder to get a pair of golf gloves from the sportswear section. Then it's back up the ladder, screwdriver in back pocket, calfskin protecting fingertips. The whole enterprise takes him longer than expected. Three more trips up and down the ladder are required as the bulb he originally forgot to bring up is not, as it turns out, the right wattage. He is back in the storeroom when the door chimes sound.

"Hello? Anybody in here? Hello?" reaches him in the utility closet. He accidentally kicks the broom hurrying out to the floor.

"Dammit. Hello?" he answers back.

And there she is.

"Hi," she says. Her hair, he notes, is shorter. "You're closing, aren't you. I — for some reason I thought you closed later. I forgot. I swear my head's been cut off these days, I'm just not thinking . . . sorry. I'll just come back."

"No!" Henry says. Indoor voice, he tells himself. One day everyone woke up and decided to start using this phrase all at once. As if *be quiet* is too harsh. Young mothers now gently suggest their kids use their *indoor voices* when they come to the store for school uniform fittings.

"No. It's a good time," Henry says. "I was just — I was — how are you? Wow. You look great."

"Oh, thanks," Cathy says. She looks down and runs a hand through her hair. Still self-conscious, he thinks. "Yeah, well, I came as a customer, actually. But you're closing so I'll just come back tomorrow."

"It's fine. Perfect time. Really. Wait, come sit down," he says. He gestures for her to take the first seat on the platform in front of the three-way mirror. "How are you? God, it's been a while. How's it going? You look great. Really great."

"I can't stay long," she says. Still standing she shifts her weight to her left side. "I just need to look at a couple of things."

"You cut your hair," he says. "It looks great."

They both laugh at his repetition. Still the laugh, while relieving some of the nervous tension, is an awkward one.

"Sorry," Henry says. "What are you looking for? You in the market for men's clothes all of the sudden?"

"Um, it's not for me, really," she says, "but for the groomsmen. My fiancé's from California and doesn't know the area so I told him I knew just the place."

He wonders if she, too, felt the air pressure drop. If she hears a rushing sound in her ears as he now does. He looks down and picks up a pin the vacuum cleaner must have missed.

When Henry looks up, the walls on either side of them suddenly move. Closing in on them. Like in *Star Wars* when they're trapped in a giant trash compactor. Or was it *Raiders of the Lost Ark?* Henry can't remember. He could swear it was Princess Leia — her white robes wet and clingy — down there with Harrison Ford, but then again maybe it was that tomboy love interest in the later film. The girl who could drink everyone under the table. Huh.

With horror he realizes his shallow breathing — mouth open like a panting dog — is audible.

"Are you okay?" Cathy asks. She puts her hand on his arm and they both look down before she hastily removes it.

"You're getting married," he says. He works on evening out his breath.

"I'm getting married."

Whooooosh. A conch shell sound parents tell children is really the sound of the sea.

"Congratulations," he hears himself say. "That's just great."

The next thing he knows, he is giving her a hug.

He looks away, but since they're in front the three-way mirror he cannot escape

Cathy. In triplicate. From every angle. She hasn't properly brushed her hair in the back, he notes.

"You guys still rent tuxes, right?" she is saying. He is watching her mouth move in profile. "I mean, it's been a long time. I remember you used to. Rent tuxes. Right?"

"Wow," Henry says.

"Yeah," she says. "It's exciting. It's just . . . well . . ."

"Awkward, yeah, I know," Henry says. "It's okay. I'm okay."

But just as he is saying this she is saying, "Oh, no, actually I was going to say that it's just overwhelming, all the stuff that goes into planning a wedding."

Henry knows he must look her in the eye. This is the moment to look her in the eye, he tells himself. But his stare is instead fixed on the pant rack.

"Wow," he says, looking back down at the carpet, this time searching for more pins. "So, wait, what's his name?"

"You don't know him. His name's Albert. Al. He's from Pershing."

"Wow."

"Yeah, you said that," she says. "Anyway, I better come back tomorrow."

She stands and pushes her purse strap up her shoulder.

"No, don't go," he says. He leaps up. "Stay. Just a second more. Just stay for a second more. I can help you find whatever you're looking for."

"I can't, Henry," she says. "I really have to go now. I was just going to do a quick once-over and then get going. I'll have more time tomorrow."

"But . . ."

"Yeah?"

"I don't know," Henry says. "It's just . . . I don't know. . . ."

"What?"

"You never called me back," is all he can think of to say.

"Huh?"

"You never called me back that time I called you. You said you were just going out for about an hour to run and do something and I waited and you never called me back."

Her mouth drops open.

This is the part, he thinks to himself. Here it is. The denouement of the book. Of the screenplay. Of the film. He personally conjures up the adverbs: Frantically, fearfully, hopefully. *Frantically* he searches her face for a clue to what will be said. Other than the momentarily opened mouth, which shuts when she realizes he is scrutinizing her, there is nothing on her face, in her eyes, that betrays her thoughts. *Fearfully* he thinks she will be scared away by his pleading tone. *Hopefully* he imagines this to be the part where she drops her purse and flings herself into his arms and says something along the lines of "I lost your number and then too much time passed and I figured you'd moved on so I didn't call you back but it killed me not calling you back and as a matter of fact I've never gotten over you, Henry, never and I've been working up the courage just to come in here to see you again and I'm not getting married I just said that in case you were already married so you wouldn't feel sorry for me, oh, Henry, I love you."

This is what he is preparing for. He even shifts his weight so that she can throw herself into his arms.

"Oh, my God, Henry. That was almost six years ago," she says. She pulls her purse in closer to her body. "Oh, my God."

The chimes sound as she exits.

1986

"Why does there have to be more?" he asked her. They were lying on his couch, post-intercourse, Henry drawing circles on her bare shoulder. He was quite sure the occupants of 10D could hear their every word, every movement, because he has, in the past, heard every word of theirs.

"I just can't stand it anymore," she said, standing, pulling her shirt from the pile of tangled clothing on the floor by the brass-and-glass coffee table he had just polished the night before. She is hunting for her panties. Henry reaches for his boxers and steps into them, flaccid.

"I can't," she continues, pulling her turtle-neck over her head. "We never should've gotten back together. Jesus, what was I thinking? Every day it's the same thing with you, day in and day out. The same. How do you not lose your mind? I can't even stand that we keep the same radio station on at work every day. I've been begging to switch it for weeks now, just a couple of days a week, switch to something else. But *you,* you're like a gerbil on a wheel in a cage. Five-fifteen, God forbid anything interfere with your five-fifteen *appointment.* I knew this was a mistake. But you called and I thought well this time things might be dif-ferent. This time he'll have his priorities straight. This time he'll be ready to go. What the hell was I thinking?"

She is fully dressed now.

"Marry me," he said.

"What? What did you just say?"

"Marry me." Henry kneels down on one knee.

"Oh, Jesus," she says, turning away. "Get up, Henry. Don't do this."

"Cathy Nicholas," he says, "will you do me the honor of becoming my wife?"

"What the hell are you doing? Huh? I'm breaking up with you and you're *proposing? Jesus.* Amazing."

He stands. "What? Why not get married? I love you. You know I do. I'd do anything for you. . . ."

"Except move away. You'll do anything for me except move away from here. To the city. To wherever. You won't leave."

"But why do we have to leave? Huh? Is it so terrible here?"

Cathy opens her mouth to speak but stops herself.

He practically whispers this part: "I can't leave and you know it."

He is aware that his voice is cracking back a lump in his throat.

"It's just I want something different," she says. "I came from a place like this. I always swore I'd get out. Live in the real world."

"And this isn't the real world, is what

you're saying. This, this lamp," he says, voice stronger now, pacing the room, "this lamp isn't real. This chair. This chair is fake. This isn't a real chair."

"You know what I mean."

"No. No, I don't. What's real, Cathy? I've never been real to you. I've always just filled up space until something better comes along. You think I don't know that? You think I don't know you're killing time with me? But nothing better has come along, has it? Huh? Maybe *I'm* real. Did you ever think of that? Maybe it's me that's real. This town that's real. Maybe everywhere else is fake. Did you ever think about that?"

She hangs her head. When she looks back up she doesn't have to say the words. He just goes to the door to unbolt the top lock she always has such trouble with.

They never said goodbye. That was the last time he saw Cathy Nicholas. Until this day. The day she came in to look at tuxedoes for her fiancé and his groomsmen.

"I guess *he's* real," Henry says out loud.

He looks over his shoulder at the freshly lighted exit sign. On his way out the door he touches each rack he passes by. Cotton. Gabardine. Wool. Pressed wool. Worsted wool. Polyester. Silk. He ticks the fabric talismans off in his mind. He turns off the overhead light and locks the glass door.

It is exactly five-fifteen when he pulls up to the house.

Henry pushes at the front door that now catches and has to be kicked from the bottom in order to fully open. Another mental note to get someone over here to fix that.

"Hey, Mom," he says as he drapes his coat on the coatrack filled with faded old jackets and windbreakers and a baseball cap.

She is in the living room. Eyes fixed to the television he bought for them a few years ago. He was quite pleased with the upgrade. A clearer picture, a wider screen and not so thick, so that the table it rested on (a low-ish cabinet, one wobbly leg, with books stacked in the shelf beneath the set) could be pushed back, closer to the wall, affording a few more inches of a living room that over the years felt smaller and smaller to him. Look at this, he began the show: finally an easy remote control — one that works — so you don't have to get up to change the channel. And look, no antennae on top to adjust — it'll pick up the stations without it. And look at this and this. And look at that, he'd pointed out all the features that had so impressed him at the electronics store half an hour away. And I've got a power strip back there now so you won't have to worry about it surging. See how good the picture looks? And that's on every station, even channel four. You know how that used to be so grainy? See that, there? It's clear. And see this? His thumb clicking on the volume button then the channel selector. It's so easy, he said.

The presentation was useless. He saw it the minute he looked at her. His mother appeared dwarfed by televised progress. As if the extra four inches of screen had been subtracted from her frame. A trade-off he immediately regretted.

This Henry realized once he placed the remote control in her lap. She'd looked at it as if it were an unwanted stray cat that appeared out of nowhere, moved in, jumping on her small lap, hoping to be pet. To be welcomed. She'd looked down at it — the remote — and back up at him in wonderment. Her eyes, formerly large and, while vacant, at least beautiful still. Dark brown. So dark her pupils were indistinguishable. Eyes he had inherited. That moment, though, the time he'd made the gift of the television, they were hollow. Empty. He tried to lock them with his. At least they used to *do* something, he'd thought at the time. At least they'd cry. Or squint in anger. Or occasionally curl up into a smile: forced up by now-wizened cheekbones.

"What's this?" Henry's father said when he came in the door to the new television. His tone accusatory, as if he'd found a dog had soiled the carpet.

"Hey, Mom?" Henry asks over the volume, increasing over the years to near deafening levels. Reflecting the decline, too, in his parents' hearing.

"What?" she says.

"Just coming by to say hi," Henry says. He crosses the room into the kitchen to locate a smell that had greeted him on entry. He knew it wasn't coming from the refrigerator because he'd just brought over fresh groceries two days earlier. In the cabinets no cans were found to be leaking. Baked beans, Campbell's soups, cling peaches — all appeared all right. It had to be the trash.

The foot pedal releases a foul odor so putrid he has to let the cover fall back down in order to take a deeper breath and hold it this time so he can see in to what it was. Opening it again, even through held breath, the stink must have entered through his ears, he thinks, because he can stand it no longer and reaches around the rim for the edges of the plastic trash can liner. He cinches it up and carries it out.

"Mom? What was that that smelled so bad?"

"I can't see with you standing there," she says, leaning her tiny body to one side so she can see past him. He moves to block her again.

"I'm asking you a question. What did you and Dad eat that smells so bad?"

"Your father isn't here," she says, leaning to the other side. "Move, I can't see."

"I know he's not here, Mom," Henry says. Blocking again.

"Henry Thompson Powell, if you don't move this second," she says in her old I'm-your-mother-and-you-better-listen-to-me voice. He finds it strangely comforting.

When he moves away she gyroscopes back to center for *Wheel of Fortune.* Henry goes into his father's study to leave a note and finds his note from the day before still there, exactly where he left it. Usually his notes were balled up and tossed into the trash, leaving a clean fresh yellow sheet for the following day. This was highly unusual and not at all like his father to overlook the very thing smack in the middle of his desk.

Upstairs he finds their bed unmade . . .

another red flag. Henry's father had made the bed every single morning of their married life. Spread pulled so tight you could bounce a quarter off of it.

"I'll see you tomorrow, Mom," he says, shrugging on his coat.

The park is his first stop. In all the years since his high school discovery of his father's "new job" he has never once let on that he knows the secret. At first he thought he would keep it to be used in case of emergency — some kind of blackmail he tucked away to be trotted out triumphantly if a wish needed to be granted and his father wanted badly enough to keep this from his mother.

But news of the football scholarship — a full ride, they'd promised him — had distracted him at first and then there were no other occasions that would have called for his blowing his father's cover.

It had fallen to Henry to get himself ready for college. All the money he'd made at Baxter's went to bed linens, toiletries, an art poster — Van Gogh's *Starry Night* — he regretted the minute he got to his dorm and saw others unfurling Farrah with hard nipples and race cars and rock bands, tacking them to their painted cinder-blocked walls with school-approved tacking paste that could be removed easily once the school year was over. He'd put the poster tube in the back corner of his tiny closet.

School supplies like paper, notebooks, pens and pencils were all covered by the scholarship. So were textbooks. And the meal plan. So it was okay that Henry had only seventy-five dollars in his pocket when he arrived at school. The bookstore was filled with T-shirts that read, "Westerfield: the Harvard of New Jersey," which he had thought quite clever until years later when he saw someone in a shirt that read: "Vanderbilt: the Harvard of the South."

He assumed he'd find a job before the money ran out not realizing being on the football team *was* a job in and of itself. His dorm-mates had a seemingly endless supply of money they used indiscriminately to make long phone calls on the single pay phone in the middle of his hall and to drink bottomless pitchers of beer. Henry was relieved to know he had a curfew — all the players did, even the upperclassmen. It provided a built-in excuse not to go anywhere that would have required a cover charge or alcoholic beverages.

By the end of the first month at school he had been proud that he had only spent five dollars and fifty-three cents but was dismayed to realize he had no idea what he'd spent even that meager amount on.

When his father called him home he had not thought of the Park Bench Blackmail Plan. It had not even occurred to him. When it did cross his mind — on the achingly long drive back with the guy he had found on the bulletin board, a guy who didn't talk much and had a penchant for country music radio stations — he knew it would not have worked. His father would never have been cowed by an idle threat from Henry. Besides, in his mother's state this bombshell of information would have been disappointingly ignored.

It is still light out when he pulls up to the far end of the park.

Henry had not realized the depth of his worry until the moment he sees his father. Alive. At least he's alive, Henry thinks.

But walking across the brown grass in his Allen Edmonds shoes crunching on sticks and pinecones, his heart quickens to see that his father is not much more than alive. In a blinding flash, he sees his father as the rest of the world sees him. An old man in a worn suit, frayed at the cuffs and at the pocket openings. A suit that, on his father's shrinking frame, appears comically large — the shoulder pads extending at least two inches past the skeleton underneath. A grim circus clown suit. His father's face is crumpled. Dilapidated like a gloomy house kids throw rocks at and dare each other to go near in famous Gothic Southern novels.

"Dad?" he says. He is standing in front of his father but kneels when he sees his father cannot seem to move his neck. His eyes darted up to Henry's face when he approached but they appear to be the only thing working in Edgar Powell's body. Immediately Henry sees his father has also wet himself. And sat in it. Most likely overnight.

"Dad, let's get you into the car," Henry says. But this is easier to say than do as Edgar Powell is stiff in the seated position, briefcase neatly at his feet, never opened. A can of diet Coke rolls back and forth on the paved path a few inches from the bench.

"On three," he says, recalling paramedics from long ago. He finds he does not mind reaching his arm underneath his father's bottom. This is my father, he thinks. This is the man who invented me. His other arm is behind his father's head, along his neck so that Edgar Powell's head is up against

Henry's chest. "One, two, three."

It takes all Henry's strength to lift his father. "Okay, okay, I got you," he says between breaths. It is all he can do to get to his car. "It's okay, Dad."

The tiny, raspy groans scare Henry. It is the only noise his father makes.

Henry balances his father on the hood of his car while he fumbles the passenger side door open, and then it's a real trick getting him into the car but he does it and is soon speeding to the hospital.

"Your father's had a stroke," the doctor is saying. Henry nods yes yes I expected so. He can't seem to speak, though. As if they'd both lost the ability to talk.

"We're going to keep him here awhile to assess the damage," the man is saying. He has a white coat on and Henry does not know what to make of this: the doctor has the very same Allen Edmonds shoes on that he does.

"Why don't you go home and get some sleep," he tells Henry. "We'll know more in the morning."

They had had to wait four and a half hours for his father to be seen and assigned a room and doctor. Four and a half hours in the emergency waiting room filled with unrecognizable faces Henry kept hoping would become recognizable. He searched the face of everyone rushing through the sliding glass ER doors but no one was familiar to him. They wouldn't be, of course, because they were in the hospital two towns to the west of their own. But they were *almost* familiar. Henry thinks of these people he would know intimately if he lived here. A parallel universe to his own. Their features are not much different from his. Having read a month-old *Time* magazine cover to cover and then a two-year-old *Forbes,* he sized everyone in the ER waiting room. Literally. Size 38 waist, I'll bet, he'd think. 42 Long for that guy. A game that lost its amusement almost as soon as it started.

And all the while Edgar Powell sitting, stone faced and brittle next to him. Waking rigor mortis setting in. Henry did not mind the smell of urine. It was a sweet smell that reminded him of childhood bed wettings that had temporarily won his mother's albeit negative attention.

"Can't he lie down?" Henry had asked on checking in. "He's got to lie down."

"I'm sorry, sir," the nurse had said. "All our beds are taken right now. Sorry." But she did not look sorry in the least. Not one bit.

The admitting nurse asked questions Henry was horrified to realize he had no answers for. He knew his father's birthday. And that he was born in 1929. But he had no idea if his father had any allergies. He and the nurse tried to get a response from Edgar on this but were unsuccessful. No surgeries, Henry was almost positive. Their insurance? No idea. Henry searched his father's soggy wallet for a card and found none. He was surprised, though, to find a library card as he had never seen his father enter a library in all his life. Any family history of strokes? Aneurisms? Heart disease? Diabetes? Mumps? Measles? Cancer? The list was endless and Henry hung his head in despair. He knew nothing about this family. Nothing.

What about *your* insurance, the nurse asked Henry. Sure, sure, he handed over his card, sorry that his father had to see this. This is just the sort of thing his father would hate. Henry is ashamed he ever thought of blackmailing his father about the park bench.

"Is he going to be okay?" Henry asks the doctor still writing things onto his father's metal medical chart. He has found his voice again. "Is he going to recover?"

"Let's talk tomorrow when we get test results back and we know more. I'm off first thing so you'll be seeing Dr. Bellcomb. He's a specialist in the field. He'll be able to answer all your questions then."

Nothing makes a man feel smaller than being dismissed from a busy and preoccupied emergency room.

Thus Henry shrinks out through the sliding glass doors. Shoulders sloped. Arms dangling Museum of Natural History–style.

Henry drives toward his apartment with the windows open in spite of the chill, so he can air the car out . . . the passenger seat still smelling of his father's decay. There is now a freeway that speeds him back to the town limits and he chooses the exit one before his own, the long way. Off the exit ramp he turns right and passes the post office. Rights and lefts he knows by heart. Slowly he reaches Main Street. Where there was once a dollar store there is now a ladies boutique, fancy purses primly winking from the storefront. The flag has been taken down from in front of the post office as is proper. Henry remembers flag etiquette from middle school when they all learned it during the end of the Vietnam War. Suburbs like his were resolute in their defiance of protests going on in the rest of the country. Hippies lived somewhere else, not in Henry's town, which seemed proud of the moat of indifference it had created around itself. Still, at that time, flags were hung on every other house (he counted fourteen on his way to school one morning) and Mr. Lee taught them that if a flag is not illuminated in darkness it must be taken down altogether. Or if it rains. Flags should never fly in inclement weather.

The old boarded-up store that never used to keep a tenant is now Pier One, selling low-priced wicker to the throngs of people who must want it, judging from the stacked chairs and matching tables they have on display. Further up Main is Cup-a-Joe, which always hurts his heart to look at. It is now Java Joe's, its apron-wearing employees numerous and referred to as baristas. Its prices tripled overnight. The hardware store is still here, and so, of course, is Baxter's. Two stalwarts that sneer at the young newcomers as if to say "We've been here longer than you were alive and we'll be here when you go, thank you very much." A right on Bridge, left on Elm (there must be an Elm Street in every town, Henry thinks) and finally another left onto a leafy street called

Stony Gate. The name has perplexed Henry for as long as he can remember for there are no stony gates on the street nor have there ever been. And there it is. Fox Run. He slows while driving past and is comforted to see it has not changed. The buildings with their ivy-covered stone walls that look dirty now because it is the time of year for ivy to fall off so only the brown vines remain. They look dead but Henry knows they will regenerate again in the spring, miraculously sprouting green as they do every year. Farther down the hill from campus is the field. His car tires crunch on the gravel and he puts the car into Park but keeps it running so the lights can illuminate at least the fifty-yard line. He stares out, motor running, windows still open, heat pouring out of vents he has to readjust so they do not hit him directly.

The play has worked. Twenty-four. He catches the ball, feeling it warm still from Wilson's pass, tucks it in close to his body for the crisscross run that takes him roughly ten yards away from where they knew the defensive blockers would gather, into a zone where he can pass to the running back. Ted Marshall. Marshall then is supposed to run it into the end zone. But where is Marshall?

He remembers taking a second to sweep the field looking for Marshall — a split second — and seeing it filled with the opposing team now bearing down in his direction. Marshall's gone.

Run. He thinks this word over and over as his long legs carry him, jump him over and around obstacles threatening to take him down. Run. Run. Run. Ten more yards. Twenty. Thirty. Forty.

And then he is there. Alone in the end zone. As shocked as everyone else appears to be. At first he does not know what to do — Marshall should have been there, he thinks. His teammates have broken free of the end-of-season worn-out white line of lime that keeps them on the sidelines, off the field of play. They are charging toward him.

"We're going to state! We're going to state!" The shouts surround him. Arms reach around him, hoisting him up on shoulders and he is bumpily carried along part of the field, toward the coach. In the dusk, his smile real, his happiness completely filling him so that he feels he might burst wide open. He raises his fist in the air like theirs all are but his is the one noticed, his is the one they all see from the sidelines. The Murrays turn to leave now that they are sure their dead boy's team will carry on just fine without him. Parents of the rest of the players clap and cheer. But in Henry's head there is silence. Beautiful, complete silence.

When he is deposited back down, the Fridge gives him a huge bear hug that lifts him again off the ground.

He trots past the team, past the coach who says "good work out there, son," past the parents who say things like "way to go, Welly," and "good job." Off to the side of the regulars, the ones who come to every game, the ones who know which number is which player, who sometimes even argue helplessly against a referee's call, to where Edgar Powell is buttoned up against the cold in his winter overcoat, a dress coat that fits handsomely over his three-piece suit. Henry slows his approach and his father looks down at first, but when his son is right there in front of him he looks up.

"I'm proud of you, Henry," he says. He extends his hand and Henry takes it. Firmly shaking it. When his father's grip begins to relax Henry tightens up his own, reluctant to let this moment end.

"Thanks, Dad."

With a sliver of hesitation, just a tiny sneeze of a moment, Henry puts the car into

Reverse, backs out of the parking lot and back into 1999.

CHAPTER NINETEEN

2000

Henry is looking forward to his lunch. He made a week's worth of lasagna the night before and purposely did not eat any for dinner because his intention is only to eat it for lunch and, anyway, he has always been of the belief that most Italian dishes are better the next day.

He hangs his overcoat in his locker, pushing the shoulders sideways so when he shuts the locker door it won't slide off the hanger in the banging. He keeps meaning to switch out hangers for one from the store that is meant to keep this from happening (the kind with a thin foam grip on the arms) but once the locker door is shut he forgets all about it. He puts his Tupperware container in the minifridge and sees that Mr. Beardsley, too, has brought in a lunch. Recovering from hip-replacement surgery has prevented his boss from walking up the street to Larry's Diner like Henry does most days. They have never eaten lunch together as they spell each other on the floor. Which is a relief to Henry, who is accustomed to reading the newspaper silently while he eats. And to Mr. Beardsley reading the newspaper is a group activity over which he presides, happily doling out topics worthy of discussion. "Well, I'll be damned," he might say, looking up to catch his companion's attention and then will proceed to read aloud whatever it is that has caught his eye. This happens every eight minutes or so. Henry timed it a while back one day when they technically did not even need to open the store, the snow was so bad no one was leaving their homes. But it had been a snow day for schoolchildren and Mr. Beardsley called him to tell him to please find a way in because mothers might take advantage of the day off to get errands done. But not a single soul entered so Mr. Beardsley read the paper sitting there at the counter by the cash register. Every eight minutes reading some inanity out loud to Henry. Never anything that might interest him (never sports). "The jury awarded two-point-nine million dollars to that woman who sued McDonald's for being scalded by coffee. Can you believe that?" or "Wow. Turns out Ron Brown was on that plane that went down in Croatia. Poor guy." Or "Chrysler and Daimler-Benz are merging. Huh. What do you make of that?"

Henry emerges from the back room and sees Mr. Beardsley waving the sign at him indicating that it is time.

"You're the traditional town crier," Mr. Beardsley says as Henry nears. "You've always been the one to put the sign in the window. So, my dear sir —" he says this part bowing, making a big show of the first day of the sale "— would you be so kind as to fill your Baxter's role with the same flourish and gusto with which . . ."

"All right, all right," Henry says, taking the sign from him. Mr. Beardsley was trailing off, anyway.

He carefully puts it in the same corner up in the front window and unlocks the doors while he is there even though it is only a quarter until ten. Fifteen minutes early. Lately he has found he has less energy to run back and forth across the store so he multitasks whenever he can. "Multitask" — a term he has only recently and somewhat begrudgingly absorbed. Typically Henry avoids words or expressions that appear out of nowhere and threaten to disappear just as quickly. "Twenty-four-seven" is one such example he cannot abide. No sirree. "No sirree," he proudly notes, transcends time.

They sit and wait. Henry busying himself with making sure the shirts on the ladder display are equally spaced.

Late morning, things really pick up and Henry is relieved for the break in monotony. A thirty-something man comes in and though he asks questions about a sport coat he ends up buying a golf shirt in a loud color that, in Henry's estimation, will never look good on him, and a pair of Dockers. Another, older, man comes in to see if any of the dress shirts are on sale and Henry tells him why yes they are in fact everything in the store is on sale and the old man nods and says I'll be right back and never is.

The mothers come, though. The mothers always come, Henry thinks. And somewhere along the line in the past few years mothers got more attractive. He notes the flat bellies where paunches used to be. Flat bellies on women wearing tight jeans (how else would he know about the flatness?) with sometimes two children in tow. He cannot imagine his own mother ever looking like this. So "put on" as if going shopping in town were an event. For her it had been, yes, somewhat social when they were very young, but she never got *dressed* for it in the way these women seem to.

Soon it is lunch and Henry retreats to the quiet of the back room for the lasagna. He unfolds the newspaper on the table next to his container but hesitates, trying to remember what it was he told himself he'd think about at his earliest free minute. What was it, what was it? he wonders. And then poof the thought hiccups its way back into his mind: that girl who used to sit one row in front of him in Western Civ. It was a survey course so it was in the auditorium, which had seemed like a treat to Henry. To have class in upholstered seats. Like it was a Broadway show. He loved that class in all its Feudal Law and Spanish Inquisition glory. All that and a redhead in front of him. He hadn't even minded the fact that it was a 9:00 a.m. class. Mondays, Wednesdays, Fridays.

Her name was Rita. He is pleased he remembers this part. Rita. He'd borrowed her notes several times after he'd missed class — regrettably — for away games. She wrote lowercase *a* like a typewriter would. In the margins of his notes he'd tried to do the same but his *a* looked like a cowering *d,* ashamed of itself for some alphabetical misdeed.

He'd masturbated to the thought of Rita plenty of times but never found the courage to ask her out. Something about her told him he'd have been rejected. Maybe it was the way she flicked her hair over her shoulder. She was nice about lending him her notes to be photocopied in the student center where there was always a line for the machine, but once when he suggested they meet at The Pub (across the street from campus) for him to return her notebook she'd said "Um, would you mind just leaving it for me at the front desk at Taubman?" Taubman was her dorm.

Rita. Rita. How'd he think of her again? Oh yes. He'd had a customer that morning who'd had the same color hair. Red but not too red. The kind of red that can look brown in a certain light. Not stripper red. This woman was looking for something for her father. He'd liked the way she rolled her eyes when she saw the price on the golf shirt he'd shown her. A natural eye roll, not a socialist one, for his benefit ("I'm with you, man. I'm not one of *them,*" the roll said), but genuine surprise that something as simple as a forest-green golf shirt could cost over one hundred dollars. She had tried to fold it back up before he took it from her gently. "Oh, don't worry about that," he said. "I'll take care of it." "Sorry," she had said.

He'd answered "That's what I'm here for" and regretted the clear indication that he was merely being nice to her because he was an employee.

"I was thinking of something around fifty dollars," she said. "Maybe a windbreaker? My dad likes to hike. I'm thinking something light would be good — he can tie it around his waist just in case."

Henry resists the urge to tell her men don't like tying things around their waists and instead nods approvingly and leads her over to sportswear.

Rita had huge breasts. He remembered that. Huge. Sitting behind and slightly above her he'd noticed — on a day when she wore a tank top (that fall semester had been unseasonably warm up until November) — her bra straps digging canals into her shoulders, they were that big. She sat with someone — a blonde? — who appeared to be a close friend in that they whispered a lot to each other even during class. But Rita's friend was petite and high-breasted and threw Rita into Ethel Mertz relief when they were side by side. Rita's breasts parted crowds during the busy time between classes and it wasn't long after the Taubman book drop that he saw her walking with a loud guy he knew from his dorm who always wore a Schaefer Beer T-shirt that read The One Beer to Have When You're Having More Than One underneath the logo.

Henry finds himself hard thinking about Rita. And he realizes that is why he is thinking about her. He hasn't masturbated in days. Can't even remember the last time. He keeps a travel-size bottle of Jergens lotion in his locker for just such occasions but just as he opens his locker he thinks of the redhead he had waited on. When he'd asked her what kind of windbreaker her father would prefer (over the head or zipper-down) she'd said, "I don't know. He's your age about — what kind would *you* want?"

This thought deflates him and it's all for the best, Henry sighs to himself, closing his locker, because Ramon walks in.

"Beardsley's calling you," he says. "He wants to know what's taking you so long?"

"Sorry but it's getting crazy out here," Mr. Beardsley says when Henry comes back onto the floor.

He looks around and realizes it is not that

it is crazy, it is that Mr. Beardsley either got lonely, which he is doing with more frequency these days when Henry leaves the floor even for the shortest period of time, or else he is hungry, too, and wants to take *his* lunch break.

"Okay. Whew —" Mr. Beardsley wipes his brow as if sweat has developed there "— now that it's a bit more under control I think I might go have a bite in the back as well."

The wind is blowing hard up Main Street. An unforgiving, unrelenting wind that whips the snow off branches and in doing so makes it appear as if it is snowing all over again. Every customer entering the store is pushed in by the winter weather, on which nearly all of them comment. "It's horrible out there," one will say. "Cold enough for you?" from another. Most step inside so quickly they don't mind, notice or are at all grateful for the fact that Henry and Mr. Beardsley tightened the springs on the front doors this fall so they shut quicker. Every little bit helps, said Mr. Beardsley at the time: he is becoming more concerned with heating costs and in the warmer summer months, air-conditioning. He'd determined, Mr. Beardsley had, that the time it took for the door to float shut would allow too much cold air to cause the thermostat to misread the overall store temperature and therefore remain engaged for much longer than was actually necessary.

So they tightened the springs. A move Henry considers an act of genius because just now Neal Peterson flings the door open to add pomp to the circumstance of his arrival but the door — with its newly tightened springs — slams his backside.

He tries to pretend it has not happened but Henry's grin will not allow it.

"Neal Peterson." Henry walks to him, hand extended. Emboldened by Peterson's humbling. "How the heck are you?"

For many, aging is a contest. Some choose to beat back nature and throw themselves into exercise, a healthful eating regimen, perhaps a disavowal of old vices bent on defeating them. Others make peace with it and, while not ignoring the fact that their bodies are shifting, seem almost amused by the weight redistributing itself, lines — wrinkles — reminding them of past laughs or frowns. Then there are those who give in to it altogether.

Neal Peterson has fallen into the latter bracket — shocking to Henry as he'd over-estimated Peterson's vanity. With a Ted Kennedy sort of bloating that wears just fine with Top-Siders and a ketch on the open seas but appears less jovial, more pathetic in town, Peterson looks much older than Henry. Henry wonders if it is still referred to as premature balding if the subject is forty — that wouldn't be premature, then, would it? he thinks. Peterson has lost all the hair on top of his head, only a Caesar laurel leaf wreath of hair remains. His cheeks, now fat, are shiny not from the cold — that sort of redness generally wears off once inside the store if wind-caused — but from drink. Henry assumes the down parka is constraining him to the point of his arms not being able to properly fall to his sides, but when Peterson unzips his coat it affords no extra room for movement. All of Peterson's clothes are too tight.

"Good, I'm fine," he says, shaking Henry's hand. "I *thought* I might find you here."

Henry knows this is Peterson's way of volleying back for the smirk Henry broke out into at his botched entry. The emphasis on *thought* implies, Henry knows, an expectation on Neal Peterson's part, of dormancy.

"Yep, I'm here," Henry says. You will not intimidate me, you big jerk. For a second he considers thinking a much stronger word, the kind Geigan might use for instance, but decides against it because he will not sink to that level for someone like Neal Peterson and besides these are just his thoughts. So maybe he should have thought the word *asshole* like he really wanted to. Henry has, of late, become troubled by his errant thought patterns appearing out of nowhere. Recently he had a similar thought about a much worse word. Henry Powell is not a racist, he thought to himself a few weeks ago. Not by the most remote definition even, no sir, he is color-blind and proud of it, thank you very much. It sickens him to think that just a few weeks ago, while treating himself to a dinner out and being waited on by a new server at a new restaurant called Imogene's down the road, a certain ugly word whispered itself into his ear. A word that has shaken him to the core. Called into question everything he thought he was. The n-word. A tiny moment that, if converted to a video image, would have amounted to a subliminal message inserted into a television commercial, not even a second in length. A burp in time. He had looked into her beautiful black face and thought the n-word. Really what he'd thought was "what if I lost control of my faculties for just one teensy second and said the n-word out loud?" But that counts as having thought the word and Henry is disgusted with himself for it.

So Henry thinks of Neal Peterson as a jerk not an asshole.

Two more customers enter immediately after Peterson and they are the sort that like to be hard sold. It used to confound Henry, this kind of person. The type that wants to buy *something,* they just don't know what. So they will offer themselves up as suggestible — a phenomenon Henry remembers learning about in Interpersonal Communications that fall semester. He and his fellow students had read that children especially can be highly suggestible in interview situations. There was an experiment offered up as evidence: "Your mother likes to cook you dinner, doesn't she?" and the child is nodding yes yes she loves to cook me dinner of course she loves cooking me dinner (the interviewer nodding encouragingly). But the mother had expressly stated she hates the kitchen and cooking and anything having to do with it within the child's hearing not moments before being interviewed.

These customers come in and don't brush him off right away when he asks if they are looking for something special. "Noooo, not *really*" will draw out. Their hand will touch this sweater and that, feel the arm of this hunting (but not really *hunting*) jacket — the English kind — remarking on how surprisingly soft it feels ("Huh. It looks so stiff on the hanger" they'll murmur). "No, not *really*" is lingering in the air, ready to be refuted by an invisible and unspoken "Sure you are. You *know* you're looking for something. Let me show you what I think you should buy today . . ." and Henry obliges, even though he was at first unfamiliar with their nonverbal cues.

The customers stomping off the cold after Peterson are a young married couple well matched in their mutual desire to spend money that exhibits itself almost immediately, before the cold has left their nostrils. "Oh, honey, look, here's that flannel overshirt thingey you saw in that catalog the other night," the wife calls out to her husband. The husband is sizing up the dress shirts, pants, socks, all of it, happy to be inside out of the cold and with his pretty wife's company in this new town of theirs in a store that hasn't yet overpriced every goddamn thing like Ralph Lauren who used to have similar weekend-in-the-Northeast clothing at prices those who didn't own weekend homes in the Northeast could afford but now, no, now he has everything priced so high it's like natural selection, like you're only allowed to buy these clothes if you own a weekend home, but places like this are throwbacks, the real deals the way it should be in small towns outside larger cities in the Northeast so fuck you Ralph Lauren we found the back door.

"Those flannel shirts are the most popular things we carry," Henry tells the wife. Her suggestible eyes sparkle and she claws her way down the rack to find one in her husband's size. Before someone comes in and snatches it from her.

"Can you put this up at the register?" she asks him, "I know he's going to want it but I don't want to carry it around."

"No problem," Henry says. "What's your name and I'll put it up there under your name." This part is sneaky, Henry knows. But still it's not like they're friends or anything. Telling her he'll put it up under her name implies throngs. And confusion. And a flannel shirt — size medium — up for grabs because someone else sees it on the counter put aside and you know how that can increase the odds of someone else wanting something. When it's earmarked for someone else — good as sold. Someone else has determined that this shirt — flannel, size medium — is good enough to purchase so why didn't you notice it on your way in? How could you have passed it up? It's not sold yet, they'll ask, looking over their shoulder to make sure this is not overheard. Can I just take it? I mean the person who asked you to put it aside might have changed his mind. And I'm here, right here, with my wallet out, ready to pay cash. Yes, she better attach her name to it now, he implies.

"Oh, great. Yes. Kelly." And he watches her move to the cashmere sweaters. She is not put off by the unenviable cost of cashmere, many don't fully understand its softness or its price but those who do swear by it, especially in small towns outside larger Northeastern cities. Especially Ralph Lauren. He watches her sort through the stack for a medium, first daintily, then, not seeing any mediums, more desperately, until yes aah at last here is a medium in just the right shade of gray. He holds his arms out for it as she approaches. "Can you add this to the pile?" she asks, already looking past him to the down vests.

"No problem. It'll be up here whenever you're ready."

Her husband appears to be in one of the

fitting rooms and so, too, does Neal Peterson so Henry makes his way there to see if he can bring any other size to them rather than their having to leave the dressing room.

"Neal? You doing okay?" he asks through the saloon doors.

"Yeah," Neal says. He pokes his head out but it is so large the door can only come closed so far and Henry is able to see past him an altogether unflattering and unfavorable view of Neal Peterson's backside. "Could you, ah, maybe grab these in the next larger size?" He has shoved an inside-out pair of slacks at Henry. The door shuts and Henry reaches his arm first down one pant leg, pulling it through, then the other. He tries not to think about the warmth of the pants, tries not to picture Peterson sweatily squeezing himself into what used to be his old size, tries not to take pleasure in the fact that he himself wears the same size waist he has for years not counting the bump-up once he stopped playing football and his body changed accordingly no let's not count that — who would? — it's really remarkable now that I think about it that I haven't gained much weight at all since those days.

Henry passes two pair of pants over the dressing room door, one the size Peterson requested, the other the next size up from that. "Here you go," he says.

He pictures Peterson standing there in his boxers looking at both pants and knows he is wondering whether Henry is trying to be a dick by implying he will need an even larger size than was expected or whether Powell is just a damn good salesperson, doing him a favor in not having to go back and raise the number again.

Henry knocks on the dressing room next to Peterson's. "Can I help you with anything?" he asks. But he knows it is unnecessary because Kelly the wife is already heading toward her husband with an armful of alternate sizes of the pants all newcomers snap up before anything else. Pants Mr. Beardsley has shipped in especially from a supplier not terribly far away. Pants that define the store for if a stranger asks an old-timer what Baxter's sells the old-timer will invariably and not without a glint of pride answer that this was the only place *off-island* to find true Nantucket Reds. Of course, the wink and nod among a certain set is that they cannot be *true* Nantucket red pants because once they leave the island (in boxes stacked in the belly of the Woods Hole ferry) they cease to matter. *True* Nantucket reds are worn — and faded properly — on boats bobbing on the Massachusetts Atlantic with Martha's Vineyard in sight. And so the joke is on the young married couples who buy them hoping to be accepted into worn-preppy circles, speaking a code they will never quite crack because their Nantucket reds remain more cranberry than soft fall-leaf colored. Had they seen Henry Powell outside the store, not a salesman just a man walking down Main Street — good posture, clothing just this side of threadbare, loafers shined but supple from years of wear — they would sniff an air of what it is they would like to bottle and spray all over themselves. That I've-been-here-all-along-before-it-was-desirable scent that they, the city dwellers turned suburbanites, try to affect with their khakis, their L. L. Bean moccasins tied just loosely enough to achieve a bored scuffle, their pink-and-green-colored sweaters draped across shoulders, arms carefully folded across both male and female chests.

"Hey, Welly." Neal Peterson is standing in front of the three-faced mirror outside the dressing rooms. "You still do alterations, right?"

"Yep," Henry says. "Let me grab some pins."

Henry works on the left leg first. "So how've you been?"

"Good, good, never been better," Neal Peterson says.

It occurs to Henry that people who refer to themselves as never having been better usually were in fact very much better. He pauses and looks at Neal's face in the mirror and sees a crinkle in his forehead that is there even though Neal's eyebrows appear to be relaxed.

"Yeah?" Henry asks, pinning slowly.

"The divorce was final just before the holidays, actually," Peterson says. "Merry fucking Christmas, huh? My lawyer calls two days before Christmas. Done deal. Merry Christmas."

"Jesus" is all Henry can think of to say. "I'm sorry, man. I didn't know. You got married when, like five years or so ago?"

"Thirteen years ago, man. 1987."

Henry stops pinning for a moment. 1987 was thirteen years ago. Thirteen years ago?

And he is genuinely sorry even though he knows Neal Peterson probably had it coming.

"Are you still in Danfield or are you moving?" Henry asks. He works faster, eager to finish this as he is less interested now in seeing Neal Peterson humbled.

"Oh, I'm staying there. For now. We're putting the house on the market and then I'll probably find something smaller but still close by. Close to the kids."

"Sounds like a plan."

Peterson flips half of the pinned pair over the door but keeps talking as he squeezes himself back into his clothes.

"So, when can I pick these up?"

"What about next Thursday?"

"Anytime's fine."

Not only does Henry find himself feeling guilty for his earlier satisfaction in letting out Peterson's much larger waist but he is surprised to feel a whoosh of weird love for this man, for their shared history. This man, who used to twirl his shower towel and dip the end in the puddle of water near the communal locker room drain, whipping it at Henry — Welly — or Wilson or the Fridge. This man who wore sunglasses inside. Who wore his clothes Miami Vice–style for a while before returning to tried-and-true wales and country club colors.

"I can get them to you sooner, actually," Henry says, wanting to do something nice for Neal Peterson. "Why don't I call you when we get them back. I'll put a rush on them."

"You don't have to. But thanks."

For a split second Henry worries he might lose control and hug him. He takes a step back and writes up the alteration ticket. Poor Neal Peterson, Henry thinks. I'll get his pants for him by the day after tomorrow. That'll be something. He won't believe how fast I'll get them back.

"So I'll see you," Neal Peterson says. "Good sale this year, huh?"

"Never better," Henry says, immediately aware of the symmetry of his reply and regrets it as he does not want to leave Peterson with the thought that he is mocking him. So he adds "good crowds" and hopes that will make up for it.

Neal Peterson ducks his head and shoves his hands into his parka pockets in preparation for the winter assault. He pushes the door with his shoulder and stumbles back out into the world.

Mr. Beardsley comes back out from his abbreviated lunch hour and asks what he'd missed.

Thirteen years. "Not too much," says Henry. "I'm holding these aside for Kelly over there." He is speaking in a regular volume — nothing wrong with her overhearing this, in fact maybe she should — and knows Mr. Beardsley is pleased with his salesmanship. He smiles broadly, then, in an unusual show of restraint for Mr. Beardsley, mutes it. It occurs to Henry they have traded places, demeanor wise.

Within ten minutes the door coughs up another face from Fox Run Class of 1978. Mike Dean, smiling, shaking his head, pulling a leather glove off his right hand now extending to Henry.

"Good thing I wasn't holding my breath," he says, and *pow,* Henry vaguely recalls a plan that called for them having drinks or maybe they were supposed to meet for dinner or oh no was Henry supposed to be helping Mike find a job now that he was back in town?

"Michael Dean," he says, shaking Dean's cold hand. He is hoping Mike will fill him in on what it was he clearly forgot to do.

"Or maybe it was a football game that kept you?" Mike says. "Just like old times, huh?"

Henry sees the smile is not as good-natured as it appeared from a Monet distance. Up close the brush strokes show how it is constructed, lips turning up over hurt.

"I'm so sorry, Mike," he says, still unsure

of what he had done. He shakes his head and lets it hang, a signal to Mike to forgive him and perhaps oh I hope maybe explain what the heck he is talking about.

"That's all right," Mike says. "I like Blackie's. You know — in all those years I'd never been in there. It's not a bad place. I can see why you guys all hung out there. I had a few drinks that night and then went back into the city after you didn't show."

The memory bolts into his brain: it was the night his father had the stroke. That's exactly when it was. They'd made a plan to meet there for drinks but he had ended up in that antiseptic hospital waiting room with his father while Mike drank alone and gave up on his old friend.

Henry tries to make a smooth transition into his explanation because he doesn't want Mike to realize he has only now just remembered the transgression. He looks up from his hangdog expression.

"Mike, I'm so sorry," he says again, "but my father had a stroke that day. I spent that night in the hospital with him. I should have called the bar to tell you. . . ."

"Oh, Jesus," Mike says, holding up his hands in surrender, the strings of resentment floating up and out of each fingertip, "I didn't know. I'm sorry, man. How's he doing? I feel like such a jerk. I'm sorry I gave you shit just then. I didn't know. How's your father doing?"

"Oh, God, no problem. I feel bad I left you hanging."

"My mother had a stroke a few years ago, actually," Dean says. "Left her whole left side paralyzed but she was right-handed so she still can write and eat and stuff. She's pretty good considering. They said it was rare — her age, no family history. Thank God, huh? Did he go through rehab, your dad?"

"Um, no, actually," Henry says, straightening up so the words can come out and he can get moving. "He died not long after."

"Oh, *Jesus,*" Mike says.

"Oh, it's fine. I'm fine," he says. "It was quick. They said he didn't suffer, so . . ." The intentional trail off.

Mike reaches out to pat Henry's back but Henry has anticipated this and takes a step back, scans the room and makes every attempt to appear busy busy busy so busy he can't spend too much more time with this customer he absolutely must must must get back to Kelly and her husband they no doubt need some help by now.

"I can see you're busy," Mike says, "so I'll get out of your hair. Just came in to see you, give the sale a shot you know. . . .''

"Yeah, yeah, take a look around. We've got some good stuff marked down. I've got to go check on a couple of people but let me know if you need anything.''

"Will do.''

Mike walks away through formal wear back to sporting goods, past the racks set in the middle of the store with the *priced to move* sign above them, sport coats and slacks shoved aside for the aisles these sale racks create.

With the flip of a switch Henry is standing in the hospital corridor, a small dark man in a green jumpsuit guiding a powerful-looking floor buffer that threatens to break loose from his grip at any moment. Henry watched the back-and-forth polishing and waited for the nurse to finish checking his father's catheter. When she comes out he smiles at her and pauses before going back in. The sight of his father's slack face, tubes up his nose, in his arms, snaking out from under the sheets, all of it makes him nauseous. Luckily, though, his father is unconscious and so does not see the sickened look on Henry's face.

He had called every Powell in the Portland

phone book, dialing information over and over again as the operator will only give two numbers for each call and unfortunately there are twelve B. Powells in the area code. Of the twelve, seven are home — "Sorry, wrong number" a secret relief to hear — but five are still unaccounted for. One is Brenda but he leaves a message, anyway. This way, he can say "Hey, I called every Powell in the phone book" later on, if necessary. So really four are still in play. "Who doesn't give his own brother his phone number?" he says out loud.

Mr. Beardsley was really good about letting Henry take the time off. They both knew it was fair as Henry has never taken vacation time, not once. Still, Mr. Beardsley did not need to be so kind in his "Oh, God, Henry. Of course. Go. Take all the time you need. Your father needs you so of course. You're a good son," he'd said. Words that had not registered at the time but revisited him in the single wooden chair beside his father's bed. That uncomfortable chair with a low back that Henry was convinced was meant to discourage anyone from even napping, much less spending the night. Which had not even occurred to Henry.

That first night — the night Henry left his

father in the hospital — after passing the football field, he returned to his apartment and packed a small overnight bag. Just the essentials and one change of clothes for the following day. Mechanically he packed his dop kit, stiff from disuse. Toothbrush, toothpaste, Old Spice deodorant, a tiny travel-size dental floss he had gotten from his dentist after his most recent visit. A comb. He zipped it up and placed it carefully on top of the underwear and pajamas already folded into the sail bag.

The floating Henry, the one hovering above watching all his motions, guides him over to the night table where he reaches behind to the outlet and unplugs his alarm clock, just in case. A strange thing to bring but floating Henry insists and so the cord is wrapped around it and it is stowed on top of the dop kit.

"Hi, Mom, I'm back," Henry says only fifteen minutes later. He closes the door quietly and sets his bag down.

The volume is still high but does not appear to keep his mother awake. She has listed over to the side in sleep and Henry, for the second time that night, carries his parent in his arms.

"David?" she murmurs into his chest.

"No, Mom," he says, huffing up the stairs

to the master bedroom. "It's me, Henry."

"Henry."

He unties the front of his mother's robe — she no longer bothers with regular clothes, just different nightgowns underneath a now paper-thin L. L. Bean robe — and slips her arms out of it one at a time.

"Mom? Mom, wake up, okay?"

"What? Henry? What is it?" The flash of recognition in her eyes is what hurts now. That flash, so rare, gets his hopes up that maybe the long nightmare is over. Maybe she is back, he thinks every time the flash occurs. But it is gone as fast as it arrived.

"I'm walking you over to brush your teeth, okay? Let's get your teeth brushed."

He wets her toothbrush and squeezes a line of Colgate on top.

"Here you go, Mom."

"I think I know how to brush my teeth," she says. Still, she moves it listlessly across her teeth, not brushing so much as rubbing it along.

Henry fills a glass with water so she can rinse and spit, amazed that he can do this so well. Pleased he is the type that snaps into action with ease. Floating Henry watches the display: parenting a parent is nothing else if not an out-of-body experience. I am here, Henry thinks. I am here and I will take care of all of it.

When her arm slows he gently jostles her, "Almost done," he says. And the arm moves again.

"Okay, here you go," he says, handing her the glass, his other hand on her back, in between her shoulder blades, ever so gently pressing her forward so her spit can hit the center of the shallow bathroom sink. "Good," he says. And he turns on the water to rinse his mother's spittle down the drain.

He walks her back to bed and watches as she does what comes most naturally to her: sliding into the bed, covers already pulled back. The lights turned off, he goes back downstairs to the dusty front hall for his bag and then back up to his old bedroom. He opens the door and an Egyptian-crypt staleness wafts out.

"Ugh," he says aloud. He flips on the overhead light and takes in the room: the single bed still made up in flannel sheets that certainly need to be washed as they had not been in years. The room is packed: over his small desk, the Fox Run trophies, varsity letter, Doobie Brothers poster, the flying, geometric *VH* for Van Halen, too, several newspaper clippings in which he was mentioned (now browned and curling wherever not tacked down), the St. Paulie girl on the ceiling, and then, of course, the Westerfield pennant jauntily stuck at a tilt on the wall across from his bed, next to the light switch. It had come in the freshman orientation packet and he had taken great pleasure in hanging it.

He took his alarm clock out of the bag and plugged it in on his nightstand, pressing the "time set" button with one finger and the "forward" with the other. Setting the time. It is just past midnight.

The following days were spent coming and going from the hospital. Whole days passed without Henry using more than a hand towel to wipe his mouth after brushing his teeth. His lack of personal hygiene a reiteration of impermanence — he'd found himself thinking several times that he would take a good long shower once he returned home, to his apartment.

But Edgar Powell took a turn for the worse — "too much time passed after the stroke," the doctor had said. "It's highly unlikely we'll see any sort of significant recovery." And then "I'm sorry" mumbled in haste. Within days his father was dead. And Henry's first thought, the first thing that popped into his head when the nurse on duty called to say his father "passed" was, he *passed?* Like he *passed gas?*

It comes back to him full force: it was a dot com. Henry remembers now. Mike's business going belly up. He had to move back to town because he lost it all when the bubble burst. God, I'm such a jerk, he thinks. He's always been a good guy. A really good guy come to think of it. And here I stand him up so he's forced to pay for drinks I was going to pay for because he hasn't got the money. And he's back here and so nice about it really.

"Hey, Mike?" he walks over to his old friend. "Can we try again? How about this weekend? We can watch college championships at that new place down the street on Sunday if you're up for it. I swear I'll be there this time." He says this with a no-hard-feelings smile.

Mike exhales and appears relieved for the clean slate this invitation is providing. Eagerly he nods. "How about you come over to my place and we can watch. I just got a new TV. All the work's finally done. You've got to come see it."

"Sounds good. Before you go just leave me your address. What time is good? I think the Notre Dame game starts at five."

"Five's perfect. Here's my card."

"You got a new job? Where're you working?"

"No, not really. Just had these printed up to make things easier."

Henry finds the fact that Mike Dean has a card but no job uncommonly sad. A face-saving move. Things must be worse than he had thought and here he had always assumed Michael Dean would surprise all of them with his success. All those brains, all that education (Henry seems to recall Dean went to Harvard), and he's unemployed and handing out cards with just a name and address and an e-mail. Then again, maybe he's onto something, Henry thinks. Maybe *I* should get cards made up. Not with Baxter's on them — Jesus, no — but like this one. Come to think of it that *would* make things easier, dammit. How grown-up to be able to hand someone a card like this one. Heavy stock. Here's how you can reach me, accompanied by a James Bond flick of the wrist. This is a damn good idea. Damn good.

Kelly and her husband appear to be satisfied with their loot and the promise of the new life these clothes will afford them. The husband is sliding his leather wallet out of his back pocket, Kelly is sorting through the items she is carrying over to the register, to be added to the two already on hold.

"I think we're good to go," the husband says to Henry.

Henry carefully folds each sweater, each shirt, the down vest, the flannel jacket, and of course the Nantucket Reds, ringing each up as he folds.

Mr. Beardsley, beaming, stands behind the counter next to Henry and makes conversation. "We've got raincoats fifty percent off, just so you know." To which the husband replies, "Oh, Jeez, we've got foul-weather gear up to here." He holds his hand above his own head to indicate the size of the pile. "We're Noah without the ark, heh."

Henry accepts the credit card and the implication that, since it was handed over before the final tally was made, this couple does not care about hearing the total. What he cannot accept is the fact that raincoats are now referred to as foul-weather gear. When did that happen? It's foul-weather gear if you're the Gordon's fisherman, Henry thinks, but when you're driving down Main Street on your way to the supermarket, it's a raincoat. Or a slicker. He could accept that term. But foul-weather gear? Come *on*.

He fits the card into the four tiny brackets

and takes a blank receipt, with its three tissues of carbon paper separating each level of nearly equally thin paper, and places it carefully on top of the card. Henry has always enjoyed the clunking sound of the slider across the imprint machine — back and forth it goes, pressing the raised credit card number all the way through the receipt. It is as satisfying in sound as it is in action. In much the same way pressing elevator buttons is thrilling for little children lifted up by amused parents.

Mr. Beardsley flutters to this customer and that throughout the rest of the day and, while Henry does, too, he finds himself already planning what to bring to Mike's house on Sunday. The poor guy is out of work, probably spent whatever he had in severance — is it severance if a company goes out of business or is severance when you get fired, he cannot be sure — on doing work to his apartment or condominium back in a town to which he probably never thought he would return.

He helps a short woman reach a peacoat for her son and thinks maybe he will bring chips and salsa along with beer.

He imagines hanging out with Mike the way he used to with Tom Geigan before Geigan got married and moved into a tiny brick house he is perpetually working on. Do-it-yourselfers, Geigan and his wife. Henry pitched in when it came to moving their few belongings into the house (and was as startled as they were to find that even just that one U-Haul's worth of boxes and furniture packed their home so tight it sometimes required a sideways turn between chairs in order to pass through a single room and the surplus of chairs had the unfortunate effect of lowering the ceiling). But when it came to tuck-pointing and cabinet replacement he bowed out and Geigan halfheartedly called him a "pussy" though never held it against him.

Yes, now that he thinks about it, Henry and Mike have possibilities. It'll be nice to have someone in the same boat, he thinks.

He helps a tall man find a jacket with sleeves long enough but that will require taking in along the back seam (the man has length not girth) and Henry rethinks the chips and salsa. Beers from around the world would be cool, he thinks, pinching and pinning the jacket from top to bottom down the man's spine. Finding beers from different countries. Beer from Poland. What's that one called? Oh, anyway. People think about German beer but there's beer from all over. Belgium. There's John Courage from England. He'll like that. It's kind of bitter but it's an amber, it's a good winter beer. Gives you a real thick head. Hint of fruit in it. There are always the Mexican ones: Tecate. Dos Equis. Foster's is big, too. Australian. He'll have had that, though, so maybe that's too obvious. I'll just go to the store and see what they've got.

The store Henry is thinking of is almost an hour away, just outside the city, but well worth the trip as it carries hard-to-find liquor and beer at warehouse prices. Since it opened in 1985, when skyrocketing incomes allowed for more than Pabst and Schlitz — indeed craved more if only to showcase a worldliness Wall Streeters were eager to cultivate — Henry has been there with some frequency, picking out a different six-pack each time, secretly appreciating his own sense of adventure.

We could make it a regular Sunday night thing, he thinks, carrying the jacket up to the register unconcerned that a pin or two fell out on the trip through the store. He knows pinning all the way around sleeves, cuffs or along seams is overkill — the tailor only needs one or two to lead the way. One week at his place with a beer I chose, the next week at mine and he brings the beer.

"When can I pick it up?" the long-armed

customer asks.

"Huh? Oh, ah, how about next Saturday?" he says.

Unlike other years, this year has brought only a few familiar faces into the store, a discomfiting fact that sticks in the back of Henry's mind like the forgotten toothbrush on the way to the airport. Whenever someone he *does* know walks through the door (Neal Peterson aside but then that turned out so different from how he thought it would which tells him not to be so judgmental and jeez next time I sure won't be judgmental that's for sure, he thinks), he is Giving Tree happy, branches shaking with delight over the return of whomever has remembered his store, remembered him.

Ted Marshall is therefore practically hugged when he stops in, surprised to see Henry but still warm, friendly and, Henry thinks, grateful for the chance to reminisce.

"Whoa, now *there's* the man," Henry says, rushing over to his old teammate from a middle-aged woman who did not really need his help, anyway. She'd been trying on fleece pullovers meant for men but she is large so it made sense in her case. She had been at it for nearly twenty minutes but none pleased her as they all seemed to hit in a very unflattering place along her hips.

"Hey . . . there," Marshall says. Henry does not hear the hesitation in his voice as a stall for name recollection but rather as something Marshall has picked up along the way. A nervous tick, that sort of thing.

"How the heck are you? Ted Marshall. Wow. You look exactly the same. But then you used to be the invisible man, heh. On the field, I mean."

"Aah, Henry," Marshall says, not even trying to cover up the fact that Henry's name has only just come to him. How could he not remember me he was always a flake this Marshall so I shouldn't be surprised still that's just bad form if you ask me, he thinks.

"How are you, man?" Marshall is still shaking Henry's hand.

"Good, good. Where are you these days?"

"Colorado," Marshall says, scoping out the store, nodding as he turns back to Henry. "Boulder."

"Nice place," Henry says. "I hear it's great out there."

"It's great. Unbelievable, actually. So the sale, huh? Still going strong every year?"

"Yep." Henry looks around and is pleased to see it is busy, the bustle somehow adding clout to his being there. "Still going strong. Like the '78 Wildcats, huh? Right?"

Marshall looks back at Henry and cocks his head to the side and smirks. "Yeah, right. Hey, where are those khakis? You know the ones? The red ones?"

"Nantucket Reds. They're right over here," Henry says, leading the way. "Just follow me. Kind of like you did that game, remember? I looked for you, man. I looked all over that field. Here they are. I have to tell you I can't picture Nantucket Reds in Boulder to be honest. . . ."

"Oh, Jesus, no," Marshall says. His chuckle warm and inclusive like an elbow in the ribs urging Henry to laugh along with him. "We've got a party coming up and it's an eighties theme so I thought these'd be perfect. I hate costume stuff but my wife, you know, she's hell-bent on us going along with it. I just wish I'd hung on to mine from back then. I figure these and one of those madras shirts you guys have — there! There they are! I'll be damned. This is perfect. Now I'm done. I just need these in a thirty-two. I can have my tailor hem them once I get home. Hey, do me a favor and grab a medium in that madras, would you?"

Marshall's fingers click along the row of pants to find his size.

"No problem," Henry says. "I'm going long. I'm going long." He is holding his arms up for the imaginary football, hoping Marshall will look up and play along and when he does not Henry becomes aware that several shoppers are looking at him so he shoves his hands in his blazer pockets and hurries over to the summer shirt rack. Medium, medium, no. A large and two smalls. No medium. Huh. He looks over at Marshall and takes a large, figuring his tailor can also make the proper adjustments to the shirt while he's at it with the Reds.

"Sorry, pal, no mediums."

Mike Dean would hate this guy, Henry thinks. He seems to recall Marshall being one of the bullies that tormented Mike but then so many did.

"Hey, when did Blackie's close?" Marshall says, handing his credit card across the counter. "And wow, I can't believe all the restaurants. We're going to Terra Firma tonight." And then, he stammers, "With, ah, my parents. Is it any good?"

"I hear it's pretty good," Henry says. "Loud but good. If you're in town long enough you should try Imogene's. It's around the corner, across from the movie theater. It's great."

"Yeah, and the movie theater's now a multiplex? Wow. I remember when there was just that one choice and then they bumped out to two screens and everyone thought it was such a big deal, having two movies to choose from. Remember that? Now it's a multiplex. Huh. I have to say I thought Blackie's would always be here. I wanted to take my wife there for a beer before dinner."

"Blackie's closed last year, I think it was. It hung on a long time but the rents are unbelievable now. Bud — remember the bartender, Bud? — he's down in Florida now. Some retirement village where they all drive around in golf carts. Even to the market."

"Bud the bartender. Man, I haven't thought of him in years." Marshall smiles a faraway smile. His signature is offhand and completely illegible. "Hey, thanks. And good to see you."

Just like that he is gone.

I never did like him, Henry thinks. He was always such a flake, never there when you needed him. Not really a team player. I really did look around for him that time. Okay, maybe I didn't *study* the field for him but I didn't have time. They were coming at me so I had to run. Maybe he's still holding that against me: that I made the touchdown not him. That's probably it. Why he was so quick to leave. Heck, I might hold a grudge if the tables were turned. The scout was there, after all, and maybe he thinks it should have been him. But he was fine, I think. He ended up at Princeton so it must not have been the scout so much as the way the team thought of him after that. You could just tell. They didn't look at him the same way. Not the way they looked at me, that's for sure. So come to think of it, that explains a lot. Maybe I should stop by Terra Firma later and really shake his hand. An apology shake: the kind that's tighter, moves up and down a few times for the grip to sink in so words aren't needed. I show up, give him the apology handshake and let him know I'm sorry, that I hope he lets it go. He shouldn't be letting it eat him up after all this time. He needs to let it go. This is great. This is a great idea.

Henry pulls out the phone book but it is a year old and Terra Firma is new so he has to call information to get the number for the restaurant.

"Hi, this is Henry Powell," he says to the smooth voice of the hostess he knows is required to wear black head-to-toe because that is what everyone is used to in the city and the town does not want the newcomers

— the city transplants — to feel they'd made a mistake moving to a town that might appear completely out of touch. "From up the street? Baxter's?"

"What can I do for you?" she asks.

"I'm wanting to come in to surprise an old friend who's having dinner there later tonight. Can you tell me what time the Marshall reservation is?"

"Marshall, Marshall," she says. He can tell she is moving a forefinger down a long list of names in the reservation book. "Oh, here they are. Marshall party of ten. Eight-thirty."

Party of ten? Henry was sure he'd said they were just having dinner with his parents. Huh.

"Is there anything else I can help you with?"

"Oh —" Henry had almost forgotten he was still on the phone "— no. That's it. Thanks."

Who eats at eight-thirty? That's kind of late. But he's still on Colorado time so I suppose it makes sense.

Mr. Beardsley's voice coming from right behind him startles Henry.

"They're back" is all he says.

"Who's back?" Henry asks, looking around the store for a reference point. There are only two people sifting through the half-off bins and neither of them looks familiar.

"Schmidt and Logan. They're back and they're interested."

"I'm still not following. Schmidt and Logan?" He racks his brain, hoping it will come to him.

"I told you about them years ago," Mr. Beardsley says. "They're the turn-around ones. They specialize in clothing stores. Stores like these. Remember? They were interested in beefing us up all those years ago. When was that . . . in the eighties sometime. You remember."

And Henry does recall a fragment of conversation, a wide smile from Mr. Beardsley, excitement, something like that he is sure of it now. "Oh, yeah. I remember. They worked on Clarke's, right? Clarke's in Westtown?"

He's pleased he can give Mr. Beardsley this: a clear sign he has indeed been listening to him all these years. The problem is Mr. Beardsley has no wide smile, no excitement, no pleasure in Henry's gift of recollection of the tiniest of details.

"So what's the problem? That's good, right? They're interested in beefing us up. What's wrong with that?"

Mr. Beardsley shakes his head. "It's not

good this time. They've got partners, architects, *planners.*"

"Still not following," Henry says. Hearing the door announce another customer he says, "I'll be right back."

"Can I help you find something in particular?" Henry asks then realizes he knows this face. "I'll be darned. Craig Eddy, right?"

They shake hands, the tutor and his old protégé. "Hey," Craig says. Henry sees he is no longer shy but still appears a bit starstruck so Henry tries to put him at ease.

"How are you? Good to see you," he says, clapping him on the back that is filled out now. "How's Hampden-Sydney? You home for the holidays?"

"Oh, um, I graduated a while ago," Craig says.

"Of course you did, jeez, what's my problem? Congratulations," Henry says, clapping him again on the back. "Any trouble finding a job? What was your major again? Your mom came in the store not too long ago and told me but I can't remember. History?"

"Yeah, history. But I didn't really do much with it, actually. I'm working in the family business now. I guess it's been about fourteen years now or so."

Henry hears a rushing sound and looks to

the front door to see if it's the blustery wind that sometimes keeps the door from shutting completely in spite of the tightened springs. But no the doors are sealed up shut. Henry pushes on, noting a physical really should be scheduled. It had been a while since his last checkup.

"Yeah." Craig is continuing in a kind attempt to fill the silence and to now put his old football tutor at ease. "I'm in the city. Banking. Same old boring thing every single day. But the 'rents are happy so I guess that's something."

Henry smiles. "So true. So true."

"Next time you're in town I'd love to take you to the club," Craig says. "You play squash? We could have a game then grab a bite after."

"You bet. I'd love it," Henry says, even though he has never played squash. "Say, what can I help you with today?"

"You know what I need?" Craig says, looking around, "I need a cummerbund."

Henry sees that Craig has warmed up to him and he is happy he now feels comfortable around his old tutor, comfortable enough to be as forthright in asking for help. So many don't, he thinks. So many are still cowed a bit. I'm glad, Henry thinks to himself, I'm glad this one's not.

"What's the occasion?" he says, leading the way to the formal wear section.

"I'm getting married, actually," Craig says.

Henry turns and shakes his hand again. "Congratulations! That's wonderful news." Can this kid be old enough to get married? Must have gotten someone in trouble. Poor kid. Trapped at such a young age.

"The thing is I have this bow tie," Craig says, reaching into one of the many interior pockets in his parka. "It's small, I know, and I hate it but my mom's bent on me wearing it. Belonged to her father and all. That's why it's faded and I wonder if you have anything that'll go with it."

Henry is again happy to know Craig is confiding in him, trusting him with this task. Letting him in. He pledges himself to this mission of Craig's.

"Ah, let's see." He reaches for the tie and handles it carefully, it being an heirloom and all. Funny how Craig just bunched it up in his pocket, devil may care. Henry holds it museum-artifact style. "Yes, it's small. Thinner. That's how they wore them in those days. We've gotten to be a bigger generation all around, you know. Taller, wider, bigger boned."

He holds the bow tie up against the assortment of cummerbunds they keep well stocked at Baxter's. The black silk is indeed faded and no doubt will become more so after being dry cleaned before the wedding. One is too pitch-black, another flat-out gray. The bow tie is in fact now presenting a host of problems Henry had not counted on.

"It doesn't have to match exactly," Craig says, noting the differing shades of black just a wee bit off. "Frankly I just want to be able to say I tried. I'd love to toss it but Mom won't hear of it. How about that one there, that plain black one. It's close enough."

But it isn't close not at all and we can do much better, Henry thinks.

"Let me ask you," Henry says, "when's the wedding? I have someone I can call who could send something over."

"It's next weekend so don't worry about it. This one's fine. Seriously. I'm so tired of all this wedding planning . . . can't wait for it to be over, frankly."

Craig takes the pitch-black cummerbund and turns to go.

"Are you sure? Because I could make a call. . . ."

"Totally. This is just right." Craig stuffs the bow tie back into his pocket and this bothers Henry all over again.

"Okay, all right," he says. "What else? You

437

need anything else? Cuff links?"

"This is it. Olivia's taken care of every goddamned detail so this is it. This was all I had to do. This and groom's gifts. You should've seen her face when I told her it was flasks. They're sterling, though, so that calmed her down. We compromised and settled on the block monogramming. At least there's that."

Henry is surprised and a touch saddened to see young Craig already so jaded. Like he is fifty and has already been married for so long it's the flaws he's commenting on, not the rest: not the beauty, the love, all that.

He would never talk about Cathy in this way, the hint of disgust crackling through every sentence like Morse code. He wouldn't do it. It's not a nice thing to do, he thinks.

"Hey, good to see you," Craig says after he's fished the money from his wallet and accepted the change.

"You, too," Henry says, "and congratulations again. Give my best to the bride."

"Remember, next time you're in the city look me up and we'll have a game."

"You got it."

Not long after Craig leaves, Mr. Beardsley is by his side, looking across the store, temporarily emptied of customers, shaking his head.

"I just can't believe it," he says, "after all this time. We've weathered so much, you and me." The pat on Henry's back is paternal and gives Henry a pit in his stomach with the realization that he has spent more of his life with Ned Beardsley than perhaps anyone else. Except, of course, his mother. But that is another story altogether.

"So what's going on?" he asks, but he is already catching on and it doesn't feel good, no, not at all.

"They're closing us down," Mr. Beardsley says. "That's just between you, me and the fence post if you catch my drift. People get wind of that and it's over before we want it to be. So we've got to carry on like nothing's happening."

"How do you know they'll close us down? Maybe they just want to change things up, move things around. Expand even." Yes yes that's it, Henry thinks, a surge of relief coming at the thought. "They could knock that wall down, the one that juts out over there. I've always thought it could really open things up, knocking that one down. Over there, see? If they pulled that out sportswear would be easier to see. Easier to get to.

Seems like that's the most popular part, anyway."

The pats are back and frankly they bewilder Henry. Mr. Beardsley's determination to remain pessimistic is unlike him and it is unsettling.

"It's over, my boy. It was only a matter of time. I knew that. These past years everything's going upscale, newer, *hip.*" Mr. Beardsley's lip curls in disgust with this last word. "Rents are skyrocketing. The owners of the building refused to renew the lease a few months ago and the writing was on the wall. I didn't want to tell you but that's the way it is. Better you get used to the idea. Plan for the future. For what you'll do next."

That wall could really come out, Henry thinks, and then customers would see yes they'd see we're just as contemporary as everyone else and besides everything can't be hip they'll need the staples, the stalwarts of the wardrobe, and that can only come from here, he thinks in one jumbled thought.

"I've put a down payment on a place in Florida," Mr. Beardsley is saying. "My sister's been at me to come down and this time of year it makes sense, that warm weather. Palm trees. Sand. It's a condo and it's got a spare bedroom so whenever you want you can come down and visit. Stay awhile. Put your feet up."

Henry is aware of his collar cutting into his neck and he pulls at it thinking he should really retire this shirt. It has not fit in a while. Today in fact he thought he'd give it one last shot, reluctant to turn it into a rag without checking one last time. But it is tight and right now feels like it is constricting the blood flow to his brain.

He checks his watch and sees it is almost time to go home. He'll think about this on the way home, he tells himself. Not now. Not with this damn shirt turning into a vice.

As if reading his thoughts Mr. Beardsley says, "Why don't you take off early, Henry. I can handle things from here. It's almost closing time, anyway."

"Okay," he says. He stalks off to the back room, to his locker where, he remembers, the Tupperware container that held his lunch awaits the dishwasher.

On his way back he loosens his tie — the Westerfield tie he bought at the college bookstore before driving off that cold day for the last time — and undoes the top button on the blue oxford cloth shirt. By the evening's end he'll have ripped it up and gotten four good-size rags out of it.

He touches the pocket of his gray flannel pants to be sure his car keys are there and takes the Tupperware and goes out the back door so he does not have to wait on a customer that might have rushed in at the last minute. Down the alley he walks, noting the Dumpsters, some new, some old, many jam-packed with fresh cardboard boxes indicating new shipments. Pier One sure seemed to get a lot of new stuff, he thinks, since the delivery two days ago. How can they fit it all in? Every damn surface of the store is covered with scented candles, napkin rings, rattan place mats, lamps even. And still they're getting shipments. He turns into the walkway between that store and the one next to it, under construction but with signs over the brown paper neatly covering all the front windows — signs that announce the arrival of Barnes & Noble. Opening soon, it says.

And now he has to double back up Main Street to where his Jeep is parked. Meters are going in. Identical holes in the pavement every few feet warn of the upcoming need for quarters.

He turns the key in the ignition and the radio, still on from his morning drive, coughs up Santana, but not really Santana, he thinks, because it's got this new lead singer who doesn't know crap about singing. Still he does not turn it down so "Smooth" plays as he backs out of his parking space. He makes that right turn at the light and takes a circuitous way home, the way that carries him past his old apartment complex. It only takes nine minutes to pull up to the front of the low clapboard building. Many of the doorways still have wreathes on them. They never used to do that when he lived there, he thinks. But maybe they did and he just didn't notice. The parking lot has been shoveled, as have all the walkways to the ground-floor units. The building superintendent was also very good about shoveling the exposed stairs leading to the second floor.

They had been good about letting him out of his lease, he remembers. They had first offered condolences about his father and had not even asked to see the letter he had procured from his mother's doctor spelling out the reasons she could not live alone, why she would need the care her son would provide. He had offered it to the complex owner, who dismissively waved it away as if insulted by the inference that he was distrustful of one of his oldest tenants.

"No, no, don't be silly," he had said, wiping his mouth and working on something apparently lodged in a molar. Henry had interrupted his lunch. "It's no problem. I completely understand."

"Are you sure? I don't want to leave you in the lurch," Henry said.

Henry had been relieved to know they had found a tenant quickly, before he had ferried the last of his things over to his parents' house. Surprised at the new rent — so much higher than what he'd been paying, nearly three times higher! — but still, relieved that he had not inconvenienced the owner. The couple moving in was expecting their first child and Henry thought how nice it would be to think of them in this place he had lived in for nearly twenty years. The pregnant wife came by one day unannounced, apologetically holding a tape measure, so sorry to bother him but would he mind if she got a head start on some of the things they needed to take care of before moving day. He had given her the tour even though he knew she had seen it before, pointing out that the shower handle had to be turned almost all the way to the red dot for the hot water to kick in, just at first, then it could move back to center just fine. It was really only for the first minute or so and come to think of it, it was never such a big problem.

She had seemed grateful for the tip and then waddled off to measure the front window for the blinds they were planning on putting in. The vertical ones were hopelessly out of date, Henry acknowledged with a shade of embarrassment that he had been able to live with them for so long. Horizontal would be so much better, he said to her. Yes, I was meaning to get to that, he had said. And then she was gone. He pushed aside two of the long dusty metal strips to watch her take the stairs carefully, holding the banister on the way down.

After a few minutes he puts the Jeep back into Drive and wonders what they ended up having: a boy or a girl. He would like to know, to be able to picture the child — crawling or maybe even walking by now — in the place. He is sure they childproofed the apartment but maybe they missed the outlet behind where his bed had been. Then again he reminds himself his bed had been moved out and they had no doubt plugged up that outlet before moving theirs in — they seemed like such a thorough couple, what with her thinking to measure for blinds in advance of the move.

Henry finally switches the top-forty station

when Savage Garden comes on. That's enough, he thinks. He prefers the classic rock one, anyway. But it is still in a commercial break (these commercial breaks get longer and longer, he grumbles) by the time he pulls into the driveway.

He no longer calls out for his mother when he comes in the front door. No need. He knows she is most likely asleep and this buys him time to get a handle on what to make them for dinner. He should eat before going to the restaurant. Have some food in his stomach in case they invite him to sit and have a drink. He has noticed lately that his tolerance is not what it used to be: two beers and he really feels the effects. Does not get drunk, mind you, but how awful would it be to show up at Terra Firma, embrace Ted Marshall and then overdrink in a manner that might require yet another apology.

From the freezer he takes a Stouffer's frozen pizza — the French bread kind his mother likes (he is a thin-crust man but this does not bother him, this bump-up in carbohydrates) and preheats the oven before climbing the stairs to check on her and then figure out what to wear later on.

"Henry? Is that you?" She calls to him once he is at the landing in front of the master bedroom that once felt so large to him and now seems suffocating.

Ah, that word again, the screenwriter says. Yes, Henry still imagines his life would make a fine movie. Maybe not the blockbuster he had once thought but one of those arty, Sundancey things that are all the rage now. Something quiet but powerful. Something that carried with it a grace, a magnificence . . . dignity.

Interesting choice of words, the bespectacled writer says. Henry imagines him to look like that actor on *ER* who was also in *Top Gun* but whose name always escapes him in its ordinariness. That is what the screenwriter looks like, though, to Henry. Why, why is it an *interesting choice of words?* he asks. It *is* suffocating in there, wouldn't you say? She's got things on every flat surface. Pictures in frames, piles of letters (mostly condolence letters but some old, like the ones Henry wrote her from college when he had pictured his father reading them aloud to her, both smiling in pride at the success of their golden boy), unread magazines she insisted on subscribing to: *Ladies' Home Journal, House & Garden* (he had had to convince her several times that *HG* was in fact the same magazine just a new logo), *Gourmet.* It's suffocating in there I tell you.

There's that word again, the writer says. It trips off nothing from you? Because I could sure use a flashback right about here. You haven't had a Brad flashback in a while and it would certainly even things out on my end. Remember? Brad used that word that last fight? Well, not the *last* fight. The writer flips back through his reporter-style notebook to earlier scribbling he had taken marking older, deeper conversations. But the second-to-last fight, he says.

I know the one you're thinking of, Henry says. He is quiet and uncomfortably aware that the oven is on and has heated up to 375 degrees by now.

I have to go and check on her and then I've got to get dinner going so no, in answer to your question, it does not "trip off" anything from me.

I'll get back to it, the writer says. He is smug, this *ER* doctor look-alike.

Anthony Edwards. That's it. Darn it. Why can't I ever remember that name? Henry shakes his head as he enters his mother's room after a double knock to let her know ready or not he is coming in.

"Hey, Mom," he says, turning on a lamp

on the side table next to the worn chintz-covered chair that has not been sat in in decades. He is pleased to see her sitting up, reading even, in her flannel Lanz nightgown. Her thin hair is a mess in the back: hospital hair, he thinks. Without the hospital.

"You getting hungry?"

"Not particularly," she says.

"I'm making that French bread pizza," he says, "so I'll bring it up when it's ready. You should get something in your stomach."

Her head is tilted back down toward the magazine in her lap and when he moves closer he sees it is *House Beautiful,* a new subscription he had gotten her for Christmas, tying a note around the current issue, letting her know there were more to come. The trouble is, the magazine is upside down. He gently takes it from her and turns it the right way up before leaving the room.

The frozen pizza clinks onto the cookie sheet. He slides it into the oven, the burst of heat feels good. The house is kept cold, as it has always been. Five to ten degrees colder than most households. The Powells had taken Yankee pride in reaching for lap blankets and sweaters rather than waste that oil on heating rooms that might not be entered.

In his room he removes his jacket and practically rips the old oxford cloth shirt off in frustration at its failure to last. But instead of changing from slacks into jeans, as he normally does, he keeps his pants on and reached for a fresh shirt. Terra Firma is the sort of place that, while not exactly requiring a jacket, sniffs at patrons who come in with anything less, so he puts his blazer back on. The brass buttons had been cut from one of his father's old jackets after he died, Civil War battlefield–style. They were good solid buttons with some type of insignia on them that made them look like they might even pass for a family coat of arms. He regretted not having asked his father about them for he was sure they carried some meaning. Once polished they looked super on his blue blazer, like he had a whole new jacket, really. He looked at himself in the full-length mirror attached to the inside of the closet door that could not open all the way because the bed got in the way. So Henry had to stand halfway in his closet with its high and unadorned light bulb (not counting the pull chain, but a pull chain is hardly an adornment) and even then he never really knew how he looked until he got to work because he had to stand so garishly close.

The closet door had not always hit the edge of the bed. He had not accounted for it when he rearranged his room after moving back in. The single bed was the first thing to go, replaced after calling a toll-free number that promised quick delivery and removal of the old box spring and mattress. The double bed was higher than his old single — a *pillowtop* that sounded like a fine idea when he ordered it but in the end meant an annoying search for sheet sets made for extra-deep mattresses. At first the bed seemed to take over the room but it opened up after Henry winched his old desk and chair out, moving them to the basement in case someone, somewhere along the way needed a kid-size desk and chair set. Carefully he pulled the old posters off the walls. *The Mod Squad.* He had masturbated to Peggy Lipton. Some album cover posters: *Chicago V, Goodbye Yellow Brick Road, Frampton Comes Alive.* The iconic Farrah. The *Rocky* movie poster: Sylvester Stallone in his gray sweatsuit, arms up in victory for his climbing those Philadelphia stairs. Best scene in the movie, Henry had thought at the time, carefully pulling it off so the Scotch tape would not take any paint with it. The college pennant was the last thing peeled off. The walls were finally a clean slate, which left Henry with a problem he stupidly had not anticipated: what to put back up. Plus, the posters had been up for so long the squares beneath them showed the original, whiter shade of paint. So Henry would have to repaint after all. Darn it, he had thought, moving his new bed and box spring and frame into the middle of the room. It took some effort to move his chest of drawers away from the wall, even after he had pulled the drawers out to stack them neatly on top of the bed. The whole thing was a mess and it bothered Henry very much. He borrowed a blue plastic tarp from Geigan and went to the old hardware store to pick up fresh paint. Once again and so many years later the choices overwhelmed and depressed him so he settled on an off-white, creamy eggshell rather than have to go with a color he most certainly would regret in time. Colors were just plain risky.

It had taken him two days to do the job he thought he could finish in one night after work. He had not counted on having to take such care with that intersection of wall and ceiling. The walls were the easy part. But the corners were murder so it stretched out for two whole days. He had slept on the couch, on his side with his legs bent so he could fit. Two restless nights (he had had to let the paint dry before pushing the furniture back in to place) that left him cranky and with a crick in his neck.

The first thing up on the walls was *Starry Night* but it had remained curled up in its museum tube since its exile in the old Westerfield closet so it refused to stay flat. Henry had to nail in the corners to keep them shackled there.

The pizza. He runs downstairs to pull it out of the oven just in time.

He works, he cooks, he takes care of his mother: *Henry Powell, ladies and gentlemen.* The applause rushes him up to the stage, to the podium where an award is handed him by a beautiful, young woman who quickly moves to the side so as not to get in the camera frame.

The oven mitt is old and is worn through exactly where oven mitts should not be worn through: in the thumb and forefinger, so Henry waves his hand in the air after dumping the cookie sheet on the counter. He makes a mental note to purchase a new oven mitt but knows this will never get done as even as he makes the mental note he crosses it off as useless to waste mind-space on such minutia.

When it cools he cuts two small pieces, puts them on a plate and carries it on a tray up to his mother. As he climbs the stairs he is seized with the urge to call out "Coming, Mother" Anthony Perkins–style.

Instead he opens her door and sets the tray on the spot that used to be reserved for Edgar Powell.

"Here you go, Mom," he says.

Though he has by no means tiptoed in and in fact has made no effort to be quiet, his mother appears startled to see him standing at the edge of the bed.

"There's your dinner," he says. "You didn't have much for breakfast and I see you didn't touch the sandwich I made you so you really should eat this."

"All right," she says. She shimmies up and rearranges the pillows behind her back, ready to receive her meal.

"I'm going out in a little bit but I'll be back soon," he tells her, standing now.

Henry eats his now cold and crusty French bread pizza on an unfolded TV table watching old *M*A*S*H* reruns. A nice tall cold glass of milk. He checks his watch frequently so dinner is enjoyed in haste and yes, nervousness.

At precisely eight-thirty-five Henry chooses his Chesterfield overcoat with the wives in mind. It is the kind of coat that looks good on just about any man. Gray herringbone, long, lined and fitting just right in the shoulders over a blazer (some overcompensate, he thinks). Henry has always noticed his posture is better when wearing it and that is what the wives will notice first. Posture. And the fact that he still has a good full head of hair, unlike Ted Marshall. But no, he chides himself, no, this night is about burying the hatchet. Reaching out. Healing old wounds. And perhaps forging new friendships.

With no mirror but the fish-eye one in the eagle frame that hangs over the front hall table Henry can only run a hand through his hair and hope that the rest looks all right.

It is eight-forty now and Henry knows this is perfect timing: he has allowed for their being a little late to the restaurant and then, coats checked, settling in at the table. He backs the Jeep out of the driveway and within minutes is pulling into a space just before the restaurant. He does not want them to see his Jeep — it is the element of surprise that lends a sweeter air to this unexpected détente.

He locks the Jeep door, pushes his shoulders back, posture excellent and exhales, watching his breath crystallize in the winter air. Just to be sure they are here — how awful for him to be the first there ("Henry? What're *you* doing here?" would ruin the impact and importance of his apology. How anticlimactic) — he stands at the edge of the front window and is grateful it is already partially fogged up. He peeks in and sees the tables are nearly all full, glasses clinking, laughter, the murmur of a crowd happy to be in such a warm and inviting place and not out in that brutal cold. And there it is. In the middle of the whole place. There it is. The party of ten. Tables pushed together, recessed lighting shining down. The rest of the room seems to orbit this table.

The whooshing sound races back into Henry's head, the same sound he experienced earlier with Craig Eddy. He feels light-headed and a tad sick to his stomach to see Ted Marshall, a woman at his side, Steve Wilson (Steve *Wilson,* he is most stunned at this as he had always thought of Wilson as his own), a woman at *his* side, the Fridge, the girl they had called "Boots," Neal Peterson, and "Figger" Newton, who, ironically, looks younger than the rest of them except for Steve Wilson, who looks more or less the same. All raise their glasses and Marshall is making a toast. Laughter as Boots insists on clinking with each person . . . even the woman sitting catty-corner from her, next to Figger Newton.

For the first time ever, Henry's shoulders shift forward and down in the Chesterfield. Into what any passerby would call bad posture.

CHAPTER TWENTY

2000

At last Sunday arrives and Henry wakes up with a Christmas Day feeling. Making breakfast for his mother, who will only pick at it, is not a chore but a way to advance time. Showering, always pleasurable, is, on this day, perfunctory only because Henry has very little patience. He is, in other words, excited about the trip to Mike Dean's house.

The day before he had settled on one six-pack of Foster's (so as not to seem too sophisticated) and one very obscure Polish beer he knew came in only rarely. On his way out of the store just for the heck of it, he thought at the time, Henry grabbed a bag of tortilla chips and a jar of Paul Newman's salsa (medium spicy: mild might make him appear wimpy, full-on spicy would most assuredly make him look like he is trying to be macho).

Mike will appreciate his thoughtfulness. He will appreciate the companionship. He will appreciate the chance to reminisce. Henry smiles at his own largesse, glad to be making such an effort with his old misfit of a friend, happy to have an even playing field now, what with him no longer a football player and all and Mike out of work.

Henry tucks Mike's calling card into the pocket of his down jacket in advance. He makes a fresh pot of coffee.

He cannot recall the exact year the rash developed on his right arm but there it was. Angry, itchy and red. His mother drove him to the doctor, driving the boat of the family station wagon to the back of the old Victorian home that had been converted into doctors' offices but had not the space for cars to park. Henry's mother had had to back out and very nearly hit the mailbox before turning to pull up along the curb in front.

It was this particular doctor visit that Henry first noticed the waiting room full not of squirmy children and young mothers and *Highlights* magazine but of women. All women. His mother's age. Other mothers of kids he went to school with. There was Mrs. Hartley. And Mrs. Childers. Mrs. Marshall.

Mrs. Evans was leafing through a magazine and did not look up when they walked in but he knew her from the bleach-blond hair. His mother greeted them all by name and Henry was mortified to hear her divulge the nature of their visit but none of the women seemed to care a whit about his rash and he was relieved and scratched at his arm until the nurse called his name. When his mother serenely walked past the others, he could tell she was pleased they got to go in first, even though the others had been waiting longer.

The rash was instantly recognized and diagnosed as poison oak and the doctor gave them a bottle of pink ointment and warned Henry not to scratch too much or he would scar himself for life. He got up to go and his mother told him she had something to ask the doctor and so she would see him back out in the waiting room in a moment.

They stopped at the pharmacy on their way home.

Abracadabra it is 2000 again and, opening the door to her room, Henry confronts the shell of the woman who has been slowly rotting ever since.

This is a good place for us to talk about Cathy, you know, Henry's biographer says when Henry comes back out of the master bedroom. I've been holding off but we've got to talk about Cathy, he says, scratching his head and following Henry back downstairs. You can't avoid it forever.

What are you, a shrink? Henry asks. He arranges the Sunday paper in stacks: one stack is the sections he will most likely not get to; another is the front section which he will tackle first; the third is pure throwaway.

No, the biographer says, pulling out a chair, clicking the tip of his ballpoint pen in and out of its body. I think the story needs it. Your readers will want to know.

Know what? Henry asks.

Like . . . do you ever think about her? She's married by now, right?

No, Henry says. I don't ever think of her. Next subject.

They both know that is a lie. Henry considers it a successful *hour* if he has not thought of her. He had tried to go a whole day not thinking of her but that was impossible so he broke it down to waking hours and slowly weaned his way down. Like a smoker cutting back from a pack a day so by the end it is one cigarette a day, savored until the filter is practically burning his fingers. If he has been really good he will allow himself a long thought of her at the end of the day, in his bed, staring up at the ceiling. He tries not to think of her so he can earn this reward. But it is never easy.

Anyway, this man, this biographer, cannot possibly understand how complicated it is, Henry thinks. Because it is not just *thoughts* of Cathy but it is her *presence,* like a ghost, in every room, across every street, in every shop, the next car over at every stoplight, that is the hardest to give up. He searches every crowd for her face, his heart simultaneously leaping at and being sickened by the thought of bumping into her unexpectedly. He keeps himself close shaven, hair clean and combed, clothes pressed if necessary but if casual then at least presentable in an outdoor-catalog way, just in case he sees her. Every single time the door chimes are set off at Baxter's there is, to Henry, the very real possibility it could be her entering the store again. In the movie theater he studies the backs of the heads in front of him, looking for her hair. In the supermarket he holds his breath each time he turns his cart into another aisle, in case she is there, buying baking soda or cereal or bread or or or . . .

Other thoughts are effortlessly removed from his mind. Like the picture of the small class reunion to which he was not invited. Deleted. Or the shot of his mother wasting away in her airless bedroom. Deleted. Right now he is needed elsewhere. At Mike Dean's. Where he can be appreciated, not ignored or struggling to clink glasses with Boots.

He settles on his jeans and a red-and-black flannel shirt over a white Woolrich turtleneck. A warm, laid-back, Sunday-football outfit.

And soon he is backing the Jeep out of the driveway, beer in the passenger seat, chips and salsa in the back. He has taken Mike's card out and has it handy under his right thigh where he can access it for the exact house number in between shifting.

The street is unfamiliar to him. It is a somewhat new one, paved to access the larger condominium communities and newly constructed mega-homes on what used to be considered the outskirts of town but is now folded into the same zip code as if the town has merely tailored its pants to accommodate holiday indulgence.

The numbers climb quickly and Henry drives slowly. The first gated community is called Stoney Brook and consists of identical brick town houses symmetrically dotting a black tar cul de sac lined by empty newly poured cement sidewalks. The streetlights work but their glow is too bright and not a single home is lit from within. No one would be outside this time of year, he thinks, as it is so cold outside. But then he and Brad used to have snowball fights long after it got dark. Until they were quite sure frostbite had set in to their fingers, the sticky snow nearly breaking the tips of their wool mittens. The absence of human beings or parked cars gives the whole place an Armegeddon feel.

The next and very similar cluster of homes are the single-family variety, tucked neatly behind a warmly lit guard booth with a sign overhead that reads Bridle Path. But the numbers do not match Mike's card so Henry drives on.

It is one full mile before he reaches a mailbox that sits at the end of a very long driveway leading in a stick-straight line to a very large house that glows from a distance as every light in every room is on. The next mailbox has ducks on it but a hedge hides the home it belongs to.

These houses appear to Henry to be on steroids and they confuse him: there is no way Mike Dean could be living here. He checks Mike's card against the street sign he sees at the first and only intersection he has encountered in these outer banks of the town's civilization. He is on the right street. He appears to be going in the right direction as the numbers are getting higher. But how can this be?

All that is seen of 1342 Granville from the road are squat lights lining a shoveled and winding driveway. This can't be right, he thinks as he drives his Jeep up to the curve in front of the massive colonial.

"You found the place okay," Mike calls out from a warm haze of an open door that is spilling central heating out into the night.

"Nice digs," Henry answers, reaching uneasily for the beer and bag that holds the chips and salsa.

"Oh, thanks," Mike says. In one motion he claps Henry on the back and takes the beer from him, host-style. "Thanks," he says, "I love Foster's. Jesus, it's freezing out here." The door seals shut, the glow enveloping Henry, thawing him out. "Give me your coat," Mike says. He is gracious the way people who entertain a lot are. Confident and generous.

Henry's head is moving sprinkler-style, taking in the front hall, the two-story ceiling above, the sweeping Scarlett O'Hara staircase. "What're you doing here?" Henry asks, momentarily forgetting the printed card he holds in his pocket, "are you house-sitting?"

Mike laughs from the front hall closet where, Henry notes, his coat is now hanging on a fat cedar hanger that slopes just right. He imagines — in a quick flash — his coat getting spoiled in that closet, refusing to go home with Henry, home to a poking coatrack that does not appreciate its need for width.

"Naw." Mike shuts the door and motions for Henry to follow him in to a large cushioned room with a suede L-shaped sectional couch and a projector-style big-screen television, the kind with the red, blue and yellow round spotlights that miraculously combine to produce a clear picture but look strange when you look back at them.

"I've been working on this place for almost two years now, God — has it been that long?" But his answer is rehearsed, Henry can tell. The same speech he gives all newcomers when he is about to embark on the grand tour. "Lucky for me I got out right before the bubble burst. What can I get you? Should we crack into the Foster's? And I love this Polish one here. I've got a guy that sends me a case every couple of months. I can't believe you know it."

Henry feels like he is swimming the back stroke, looking over his own shoulder through the splash of water to the end of the pool, which is never quite what he expects so he either swims into it too hard or tapers off too soon. All he can say is, "Bubble?"

"Bubble," Mike says. His tone is like a hand waving in front of Henry's hypnotized face. "Bubble. The *dot com* bubble." Mike pours the two beers into chilled glasses. "I'll tell you what, you need an Aeron chair, I can set you up." He raises his glass with a laugh, assuming Henry can commiserate with him on the surplus of luxury ergonomic office chairs. "I've got a couple hundred of them in a storage unit in Norwalk."

But Mike's voice sounds tinny and faraway. Henry's peripheral vision is narrowing and suddenly the preshow on the big screen sounds too loud and jumbled up with other, more mysterious and equally annoying sounds in the way of huge chain electronic stores. Pop: it all comes together. The tastefully worn Persian rug underfoot, the architectural lighting overhead.

Mike is not unemployed. Mike is a dot-com millionaire, retired early.

The chips are poured into a bowl he is told came from Costa Rica ("they don't cut trees down to make these things . . . they only use 'fallen trees'— talk about environmentally friendly"), the salsa into a smaller glass dish that also has a story ("we had these made up for everyone when we moved into our first loft south of Mission," he said in an aw-shucks-wasn't-that-quaint-back-then-before-we-became-mega-successful way, ("we wanted continuity, fluidity, a *common thread* from desk to desk. This big open space. We lasted there about two months and then went to the Valley and hired like crazy").

But to Henry the chips lack adequate salt and therefore have no taste. The salsa is watery and messy and not spicy enough for him. The beer, too, is a complete disappointment. There is an ample head on it but to Henry it tastes flat. He finds himself imagining his mother in an Edvard Munch scream, calling out for him and here he is watching a football game letting her down again and how can I continually be so selfish it's like a letter to Dear Abby where the mother writes in and says her son is never there when she really really needs him signed Miffed Mother and Dear Abby replies that yes indeed he sounds like a selfish boy but then maybe it's just a phase she has to weather.

The conversation is stilted. It goes something like this:

Mike: "I'm so sorry about your dad, Henry. I didn't know."

Henry: "Oh, well. No . . . it's totally fine. He didn't suffer."

Mike: "At least he didn't suffer. Yeah."

Both look at the game that mocks them in its glorious boisterousness: cheerleaders and spectators so rip-roaring happy it amplifies the silence that echoes through the new home that is more a house than a home.

Mike: "So, Baxter's, huh? How's it going?"

Henry: "Aw, man! Did you see that? That was definitely offside. What'd you say? Oh, yeah, Baxter's. It's good. It's great."

Mike: "Offside?"

Henry knows Mike has no interest in football but they both make an effort to comment whenever they can on the action on the screen.

Henry: "I guess not. I thought it was offside."

At half time they both pretend to be engrossed by the commentary so they aren't forced to make conversation.

By the end of the game, Henry stands and

stretches and says he had better head out, purposely not saying head *home* because that might invite Mike to ask where home is (he has managed to avoid this question all evening — calling attention to some action on the field whenever the question threatened to humiliate him).

They shake hands and Henry hears the door seal up behind him. The fortress has spit him out, he thinks. The Jeep is freezing inside but Henry knows not to turn on the heater until he has had the engine running at least ten minutes. Otherwise it blows cold air.

Home. The front walk. The box hedge along the picture window. The house dark. The door knocker — a lion holding a big ring in its mouth. The mail slot. All of it miserably duller after the shiny spectacle of Mike Dean's. He opens the door and steps on the restaurant menus scattered on the floor just inside. Takeout menus are a phenomenon that baffles him in their sudden appearance. Takeout used to mean the hot dog stand or even McDonald's in Westtown. But now, day and night, these delivery menus force their way in through the rectangle that has only a strip of brass to keep the world out, the menus contemptuous in their insinuation that Henry lives a life that would prevent him from leaving home. Sometimes he wonders if they are not malevolent but rather are calling for help, messages in bottles bobbing up to him from an isolated island he might never find.

He opens the door to his mother's room that smells like an unopened library book and sees that she is in bed, asleep. He takes her dinner tray downstairs and washes up. Henry imagines it takes Mike Dean a long time to work his way through the house before going upstairs to bed. His house requires "closing up." Locks on French doors checked. Multiple light switches. The odd lamp here and there. When Mike gets married — and Henry considers it only a matter of time as he has everything in place for a bride — he sees the couple tickling each other on their way up that wide staircase, one of them remembering with a groan that the ground floor is still on fire with lights. The job of reaching all the switches so arduous they have to make deals with each other to get it done. "I closed up last night. It's your turn," or, "Just help me and we can go up together." Henry has always thought the turning off of lights in the evening the death of another day. And in his case it is one light, the kitchen light that needs switching off, the glow from the television gone once Power is depressed on the remote. The streetlight is close enough to illuminate the house so he can move through the musty living room and hallway to the stairs. He climbs them and closes himself up in his room.

Henry undresses himself, carefully hanging up his black-and-red checkered over-shirt, sniffing at the turtleneck to see if it can stand another wear before laundering. He decides it can and folds it and neatly sets it back into his shirt drawer. Floating Henry stares down from the ceiling approvingly, proud that he is the sort of person who designates piles inside this shirt drawer. One pile is turtlenecks — the mock variety lower down underneath as he wears them with less frequency feeling foppish every time. One pile is undershirts — he had a real dilemma on his hands putting the undershirts in his regular shirt drawer and not in with his underwear as, technically, undershirts *are* underwear. But he threw his hands up and bucked the system and there they sit, next to turtlenecks and on the other side of regular T-shirts. In wintertime he switches out the pile and puts the long-sleeved T-shirts on top, short sleeves on bottom. Floating Henry is watching his every move and is glad for his own organizational skills.

Lying in bed earlier than usual, Henry has time to think and at first panics that he can no longer conjure up Cathy's face. The harder he tries to the more amorphous the image. He had combed the wedding announcements following her visit to the store on behalf of her fiancé but nothing had appeared in any of the area newspapers on wood poles in the library. Turning over onto his side he decides it must simply be enough to think of her moving around in the same world. Breathing the same air. Maybe even lying in her bed at this precise moment, also trying to get to sleep. This lifts his spirits considerably and he is able to go to bed satisfied.

CHAPTER
TWENTY-ONE

2001

"Here's the plan," Mr. Beardsley says, clipboard clutched against his left forearm, pen in his right hand. "I've put an ad in this Friday's paper announcing the sale. On Thursday they're coming in to look at fixtures and to get paperwork from me — records, receipts that kind of thing. On Friday I'll be asking you, Henry, to stay a bit late — I know you have an obligation around five o'clock but if you could come back here after and give me a hand I'd appreciate it. And Ramon, on Saturday if you could plan on being here along with Henry and me after close that'd be great. The sale will last all day Saturday, Sunday and Monday. Monday night it's lights out. They'll take care of the inventory we can't move out. But it's in our best interest to sell as much as we can because whatever's left over will have to be deducted from the final purchase price and that means paychecks will be affected. There's no way around that, I'm afraid."

Henry's eyes sweep the floor, taking it all in. It'll have to be some sale, he thinks. The smaller items, the accessories, will be the hardest push. Nothing you haven't tackled before, the biographer's voice whispers in his ear. You're Henry Powell after all. Yes yes that's true I *am* a darn good salesman and this time I'll put everything I've got into it. I've been holding back a little up until now but *this* time this time I'll dazzle them all I'll take the toughest things to sell, the others are weaker, I'm the strongest on the team it's up to me.

"Sound all right?" Mr. Beardsley asks them both. Ramon and Henry nod silently. Henry pledging to carry the team, bring them into the end zone triumphantly.

"Did they say what they're going to do with the building?" Ramon asks. Henry thinks: that's in bad taste right now, Ramon. He, personally, has not asked this question, imagining it to be too painful for Mr. Beardsley to have to utter the words. It's not like he has not wondered about it, too, but this is what separates Ramon and Henry: tact. Still . . . he looks at Mr. Beardsley and awaits the answer.

"Restoration Hardware," Mr. Beardsley says. He is looking down at his clipboard when he says this, as though it is a minor detail, an afterthought that means nothing. Something else to check off on the clipboard. He clears his throat and looks back up. "So we've got the plan, eh?"

Nods again.

"I'll be in the back room if anyone needs me."

"You got it," Henry says, and the eyes in the back of his head tell him Ramon is thinking he's a suck-up but what the hell did Ramon ever care, anyway. To Ramon it's always been a job, just a job, and he's got another one lined up down at Pier One so what the hell does he care, anyway?

The rest of the morning Henry daydreams about the past three weeks.

Three weeks ago he had gone for his weekly lunch at Larry's Diner and ordered a grilled cheese up at the counter. Shaking it up, he thought to himself, as he had always taken a booth by the window, ordering Philly cheese steak. On the stool next to him was a woman he had recognized from the cereal aisle at the supermarket a few days earlier.

"Hi," he said to her, pulling two napkins

from the dispenser bracketed by a Heinz ketchup bottle but he knew was refilled with another, cheaper brand, and yellow mustard with a dot of dried mustard at the end of the funnel top so that when it was squeezed the hardened bit mixed in with the glop, unless a diner paid close attention and squirted it first to the side of their meal. He unfolds one of the napkins and puts it lengthwise on one thigh and does the same with the other. In preparation for his grilled cheese.

"Hi," she said, wiping her mouth but not quite. "I know you from somewhere," she said. "Where do I know you from?"

"I think I saw you a few days ago at the A & P," Henry said. He is gratified she has recognized him, too.

"Ooh, yeah. That's where I saw you. You were getting Cheerios."

Attention to details, attention to *my* details, this is good, he thinks.

"I'm Henry," he holds his hand out, "Henry Powell."

She switches her hamburger to her left hand and wipes her right before shaking his. "I'm Celeste." Several used napkins are balled up and littering the space around her plate.

"Are you new in town?" He is aware of

the cliché but cannot think of another way of phrasing this question and she very well might be new and might appreciate his effort to welcome her.

"I moved here about six months ago," she says, nodding. "From the city. My parents are here and they're at that stage, you know? That stage where they kind of need me around more? When I lived in the city I barely got out here and they're still pretty new here, too, and don't have many friends so it was move out or get the guilt trip every time I talked to them on the phone, so . . ." She shrugs as if the decision was a light one. Then she reaches for another napkin from the dispenser. "I figured what the hey. I was sick of the city, anyway. Burned out. Ready for a change I guess."

Her talk was quick, the information so freely flowing Henry forgot to thank Michelle for his sandwich.

"Where do you live?" he asks her.

"I'm staying with my parents right now — I know, I know — but it's really just until I can find a place of my own and I haven't figured out where that is yet, you know? But I have my eye out and plus they've got the space and it's a nice place so I'm not really in any kind of hurry. Casing the joint, you know? I don't want to take the plunge and buy something and then find out it's not convenient. I want to be able to be close to them if I need to get there quickly God forbid but far enough away so that I have a *life.*"

Henry is watching her mouth move and notices she has dimples even when she is not smiling. Her hair is dirty blond and very thick so that when it is pushed behind her ears they stick out but not in an unattractive way. He cannot be sure since she is on a counter stool but she appears small. Her wrists are tiny, like a child's, he could easily form a finger bracelet around them, he thinks. Her skin is pale, the kind of skin that has been sunblock-protected for years, maybe even also guarded by a floppy summer hat that will stand her in good stead when she is older and her peers are all wrinkled from sunbathing.

She takes a bite of her hamburger, wipes her mouth, and says with her mouth so full her words are barely understood: "God, I talk too much. Sorry. What about you?"

"No, no," he says to the talking-too-much part. "Me? Not much to tell, actually. I'm from here. In the same boat you are, kind of."

"Yeah?"

"My mom's not well," he says, "so I'm

taking care of her. . . ."

"Thank *God* I'm not the only one," Celeste says. She swivels her seat to face him, chewing still. "My friends all think I'm crazy but you know what? I don't care. It's the right thing to do. And plus you can only push your way down the crowded sidewalk for so long before you get bruised, you know? I'm tired of it. Maybe I'll go back sometime but I'm sick of it."

Henry imagines her to be an artist of some kind. A painter? She is wearing a flowery, bohemian hippie skirt that grazes the diner floor it is so long and a bright red T-shirt that is just a wee bit off the color of red mingled in the pattern of the skirt. But she pulls it off, he thinks, but wonders how.

"Do you want to go out sometime?" Henry hears his words and holds his breath, wishing he could vacuum them back into his mouth, suction the thought back into his brain. She's just being nice, he thinks, making lunchtime conversation, and now I've gone and ruined it and she'll turn back to her burger and there'll be that awkward thing the next time I run into her in the market and she'll be with a boyfriend and after I walk away she'll whisper to him that's that guy I told you about the one that hit on me at the diner that time, remember?

"Sure," Celeste says without hesitation.

Henry hopes his exhalation is not as audible as it seems to his inner ears.

"That'd be nice, actually," she continues easily, "since all I've been doing is hanging out with eighty-year-olds for the past six months. But, wait. I hope you aren't asking me out because you feel sorry for me because you shouldn't. Feel sorry for me I mean. I don't mean you shouldn't ask me out, I just mean you shouldn't feel sorry for me. I've never had a problem meeting people before so it's not that but to tell you the truth I haven't been on a date since I moved here. I was in a long-term relationship that finished just before I moved. But now you're thinking I moved out here like a rebound from that but I didn't. I'd been thinking about it for a long time and plus I knew it wasn't going anywhere with Lars. That's his name. He had long hair and it always sort of bothered me. It's a metaphor, you know? Like he didn't ever want to grow up or something Peter Pan–ish. Oh, God, Celeste, shut *up*. See? I talk too much."

"No," Henry says. He smiles. "It's fine. It's good."

"And look you haven't even touched your lunch. Jeez, I'm sorry. I'll stop now."

"How about this weekend?" Henry asks, admiring her long graceful fingers and then her delicate nose and her wide eyes. How can this girl not have had a date in six months? he wonders.

"This weekend would be great."

"Maybe dinner on Saturday? I could pick you up at around seven."

"Seven sounds fine. I better get going," she says, chewing the last bite while fishing in her bag for the money to leave on top of the ticket the waitress had left in front of her. "Oh, let me give you my phone number before I forget. Call me and we can make the plans." She pulls a napkin out of the dispenser and scrawls her name and address on it with a sharpie marker. The napkin hits a puddle of ketchup so it looks like her address is bleeding. "See you Saturday then." And she is gone with a wave.

On their first date Henry and Celeste went to Imogene's and Henry admired her cheekbones, which made her eyes look catlike when she smiled but did not take up any unnecessary room on her face when it was at rest, allowing her eyes to widen back up properly. And guiltily Henry thought to himself that Cathy's eyes were, as best he could remember, beady and small and —

dare he say it — suspiciously like the rat's eyes in the Charlotte's Web movie. The rat voiced by Paul Lynde.

On their second date they went to Terra Firma and Henry noticed she cocked her head to the side when he spoke, turning her ear toward him so his every word was absorbed. Feeling a tad disloyal he seemed to recall Cathy appearing preoccupied when he spoke. In fact, sometimes when he and Cathy had gone out to dinner and he began to speak she picked up the menu while she listened and maybe she never listened to me now that I think about it.

For their third date Celeste prepared a picnic and Henry complimented her on her cooking (fried chicken) and really meant it. Like all picnics do, this one required a fair bit of kissing and Henry became easily aroused as Celeste was forthright with her tongue. Cathy had thin lips that had to be wrenched open by his own tongue and this had secretly bothered him all along.

On their fourth date they drove out to an orchard that allowed them to pick their own apples and Henry was charmed by her reach. After she pulled her first apple she said "Woo-ee, that was neat" and plunked the fruit into the basket he was carrying and jumped up to reach another.

Somewhere in the middle of dates five and six (both dinner dates), Henry found himself falling asleep to thoughts of Celeste not Cathy, and the transformation was as complete as it was inevitable.

This day, this second-to-last Monday, feels like a death march as Mr. Beardsley had insisted on keeping the news of the store's closing a secret until the ad announced it that Sunday. His thinking: people would be so shocked at the news they would flock to the place almost involuntarily and buy things out of sympathy or in attempts to take a piece of the town history with them before it all disappeared. Henry had told Celeste (and knew Ramon had told his wife as he would have had to since he already got that new job) and she offered to put a word in with her boss at the newly opened avante guard restaurant called 20/90 where she had secured a hostess position with some ease. Henry said no thanks and did not tell her he could not see himself working in a restaurant because he had not wanted to hurt her feelings. But he could not see himself working in a restaurant. Especially one whose name was pretentiously indecipherable.

Henry tries to see the store as a customer

might, thinking to himself that it would be smart to do his own shopping before the end of the week but he cannot think of what he needs. Celeste mentioned she likes to hike so maybe a fleece pullover from outerwear but he already had one — pilled and with a zipper that broke long ago at a Fox Run game he went to one Friday night after work and after checking on his mother — still he could not justify buying a second one.

Celeste also talked about going to dinner in the city one weekend and he knows that will call for something dressy, but he has nearly forty ties and several jackets and even a good worsted wool suit that was old but still fit him by golly so why the heck would he want another plus if anything is timeless it is a worsted wool suit. And his Chesterfield. Both were perfect for a city dinner.

Otherwise Henry could find nothing in the store that he felt was lacking in his own wardrobe.

"Hard to believe it'll all be gone, eh?" Mr. Beardsley asks him. You know what I won't miss, Henry thinks to himself, I won't miss the way everyone sneaks up from behind with their questions like a man can't have a minute to himself just one goddamn minute. No sirree, I won't miss that at all.

485

"Have you given any more thought to what you'll do next?" Mr. Beardsley asks.

"What? Oh, um . . ." Henry says, not wanting the conversation to go any further, hoping to buy a little time until a customer perhaps enters the store and pulls focus.

"What are you going to do once the store closes?" Mr. Beardsley repeats. "I've been so busy with all this and my condo closing I haven't had the chance to ask you. I'd of course be happy to be a reference for you if you'd like. Nothing but praise for my boy Henry."

"Oh, thanks," Henry says. "But I don't know yet. What I'm going to do next, I mean. But thanks. I'll put you down as a reference, I'm sure."

Here is what Henry is thinking and frankly has been thinking ever since Mr. Beardsley broke the news to him about the store closing: How in the hell can Beardsley act like he *doesn't really care,* I mean really care? All these years. He *used* to really care. He used to say all that stuff about all of us being "in it together." Being the "stalwarts" of the town. The "anchor" that keeps the town from becoming like any other. And now *now* when it's do or die he's just given up and you know what? He even seems *happy* about it. I'll just say it: he's downright *relieved.* Sure, he *says* "hard to believe it'll all be gone" but he doesn't seem *sad* about it. It's been his *life* up until now. So what was all that about anchors and stalwarts? Huh? What was all that? I *bought* all that. Goddammit, I *bought* all that.

CHAPTER
TWENTY-TWO

2001

"The ad is out," Mr. Beardsley says, holding up the *County Register* on his way into the store. Henry arrived earlier, to clean out his locker so he would not forget. Not that he would forget but it is something everyone wants to do in private: this erasure of oneself from one's workplace.

"Did you see it?" Mr. Beardsley asks him. They are standing by the counter and Henry is disgusted to see that his boss appears triumphant about the advertisement. His mind wanders from the huge lettering that screams at him from the ad between Mr. Beardsley's fat fingers (it is a two-page spread that contains the phrase "closing our doors forever," and that is just too much really if you were to ask Henry).

Henry walks away from the counter and busies himself with straightening the already pinprick precision of the sport coat display. Shoulders standing at West Point attention. An honor guard ignorant of the fact that within twenty-four hours they will be molested by greedy, grubby fingers eager to cash in on their demise. At least, Henry thinks, they could have a dignified ending. He realizes, standing there overlooking his kingdom, that he is hoping nothing sells. Paychecks be damned. No money is worth this . . . this . . . humiliation for what was, until now, a noble life. Yes, yes, that's it: *Not one item should leave this place from this moment forward.* Let them be captains, stoically and bravely going down with the ship. Saluting from the top of the bow before it is submerged in the deep water, never to be salvaged. Let the store have a worthy death, one that is equal to its courtly distinction.

He walks into the back room and sees himself, eighteen, lettering a length of masking tape to go up on top of the locker his new boss had assigned him. *Henry Powell.* Just like the locker at Fox Run. Then at the spectacular Westerfield. There he had no need for the sticky tan tape, his locker already had his name on it, printed up by a label maker. But here, standing here, he sees the same tape he affixed twenty-three years before.

He slides the edge of his thumbnail under an edge and eases it off of the metal but it rips into shards that have to be individually peeled and this ruins the moment for him. It should have come off in one long elegant piece, he thinks. More annoying is the fact that this lyrically melancholy moment ends with him having to shake the tape fragments into the waste basket but they cling to him and he has to pick them off, little pieces of his life . . . into the garbage.

Saturday

"This is the last time," Mr. Beardsley says, producing the sign from the back room, carrying it to him offhandedly, hurriedly, even nicking the shirts hanging from the leisure-wear circle with the edge of it but not even glancing back at them, Henry notes. "And it falls to you, as always, our town crier. Mr. Football Hero. Will you do the honors?"

And for the first time Henry is not annoyed at Mr. Beardsley's show of ceremony (in fact he thinks this time around it could have reached greater heights in its flourish but . . .) but is proud to place the sign in the front window. Same place. Lower corner by the front door. Stately. One sign. He likes this . . . that they are not shouting out their off-season sale . . . they are not pleading for business but simply alerting whomever might care that if they so choose they can find a bargain here within this establishment.

Celeste is the first through the door but is only coming to bring Henry coffee from Java Joe's, blowing on her own while handing him his. "Good luck today," she says. It is anticlimactic to all three of them, standing there facing the front door.

Ramon thinking: They better haul ass and move this shit, I need that extra money but then fuck the feds they'll just take out what they do and it'll suck so I'm not even gonna think about it but they better haul ass, these two with their sticks up their asses about clothes. It's just *clothes.*

Mr. Beardsley thinking: I wonder if I should double-confirm the movers? That man seemed pretty spacey when he came out to give me the estimate — yes, I'll double-confirm when I call to confirm the flight and I better not forget to make a copy of the pink slip for the car just in case.

Henry thinking: This coffee is worth that extra price. I think Joe used to water it down before and I like how now you can watch them pack the grounds into the espresso scoop getting as much as they can in there so it's brewed just right nice and strong and that sure was thoughtful of Celeste to bring it to me she had a late night last night at the restaurant so she must have woken up early just for me that was nice.

The day is filled with unfamiliar faces Henry barely takes time to look at. He finds himself moving slowly for differing requests: Can you reach this? Do you have a 36 in the back maybe? Is everything you have out or is there more in the back — I'm looking for this in brown not black?

"Sure I can reach it for you" comes out wooden, his arm-raising perfunctory.

"No, if you can't find a 36 out here it means we're all out" sounds rude.

"Everything we have is out on the floor and it never came in brown, just black" is just plain brusque.

The store closes and Mr. Beardsley says, "I think tomorrow will be better. Saturdays are errand days. Tomorrow we should see more people in here. More of our old-timers. Ramon, can you bring out the vacuum? Henry, will you straighten up the outerwear section? Why can't people hang things back up once they've tried them on? It never ceases to amaze me."

And Henry is happy that it is the Mr.

Beardsley of old who is barking these orders. Keeping up appearances. The vacuuming is a nice touch. Of course we should vacuum, he thinks.

By the time they are finished readying the store for the second day of the sale Henry's limbs are aching. Not his back but his arms. His legs. Twitching like they used to after two-a-days and games at Fox Run.

"You can't come to the game, Mom," he said the day she had gotten herself dressed up like she used to, when he was a little boy. She had had two whole days of normalcy, of cooking without complaint and without incident. Two whole days of looking him in the eye and asking relevant questions like "How was school today? Is the coach being too hard on you?" followed by genuine concern for his well-being. "I just worry about you that's all. Can't a mother worry about her son?"

But Henry knew two days was her limit. He saw her summer clothing and knew it was only a matter of time for it was cold outside and her dressing for June or July tipped her hand.

"Why not?" she asked him, standing there in her Pappagallo shoes, her A-line skirt, her matching headband, her Bermuda bag on its wooden handle. "I'm all ready to go."

"First of all," Henry says, scrambling for a reason, *one* reason, something that would not hurt her feelings but that would seem plausible even understandable, "first of all it's an away game and we're all taking the bus." It was not an away game but how would she know that? he reasoned.

"I'll follow you in the station wagon."

"But I don't know who we're playing, which school, and last time moms followed in their cars some got lost and then they got mad at the coach for not handing out directions and then he took it out on us in practice the next day. He called us mama's boys," Henry says, knowing this is not true but it *rings* true so what's the harm? "So please don't bother. It's not a big game, anyway. Come to the Rye game. That's a big one later on in the season. That'd be great if you could come to that." He says this knowing she will forget all about the Rye game when the next prescription gets filled. He's not worried about that part.

Still, he held his breath as she considered his words and he imagined them to be like spaghetti noodles thrown onto the wall, the cook hoping they'll stick.

"That coach works you so hard already,"

she said, "I can't believe he would call you mama's boys. I wouldn't get lost but just in case I won't come. Far be it for me to be the mother who gets lost and then everyone would hate me for making their boys suffer."

She pats him on the back and walks into the kitchen.

This is a triumph of gargantuan proportions. When he was sure she was safely out of sight he raised his fists in a victory sign, grabbed his bag and was out the door with a "see you later" and without another thought.

Until. Until midway through the game he glanced over (funny, he never glanced at the crowd of random student supporters or parents), but this time he happened to look over and there she was. In front of the wood-trimmed station wagon, freezing no doubt, but with her arms by her sides, one hand prissily holding that Bermuda bag, looking directly at him. He had to look away when the coach called an offense huddle but on his way over he turned again to see her and she was gone.

When he returned that night she was already asleep, prescription filled, standing guard on her nightstand.

He ate his dinner alone that night, legs

twitching from the running he had done in the game they had again won.

Sunday

The store is again filled in waves mostly by people Henry knows from other stores in town, people who normally would not be able to afford shopping at Baxter's but are now taking advantage of the deeply discounted items he wishes were still out of their reach. It is a terrible thought and Henry feels momentarily bad for even suggesting it to his own self but really, this — these clothes, this store — has been what has set him apart from the rest. Now with all of them scrabbling for the very same items hanging in his closet at home there will be no differentiation whatsoever. Henry vows never to think this thought again, it is so deplorable of him to have even considered it for a moment. He banishes it from his brain and sets to work helping any and all who walk through the doors on this Sunday to prove he is in fact a good person, an egalitarian, impartial, unbiased, that's me, he thinks.

At five-fifteen he tells Mr. Beardsley he will return and rushes out to his car, sick with the thought that he is missing his time slot, hoping she is asleep and does not notice. On his way up Main Street he pictures her looking at the clock by her bed, under her lamp, seeing that it is five-twenty now and wondering, *worrying,* about him. Maybe he drowned, he fears she is thinking . . . *maybe he drowned, too.*

And he breaks the speed limit to get home, pushes the door open, drops his keys on the front hall table.

"Mom?"

She is not asleep but has been looking out the window (worrying? Was she worrying?) and turns her head slowly to face him.

"You okay?" he asks, breathless (he makes a mental note to see his doctor about his lungs. Lately he's become out of breath at the slightest of exertions).

"David?" she says, staring at the television set.

"No, Mom. It's me," he says. "Henry." Then adds, "You okay?"

When he opens the curtains the brightness surprises her.

"Are you just home from football? How was practice?"

"I'm home from work, Mom," he says, lifting her up and off the couch to carry her to her bedroom. "Remember?"

She shimmies down under the sheets he neatly tucks around her, burrito-style. She smiles up at him and closes her eyes. He waits a moment before turning out the light and becomes frightened that this might be the last time he sees her alive. The thought so alarms him that he shakes her awake.

"How was work?" she says, eyes wide at the interruption in her drifting off to sleep.

Yes, how was work? asks the biographer, now bearded and sitting back in the shadows on that slipcovered chair that is never used. What is it, Henry? They both ask him with their eyes.

He waits a moment and before her eyes close again he says, "You know what? It was a hard day," he says. Then, "Bye, Mom. I'm going out for a while but I'll be back later, okay? I'll check on you later."

Back at the store Ramon is vacuuming and Mr. Beardsley is busy with the receipts for the day.

"How'd we do?" Henry asks, after locking the door behind him. As if hoards of shoppers would try to enter the store after hours.

"We did okay," Mr. Beardsley says. "We did just fine. Will you handle outerwear again? I swear it's like these people are animals. I remember our old customers. Remember, Henry? Mr. Warren? Mr. Childers? None of them would just drop coats that didn't fit onto the floor. It wouldn't even occur to them. But these people . . . well, it just goes to show you — it's time to go. It's a sign, I guess."

At the end of the day again Henry limps home after cleaning up and restoring order, once again readying the store for its last day of business.

Celeste calls and suggests a movie but he declines, telling her he is too tired and will see her later. She asks him if he is blowing her off and he says no, of course not, no, I'm just really tired and he means it in fact he cannot imagine her thinking for one second he is blowing her off but instead convinces himself she will no doubt be the one to break it off. When she sees I'm unemployed and have no plan. Celeste is the type to have a plan so it will be Celeste who blows me off. And I won't blame her. No sirree.

Monday
September 10
The last day.

A nice ending if I do say so myself, the biographer says to Henry from the passenger seat of the Jeep on his way in to work. Store closing, Henry leaving — there's symmetry to that, don't you think? He makes a note about brackets and bookends and turns in his seat to face Henry. What do you think? What are your thoughts on this day, Henry Powell? He is laughing asking this, trying to make himself sound more formal. For a second Henry wants to clock him for his flippant tone.

But really it worries Henry that he has no thoughts whatsoever.

That's not entirely true, though, is it? the biographer asks.

I guess not. Henry pauses before saying: Here is what I am thinking, if you really need to know.

I'm thinking it's just another day. It's just another day. All these people — they're hurrying for just another day of work. They're hurrying in to Java Joe's for another cup of coffee (he curls his lip when he says the name of the place for emphasis of its being able to do what Baxter's cannot . . . stay afloat). To them nothing's different, he says.

And to you? What about you? his passenger asks.

Henry imagines that this writer is trying to squeeze out a dramatic chapter title from him. He's lazy, Henry thinks. All this time asking me for answers: he should be able to figure it out for his goddamned self. I'm tired of carrying him. Doing the heavy lifting.

You wanted to know what I'm thinking, Henry says. That's what I'm thinking. I'm thinking it's weird these people are having just another day.

When you're not, says the biographer.

Henry has already parked his car in front of the store and turned off the engine. He looks out the driver's-side window and watches the spaces start filling up, people fishing in pockets for quarters now necessary to visit downtown.

When I'm not, Henry says.

The customers — these last cherished customers — are again annoyingly unremarkable in their demeanor and in their purchases and it occurs to Henry that this is the way all things highly anticipated end up. The way Christmas Eve is so much better than Christmas Day. He had thought the sale would draw in old friends, acquaintances at least, people who would appreciate the gravity of the situation. People who would know what it meant to have this store close. But then everything is possible on Christmas Eve.

Mr. Beardsley is busy with the agent representing Schmidt and Logan, keys are turned over, papers, file folders, murmured reminders to call about this and that over the next few days. The building owner is there, too. But Henry sees them as outlines of human beings, mouths moving, hands shaking, backs patted, fingers pointing toward the door, the men standing aside so the agent, the only female, can be the first out — gentlemen all. But this is a black-and-white cartoon to Henry . . . like stills on a drafting table at Disney — stage one, before they are handed over to the next animator to be filled in with color and life. Their movements are the stills — piled on top of one another — flipped by the thumb to show the action, moving clumsily because, after all, it is stage one of animation.

Then Mr. Beardsley is approaching. "Henry? It's time to go."

"Can I . . . ah . . . can I just have a moment?" Thankfully Mr. Beardsley sees that this is a difficult and meaningful request and so says nothing but retreats to the others and ushers them all out.

The racks are still filled. Not to brimming, no. A lot has sold. The herd has been culled, Henry thinks. As he looks around it seems the remaining clothes are calling out to him. The tweed jackets bending at their patched

502

sleeves to wave. The shirts, those classic oxford cloths, intertwine arms and drink toasts like lovers do to each other at champagne-fueled weddings. The pants bend at the knees and look like they, too, are moving, dancing? Or are they all beckoning? Begging him not to leave. Not to leave them alone. Not like this.

And then Mr. Beardsley is calling from the front door: "Henry? It's time, son."

He takes one last look around and knows the clothes were pushing him out. Pushing him on. Waving goodbye. Making it all right for him to go out into the world.

"Where do you want to go?" Celeste asks. She is waiting for him on the sidewalk. Mr. Beardsley is turning the key in the lock and Henry is watching, wishing Celeste would also take in the enormity of that key turning that one last time. But how could she know?

Mr. Beardsley knows. He turns from the door and smiles at Henry and nods. He passes Henry wordlessly and pats him on the back one last time. Before getting into his car he says, "I'll call you before I leave and we can get a beer, okay?" and Henry says "Yeah, sounds good" and Mr. Beardsley is off.

"So where should we go?" Celeste asks, slipping her arm into the crook of his.

"I don't care but first I've got to go do something," he says. It is only a few minutes after five o'clock so he has time.

"I know. I'll come with you," she says.

He is too exhausted, too drained, too preoccupied to say no or to come up with an alternative and, anyway, she is instantly in the seat next to him in the Jeep. The seat where the biographer sat only hours ago.

"Don't forget to put your seat belt on," she says, fastening hers into its docking station.

He looks out the windshield before starting the car up and there it is. Without exclamation of the point. Without the finality of a dot. Entirely without punctuation. The sign he had — for years — tucked neatly into the corner of the front window. The three words a swift superlative: existential and morbid and yes yes hopeful. Capitalized to boot.

Everything must go

ABOUT THE AUTHOR

Former print journalist **Elizabeth Flock** reported for *Time* and *People* magazines before becoming an on-air correspondent for CBS. Her acclaimed debut novel, *But Inside I'm Screaming*, chronicled the inner struggle of a young reporter. But it was her second novel, *New York Times* bestseller *Me & Emma*, that earned her the praise of critics and fans alike. Elizabeth lives with her husband and two stepdaughters in Chicago.

The employees of Thorndike Press hope you have enjoyed this Large Print book. All our Thorndike and Wheeler Large Print titles are designed for easy reading, and all our books are made to last. Other Thorndike Press Large Print books are available at your library, through selected bookstores, or directly from us.

For information about titles, please call:
(800) 223-1244

or visit our Web site at:
www.gale.com/thorndike
www.gale.com/wheeler

To share your comments, please write:
Publisher
Thorndike Press
295 Kennedy Memorial Drive
Waterville, ME 04901